KING
AND
EMPEROR

KING
AND
EMPEROR

HARRY HARRISON
JOHN HOLM

A TOM DOHERTY ASSOCIATES BOOK   NEW YORK

KING AND EMPEROR

Copyright © 1996 by Harry Harrison and John Holm

This book is printed on acid-free paper.

A Tor Book
Published by Tom Doherty Associates, Inc.
175 Fifth Avenue
New York, NY 10010

Tor Books on the World Wide Web:
http://www.tor.com

Tor® is a registered trademark of Tom Doherty Associates, Inc.

Library of Congress Cataloging-in-Publication Data

Harrison, Harry.
    King and emperor / by Harry Harrison.—1st ed.
       p.   cm.—(The hammer and the cross ; bk. 3)
    "A Tom Doherty Associates book."
    ISBN 0-312-85692-X
    1. Great Britain—History—Anglo-Saxon period, 449–1066—Fiction.
2. Vikings—Fiction.   I. Title.   II. Series: Harrison, Harry.
Hammer and the cross ; bk. 3.
PS3558.A667K56 1996
813'.54—dc20   95-53325
                                                    CIP

First Edition: July 1996

Printed in the United States of America

0 9 8 7 6 5 4 3 2 1

KING
AND
EMPEROR

STAMFORD —
MARCH, ANNO DOMINI 875

J ust a village," they said. "A few huts by the roadside. Capital of the North! It's not even Capital of the Fen. Never been anything, never will be."

The inhabitants of Stamford, both the old ones and the many more numerous incomers, bore the taunts of their neighbors easily. They could afford to. For whatever its history, whatever its native merit or lack of it, Stamford was now chief residence of the King of the North, once a co-king, once a jarl, before that a mere carl of the Great Army now destroyed, before that, almost, a thrall in a fenland village. Now they called him the One King, for so he had proved himself, and to his name and title, King Shef, his Norse subjects added the nick-name *Sigrsaell,* his English ones, with the same meaning and in almost the same word *Sigesaelig:* the Victorious. Truly he was a king who ruled by his word alone. If he declared humble Stamford the Capital of the North, then so it must be.

After his now-legendary defeat of the Ragnarsson brothers in the great battle of the Braethraborg in the year 868 of the Christians' count, that itself following on his defeat of the King of the Swedes in single combat at the Kingdom Oak of Uppsala, Shef the One King had received the submission of all the petty kings of the Scandinavian lands, of Denmark, Sweden and Norway as well. His fleets filled by levies from his under-kings, prominent among them Olaf of Norway and his own comrade Guthmund of Sweden, he had returned with massive force to the island of Britain, regaining power not only over the kingdom of the East and Middle Angles which he had been granted previously, but rapidly overawing also the petty rulers of Northumbria and the southern shires, and after them exacting submission further from the Scots, the Picts and Welsh. In the year 869 King Shef had launched the great circumnavigation of the island of Britain, which set out from the port of London, cruised to the north along the English and Scottish coasts, descended like a cloud on the disbelieving pirate-jarls of the Orkneys and Shetlands, left them chastened and afraid, and then turned south and west again through the many islands of the Scots and down the lawless western coasts to Land's End itself. Only there did it recognize friendly power, sheathe its talons, and sail east in company with the escort-ships of Alfred, King of the West Saxons, till it reached home harbor once more.

Since then the inhabitants of Stamford could boast that they sheltered a king whose power was uncontested from the westernmost isle of Scilly to the tip of the North Cape itself, two thousand miles north and east. Uncontested and—most said—shared only in theory with King Alfred, whose narrow boundaries King Shef persistently continued to honor, in obedience to the agreement of co-kingship the two had entered into in dark days of threat almost ten years before.

What the inhabitants of Stamford could not say, and did not care to think about, was why the greatest king the North had known since the times of the Caesars should make his home in the rural mud of Middle Anglia. The king's advisers had said the same thing, many times. Rule from Winchester, some said, to be frowned down by an angry one-eyed stare: for Winchester remained the capital of Alfred and the South. Rule from York, suggested others, from the stone walls that the king himself had stormed. London, said others, long a wretched backwater without a king or a court to fill it, but now increasingly the rich center of trade from the fur-lands of the North to the vineyards of the South, crowded with ships carrying hops, honey, grain, leather, tallow, wool, iron, grindstones and a thousand luxury goods: all paying toll to the officers of the co-kings, Shef's on the north bank and Alfred's on the south. No, said the many Danes among his counselors, rule from the ancient stronghold of the Skjöldung kings, from Hlethraborg itself, for it is the center of your dominions.

The king rejected them all. He would have chosen a town in the fen-lands themselves if it had been possible, for he was a child of the fens. But much of the year Ely stood inaccessible in the swamp, and Cambridge little better. In Stamford he was at least on the Great North Road of the Romans, now relaid with hard stone on his own instructions. It was there, he declared, that he would set the *Wisdom-hus,* the House of Wisdom, that would be the central achievement of his rule: the new College of the Asgarth-Way, not replacing but overshadowing the old one at Kaupang in Norway. There all priests of the Way would be welcome, to teach their crafts, to learn crafts from others.

It was part of the Wayman law that all priests should pay their way by work, not living from tithes and soul-taxes like the priests of the Christians. Nevertheless the king had given to the College a skilled reckoner, once a Christian priest himself, Father Boniface, to give money to any Way-priest for his own support, such money to be repaid when convenient in work, in knowledge or in good silver. From all over the north priests came, now, to learn the craft of milling, by watermill or windmill, and dispersed again, taking with them the knowledge of how to grind corn, but also how to beat out iron with powered trip-hammers and draft-bellows, how to adapt the new power to many tasks once carried out by slave-muscles alone. Father Boniface, by the king's permission but without his direct knowledge, often lent money to such visitors in return for a share of the profits of some new mill for five, ten or twenty years into the future.

The silver that flowed into the coffers of the king, and the coffers of the Way, would once have brought ten thousand Vikings on the trail of loot. But across the North there were now not even many bearded corpses dangling on coastal gibbets as a warning to their kind. Royal warships patrolled the seas and the port-approaches, the few towns and fjords that kept to their old piratical customs were visited one after another by overwhelming fleets drawn from the powers of too many sub-kings to resist.

What Stamford did not know, did not wish to know, was that its very insignificance and lack of history had been a recommendation to the king. He had said in the end to the chief of his advisers, Thorvin priest of Thor, whom he had set over the College as its director: "Thorvin, the place for new knowledge is somewhere where there is no old history, no old tradition for people to imitate and follow and misunderstand. I have always said that as important as new knowledge is old knowledge which no-one has recognised. But worse than anything is old knowledge which has become holy, unquestioned, so well known to everybody that no-one thinks about it any more. We will begin again, you and I, somewhere that no-one has heard of. Where there will be no stink of ink and parchment in the air!"

"There is nothing wrong with ink and parchment," Thorvin had replied. "Or vellum for that matter. The Way has its books of holy songs. Even your steelmaster Udd has learnt to write down what he knows."

The King frowned, reconsidering what he meant. "I have nothing against books and writing, as a craft," he said. "But folk who study books alone come to think there is nothing in the world outside them. They make book into Bible, and that is old knowledge become old lore. I want new knowledge, or old knowledge recognised. So here in Stamford at the House of Wisdom we will establish this as a rule. Anyone, man or woman, Way-folk or Christian, who brings us new knowledge or shows us some new and useful way to use old knowledge, will be better rewarded than they would be for years of toil. Or years of Viking robbery. I want no more Ragnarsson heroes. Let people show their courage some other way!''

By the year of Our Lord 875—for the chroniclers of the Asgarth Way kept to the Christian count while they rejected the Christian Lord—his capital was established, his policy bearing fruit: sometimes sweet, as often sour.

CHAPTER ONE

Hhigh in the sky, small white clouds scudded before the strong wind from the south-west. Their shadows raced across the bright green of new grass, across the strong rich brown of plow-furrows, the heavy horse teams drawing slow lines across the springtime fields. In between the sun shone, hot and welcome on England emerging from its winter sleep. Emerging too, many said, from the long dark into a new day and a new spring under its young ruler and his iconoclastic but fortunate rule.

In the market place of rustic Stamford maybe as many as two thousand people were gathered to witness the strange experiment that had been promised. The thanes and churls crowded in from the fields, wives and children with them, pushing back their hoods to take the sun, even shedding their cloaks with due caution against the return of the spring showers. The slow heavy faces showed pleasure, wonder, even excitement. For today some-one would indeed show a new kind of courage that not even Ivar the Boneless or his brother Sigurth the Snake-eye might have matched. Today a man would leap from the great stone tower of the House of Wisdom itself. And fly!

Or so it was said. The crowd would be happy to see flight, to tell their children and grandchildren about it ever after. But they would be happy also to see dramatic fall. They munched bread and good blood-sausage in even-tempered expectation of either.

A blare of horns set the spectators moving slowly to either side of the square, as towards them from the king's great hall came the king himself and his guests and officers. At the head, walking with deliberate ceremonial just behind the troop of champions blasting challenge from their enormous, long-preserved aurochs horns, came the two kings themselves, Shef and his guest and partner Saxon Alfred. Those who had not seen them before stared uncertainly at the contrasting figures, wondering—till their better-informed neighbors hissed the truth in their ears—which was the mighty one, which the tolerated partner. Indeed it was Alfred who caught the eye, dressed like a king in scarlet cloak, sky-blue tunic, gold circlet on yellow hair, left hand resting easily on the gold hilt of an ancient sword.

The man beside him wore scarlet also, a cloak of wool woven so fine it seemed as soft as its magnificent silk lining. But the tunic and breeches beneath it were plain dark gray. The king carried no sword, indeed no weapon at all, stalking along with his thumbs in his belt like a churl coming home from the plow. And yet, if one looked closer, it seemed possible that this was after all the man the Norse-folk called *Ivarsbani, Sigurtharbani,* the man who had killed both Ivar the Boneless and Sigurth the Snake-eye with his own hands, and King Kjallak the Strong of the Swedes as well. Had overthrown too the power of Charles the Bald and his Frankish horsemen at Hastings, in the year of Our Lord 866.

The king was now in his late twenties, and he had the body of a swordsmith in his prime: broad shoulders, powerful hands, a stride that swung from the hips, a waist so narrow he might have traded belts with his wife—if he had had one. Yet his face was that of a man much older. The black hair was streaked, and more than streaked with gray over the temples. More gray showed in the short clipped beard. The king's right eye was covered with a plain black patch, but round it men could see the flesh drawn in, wasted, the one cheek hollow. Lines of care ran across his brow, an expression of constant pain. Or was it regret? Men said that he had returned from his duel with the last of the Ragnarssons friendless and alone, having bought his life and his victory with the loss of others. Some said he had left his luck behind on the battlefield with his dead friends. Others, better-informed, said that his luck was so great that he drained it from others, brought death to those who came too close.

Whatever the truth, the king felt no need to display wealth or rank or power. He wore no crown, no fine jewelry, gave no employment to cunning goldsmiths. Round his arms, though, there ran half a score of golden bracelets, plain and unworked: worn without show, as if they were merely money.

Behind the two kings came their retinues, chamberlains, bodyguards, Shef's swordbearer, Viking sub-kings and English aldermen of shires anxious to be near the center of power. Close on Shef's heels strode one man who brought murmurs of wonder to the rustics in from the fields, a man nearer seven foot than six, and one who would never see twenty stone again, nor twenty-five, a man head and shoulders above all but the mightiest even of the picked bodyguards: Brand the Viking, Champion now of all of

Norway and not only of his native Halogaland, rumored in whispers even in the depths of England to be the relative of trolls and a kinsman of marbendills of the deep. Few knew the truth of what had happened when the king had been hunted into the farthest north, and few dared to enquire.

"But where is the man who is to fly?" whispered one anxious rustic to his town-dwelling cousin. "The man dressed like a bird?"

"Already in the Wisdom House with the priests," came the reply. "He feared his feather-hame, his coat of birds' feathers, might be crushed in the press. Follow the kings now, and we shall see."

Slowly the crowd closed in behind the royal procession, and trailed them down the hard stone of the Great North Road itself. Not to the town walls, for in demonstration of power Stamford had none: its defenses lay far out at sea, in the catapult-mounting battleships that had crushed Vikings and Franks alike. But to the edge of the wooden huts of the common folk, where beyond them in a meadow stood the great square of dormitories, workshops, forges, stables and storerooms that was the College of the Way in England, with lifting over it the tall sails of windmills. And at its center the stone tower Shef had ordered to outstrip the works of the Christian kings: sixty feet high and forty square, its blocks of stone so massive that visiting churls could not believe they had been raised by men with cranes and counter-weights, but told strange tales of devils compelled by magic.

The kings and dignitaries entered the high iron-bound doorway. The common crowd spread itself round in an expectant semi-circle, gaping up.

As he reached the top of the staircase, Shef stepped ahead of his co-king for the first time and walked out onto the flat roof, surrounded by battlements. Thorvin was there to meet him, dressed as always in the plain but shining white of a priest of the Way, silver hammer round his neck as a sign of his devotion to Thor, a real double-headed hammer tucked into his belt as a reminder of his craft. Behind him, but surrounded by other priests, was the man who was to fly.

Shef walked thoughtfully towards him. The man was dressed in a woolen suit of the plainest homespun, but not the usual tunic and breeches. Instead what he wore seemed to have been cut and sewn as one piece, to fit as tightly as possible. But round him and disguising his body-suit was a cape. Shef looked closer, still unspeaking. Thousands upon thousands of feathers, not stuck into some other material, wool or linen, but sewn tightly, quill to quill. The cape was strapped with sinews to wrists and ankles, stitched also along the line of the shoulders and down the back. It hung loose, though, round the man's sides.

Suddenly the man, meeting the king's eye, threw his arms wide and straddled his legs. The cape took shape, like a web, like a sail. Shef nodded, recognizing what was intended.

"Where do you come from?"

The bird-man nodded respectfully towards Alfred, standing a pace behind Shef. "From the land of Alfred King, my lord. From Wiltshire."

Shef forbore to ask why he had come to the land of another king. Only one king paid silver for new knowledge, and at a rate that drew experimenters from all across the Northern lands.

"What gave you the idea?"

The bird-man drew himself up, as if ready with a prepared speech. "I was born and baptized a Christian, lord, but years ago I heard the teachings of the Way. And I heard the story of the greatest of smiths, of Völund the Wise, whom we English call Wayland Smith. It came to me that if he could rise and fly from his enemies, then so might I. Since then I have spared no effort in making this garment, the last of many I have tried. For it says in the 'Lay of Völund,' 'Laughing, he rose aloft, flew with feather-hame.' And I believe the words of the gods are true, truer than the Christians' stories. See, I have made myself a sign in token of my devotion."

Moving carefully, the man pulled forward a silver pair of wings, hanging from a chain round his neck.

In response Shef pulled from under his tunic the sign he himself bore, the *kraki*, the pole-ladder of his own patron and perhaps-father, the little-known god Rig.

"None have worn the wings of Völund before," Shef remarked to Thorvin.

"Few wore the ladder of Rig either."

Shef nodded. "Success changes many things. But tell me, devotee of Völund—what makes you think you can fly with this cape, besides the words of the lay."

The bird-man looked surprised. "Is it not obvious, lord? Birds fly. They have feathers. If men had feathers, they would fly."

"Why has it not been done before?"

"Other men have not my faith."

Shef nodded once more, leapt suddenly up to the top of the battlements, stood on the narrow stone lip. His bodyguards moved forward urgently, were met by the bulk of Brand. "Easy, easy," he growled. "The king is not a Halogalander, but he is something of a seaman now. He will not fall off a flat ledge in broad daylight."

Shef looked down, saw two thousand faces staring up. "Back," he shouted, waving his arms. "Back from under. Give the man room."

"Do you think I will fall, lord?" asked the bird-man. "Do you mean to test my faith?"

Shef's one eye looked past him, saw in the crowd behind Alfred the face of the one woman who had accompanied them to the top of the stair: Godive, Alfred's wife, now known to all as the Lady of Wessex. His own childhood sweetheart and first love, who had left him for a kinder man. One who did not look at others to use them. Her face reproached him.

He dropped his gaze, gripped the man by the arm, careful not to disturb or disarrange his feathers.

"No," he said. "Not at all. If they are too close to the tower they will not see well. I wish them to have something to tell their children and their children's children. Not just, 'he flew too fast for me to see.' I wish you the best of fortune."

The bird-man smiled proudly, stepped first onto a block, then, carefully, onto the wall where Shef had stood. A gasp of amazement came up from the crowd below. He stood, spread his cape widely in the strong wind. It blew from behind him, Shef noted, flattening the feathers against his back. He thinks the cape is a sail, then, which will sweep him on as if he were a ship. But what if it should instead be a . . . ?

The man crouched, gathering his strength, and then suddenly leapt straight out, crying at the top of his voice, "Völund aid me!"

His arms beat the air, the cape flapping wildly. Once, and then as Shef craned forward, again, and then . . . A thud came up from the stone-flagged courtyard below, a long simultaneous groan from the crowd. Looking down, Shef saw the body lying perhaps sixteen feet from the base of the tower. Priests of the Way were already running towards him, priests of Ithun the Healer. Shef recognised among them the diminutive shape of another childhood friend, Hund the one-time slave, who shared a dog's name with himself, but was now thought the greatest leech and bone-setter of the island of Britain. Thorvin must have stationed them there. So he had shared his own misgivings.

They were looking up now, shouting. "He has broken both legs, badly smashed. But not his back."

Godive was looking over the wall now, next to her husband. "He was a brave man," she said, a note of accusation in her voice.

"He will get the best treatment we can give him," Shef replied.

"How much would you have given him if he had flown, say, a furlong?" asked Alfred.

"For a furlong? A hundred pounds of silver."

"Will you give him some now, as compensation for his injuries?"

Shef's lips tightened suddenly into a hard line, as he felt the pressure put on him, the pressure to show charity, respect good intentions. He knew Godive had left him for his ruthlessness. He did not see himself as ruthless. He did only what he needed to. He had many unknown subjects to protect as well as those who appeared before him.

"He was a brave man," he said, turning away. "But he was a fool as well. All he had to go on was words. But in the College of the Way it is works alone that count. Is that not so, Thorvin? He has taken your book of holy song and turned it into a Bible like the Christians' gospel. To be believed in, not thought about. No. I will send my leeches to him, but I will pay him nothing.''

A voice drifted up from the courtyard again. "He has his wits back. He says his mistake was to use hen's feathers, and they are earth-scratchers. Next time he will try with gull-feathers alone.''

"Don't forget,'' Shef said more loudly and to all, still answering an unspoken accusation. "I spend my subjects' silver for a purpose. All this could be snatched from us any summer. Think how many enemies we have over there.'' He pointed at right angles to the wind, out across the meadows to the south and east.

If some bird or bird-man could have followed the wave of the king across sea and land for a thousand miles, across the English Channel and then across the whole continent of Europe, it would have come in the end upon a meeting: a meeting long-prepared. For many weary months go-betweens had ridden down muddy roads and sailed stormy seas, to ask careful questions, in the languages of Byzantium and of Rome.

"If it might be that the *Imperator,* in his wisdom, might be prepared to consider thus and so; and might attempt to use such slight influence as he has with His Holiness the Pope to persuade him in his turn to reconsider such and such a formula; then (accepting the foregoing as a working possibility or if I may use your so-flexible tongue, a *hypothesis*) could it be so that in his turn the *Basileus* might turn his mind to the thoughts of so and thus?'' So spoke the Romans.

"Esteemed colleague, leaving your interesting hypothesis to one side for the moment only, if it were so that the *Basileus* might—saving at all times his orthodoxy and the rights of the Patriarch—consider a working and perhaps temporary arrangement in such and such a field of interest, might we then enquire what the attitude of the *Imperator* would be to the vexed question of the Bulgarian embassy, and the unhappy attempts of previous administrations to detach our newly-baptized converts from their faith and attach them to the allegiance of Rome?'' So replied the Greeks.

Slowly the emissaries had conversed, fenced, felt each other out, returned for further instructions. The emissaries had risen higher and higher in rank, from mere bishops and second secretaries to archbishops and influential abbots, drawing in military men, counts and strategists. Plenipotentiaries had been dispatched, only to discover that however full their powers might be, they did not dare to commit their emperors and churches on their word alone. Finally there had been no help for it but to arrange a meeting of the supreme powers, the four greatest authorities in Christendom: the Pope of Rome and the Patriarch of Constantinople, the Emperor of the Romans and the Emperor of the Greeks.

The meeting had been held up for months by the discovery that in his eyes the *Basileus* of the Greeks considered himself the true heir of the Caesars and so Emperor of the Romans as well, while the Pope bitterly resented the termination 'of Rome' being added to his title, regarding himself as the heir of St. Peter and the Pope of all Christians everywhere. Carefully formulas had been arranged, agreements reached not only as to what might be said but what might *not* under any circumstances be said. Like mating hedgehogs the powers drew together: delicately, gingerly.

Even the place of meeting had required a dozen proposals and counter-proposals. Yet now, at last, the negotiators might look out over a bluer sea than any the barbarian kings of the North would ever view: the Adriatic, looking west towards Italy, at the place where once the mightiest of Roman administrator-emperors had built his palace for retirement—Salonae of Diocletian, called already by the Slavs filtering into the region, Split.

In the end, and after days of exhausting ceremonial, the two military leaders had lost patience and dismissed all their retinues of advisers and translators and chiefs of protocol. They sat now on a balcony overlooking the sea, a pitcher of resined wine between them. All serious issues were settled, the agreements at this moment being embodied by relays of scribes writing a massive treaty in multiple copies in gold and purple ink. The only possible check now could come from the religious leaders, who had retired to talk between themselves. And each had been given the strictest and grimmest of warnings by his earthly colleague and paymaster, to cause no trouble. For there were worse things that could happen to the Church, as the *Imperator* Bruno had said to his creature Pope John, than a misunderstanding over the exact nature of the Nicene Creed.

The emperors sat quietly, then, each with an ear cocked for the return of the Churchmen, discussing their personal problems, as one ultimate ruler to another. It was perhaps the first time either had talked freely and frankly of such matters. They spoke in Latin, native to neither of them, but at least allowing them to communicate without intermediaries.

"We are alike in several ways, then," mused the Emperor of the Greeks, the *Basileus*. The imperial name he had chosen, Basil I, showed a certain lack of imagination unsurprising in one with his history.

"*Hoc ille,*" agreed the *Imperator* of the West, Bruno Emperor of the Romans as he claimed, but in reality of the Franks, the Italians and most of all of the Germans. "That's it. We are new men. Of course my family is old and distinguished. But I am not of the blood of Charlemagne."

"Nor I of the house of Leo," agreed the *Basileus*. "Tell me if I am wrong, but as I understand it there is none of the blood of Charlemagne left."

Bruno nodded. "None in the male line. Some were killed by their own vassals, like King Charles the Bald, on account of their failures in battle. I had to take measures against others myself."

"How many?" probed Basil.

"About ten. It was made easier for me in that they all seemed to have the same names. Lewis the Stammerer, Lewis the German. Three sons for each of them, and still with the same names, Charles and Lewis and Carloman. And some others of course. But it is not quite true that there is none of the blood of Charlemagne left. He has great-great-granddaughters left. One day, when all my tasks are done, I may ally myself with one."

"So your position will be stronger."

A yet fiercer look crossed Bruno's craggy, rock-hewn face. He straightened up in his chair, reached behind him for the thing that never left him, that no negotiators could persuade him to abandon. The lance with the leaf-shaped blade, its plain head now shining once more with inlaid gold crosses, set on a shaft of ash-wood barely visible beneath gold and silver wire. His ape-like shoulders stretched as he swung it before him, thumped its shaft on the marble floor.

"No! My position could not be stronger in any way. For I am the holder of the Holy Lance, the lance with which the German centurion Longinus split the heart of our blessed Savior. He who holds it, he is the heir of Charlemagne, by more than blood. I took it in battle with the heathen, brought it back to Christendom."

Reverently Bruno kissed the blade, laid the weapon down with tender care beside him. The bodyguards who had stiffened into readiness yards distant relaxed, smiled warily at each other.

The *Basileus* nodded, reflecting. He had learnt two things. That this strange count from the furthest extremity of the Franks believed his own fable. And that the stories they told of him were true. This man did not need a bodyguard, he was his own. How like the Franks to elect as their king the one the most formidable in single combat, not a *strategos* but a mere champion. And yet he might be a strategist too.

"And you," probed Bruno in his turn. "You . . . put from his throne your predecessor, Michael the Drunkard, as he was called. I take it he has left no seed behind to grow rebellion."

"None," replied Basil curtly, his pale face flushing over the dark beard.

Basil's supposed second son, Leo, is in reality the child of Michael, Bruno's spies had reported. Basil killed the Emperor his master for cuckolding him. But in any case the Greeks needed an Emperor who could stay sober long enough to marshal an army. They are pressed by the Slavs, the Bulgars, even by your own foes, the Vikings raiding down the great rivers of the east. Not twenty years ago a Viking fleet menaced Constantinople, which they call Byzantium. We do not know why Basil allowed Leo to live.

"So. We are new men, then. But neither of us has old men waiting to challenge us. And yet both of us know we have many challenges, many threats. We and Christendom at once. Tell me," Bruno asked, his face intent, "where do you see the greatest threat to us, to Christ, and to his Church. You yourself, I mean, not your generals and your advisers."

"An easy question, for me," Basil replied, "though I may not give the answer you expect. You know that your adversaries, the heathen of the North, the Vikings as you call them: you know that a generation ago they brought their ships up to Byzantium itself?"

Bruno nodded. "It surprised me when I learned it. I did not think that they could find their way across the Italian Sea. But then your secretary told me that they had not done so, had somehow brought their ships down the rivers of the East. You think they are your greatest danger? That is what I hoped . . ."

A lifted hand interrupted him. "No. I do not think that these men, fierce as they are, are the greatest menace. We bought them off, you know. The common folk say that it was the Virgin Mary who routed them, but no, I remember the negotiations. We paid them a little gold. We offered them unlimited use of the great municipal baths! They took it. To me they are fierce and greedy children. Not serious.

"No, the true danger comes not from them, mere *pagani* that they are, immature rustics. It comes from the followers of Muhammad." The *Basileus* paused for wine.

"I have never met one," Bruno prompted.

"They came from nowhere. Two hundred and fifty years ago these followers of their false Prophet came from out of the desert. Destroyed the Persian Empire. Took from us all our African provinces, and Jerusalem." The *Basileus* leaned forward. "Took the southern shore of the Italian Sea. Since then that sea has been our battleground. And on it we have been losing. You know why?"

Bruno shook his head.

"Galleys need water, all the time. Oarsmen drink faster than the fish. The side that controls the watering-grounds controls the sea. And that means the islands. *Kypros* they took, island of Venus. Then Crete. After they conquered Spain, they seized the Balearics. Now their fleets press again on Sicily. If they take that—where will Rome be? So you see, friend, they threaten you as well. How long since their armies were at the gates of your holy city?"

Opening doors, raised voices, a shuffle of feet, said that the conference of Pope and Patriarch had broken up, that the Emperors of East and West must turn their minds again to ceremonial and treaties. Bruno groped for a reply, amid several. The *Basileus* is an Easterner, he thought, like Pope Nicholas whom we killed. He does not realize that destiny lies in the West. He does not know that the Way-folk are not the greedy children bought off in his father's time. That they are worse than the followers of the Prophet, for they still have their prophet with them: the one-eye. I should have killed him when I had my sword at his throat.

And yet maybe there is no need to argue here. The *Basileus* needs my bases. I need his fleet. Not for the Arabs. Just to sweep the Channel so I can put my lancers across. But let him have his way first. For he has the one thing that the Way-folk do not . . .

The Emperors were on their feet, the churchmen approaching, all smiles. A cardinal spoke, bowing, the cardinal who had once been Archbishop Gunther of Cologne. He spoke in fluent Low German, his and Bruno's native dialect, which neither Pope nor Patriarch nor any Greek or Italian would follow. At the same time one of the Patriarch's staff broke out with a burst of demotic Greek, no doubt with the same intention.

"It's fixed. They have agreed that we may add the formula 'and the Son' to the Nicene Creed—much difference that makes—as long as we draw no conclusions about the Double Procession of the Holy Ghost from it. Our fool, the Italian, has been told he has to withdraw his bishops from the Bulgars and let Saint Cyril have a free hand teaching them to read and write. All sides have agreed in condemning the former Patriarch, Photius the bookworm, no problem there. It's fixed."

Bruno turned towards Basil as the latter heard his own secret briefing chatter to an end. The two men smiled, simultaneously, reached out their hands.

"My bases in Italy," said Bruno.

"My fleet to relieve Sicily. And then the whole Italian Sea," replied Basil.

And then the Atlantic, thought Bruno. But he held his tongue. After all he might have shed the Greeks and their Emperor before then. If he or his agents could find out the weapon that held Constantinople inviolable from the sea. The secret no Westerner knew, Roman or German or Way-man.

The secret of Greek fire.

CHAPTER TWO

Halim, *amir* of the fleet of the Fortunate of God, bin-Tulun, Caliph of Egypt, newly independent of the feeble Caliphate of Baghdad, felt no unease as his galley led its hundred fellows to sea in the darkest hour before dawn. In moments, when a keen eyesight could see sufficiently to distinguish a white thread from a black one, his muezzin would call the faithful to prayer with the traditional cry, the *shahada:*

> *God is most great!*
> *I testify that there is no God but Allah.*
> *I testify that Muhammad is the messenger of Allah.*

And so on, in the invocation that Halim had heard and repeated and obeyed forty thousand times since he reached the estate of a man and a warrior. He and his men would stretch out their mats on the rolling decks and go through their *rakat,* the prescribed ritual of prayer. But the men at the oars would not, would carry on sweeping his fleet into battle. For they were Christians, the slaves of many a lost campaign. Halim had no doubt of the outcome of this one. His soldiers were fed and rested, his slaves watered and refreshed. By the end of the summer the disorganized resistance of the *Rumi* would have come to an end, as always. And this time the whole island of Sicily would be brought once more under the rule of his master, and beyond his master the rule of the *Dar al-Islam,* the House of Submission to the Will of God.

Halim heard the call of the lookout simultaneously with the start of the ritual prayer, the *salat*. "Ships to seaward of us! Ships with the light behind them!"

It angered him, but it did not surprise him or cause him uneasiness. Over the years the Christians, those who added gods to God, had learned the rituals of their enemies, and sought from time to time to make use of them. They were mistaken in thinking that an advantage. In combat for the Faith, to abstain from prayer was permissible, even meritorious. It could be made up later. If the *Rumi* were trying to take him by surprise, they only brought their own end so much the closer.

Halim called to his steersman to swing the ship towards the dawning light, heard the master of the slaves shout orders to the port oars to cease rowing, then to accelerate to ramming speed. Halim's vessel was one of the ancient pattern that had ruled the Mediterranean Sea, the Italian Sea as the foolish *Rumi* called it, since the days of the Greek philosophers before the son of the Lady Miriam came to trouble the world. Long, thin, with little freeboard, it was heavily reinforced forward to take an iron-shod ram, with catwalks above the oarsmen's benches for the fighting men to line either side.

Halim did not rely on his ram alone. His master, bin-Tulun, was no Arab by blood, but a Turk from the central steppe lands of Asia. He had supplied a dozen of his countrymen to each ship. As they lined the sides they began to string their bows: the composition bows of Central Asia, wood at the center, sinew on the outside, the side to which the bow bent before it was strung, hard horn on the inside, all glued and assembled with fanatic care. Again and again Halim had seen the *Rumi* shot down before ever they came to a handstroke, their own weak wooden bows outranged by a hundred yards, not able to pierce even good stout leather.

As the light grew across the water Halim realized that the ships now closing on him at ramming speed like his own were not the kind he expected. Their prows were painted red, were higher out of the water than any he had seen before, and from the warships' hulls he could see sprouting not the crucifixes of the *Rumi,* but gilded pictures, icons.

Not the fleet of the Sicilians then, or their holy father in Rome, but the Red Fleet of the Byzantines, of which Halim had only heard. He felt something at his heart—not fear, for that was impossible to the true believer, nor even surprise, but intellectual worry: how could the Byzantine fleet be here, five hundred miles from its bases, more days than it could row without exhaustion? Concern, as well, that this news and what it meant should be passed to his master.

But passed it would be. Halim signaled to his steersman not to meet the charging enemy bow to bow, but to swerve aside, trusting to greater handiness, to shave away one row of oars as they passed, and pour in a deadly volley from his bowmen, each of them able to shoot a shaft a second and never miss. He ran forward himself along the starboard catwalk, drawing his saber, not with the intention of striking a blow but to encourage his men.

There would be a moment of danger here. For as he turned aside, the Greek, if he were fast enough, could accelerate and strike bow to flank, driving through below the waterline, and reversing oars instantly to shake the smaller craft off and leave her crew struggling in the water, her chained slaves drowning desperate and trapped.

Yet the slaves knew that too. As the ship swung barely fifty yards from the white water of her enemy's prow, the starboard side braked with their oars as one man, the port side slaves swung with all the strength in their bodies. Then a concerted momentary glance from both sides at each other to pick up the time, and the ship leapt forward as if it were the first stroke that any man had made that day. The bowmen bent their bows and picked their targets among the faces crowding the rail.

There was something there in the middle of the boat. Halim could not see clearly what it was, but he could see some metal contrivance, like a copper dome, lit brilliantly not only by the rising sun but by some flare or flame beneath it. Across the water, over the hiss of the oars and the blare of trumpets, came a roaring noise like that of some great beast, cut by a high and eldritch whistle. He could see two men pumping desperately at a handle, two more leveling a nozzle over the side.

Greek ships and the Greek fire. Halim had heard of this weapon, but never seen it. Few men who saw it lived to say how it should be countered. Yet he had heard one thing, which was that if its crew could be killed or distracted while they prepared its action, then it became as dangerous to its own side as to the enemy.

Halim began to shout orders to the Turks in his own craft, wishing vainly as he did so that he could shout the same warning to the hundred ships streaming in his wake, to attack, he could now see, no more than a score of the Byzantines.

As the breath filled his lungs, and the first arrows began to fly, the whistle in Halim's ears rose to a shriek, a barked command came from the vessel lunging towards him. Halim saw the nozzle swing to face him, caught a strange reek in the air, saw a glow at the mouth of the nozzle. Then the air was full of fire, searing out his eyeballs, crisping his skin so that pain struck him like a club from all directions at once. Halim breathed in death as he tried to scream, his lungs filling instantly with flame. As he fell back into the blaze that was his flagship he heard the simultaneous agony of a hundred slaves, and took it with the last flick of consciousness as the tribute for the entry of a warrior into Paradise.

* * *

The Tulunid scout boats, creeping cautiously into the water where their fleet had been barely three days before, found nothing to explain its disappearance. Except charred timbers floating, the headless corpse of a circumcised believer who had survived the burning only to meet death for refusing baptism. And still chained to the timber he had pulled free from his sunken ship in a frenzy of fear, a slave half mad with thirst. The story he croaked out sent the scout boats racing without further delay for the Egyptian shore.

News of the disaster did not outsail the fleet that caused it. A bare fortnight later, Ma'mun bin-Khaldun, commander of the faithful on the new-conquered island of Mallorca, could only watch grimly from the shore as the Byzantine fleet brushed aside the attempts at interception by his own always-manned inshore squadron, and then cruised slowly along the ranks of his massed invasion fleet, moored a hundred feet offshore, pouring out their Iblis-flame. His army had debarked months before, to set about the conquest of the island, leaving their ships with no more than an anchor-watch and a guard against surprise by the natives. As the Greeks came into sight, his few boat-keepers had quickly abandoned their charges, pulling furiously for the shore in dinghies. He would lose few men, other than the ones he would execute for fleeing without orders. Nevertheless the ships were a major loss.

Yet Ma'mun felt no great concern. Behind him he had a large and fertile island, its native inhabitants by now thoroughly tamed. He had immense stores of grain, olives, wine and beef, and could if need be support himself and his army indefinitely on the products of Mallorca itself. He had something more important than that as well, the breath of life itself to any Arab: he had water. And while the Byzantines had fire at sea, they would soon need to come to land, for water. No fleet of galleys could last long without it. They must already be at the limit of their endurance, if they had made the long passage from their bases on the islands of the Greeks.

Though there was something wrong there, Ma'mun reflected silently. If the Byzantines had indeed made the long passage down the Mediterranean, they would not be at the limit of their endurance, they would have passed it days ago. Therefore, they had not. They had touched land somewhere much closer. On his information, that was impossible. Therefore, his information was wrong. That was the dangerous element in this situation, Ma'mun concluded. Where could the Greeks have watered? In Sicily? By his understanding, Sicily was closely invested by the forces of the Tulunids, the Caliph of Egypt. Ma'mun himself had nothing but contempt for Tulun and his followers, mere Turks, barbarians from nowhere, followers in any case— till they rebelled—of the treacherous successors of Abdullah. He himself was an Umayyad and a member of the tribe of Quraysh, related by blood to the Caliph of Cordova, both of them descendants of that Abd er-Rahman who had fled the massacre in Persia when Umayyad power was broken. Nevertheless, while the Egyptians had no more love for him than he for them, he was surprised that some information or other had not reached him if Sicily had been retaken: it was not like the pale followers of Yeshua whom they mistakenly called the Christ to act so swiftly.

He would have to gain further information. Yet whatever the true state of affairs, there could be no doubt that those boats out there in the calm bay of Palma would soon be trying to find some unguarded spring or other. No doubt they hoped that he, Ma'mun, would be unable to guard every foot of shore on this rugged island. Now it would be their turn to be mistaken.

As he turned dismissively from the last moments of the destruction of his fleet, he became aware of some disturbance on the outer fringes of his guard. A young man was struggling in the grip of two warriors, calling out angrily. Angrily, not fearfully. Ma'mun signed to his guard-captain to let the young man through. If he had a word to say, let him say it. If he wasted the time of the commander of the faithful, he could go to the impaling-post as a warning to others.

The young man fretfully pulling his clothes back into place had the face of a Qurayshi too, Ma'mun noticed. Most of his army now were the descendants of Berbers, converted Spaniards, even Goths. Ma'mun had been obliged to prohibit taunts of pork-eating, so sensitive were the sons of former Christians in his ranks. But this young man had no touch of the tow-brush about him, as lean and dark-faced as Ma'mun himself. He spoke, too, like a true Arab, without evasion or deference.

"Commander, the men on those ships are not Greeks, even if the ships throw out the Greek fire. Not all of them. Many are *ferengis*, Franks."

Ma'mun raised an eyebrow. "How has it been permitted to you to see this? I have not seen it, and my eyes are keen enough to pick out the Rider of the Stars." He meant the star in Orion's sword-belt which has, invisible to all but the keenest-sighted, a tiny companion sheltered by the light of its neighbor.

The young man smiled with irritating condescension. "I have that which enables me to see better even than that."

The guard-captain standing at the young man's elbow stepped forward, aware that his master was on the edge of ordering the impaling-post to be set up. "The young man here, lord, is Mu'atiyah. A pupil of bin-Firnas."

Ma'mun hesitated, pulling his beard. He himself had been named after the great Caliph of fifty years before, who had set up the great library and center of wisdom in Baghdad. He had the greatest respect for men of learning. And there was no doubt that Abu'l Qasim Abbas bin-Firnas was the glory of Cordova for his learning and his many experiments. With less impatience in his voice he said, "Show us then, the wisdom of your master."

Smiling once more, the young Mu'atiyah pulled from his sleeve an object like a stout bottle covered in leather.

"Know," he said, "that my master, being advanced in years, found a dimness coming upon his eyes, so that he could see only that which was further away than his own arm's reach. For many years he had studied the science of making glass, and the stones from which it might be made. So, by accident, one day he discovered that if one looked through stones of a certain kind and shape, that which was too close for his eyes became as it were far away, so that he might read it. And, not by accident but by design, he studied many hours till he could find a glass shape that would do likewise for him, and restore to him the liberty of his books."

"But that is to make the close far away," replied Ma'mun. "Here we have need of the opposite."

Again the young man smiled, again provoking Ma'mun with his display of confidence. "That is what I, Mu'atiyah, have discovered. That if one takes not one but *two* glasses, and looks first through one and then through the other, the far away comes close."

Thoughtfully, Ma'mun reached over and took the leather object from the young man's hand, disregarding a look of alarm and a sudden babble of explanation. He put it to his eye, looked a moment, lowered it.

"I see only the tiniest of images."

"Not like that, lord, mighty one." The young man was at least showing agitation for the first time. It was often so with the learned, Ma'mun conceded grimly. What upset them the most was not the threat of death but the fear that they would not be able to display their abilities. He allowed the young man to take the object from his hand, reverse it so that he looked through what appeared to be the neck.

"Yes, lord. On the deck of the lead ship I see a Greek, with a curled beard, standing by an image of the holy." Ma'mun's face twisted in disgust, and he spat ritually to avert the contamination created by any image of the divine. "But by him there is a fair-haired Frank, all in metal armour. They are arguing, pointing in different directions."

"What are they saying?"

"My art deals with sight, not sound."

"Very well." Ma'mun signed to the guard-captain. "Take the young man from his place in the ranks, keep him with yourself. If I have need of his art I will send for him. If I do not, the armies of Spain have more need of wise men than of brave ones. We must keep him safe. And, Mu'atiyah, if you tell me where the Greek *amiral* means to land for water before I can see myself, I will fill your mouth with gold. If you tell me wrong I will melt it first."

He turned away, calling to his commanders of divisions. Behind him the young man raised his spyglass again, seemed to be attempting to gain a clearer view by moving his eye in and out from the eyepiece.

From time to time in his babbling flow of talk, the Mallorcan villager cast a fearful glance sideways. He had reason to feel fear. The villager had seen the fleet of great red galleys pull round the point, having burned to the water-line the ships that had brought the circumcised to Mallorca long months before. He had realized they must be searching for water, and theorized that whoever they were, the enemies of Muhammad must be his friends. So, when they came ashore and began to set up their camp, and after he had crept close enough to see the crucifixes and the saints' images raised, he had come shyly and slowly forward to volunteer his services: hoping for some reward that might keep him from starvation. Hoping too for revenge on the fierce dark-faced raiders who had stolen from him wife and son and daughters.

Yet he had not reckoned on facing quite such strange and menacing allies. The villager had no language in common with the Greek sailors, or with the German soldiers whom they transported. He had been passed on, though, from guard-post to guard-post till they found a Latin-speaking chaplain. If he spoke slowly and listened carefully, he and the Mallorcan could understand each other, for the Mallorcan's peculiar dialect was no more than the Vulgar Latin of old time, spoken badly and without a schoolmaster for generation after forgotten generation. So much the Mallorcan had expected. He had not expected to find anyone like the man who stood with a scowl on his face next to the Christian priest and his wizened informant.

Agilulf, *Ritter* of the *Lanzenorden,* once companion of the great Emperor Bruno himself, and now commander of the expedition against the Moors, stood a foot taller than either priest or villager. His height was increased by the visored iron helmet he wore, and the black plume in it that marked his rank. Yet what the villager could not understand, or hardly believe, was not the man but his dress. From head to foot Agilulf seemed to be made of iron. He wore helmet, mail shirt hanging to his knees, greaves on his calves and beneath them iron-plated boots. Iron studded his gauntlets and rimmed the long kite-shaped shield he carried: a horseman's shield, drawn out in a kite shape to protect the lancer's left leg when he charged, but carried by Agilulf on foot as if weight meant nothing to him. Nor heat. Beneath the iron he wore leather to prevent links being beaten into his flesh, beneath the leather he wore hemp to soak up the sweat. In the late afternoon heat of the Balearics in spring time, the sweat sprang out from under the hairline and dripped steadily down into his beard. He took no notice, as if to notice discomfort was beneath his dignity. To the villager, who had never seen more iron in his life than it would take to sheathe the spike on his primitive plow, the German seemed a creature from another world. The cross painted on his shield was little comfort.

"What does he say?" demanded Agilulf, tiring of listening to slow exchanges in a language he could not follow.

"He says there is a good spring half a mile away, where we could fill as many water-barrels as we wish. But he says the Moslems know of it and use it too. They will have seen us already. The main army of the invaders is a bare ten miles off. They move with the speed of the wind, he says. That is how he lost his family: taken before anyone in his village knew raiders had landed."

Agilulf nodded. He showed none of the dismay that Pedro the villager had expected. "Does he know how many men the Moslems have?"

The priest shrugged. "He says ten thousand thousand. That could mean anything over a couple of hundred."

Agilulf nodded again. "Very well. Give him some grain and a flask of wine, and let him go. I expect there are many like him skulking in these hills. Tell him when the Moslems have broken there will be a reward for heads. They can round up the stragglers for us."

Agilulf turned away, shouting orders to his men to form up the watering-party. As usual, protest and expostulation from the Greek sailors, uneasy on land, convinced that at any moment a horde of *ghazis* would rush from the woods and overwhelm them. Agilulf paused for a moment to explain his plan to the Greek commander.

"Of course they'll rush us," he said. "At dawn. My crossbowmen and your rowers will hold them in front for a few minutes. Then I and my knights and companions will take them from behind. I wish we had horses to make our charge swifter. But it will come to the same thing in the end."

The Greek looked after the iron man as he stalked on his way. The Franks, he thought. Clumsy, illiterate, heretical peasants. Why are they so confident so suddenly? They have swept out of the West like the followers of Muhammad from the East two hundred years ago. I wonder if we will find them any better than the wine-haters?

Ma'mun made no effort to conceal his dawn attack, once his men were in place. He had counted the ships of the enemy: a bare score. No matter how crowded with men they were, they could not hold more than two thousand at the very most. He had ten thousand. Now was the time to avenge the destruction of his ships. The Greek fire, he knew, could not be transported overland. He feared nothing else. He allowed his priests to call out the dawn *salat,* regardless of the warning it gave, and led his men in their ceremonial prayers. Then he drew his saber, and signaled to his commanders-of-a-thousand to lead the assault.

In full daylight the army of the faithful ran forward in the tactic that had led them to victory over army after army of Christians: in Spain, in France, in Sicily, at the gates of Rome itself. A loose wave of men with spears and swords, without the locked shields and heavy body-armor of the West, but driven on by contempt for death, assurance that those who died fighting the unbelievers would live for ever amid the houris of Paradise.

Ma'mun knew that the Christians would have some trick or other. Otherwise they would not have ventured to set up their camp on land. He had seen many tricks, seen them all fail. The sudden appearance of a row of helmeted heads, the leveled crossbows beneath them did not surprise him. He had not heard the metallic twang of the crossbows before, and watched with interest as his first wave of stormers fell or were hurled off their feet by the thump of crossbow quarrels at short range. Weapons to use against armor, he guessed, the besetting vice of Frankish tactics: eager to kill, reluctant to die. They would be slow to reload, whatever they were. The followers of Islam ran on undeterred, reached the low palisade, began to hack and stab at the defenders. Ma'mun could hear his priests calling ritual curses on those who added gods to God. He walked slowly forward, waiting for the resistance to break.

His guard-captain touched his arm, pointed silently behind him. Ma'mun frowned. Another trick, indeed! Coming out of a rocky gully to his left flank, already swinging round in a wide arc as if to cut off his retreat— his retreat!—were a line of men.

Iron men. Gray steel glittered from their weapons, their armor, their shields, their very hands and feet. Not many of them. They seemed barely two deep in file, their line a mere two hundred yards. They came on slowly. Why did they look so strange? Pulling his beard, Ma'mun realized that each carried the same weapons, carried them in the same way, even at the same angle: a short pike in the right hand, a kite-shaped shield on the left side. Had they no left-handed men in their ranks? What could make men walk together like that, as if they were a machine, as unvarying as the scoops on a *noria*, a water-wheel. With incredulity Ma'mun saw that each man was putting his foot forward at the same time, so that the line came on like a single animal, like the limbs of a crawling hundred-legged beast. He could hear a great voice shouting something in the barbarous tongue of the *ferengi*, the same word repeated again and again: "Links . . . links . . . links." At every word the feet came down again.

Ma'mun shook himself, sent runners to turn the rearmost of those attacking the palisade, called his guards round him and ran forward himself, saber drawn, to engage the iron men. A moment of delay and his men would turn, swarm round the Franks now out in the open, drag them down from all sides. Breathing hard, for he was a man of fifty winters, he reached the slowly advancing line, hacked at an iron figure with his saber of best Toledo steel.

The German facing him, no knight or *Ritter* but only a poor brother of the *Lanzenorden,* ignored the blow, merely ducking his helmet into it. He concentrated on keeping the step, keeping the line, following the battle-drill his sergeants had shouted into him. Left foot forward, thrust with the shield, lift the man in front of you back. Right foot forward, stab with the pike. Not at the man in front, ignore him. At the man to your right. *Bruder* Manfred to your left will kill the man in front of you, you kill the man in front of *Bruder* Wolfi to your right. Stab at the armpit as he raises his weapon.

Ma'mun struck one stroke against the unbelievers and died, killed by a blow he never saw. His guardsmen were cut down and trampled under foot by a line that did not even check its pace. The wave that turned back from the palisades and rushed at the iron men did not break and retire but was accepted and trodden under like stalks beneath a scythe. Their cries of encouragement and praise to God were answered only by the hoarse bellows of the sergeants: "*Links . . . links.* Straighten up there! Close up, close up! Second rank, keep your points down, stab him again, Hartman, he's only wounded. Right wheel, right shoulders there!"

As the dust rose over the churning battle, Mu'atiyah, who had not followed Ma'mun and his guards to glorious death, heard the strange machine-soldiers of the Franks grunting like laborers who have heavy loads to carry in the cornfields. From the palisades the Frankish bowmen were preparing a second volley, while the lightly-armed Greek oarsmen swarmed out, ready to drive a demoralized enemy onto the points of the iron line now fully behind them.

It was the duty of a learned man to learn, and to report his learning, Mu'atiyah reflected, dodging through the rocks and scattered scrub of the hillside. Some of the lower-born among the army were following his example, mere Berbers and Goths. He called a dozen of them round him, to act as a guard against the Christian peasants who would surely be out to avenge their stolen fields and children. They obeyed, recognizing his dress and the pure Arabic of a descendant of the Quraysh.

Somewhere on the island there would be a boat. He would take the news to his master bin-Firnas. And to the Caliph of Cordova himself. But best to speak to his master first. It would be wise to appear not as one who had fled from battle, but as one who had braved dangers to know the truth. At a safe distance Mu'atiyah turned, produced his spyglass, and looked again across the hillside to where Agilulf was directing the passionless slaughter of a mass of men trapped too close together by their enemies to lift a hand against the pikes and pole-axes.

Iron Franks, he thought. And Greek fire. It will take more than the courage of the *ghazis* to defeat those together.

* * *

Far away, in his sleep, the King of the North felt a pang of warning, a chill that seemed to strike up from the ground beneath his stout-timbered bed and down mattress. He tossed in his sleep, trying to wake up as a swimmer before sharks tries to throw himself out of the water. As unavailing. Over the years Shef had come to recognize the difference between one kind of vision and another.

This would be one of the worst kind: the kind that took him not across the surface of the earth, like a bird, or back into the old histories of men. One that took him down into the deep strongholds of the gods, the Hel-world, past the Grind, the grating that separates the living from the dead.

He seemed now to be sinking deeper and deeper, unable to see anything but earth and rock, a stink of mold in his nostrils. Yet some sense warned him that he was going to a place he had seen before. Glimpsed before. Not a place for mere men to visit.

The darkness did not lift, but a feeling of space grew around him, as if he were in some enormous cavern. Light over there, or at least a glow. He did not think his father and patron would let him go without showing him something.

Suddenly the shadows turned into a shape. A shape that without warning struck at his face, slashing out of the dark with a hiss of hatred so fierce it was like a shriek. Shef jerked convulsively in his bed, his muscles trying to hurl him back. Too late, his eye recognised the head of a monstrous serpent glaring at him, striking again, the poison fangs jerking down bare yards from his face.

The serpent was fettered, he realized. It could not reach him. It struck again, but this time not at him. Again at a target it could not reach. Not quite reach.

Below him Shef could now make it an enormous human shape, stretched out in the darkness. It was chained down by great iron fetters to a table of stone. Shef's flesh crawled as he realized what he was seeing. For this could only be Loki, the bane of Balder, father of the monster-brood, enemy of gods and men. Chained here on the orders of his father Othin to live in everlasting torment till Doomsday. Till Ragnarök.

The harsh face twisted in agony as Shef watched. He could see that the snake, while it could not reach its chained enemy, could sweep its fangs within inches of his head. The venom from them ran out, splashed on the face that could not turn away, ate away skin and flesh, not like venom, like—something Shef could not name.

But while the face twisted, something about it did not change. A set purpose, an air of craft. Looking carefully round, Shef saw that the great body was concentrating its force, was heaving all the time, heaving on the seemingly unmovable, deep-anchored fetter on the right hand. He had seen this before, Shef remembered. And he had seen that the fetter was working loose.

Yes, there was his father now. Seemingly dwarfed by the shape of Loki, by the great serpent, but standing there with perfect self-possession, ignoring the fangs now striking hatefully at him.

"You have come to gloat over my pain, Rig?" A hoarse whisper from Loki.

"No, I have come to look at your fetters."

The face of the tormented god closed, as if determined to show neither fear nor disappointment.

"No fetter can hold me for ever. Nor will my son Fenris-wolf be bound for ever by Gleipnir."

"I know. But I have come to speed things up."

Incredulously, Shef saw his father, the trickster-god, stoop, produce some metal instrument from his sleeve, begin to lever at the places where Loki's right wrist-manacle was set into the rock. The bound god seemed unable to believe what he saw either, watching motionless till the eating venom from above ran into his very eyes.

As he felt himself drawn away, returned to the world of men, Shef heard another hoarse whisper: "Why are you doing this, deceiver?"

"Think, if you wish, that I find Ragnarök too long in coming. Or that I desire freedom for Loki as well as for Thor. In any case, there is someone I mean you to meet . . ."

Shef crashed into wakefulness again, heart pounding. Me? he thought. Not me. Not me.

CHAPTER THREE

$\int$hef eyed his royal guests broodingly as they emerged from the guest hall he had had built for them. The dread of the night was still on him. It had turned the whole world a darker shade. He found himself even walking more lightly, more warily, as if at any moment the earth might split and hurl him down to what he knew lay beneath.

And yet all seemed well enough. There was his friend and partner Alfred, turning on the steps and stretching his arms out encouragingly to the sturdy toddler behind him. Little Edward half-running, half-falling into his father's catch. Behind them both, stepping forward with pleased maternal smile and a second baby slung familiarly on her hip, the face Shef could not forget. His own love, long-lost to him now, Godive, once his childhood sweetheart from the marshes, now known and loved far and wide as the Lady of Wessex. They could not see him for a moment as he stood in the shadow of the strange contrivance he meant to show off that day. He could observe unobserved.

Unobserved by those he watched. Not by his own men, who shifted uneasily and glanced at each other as they saw his silent concentration.

He ought, he knew, to at least fear and resent them. To be making plans for—if not their death, their removal. For making them safe. Many would say, though they did not dare to say it to his face, that it was a king's first duty to think of his own successor. Years ago, in the dark days of the double invasion by Charles the Bald's Franks and Ivar the Boneless's pagans, Shef and Alfred had agreed to share their luck, and their kingdoms, if they should ever hold them again. They had agreed too that each would be the other's successor if either died without an heir, and that any heir of either would inherit from both in the same situation. The deal had not seemed important at the time. Neither had much chance of living to see another winter, let alone another spring. And Godive had slept in Shef's tent, if not in his bed. He had thought, if they lived, it would only be a matter of time till her love returned, and his desire.

He had been wrong. If he died now, his kingdom fell to Alfred. And after him to the laughing toddler now being carried towards him, baby Edward. The sub-kings would ignore the agreement, of course. There was no chance that the Scandinavian kings, Olaf or Guthmund or any of the dozen others, would agree to obey an English Christian. It was doubtful if even the Mercians or Northumbrian English would accept rule by a Wessex Saxon. The One King of the North was truly One King. No-one else would be accepted by the rest.

An unstable situation. Could this be the trigger for the Ragnarök his father wanted him to know of? He ought to take a wife and breed a son as fast as possible. Everyone thought so. The court was alive with jarls' daughters and princesses of the North, paraded in the hope of catching the king's feeble attention. Ragnarök or no, he would not do it. Could not do it.

As he stepped forward out of the shadow to greet his guests, Shef creased his face into a welcoming smile. Even to those he greeted, it looked like a rictus of pain. Alfred controlled himself, managed not to shoot a glance at his wife. He had known for years that his co-king was not the boy-lover many whispered, was instead in love with his own wife. Sometimes he wished it was in him to hand her over, or to share her. But while it might be in him, it was not in her. For some reason, she seemed to hate her friend of childhood more deeply each passing year. Her resentment grew with his success: as she thought, perhaps, of what might have been.

"What have you to show us today?" asked Alfred with false-ringing good cheer.

Shef's face brightened, as it always did when he had some new thing to explain. "It is a horse-wain. But one to carry people."

"Wains have always carried people."

"Three miles to market and back. Bump into a pothole, crawl out of it. Going no faster than a walk, or the passengers would be hurled out. Even on the good stone roads we have had built, you and I"—the last two words were mere flattery, as everyone knew—"it would be torment to travel in it if the horses began to run.

"But not with this. See." Shef patted a stout post that led up from a frame above the axles. "This post holds a metal spring." He pointed to it.

"Like the steel you use for your crossbows."

"Yes. Over the spring we fit straps of the stoutest leather. And from the straps we hang—this." Shef patted the wickerwork body of the coach, setting it swaying gently. "Climb in."

Gingerly Alfred stepped up, sat on one of the two benches in the coach body, noting the way it bounced and swung like a hammock.

"Lady." Shef stood back a careful two paces to avoid any brush of hand or clothing, gestured Godive in after her husband. She climbed in, moved little Edward from the place he had seized by his father, and settled herself firmly next to Alfred. Shef climbed in too, picked up the wailing child, and sat him next to himself. He waved to the driver in front of them, who cracked his whip and set off with a dramatic jerk.

As the coach dashed at unheard-of speed down the road behind its four horses, Alfred leapt in his seat with surprise. From behind the coach there came a dismal screech, which turned into a violent noise like pigs being killed. A gap-toothed face rose grinning into view, face purple with the exertion of blowing on a bagpipe.

"My thane Cwicca. If they hear the bagpipe people know to clear the road."

And indeed the coach, swaying from side to side on its springs, was already racing for the outskirts of Stamford. Alfred realized that the road was lined with cheering churls and their wives, all caught up in the intoxication of speed. Behind them the royal escorts were stretching out their horses into a gallop, whooping like jaybirds with excitement. Godive clutched her baby daughter to her and looked anxiously at Edward, prevented from climbing out by King Shef's iron grip on his breeches.

Above the roar of the road Alfred yelled, "Is this the most useful new thing the Wisdom-House has brought you?"

"No," Shef shouted back. "There are many. Here is one coming up, I'll show you. Stop, Osmod," he bellowed to the driver, "stop for Christ's sake, I mean Thor's sake, stop, can't you, what's the matter?"

Another grinning face peered back. "Sorry, lord, the horses get excited, like, with the speed."

Alfred looked down doubtfully. The court of Stamford was a strange place. Men called Alfred *esteadig,* 'the Gracious,' for his kindness and his good humor. Just the same, his thanes and aldermen addressed him with something like respect. Even churls often spoke to his co-king as if they were both schoolboys engaged in stealing apples: and both Cwicca and Osmod, thanes though they might be called, still had the marks of slave-birth on their faces and bodies. Not long ago their only possible contact with a king would have been facing his doom on an execution-ground. It was true that Cwicca and Osmod were both survivors of the One King's strange journey to the North, and so allowed many liberties. Even so . . .

The One King had already sprung from the coach, leaving its door swinging open, and was setting off from the road to a group of churls knee-deep in mud not far away. They broke off from what they were doing, knuckled foreheads in respect. And yet they were grinning too.

"See what they're up to? What's the hardest work in clearing a new field? Not cutting the trees down. Any fool can do that with a broad-axe. No, getting the stumps out. They used to cut them off low down and then try and burn them out. Long job, and oak, or ash, or elm, they'll all grow back from almost anything.

"But what we have here"—Shef seized a long staff standing up from a complex contrivance of iron wheels and pulley-blocks—"is ropes rigged to the stoutest stump in the field. Fit the other ends round a weaker stump. Throw your weight on it"—Shef suited his actions to the words, ratcheted the staff back, threw his weight forward again, and again. Twenty yards away, with cracking noises, a stump began to heave out of the earth. A churl sprang forward, added his weight to the king's. With heave after heave, the stump tore free, to loud cheering from churls and the watching escort.

The king wiped his muddy hands on the legs of his gray breeches, waved to the churls to drag the stump free and attach the ropes to the next victim.

"England is tree country. I am turning it into grain country. This pulley machine was made in the Wisdom House by priests of Njörth—they are seamen, they know all about pulleys—and some of my catapulteers. They are used to cogwheels. My steelmaster, Udd, is in charge of making the wheels. They have to be small, but strong."

"And do you let anyone have the machine?"

Shef's turn to grin. "If they left it to me, maybe. But they don't. My fee-master in the House of Wisdom, Father Boniface, he rents them out to those with land to clear. They pay a fee for the machine. But cleared land is free for the clearers to keep. Not for ever. For three lives. Then the land reverts to the crown. I get rich from the rents of the machines. My successors"—Shef nodded at baby Edward. "They get rich when the land comes back to them."

He pointed across the flat fields of Stamfordshire to the now-familiar shape of a windmill, sails turning briskly in the breeze. "Another new thing over there. Not the windmill, you know about that. What it's attached to. Another way to make new land. Come along and I'll show you."

The horse-wain slowed dramatically as Osmod the driver turned it off the Great North Road with its stone-and-gravel surface, and took it down one of the old mud tracks. Shef seized the opportunity of relative quiet to speak again of the successes of the House of Wisdom.

"We're off to see a big thing," he went on, leaning forward in his seat towards Alfred, "but there have been some small ones that have made as much of a difference. I didn't show you how this is hitched up at the front, for instance. But when we learned from Brand and his men how to harness a horse so it could pull, we found after a while that the horse-pull can be too strong. When you turn them, they often break their traces, as the pull comes through one side or the other, not through both. Well, we kept on using thicker leather. But then some farm-churl realized—I gave him his own farm and full livestock for it—that you don't need to harness the horses to the cart. You harness them to two ends of a stout bar instead, and you harness the bar, in the middle, to the cart. That way the pull evens out.

"And that doesn't just save on leather! No. I did not realize straight away. But often the real change a machine brings is not the first good it does, but the second. The whipple-tree, we call it, means men can plow shorter lines, smaller fields, because they can turn their teams more easily. And *that* means that even poor men, with no more than an acre or two, can plow their own fields instead of depending on their lords."

"And they thank the king for it," Alfred replied thoughtfully. "They become your men, not their landlords'. It is another thing, like your machine-fees, that makes you strong."

Godive shifted in her seat. "That's why he did it. He does nothing without a reason. I learned that years ago."

Shef fell silent, stared at his muddied fingers. After a few moments Alfred broke the silence. "This new thing you are taking us to see. Tell us about it."

Shef replied in a flatter, duller tone. "Well. Round here, as you know, the land turns quickly to marsh. Some of it has always been marsh. Naturally, people try to drain it. But if you dig a channel you can't always tell which way the water will run, not down here, or if the water will even go into the channel.

"But we knew one thing." Slowly the animation was coming back into his voice. "Anyone who brews a lot of beer knows that to get it out you can either tap the barrel low down—and then you have to plug it carefully or it'll all go—or else you can suck some up through a tube and then put the end of the tube in your jug or bucket. The beer keeps on running, even though you aren't sucking any more."

"I never knew that. How?"

Shef shrugged. "No-one knows. Not yet. But once we knew that we knew what we needed. Big tubes, bigger than any man could get his mouth round. And something to suck the water through. Like a bellows in reverse. Then we could make the water run from a fen into a channel, even a channel some distance away."

The wain and its escort pulled up by the mill they had been making for, and Shef jumped out, leaving the door swinging wide once more. Round the mill ran a confusion of muddy ditches, with here and there a tube of tarred canvas leading, seemingly, simply from one drain to another.

"Again, you see, new land." Shef lowered his voice so only his royal guests could hear, not the escort. "I don't know how much. Sometimes I think there might be the worth of half a dozen shires lying waiting to be drained. And this land I do not give away. I make the mills, I pay the millers. What is gained remains royal land, to be leased out for the royal revenues."

"To your own profit again," cut in Godive, her voice like a whip. Alfred saw his scarred co-king flinch again. "Tell me, out of all this, what have you done for women?"

Shef hesitated, began to say something, checked himself. He was unsure what to name first. The mills themselves, which had released tens of thousands of female slaves from the everlasting chore of grinding grain with a hand-quern? The experiments being conducted in the Wisdom House to find a better way to spin thread than the distaff, which almost every woman in the country still carried with her wherever she went, winding incessantly? No, Shef decided, the vital thing for women had been the soap-works he had set up, where they made a harsh and gritty soap out of ashes and animal fat: no new thing in itself, but one which, Hund the leech insisted, had halved the number of women dying of child-bed fever—once the king had issued an order that all midwives must take the soap and always wash their hands.

He took too long to decide. "I thought so," said Godive and whirled away, dragging her children with her. "Everything is for men. And everything for money."

She did not trouble to lower her voice. As she swept towards the wain, the two kings, Cwicca and Osmod, the miller and his wife, the two bands of royal escorts, all stared after her. Then all except Shef turned their eyes back to him.

He dropped his gaze. "It's not like that," he muttered, the same anger growing inside him that he had felt when the man crashed from the tower and they had asked him to pay for failure nonetheless. "You can't do everything. You have to do what you know how to, first, and then see where that leads you. Women get their share of what we have done. More land, more food, more wool."

"Aye," agreed Cwicca. "A few years ago, every winter you saw little bairns in rags and barefoot every winter, crying for cold and hunger. Now they've coats at least, and hot food inside them. Because the king protects them."

"That's right," said Shef, looking up, his face suddenly fierce. "Because all this"—his arms waved at the mill, the fields, the drainage channels, the waiting wain—"all this depends on one thing. And that is force. A few years ago, if any king, if good King Edmund or King Ella had done any wise thing, as soon as he had enough silver to use, the Vikings would have been on him, to take it away and turn the land to beggary again. To keep it like this we have to sink ships and break armies!"

A growl of immediate assent from his men and Alfred's, all of whom had won their way by battle alone.

"Yes," Shef went on, "all this is well enough. And I would be happy to see women take their part of it. But what I need most, what I would pay gold for, not silver, is not a new way of hitching horses, or of draining marshes, but a new way to defeat the Emperor out there. Bruno the German. For if we have forgotten him, here in the marsh, he has not forgotten us. Rig, my father"—Shef's voice rose to a shout, and he pulled from the breast of his tunic his silver ladder-emblem—"send me a new thing to bring victory in battle! A new sword, a new shield! New crossbows, new catapults. There is no other wisdom we need more. If Ragnarök is to come, let us fight it and win!"

Their king safely out of the way for a long morning, his closest advisers and friends had seized the opportunity to discuss him. They sat, the three of them, Brand, Thorvin and Hund, near the top of the great stone tower of the House of Wisdom, in Thorvin's private chamber, looking out over the busy and fertile countryside, the green fields divided by the long white strip of the Great North Road, riders and carts passing steadily along it. With them, though, and at Thorvin's insistence, sat a fourth man: Farman priest of Frey, one of the two great visionaries of the Way. An unimpressive figure, and one who had not shared the perils of the others, but deep in the secrets of the gods, or so Thorvin insisted.

Brand the giant Norwegian had looked askance at Farman for a while, but he had known the others, at least, long enough to speak frankly. "We've got to face it," he began. "If he goes, Shef I mean, then everything will go. There's people like Guthmund, owes everything to the One King, stone-cold reliable as far as he's concerned. But would Guthmund agree to co-operate with Olaf, or Gamli, or Arnodd, or any of the other kings in Denmark or Norway? He would not. His own jarls wouldn't let him if he did. As for obeying an Englishman . . . No, this is a one-man business. The trouble is, the man's mad."

"You've said that before," said Hund the leech reprovingly, "and been proved wrong."

"All right, all right," Brand conceded. "Maybe he's not mad, just strange, he always has been. But you know what I mean all the same. He has won many battles and survived many strange events. But each one seems to take something out of him. And it isn't put back."

The other three considered the matter: Hund the leech, priest of Ithun and Englishman, Thorvin the smith, priest of Thor and Dane, Farman the visionary, a man whose race was by now forgotten.

"He lost something when he killed Sigurth," volunteered Hund. "He lost that lance. None of us knows how he came by it, exactly, but he valued it for some reason or another. They say it is the lance the new Emperor always carries with him, and Hagbarth says he saw the two fight, and Bruno run off with it. Maybe it is the good luck sign that the Christians call it, and that is what he has lost."

Brand shook his head decisively. "No. We have experts on luck here, and he has not lost that. He is as lucky as he ever was. No, it is something else. Something to do with how he feels about himself."

"He lost friends that day at the Braethraborg also," Hund suggested again. "The young man from the Ditmarsh, and Cuthred the champion. Could he feel—guilty, maybe, because he lived and they did not?"

Brand, the veteran warrior, chewed on the thought, not much liking the taste of it. "I have known things like that," he conceded eventually. "But I don't think that's it. To tell the truth"—he looked round before going on. "I think it's to do with that damned woman."

"Godive, Alfred's wife?" said Hund, shocked. He had known them both since all three were small children.

"Yes, her. She talks to him as if he was a dog, and he flinches like one that has been beaten too often. But not just her. There was the other one too, Ragnhild, the queen in Norway. She took something from him. He did not kill her, but he caused her death, and her son's. If he feels guilty it is not about the men he has hurt, but about the women. That's why he will not take another one."

A silence. This time it was Hund's turn to chew on a thought and not relish the taste of it.

"Talks to him like a dog," he said in the end. "My name means 'dog,' as you know. My master, Shef's stepfather, thought that was all I would ever be to him. But he gave Shef a dog's name too, in hatred. We see new folk smile all the time when they hear us say 'King Shef,' as if we were saying 'King Bowlegs' or 'King Fang.' Norsemen cannot even pronounce it. You know Alfred has asked him several times to take another name, one that both English and Norse could say and honor: Offa or Atli, some hero-name from the past. Yet you say his *is* a hero-name, Thorvin? Perhaps it is time you explained that to us. For I feel whatever is happening here is the gods' business as well as ours. Tell us the whole story. And tell us why the Way has accepted him in the end, as the One who is to come. The three of us here, after all, know more of his story than anyone else in the world. And Farman is our guide to the gods. Maybe between the four of us we can judge it."

Thorvin nodded, but hesitated a while, to organize his thoughts.

"It's like this," he said in the end. "There is a very old story the Danes tell. It has never been turned into a poem, and it is not part of our holy books, or not one that all accept. I used to think little of it as well. But the more I reflect on it, the more it seems to me that it has a ring about it, a stink of old age. I believe it is a true story, and that it has meaning in the same way that the lays of Völund or of dead Balder do.

"One way that it is told is this. Many years ago—about the time that Christians say their Christ was born—the Danes found themselves without a king. They had driven out the last of their royal line, that Hermoth who is said to be the favorite warrior of Othin in Valhalla, for his cruelties. But without a king the cruelties grew even worse. It was an age when brother slew brother and no man's life was safe except when he had weapons in hand.

"Then one day, on the shore of the sea, they found a shield washed up, and in the shield there was a baby boy. His head was resting on a sheaf of barley, but other than that he had nothing. They took him in and reared him, and in time he became the mightiest king the North has ever known. He was so warlike that he made peace across the North. In his time, they say, a virgin could walk unescorted from one end of the North to the other, with gold on every finger and a bag of it at her girdle, and no man would stay her or offer her so much as a foul word. Danish kings still claim, some of them, to be of his line, the Skjöldungar, the Shieldings, for he was called Skjöld after the shield they found him in.

"That is one story," Thorvin went on, "and you can see it makes a kind of sense. The shield gives the name, the Shieldings. And because the boy came from nowhere men say that the gods sent him, because they saw the misery of the Danes and pitied it.

"But in other ways it does not make much sense, and that is why I think it is genuine. Yes, Brand, I see you raise your eyebrows, but what I am telling you is that the good sense of the gods is not the same as the good sense of men. Consider: the gods pitied the misery of the Danes? Since when do our gods pity anything? We would not worship them if they did. And anyway, what about this sheaf? It is always in the story, but no one knows why. I think that is the key to understanding.

"I think that the story as we have it has been told wrong, over the years. I think the name of the king was once heard as Skjöld Skjefing, or in English Scyld Sceafing. Some storyteller somewhere took the name and made a story out of it. He said the king was called 'Shield' because—why, because he had floated to land on a shield. And he was called 'Sheaf-ing' because—because there must have been a sheaf with him. The names came from the things. Even the story about floating to land came from the idea of the hollow shield. Now, I do not think any of that was true.

"Instead I think there was a real king called 'Shield.' Many of us have names like that. Your name, Brand, means 'sword.' I have met men called Geirr, 'spear,' or Franki, 'battle-axe.' There was a king called Shield. He was called Sheaf-ing not because of having his head on a sheaf, but because he was the son of Sheaf. Or Shef."

Thorvin seemed to think he had finished his explanation. After a while Hund prompted him further. "But what does this story, this old story, mean?"

Thorvin fingered his hammer pendant. "In my view—and this is not shared by others of the College, indeed some would call me a heretic if they heard me say it, Farman, as well you know. In my view it means three things. One, these kings were remembered, or invented, for a reason. I think the reason is that they set our world on a track, a track it had not gone before. I think the war-king who made peace, Shield, he was the one who organized men into nations and gave the North law: law better than the strife of brother against brother that they had had before. I think the peace-king, Sheaf, gave us barley and crops and fields, and turned us from the ways of our ancestors, who lived like the Finns, hunting in the waste. Or like your cousins the Huldu-folk, Brand. Meat-eaters and wanderers.

"Two, I think the track they set us on was the right track, and men have never quite forgotten it. But since then we have climbed back onto the wrong track: the track of Hermoth, Othin's favorite. War and piracy. We give it proud names and call it *drengskapr,* the *hermanna vegr,* gallantry, the warriors' way. You do that, Brand, I know. But it comes down to the strong robbing the weak."

"I prefer to rob the strong," growled Brand, but Thorvin ignored him.

"I think King Shef has been sent here to return us to the right track. But that track is not the track of Hermoth, or of Othin. Indeed I think our king bears Othin's enmity. He will not sacrifice to him. He will not take his token.

"And now I come to what some would call heresy. I cannot help remembering that all this was supposed to happen at the same time as the Christians say their White Christ came. And why did he come? Why did Sheaf and Shield come? I can only say this, and it is the third opinion I hold.

"I think the world at some time endured some great maim, some great wound that could not be cured. Balder died, we say, and the light went out of the world. The Christians have their foolish story of an apple and a serpent, but it comes to the same point: the world was maimed, and it needed a healer. A healer from outside. The Christians say the healer was the Christ and the healing is done, and so we can all sit on our backsides and wait for rescue. Hah! We say maybe—or we used to say—that two kings came, to start us on our way. Then we lost it. It is my view that the king we have, not called Shef by chance, has come to set us on the right way again, like his many times grandsire. For I think that both he and his ancient namesake are the begetting of a god, the god Rig. Not older, maybe, than Othin, but wiser."

After a pause Hund said, fingering his Ithun-pendant, "I cannot see where the heresy lies in that, Thorvin. Not that we are Christians in any case to tell men what to think."

Thorvin stared into the distance, out across road and fields. "I am beginning to suggest that the Way-stories and the Christ-story are of the same kind. Both false, both garbled. Or, it may be, both true. But true fragments of a greater whole."

Brand laughed, suddenly. "And you may be right, Thorvin! But while you may persuade me, and Hund here, and even the council of the priests of the Way if you talk to them long enough, I doubt you will get far in persuading the Pope of the Christians in Rome to go along with you. And agree that maybe the Way has some truth on its side too!"

Thorvin laughed with him. "No, I shall not go to Rome and ask for an audience to put my point of view. Nor will I forget that whatever one thinks of the Christians, the Church remains our deadly enemy. And the Empire now that supports it. They say our king had Bruno the German in the şights of his crossbow that day. He should have pulled trigger."

For the first time Farman spoke, the pale thin face unaffected by emotion. "The maim," he repeated. "The maim the world has suffered, that this second Shef, or second Savior, has been sent to heal. In our myth that is the death of Balder, brought about by the tricks of Loki. But we all know that Othin tried to have Balder released from Hel, and failed, and chained Loki beneath serpent-fangs in vengeance. Vengeance may be good, but how can one see any cure?"

"If there is a cure," said Thorvin, "it will come about through something mere sense cannot predict. But our friend Shef—he is wise, but often good sense is not in him."

"And so we are back to our real question," Hund concluded. "Whether he is man or half-god, crazy or driven, what are we to do with him?"

Farman looked out at the shape of a speeding coach on the road, trailed by a plume of dust and thirty galloping horses. "I cannot be sure," he said. "I have seen nothing in my dreams of this. But from all I have heard, I would say that this man has unfinished business with the gods. Maybe it is his destiny to regain the Holy Lance, maybe to burn the gates of Rome, I do not know. But while he sits here he is rejecting it, turning his gaze away."

"Fretting about women he left behind many years ago," agreed Brand.

"It may be he needed the chance to draw breath, even to grow to be a man," Farman went on. "But he will grow no more if he stays here playing muddy games with yokels."

"We must get him on board a ship," said Thorvin. "Maybe it will take him where the gods mean him to be, like the naked child floating on the shield in the story."

"But this time he must not go alone," said Farman. "You are his friends. You must go with him. As for me—I will wait for clearer guidance."

From outside the notes of the bagpipe squealed their discordant warning.

CHAPTER FOUR

Ghaniya, half-brother to the Caliph of Cordova, well understood the importance of his mission to the North, to the savage, half-naked, fire-worshiping *majus*, the devil-people, as he thought of them. That did not prevent him from hating every moment of it. He was a man of certain and unquestioned loyalty. If he had not been, of course, he would not have survived his brother's succession to the *divan,* the cushioned throne of Cordova. His brother might be called, in honor of his great ancestor, Abd er-Rahman, the Servant of the Compassionate One, but there was no compassion in his nature. When he succeeded to his father, the sword and the bowstring had been busy. The male children of his father's harem had been considered carefully and attentively. The children of true Arabs, descendants of the Quraysh, had died soon: they might have been centers for future rebellion. The descendants of Christian slave-women had died also, if they seemed unusable: some of the best had been given posts in exile, under supervision, often on the frontier against the feeble Christian princedoms and dukedoms of the mountainous North of Spain. Ghaniya, however, had been the son of a Berber woman. His blood not pure enough to attract supporters, yet he was the child of no *mustarib* either, no would-be-Arab, as they contemptuously called the children of Christians who had converted to Islam for food, or advancement.

Ghaniya knew he was good enough to be used. Not good enough to be feared. It satisfied his ambition, at least for the time. He had no intention of risking once again the leather carpet that stood before the divan, with by it the giant slaves with their scimitars forever drawn.

It was a good sign also that he had been sent on this mission. He knew how seriously his half-brother took it, as he had taken the news from

Mallorca and from Sicily. Not that a Caliph of Cordova could fear the activities of the Christians, whether Greek or Frank. The city of Cordova in the year 875 had fully half a million inhabitants: more than the villages of Rome and Byzantium and all the capitals of all the Franks put together. Every day three thousand minarets called the faithful to prayer. Every day a thousand carts rolled into the city with food for the citizens, drawn from the immensely fertile valley of the Guadalquivir, and all of Andalusia beyond it. The Christians could not reach Cordova if all the Faithful did was merely to stand before them to block their way.

And yet er-Rahman his brother had listened with great care to the account of Mu'atiyah, the pupil of bin-Firnas: as he had also to the reports of his merchants returning from Egypt and reporting on the panic and fear among the Tulunids there. He had condescended even to explain his thoughts to his half-brother.

"We need the islands," he had said. "They guard our traders, they guard our shores. Also," he went on, "a caliph must think of the future. For many years we have pressed back the unbelievers, from the day our ancestor landed on the shore at Jeb el-Tarik, and told his men the sea was behind them and the enemy in front, and there was nothing for them but victory or death. Now we come upon a check. Is it a check, or is it the moment when the balance tilts?" Er-Rahman, knowing only a tideless sea, had no idea of the image of the tide turning, but if he had he would have used it. "If our enemies even think the balance is tilting," he concluded, "they will gain heart. We must thrust them back once more.

"And another thing. We have always known the Christians our inferiors in all the arts of civilization. Where have they such a man as bin-Firnas"— he stretched a hand to his listening pupil—"and yet now they come on our shores with weapons we cannot match. We must know more. Our enemies will not tell us. Yet our enemies have enemies too, or so we hear. The news came years ago of the defeat of a great host of the *ferengis*, the Franks, at the hands of those who were not Christians. Seek them out, my brother. Find what they know. Bring us help, or knowledge. Take with you the pupil of bin-Firnas, to report on whatever mechanic arts the savages have been able to learn."

He had waved a hand. And by doing so he had sent Ghaniya with his guards and his companions, and his adviser the pupil of bin-Firnas, on this terrible expedition into the land of everlasting wind and cold.

It had begun ill, with the ship they had taken from the port of Malaga pronounced useless as soon as they were through the straits of Jeb el-Tarik themselves. The sea grew fiercer, the wind stronger, the rowers made no progress against the current sweeping in from the ocean to the central sea of the world, the Mediterranean. Ghaniya had transferred at Cadiz to a different vessel, a ship with sails, captained and crewed by men who showed the blood of the Christians in their faces and their actions. They had been willing enough to sail north, for gold, and their families remained as hostages for their loyalty. Yet Ghaniya had doubts about their respect from the start.

Even his pork-eating crewmen had fallen silent, though, as they pressed further into the cold seas of the North. As they approached what they had heard should be their goal, the port of Lon ed-Din, gray shores beginning to show on either hand, a strange craft had sheered up to them out of the everlasting squalls of rain. A ship twice the size of theirs, with two masts made from tree-trunks, and sails towering up to the sky. High castles stood on poop and bow, with great machines on them and fierce bearded faces glowering over iron plates. The ship had not closed up, merely pulled alongside, and with deliberate routine launched a great rock into the sea ten yards ahead of Ghaniya's own bow. A long shouted exchange in some unknown language like the barking of dogs: then the ship had shifted its sails and swept leisurely away.

"They say go ahead," the *mustarib* skipper translated. "They wanted to be sure only that we were not servants of the Franks, of the Empire with whom they are at eternal war."

A good sign, Ghaniya had tried to think. The enemy of my enemy is my friend, and these are enemies of the Franks, true enough. Yet he had not liked the careless ease with which a ship of Cordova had been weighed and dismissed. Nor had he liked the strange sight of the ship. Even the supercilious Mu'atiyah, he noticed, had stood gaping after it for too long.

Shef's shipwrights had had several years of peace in which to discard or perfect the desperate makeshifts of the 860s. Prodded on by their king, and by the expert advisers of the Way, Hagbarth priest of Njörth prominent among them, they had come up with new designs taking up the best features and solving the problems of the old. The idea of the catapult-mounting battleship had stayed, much improved by the ring mounting devised by steelmaster Udd. The problem of weight high up had been solved by broadening and ballasting the hull. The terrible sluggishness of Shef's first 'Shire' class of battleships had been solved in part by developing and extending the two-mast design. The doubled sail area had meant that the fisherman's idea of the slanted and extended sail could be dropped. There were still problems, as Shef's skippers reported, sailing before the wind, for the rear sail robbed the wind of the foresail. If they could, such ships would always sail with wind on the beam. Some skippers were experimenting with a small extra sail on a topmast above the foremast, keeping half a dozen lithe lightweight boys in their crew to shin up and reef the sail when needed. Yet meanwhile one problem remained, which Brand at least had thought insoluble: weakness in the keel, now larger than any single tree-trunk could furnish.

Steelmaster Udd had dealt with that by insisting that metal could do what wood could not. Weak keels needed more bracing, that was all. In the end a combined system of bronze bolts—for even Udd had had to admit that salt water was death to the strongest steel—and massive riveted wooden ribs had strengthened the combination keels even to Atlantic levels. At last seaworthy, decked all over, mounting swiveling onagers fore and aft, with heavy crossbows lining each gunwale, the new ships of the navy of the co-kings had immediately closed the English Channel to all ships without their majesties' license. Trade from Frisia to the Loire moved only on their sufferance. Tolls on trade paid the ships' crews. And without a Viking ship at sea from end to end of the Atlantic coast, trade doubled and redoubled. The Andalusian ship, rowing slowly in the end into the port of London, found a scene of activity that might almost have been the Guadalquivir, for business if not in sheer population.

At least they had had no trouble in gaining attention. As soon as the port-reeve who came aboard had grasped that these men sought audience with his master, and that they could pay in bright gold dirhams, he had provided the embassy with horses—poor scrubs of animals, Ghaniya noticed with contempt and a certain relief—with a guide and escort, and set them firmly on their way up the road that led North to the king's capital of Stamford.

As the party rode on, Ghaniya's anxiety nevertheless increased. To a son of the Quraysh, nothing that barbarians did could seem wholly admirable, but Ghaniya was intelligent enough to read the signs. He would not exchange his own cotton for the animal fabrics that the natives wore. Yet he could feel soon enough how inadequate his cotton was for the continuous winds and the everlasting rain. He saw, too, how the mere peasants laboring in the fields did so in stout wool. The food they ate was such as the dogs of Cordova would turn from in disgust, black bread and pigs' fat, soured cows' milk and sharp biting vegetables that filled the breath. Yet they seemed to have plenty of it. He saw no pinched faces, no hands outstretched for alms.

By the side of the road, too, again and again he saw the wheels turning. The first two or three he came to, he turned from with a smile of patronage on his face. They were like the *norias* of his homeland, only the unfortunate barbarians used them not to lift water but to grind their corn; and they did so by putting the wheels in the slow-moving water and taking what force they could get from that. The fourth mill they saw, however, turned Ghaniya's smile to a frown. Here the natives had realized their error, had taken advantage of a slope to direct the water-channel above the wheel, so that it was driven by the full weight of falling water, not flowing water. And from inside the mill came not the harsh grinding of the corn-mill but the continuous Iblis-clash of a trip-hammer forging iron. It was not a thought Ghaniya could readily frame, but at the back of his mind lurked the suspicion that while the barbarians had clearly been no better than he thought them a short while ago, in a few years they seemed to have made more changes than had taken place under as many caliphs as could be remembered.

Nor did Ghaniya like the stories passed on to him about the strange king responsible for all this. It was good that he was no Christian. It was acceptable that he did not persecute Christians: no more did the great er-Rahman himself, preferring to tax them instead as he could not tax believers. It was impossible that any should believe that he was the Son of God, another Yeshua returned. Even worse, it might be, that he was not the son of the One God in whom Christian and Moslem alike believed, but of some barbarian godlet, one among many. Ghaniya felt the horror of the monotheist for the idol-worshiper.

Tempered still with fear: one day on the road they had heard terrible screeching coming towards them, and then seen on the road five hundred men marching together, bagpipers at their head and the banner floating over them of the smith's hammer. No Christian cross with it, for these were men of the Way, their alliance with the Christian Alfred no longer signaled. Ghaniya, drawing his horse aside, had marked their weapons: the usual metal-clad foot-soldiers of the *ferengis,* strong men with swords and axes, but pitifully slow to move, but with them others, small men mostly with strange heavy bows over their shoulders, and trailing the column a dozen contrivances pulled by mules, objects of rope and wood. Dart-throwers, his guide declared, or stone-throwers, catapults that could batter down any wall, pierce any armor or shielding. Ghaniya scowled most of all at the cheerful faces and the constant chatter from the marching men. These men possessed something he understood: *iqbal,* the expectation of success that breeds success.

And yet when he came to the town they called the capital, Ghaniya felt his sense of disdain and superiority rise again like the flesh of a caliph in his harem. The town would not have ranked as a suburb of Cordova. Its stone tower was new and well-made, but low and single. The market place itself had fewer men in it than a courtyard of his master. From one end of the town he could see the other! Instead of the crowd of suppliants being ranked and listed by chamberlains, one man came out to meet them, and made no pretense that his master was too busy to receive any visitor. Surely the master of such a place could feel only honor at being offered an alliance with the Caliph of Cordova, Successor of the Prophet, Deputy of Allah on Earth!

Ghaniya felt confidence again as he prepared for his audience with the master of the men and of the ships. He must impress them, he reflected, with his own wealth and with the learning of Mu'atiyah, neither of which, he was sure, the barbarians could match. It troubled him only that in this far land he must rely, for a translator, on the skills of Suleiman the Jew.

*   *   *

"What's a Jew?" muttered Shef out of the corner of his mouth. The embassy of strangers stood in front of him in his great chamber of audience, one of their party—not the leader, but the spokesman—standing in front of the others. He had just introduced himself, but the word he used meant nothing to Shef.

The advisers who stood behind him conferred briefly. Then, as Shef's own translator Father Boniface began again to put the other's credentials into English, Skaldfinn priest of Heimdall stepped forward. A linguist and interpreter, he knew all there was to be known in the North about foreign peoples.

"The Jews are the people from the East who crucified the Christian god," he said. "Apparently there are still some of them left."

"It was the Romans who crucified Christ," said Shef. "German soldiers from a Roman legion." He spoke with flat certainty, as if he had seen the event himself.

"The Christians prefer to blame the Jews."

"And these other folk, the ones in long thin robes. What do they believe?"

"We call them Mohammedans. They believe in a prophet who arose some time before ours. Their God and the Christian God seem much the same, but they do not believe in the Christ as divine, and the Christians will not accept their prophet even as a prophet. There is always war between the Mohammedan kingdoms and the Christian ones. Yet the Mohammedans accept Christian subjects, and Jewish subjects, and treat them fairly."

"Like us, then."

"Yes: except—"

"Except what?" Shef was still listening with half an ear to Boniface's long translation of what seemed the Jewish spokesman's excessively flowery string of opening compliments.

"Except that they regard all three, Mohammedan, Jew and Christian, as 'People of the Book.' They do not regard any others as sharing the same God, as these three religions do, even if they have different beliefs."

Shef pondered for a while as the double translation wandered on, the Arabic of Ghaniya heard and put into a kind of Latin by Suleiman the Jew; the Latin heard and put into the Norse-English dialect of Shef's court by Boniface. Eventually he raised a hand. The translation stopped at once.

"Tell him, Boniface, that I am told they do not consider us to be People of the Book. Now, Thorvin, show him one of our books. Show him your book of holy poems, written all in runes. Boniface, ask whether he will not say that we too are people of a book."

Ghaniya stroked his beard as the big man in white with a hammer in his belt came towards him, holding out a volume of some kind. He let Suleiman take it in case there was some sort of defilement lurking in it.

"What is it made of?" he muttered in Arabic.

"They say it is the skin of calves."

"Not pigs, then, praise Allah. They have no paper, then?"

"No. Neither paper nor scrolls."

Both men looked at the writing without comprehension. Suleiman peered closer.

"See, lord, there are no curves anywhere in this script. It is all straight lines. I think they have taken some system they have for scratching marks on wood with a knife, and made it into a kind of writing."

Shef's one sharp eye saw the very faint curl of contempt on Ghaniya's lip, and remarked to the men behind him, "They are not impressed. See, the spokesman will praise it politely and not answer our question."

"The emissary of the Caliph sees your book," tried Suleiman manfully, "and admires your penmanship. If you have no artisans skilled in the making of paper, he will send instruction. We too did not understand that art till it was shown to us by captives from a far Empire, whom we defeated in battle many years ago."

Suleiman found no Latin word for 'paper' other than *papyrium*, papyrus, known to Boniface already, though he used vellum. By the time translation reached Shef it had become 'calf-hide,' neither new nor interesting.

"Accept his offer politely and ask what brings him here."

All the advisers, English and Norse, Christians and Waymen alike, listened attentively as the story rolled out, of attacks on one island after another, of the Greek fleet and the Frankish soldiers, of the iron men and the Greek fire. As Suleiman reached the last point, Shef intervened again to ask if there was anyone in the embassy who had seen it for himself. Their group parted and a young man was urged forward: a young man with the dark aquiline face of his leader, but on it, Shef could only say, an expression of smug superiority he was not diplomat enough to conceal.

Slowly the young man was led through his tale.

"You have sharp eyes," said Shef at the end.

Mu'atiyah looked sideways at Ghaniya, received a nod, and slowly produced his spyglass.

"My master, bin-Firnas," he said, "is the wisest man in the world. First he learned to correct the weakness of his eyes, by the use of a reading-glass of the correct shape. Then one day, by his direction and the will of Allah, I discovered that two glasses will make the far-off close." He trained the stout leather-covered lens out of the open window, seemed as always to have difficulty finding the right focus.

"There," he said finally, "an unveiled maiden bends over the well, winding up water in a bucket. She is of great beauty, fit for a caliph's harem, and her arms are bare. Round her neck she wears—she wears a silver phallus, by Allah!" The young man's laugh brought a frown of disapproval from his own leader: wiser not to mock the savages, even if their women had no shame.

Shef looked at Ghaniya, received the nod of permission, took the strange object from the young man's hands, ignoring his frown of discontent. He looked at the larger end, took a cloth from a table and rubbed the lens gently, feeling its shape. Did the same at the smaller end. He had noticed before, looking through the thick bottle-glass which was the best his own world could produce for windows and that only for the greatest, how shapes were distorted by it. So that could be useful as well as a hindrance.

"Ask him why one end has to be smaller than the other."

A mutter of translation. The answer: he does not know.

"The shape at the large end bulges out. What would happen if it curved in?"

Again the mutter, again the answer.

"What happens if the tube is longer or shorter?"

This time the answer was evidently angry, the Jew's translation shorter, as if diplomatically altered. "He says it is enough that it works," came the filtered reply from Boniface.

Finally Shef put the tube to his one eye, looked where the young Arab had. "Yes," he remarked. "It is Alfwyn daughter of Edgar the groom." He inverted the tube, looked through the large end as Ma'mun had done before him, to a grunt of impatience from the Arab, handed it back without further comment.

"Well," he said, "they know some things, but they seem to have no great desire to learn any more. People of the Book, indeed, doing things because their master said so. You know what I think of that, Thorvin." Shef looked round at his advisers, aware that nothing he said could be understood by Suleiman or the others without further translation into Latin. "Is there any good reason why we should ally with them? It seems to me they need us more than we need them."

The demonstration had gone wrong, Ghaniya realized. He had thought little of their book. They had noticed—or their king had—that Mu'atiyah was a fool, for all the wisdom of his master. This was a moment when his mission hung in the balance. His voice hissed ominously as he whispered to Mu'atiyah and Suleiman together.

"Tell them of the glories of Cordova, you fools. Mu'atiyah, tell that king of theirs something about your master that even he will wonder at. And no tricks for children! He may be a savage, but he is not one to be deceived by toys!"

Both men hesitated. Suleiman was the quicker to respond. "You are a Christian priest?" he said to Boniface. "Yet you serve a king who is not of your faith? Tell your master, then, that so do I. Tell him that it would be wise for all those of us who serve masters like him and like my master to stand together. For whether we are all People of the Book or not—and I do not think his book is like my Torah or your Bible or my master's Koran—yet we are all people of the blessing. Our blessing is that we do not seek to make others share our belief by force. The Greeks burn or blind those who do not share their creed down to the last word and glossing. The Franks say to each other, 'Christians are right and pagans are wrong.' They accept no other book than their own Bible and their own reading of it. For your sake and mine, father, add your own words to what I have said, I beg you! We are the ones who will suffer first. They call me the crucifier of their Lord. What will they call you? A traitor to the Faith?''

Shef listened as Boniface, paraphrasing now rather than translating, repeated the substance of Suleiman's appeal. He noted the concern on the Jew's face. His own betrayed no response.

"Ask what the other has to say?"

Mu'atiyah had time to collect his thoughts, but they ran only to a repetition of the many virtues of his master: virtues in the Arab tradition. He had made a machine for counting out the beat of music, so that musicians might play their instruments in time. His courtyard was the glory of Cordova for the glass roof he had made over his fountain. He had found out how to make glass from ashes. His poetry—Mu'atiyah was grasping at straws by now—was famous across the world.

Shef glanced round at his advisers, ready to draw the audience to a close. Ghaniya scowled furiously at the gabbling Mu'atiyah, now shaken by the lack of interest on all faces.

"Shall I sing the one-eyed king one of the poems of my master?" he suggested. "Or one of the poems *about* my master?"

Shef grunted as he heard the translation, rose to his feet, looked Ghaniya firmly in the eye. As he drew in his breath to terminate the hearing, Boniface broke in, his quiet voice cutting across the gabble of Arabic from the young scholar.

"Pardon, lord. He has said something interesting. He offers to sing you a poem about the time his master flew. Flew from the tallest tower in Cordova. And lived, it seems."

Shef looked at the young man with deep suspicion. "Ask him what feathers he used?"

Question and answer, and Boniface's reply. "He says no feathers. He says only a fool would think men can fly like birds. They have to fly like men."

"How then?"

"He will not say. His master orders him not to speak. He says, if you want to see, come to Cordova and look."

* * *

Hours later, after a closed meeting with his council and an extended feast for his own men and their visitors, Shef headed wearily for his bed. The feast had been a struggle. His visitors had queried every dish set before them, refused pork, ham, sausages, wine, mead, beer, cider and even the 'burnt wine' that Udd had learnt to distil, sniffing it suspiciously and then rejecting it. In the end they had eaten little but bread and water. Shef feared for their health. In his world drinking plain water was a risk few cared to take. Water-drinkers died too often of the belly-ache and the running flux.

The meeting had been little better. All the way through he had been conscious of pressure, of being manipulated. What surprised him was that his advisers had been unanimous on wanting him to leave. In the past they had been anxious to hold him back from what they saw as rash expeditions. Now—though they had done so carefully—they seemed united in wanting him away. A man more interested in politics than himself might have suspected a brewing rebellion.

First it had been Brand. "The Inner Sea," he had muttered. "It's been done before. I don't suppose you know this, but the Ragnarssons"—he had spat into the fire at the mention of their name—"they tried it before ever you were on the scene. Fifteen years ago, maybe, when their father was still alive. Took a hundred ships down and stayed away two years. That was when there were five of them . . ."

"Five?" Shef had asked. He had known only four.

"Yes. Sigurth, Ivar, Halvdan, Ubbi—and their elder brother, Björn. Björn Ironside, they called him. I quite liked him," Brand reflected. "Not as crazy as the others. He was killed by a stray rock when they besieged Paris.

"Anyway, point is this: they went down there, came back two years later when everyone had got to thinking they were dead. Lost more than half their ships and two thirds of their men. But, Hel, did they come back rich! Start of the Ragnarssons' power, that was. They built the Braethraborg on it. Must be good pickings down there. You don't find gold anywhere else."

We don't need gold, we have silver enough, Shef had replied. But then it had been Hund, playing up the chances for new knowledge. A whole new science of the eye, he had suggested. And what of the flying man? No-one would give them any further details, but the way the story had slipped out, not intentionally, from a silly youth talking about poetry: that argued there was something in it. Something that none of them could even imagine. That was the most useful type of new knowledge. In any case, Hund had added, he had talked carefully to the Jew translator. It was clear that in the city of Cordova they had leeches who did not think twice about opening the body of their patients to cure them, something even Ingulf, Hund's master, had done only a few times, and Hund even fewer. And he had said besides, that there were men there who did not scruple to open the skull and search the brain. He would go south, Hund had declared. It was his duty to Ithun, his patron-deity, goddess of healing.

Thorvin had said little, though he too had offered to join any expedition that might sail. Who would direct the Wisdom-House for you, Shef had asked. Farman, said Thorvin without debate, a strange answer, for Farman shared none of Thorvin's interests in the crafts of the smith. His eyes had dwelt somberly on Shef all evening, as if wishing him to leave.

Shef stumbled into his room, dismissed the light-bearing attendants, stripped off his garments of state and threw them into a corner, rolled himself in his blankets, and wished for sleep. Even on the down mattress, so different from the boards and straw on which he had slept most of his life, sleep did not come easily. And it came haunted.

In his dream, he was looking down at a mappa. *But a true* mappa, *different immediately from the one he himself had hanging on the wall of his great study-chamber. Even more different from the many he had seen and collected from the Christian world. Most Christian maps presented the world as a T-shape, with the unknown land of Africa as the vertical beam, with Europe as one of the cross-beams and Asia as the other, the two equal in size. And the junction-point, the pivot of the world, invariably marked as Jerusalem.*

Shef's own maps were detailed towards the North and the West, fading rapidly into vagueness in the South and the East, where he refused to indicate what had not been confirmed by reliable sources. The map of his dream was neither Christian schematic nor local record. He knew intuitively that it was true. Too jagged, unexpected, and full of needless additions to be the work of imagination.

On the map, divisions were marked in colors. First Shef saw his own dominions, Britain, Denmark, Norway, Sweden, the islands between them, in a wash of brilliant red. Against them, other lands began to be marked out in blue. First the land of the Franks, facing Britain, then the whole interior of Europe, the German lands, then rippling down in a blue tide the boot-shape of Italy. The Empire of Charlemagne. Now owing allegiance again to the Holy Lance. Only carried in the hands of Charlemagne's true successor, though not his blood-successor. Bruno, new emperor.

Shef jerked as he heard a cold, quiet voice, too familiar to him now. "Easy," it said. "This is not a Hel-vision. No serpent, no Loki. Just look at the map. Look at the frontiers on it.

"See, you have only one land frontier with the Empire, at the base of Denmark. Fortified now by you from the Ditmarsh to the Baltic Sea, along the lines of the old Dannevirke, the Dane-work that King Guthfrith built. But Bruno has many frontiers. To the East . . ." and Shef saw the blue fade away to a near-colorless pallor, gently turning green. "The land of the steppe and the forest. From it any moment great armies can come. But they fade as fast as they appear. Bruno does not worry greatly about them.

"To the South-East." And suddenly Shef saw a blaze of gold sweep across from the Italian boot-top towards the depths of Asia. "The Greeks. With their great city of Byzantium, Micklegarth as Brand calls it, the Great Town. Not as rich, any more, as the lands of the Arabs. But the true heir of the Romans, and the Roman knowledge. Bruno does not fear them either, though he has plans for them. He wishes to bring them into a united Christendom, with the skill and subtlety of the Greeks and the energy and ferocity of his own Germans. Even the warriors of the steppe might quail before that. But now see the silver."

And it was there, washing across the map like a carpet unrolling, stretching over lands Shef could not imagine, far to the East of the Byzantines and deep into Africa as well. "The lands of Dar al-Islam, submission to the will of Allah," said the cold voice. "Allah the One God. No wonder that the hate is hottest between the two sides who believe alike in One God. Maybe the same god. But that neither side can agree.

"See now where lies the Dar al-Harb. The House of War." A glowing line began to thread between the silver and the blue, across the mountain-lands of Northern Spain—"robber-dukedoms," said the voice, "but strengthened now by the Lanzenorden, the soldier-monks of Christ." A flicker across southern France—"robber-holds of the Mohammedans," said the voice, "but now under threat from the reviving Empire." And then a glow around island after island, Sicily, Malta, Sardinia, Mallorca, the remaining Balearics. "They are the key," said the voice. "They control the Inner Sea." Slowly Shef saw the silver change again and again to blue. Like pincers groping round the flank of Arab Spain.

Unite the blue and gold, Shef thought. Cut off the silver and turn it blue. There will then be a great block across the world. His own red came back into focus—a thin line, an edge drawn around one corner of the block. His dominion ran from Scilly to North Cape. It seemed no more than a pencil line for thinness.

"Now there is the hinge," said the voice, already seeming to come from further away, as if it was withdrawing. The maps of the Christians showed Jerusalem, always, as the world-center, the pivot, the axle-tree of destiny. As Shef looked at it, one center spot seemed to glow, to stand out against the fading colors of his dream, to swell towards him. A spot at the heart of the Inner Sea, balancing north against south, east against west. But he did not know where it was.

His thought reached out after his fading mentor, calling: "Where? Where?"

And the voice came back, from a chill and hostile distance. "Rome," it called. "Go to Rome, my son. And there you will find your peace . . ."

Shef woke with a start and a clenching of muscles that made his bed-frame creak and brought the sleepy guard in the hallway outside to his feet. He means me to go, he thought. That was my father Rig calling.

He called me 'my son.' From a father like him, that bodes nothing but ill.

CHAPTER FIVE

As the fleet completed its fast current-assisted run down the estuary of the Thames, and turned south for the longer haul down-Channel and across the Bay of Biscay, Shef wondered again at his own reviving good humor. The omens were bad. He did not trust his visions. His own friends, he sensed, were conspiring against him. Yet he had felt his heart lift with the first heel of the deck beneath his feet.

It might be, he considered, the continuous changes he became aware of every time he boarded a ship. It was as if the pace of change, obvious enough on land, or at least on his land, accelerated at sea. He could not help comparing this voyage with the one he had begun eight years before, when he had sailed far to the north, in the end to defeat the Ragnarssons and lose the Holy Lance to his rival Bruno. Then the ships he had taken with him had been experimental, capable of one thing only: mounting a catapult. Everything about them had been a struggle. The most expert crews in the world could not have prevented them sagging eternally to leeward. And his crews had been experimental too. Fishermen as captains and landsmen from the levies as crew. Too clumsy and uncertain even to allow fires to be lit, no matter what precautions everyone took, so that it was cold food and small beer day after day, and only the hope of finding an anchorage at night that made it worth carrying kindling.

A different story now. Shef's was not a large fleet. After anxious calculation it had been decided to leave the bulk of the new two-master catapult-armed vessels to watch the ever-dangerous mouth of the Elbe. Everyone knew that the Empire had ships continually manned, in the hope of slipping out to break the blockade, maybe even make a beachhead on

English soil and carry over the feared, drilled, irresistible soldier-monks of the *Lanzenorden*—a far cry, indeed, from the poorly-disciplined knights of Charles the Bald, defeated at Hastings nine years before. So thirty ships remained on their continual rotation between the Elbe station, their home base of Norwich, and their short-stay ports on the Danish peninsula. Shef had only six with him, besides his own flagship, the *Fafnisbane*.

Yet what ships they were. They made nothing of the south-west wind that would have blocked their prototypes, tacking steadily down-Channel without difficulty, the crews handling the double sails without fuss or confusion. There was nothing, too, of the alarming swarming motion which had so terrified Shef and his dead companion Karli when they had first ridden as passengers in a true Viking longboat. Instead of swooping up and gliding down every wave, the bigger, heavier ships seemed to crush through them, stabilized by their heavy cargoes and ballast, taking the weight of the ton-and-a-quarter catapults mounted high up without strain. They had even—Brand had shaken his head in a mixture of envy and sorrow when he had first seen it—the entirely new luxury of decking. No longship had anything above its hull except the rowers' benches and the skin awnings they sometimes slung to keep off spray. Sleeping during a sea passage was a matter of rolling yourself in a blanket and lying in the bottom boards, between the thwarts if you were fortunate. Here the greater size and depth of the bronze-bolted hulls meant that permanent wooden decks could be built, with room beneath the shelter they gave to sling hammocks for the great ones, and above all for the king. Shef had grinned like a boy at the luxury of it when his skipper, Ordlaf, had shown him the new invention. And then, climbing out again, had remarked that it would improve the ships' ability to keep the sea for longer periods: valuable for the blockade detachments.

"He never enjoys anything," Ordlaf confided later to his mates. "Thinking ahead all the time. Good for no-one, if you ask me."

But Ordlaf was wrong. Shef felt keen enjoyment at every detail as he stood, finally, on the after catapult-castle, watching the coast of England fade and hearing the terrible retching sounds of the Caliph's ambassador and his men coming to terms once more with the Atlantic swell. His eye noted the skillful way his dozen ships—seven catapult-craft, and five more conventional Viking-manned longships in company as scouts—spread out into an extended 'V', five miles from arm to arm, so as to keep each other in plain sight and at the same time extend the horizon of their own lookouts. He nodded approvingly too at the new 'crows' nests' at every masthead. He would have liked to see in each of them a man armed with a far-seer like the one the Arab had shown him, but so far the secret of their manufacture had eluded him. Priests of the Way were busy at this moment in the Wisdom House, blowing glass, making different shapes from it, trying to learn in the way they had learned to make better steel and better weapons: not by logic, but by deliberate random change. The man who succeeded could name his own reward.

But meanwhile, the new ships had even a brick fireplace amidships, screened from the wind and the spray! Shef's nostrils flared to the smell of thick sausage soup, remembering again the terrible belly-pinch of his past. For all men say, he thought again, as he did many times, there is no virtue in hardship. Virtue in being able to endure it, maybe. But no-one gets better for practice.

His comfortable reflections were cut short by sudden turmoil from the fore-castle: men's voices raised, and in the middle of them—impossible, at sea—what sounded like the shrieking of a woman. An angry woman by the sound of it, as well. Shef turned for the rail and headed swiftly along the ship's seventy-foot length.

It was a woman, sure enough, but what caught Shef's eye in his first astonished instant was the sight of his childhood friend Hund the leech, standing in front of Ordlaf the skipper and bodily thrusting him back. Hund was among the slightest of men, and moreover quiet and gentle almost to a fault. To see him thrusting aside the burly Ordlaf was barely credible.

Even less credible was the sight of the woman herself. For an instant Shef's eye caught the copper hair, flash of blue eyes—they brought back a memory of some kind—but then he could notice nothing beyond her dress.

Slowly his brain took in what his eye had already registered. She wore what was certainly an imitation of the dress of a priest of the Way. White wool, bleached again and again. Round her neck a pendant, but not one he could readily recognize. Not a leech-apple, not a smith-hammer. A ski, for Ull? No: a feather, badly-crafted, but a quill nonetheless. And round her waist, certainly, a girdle of the sacred rowan-berries.

Shef became conscious of Thorvin standing by his side. Realized too that the shouting and pushing had ceased, quelled by his appearance and his fixed stare.

"Is she with you?" Shef asked Thorvin disbelievingly. "Do you have priestesses now?"

"Not with me," came a grim voice in reply. "She has no right to wear any of our marks or tokens. They should be stripped from her back, aye, shift and all."

"And then what?"

"And then over the side with her," cut in Ordlaf. "Who ever heard of a woman aboard ship?" He caught himself a moment later. "I mean to say, a distaff-bearer."

Shef had noted the spread of the *haf*-words among his seamen, even the English ones who had been brought up as Christians, like Ordlaf. Brand and his men were adamant that it was the worst of luck at sea to mention women, or cats, or Christian priests, except for the terrible luck that would be brought by sailing with one. They would not mention parts of their own ships in ordinary language either, but carefully used separate ritual terms. Now Ordlaf was doing it. But his reflections were interrupted again by a closer stare at the woman in front of him. Absently he waved to Hund, pushing forward protectively, to stand back and let him see her plain.

"I have seen you before," he remarked. "You hit me. You hurt me. I remember now. It was at Bedricsward, by—by the mighty one's camp. You were in the tent, the tent I cut open, the tent—" Shef hesitated. He could remember no ruling from Brand on this point, but something told him that Ivar the Boneless was a name as likely to annoy, or to attract, the sea-hags of Ran the goddess of the deep as any mention of women or cats. "The tent of the pale man," he finished lamely.

She nodded. "I remember you too. You had two eyes then. You slashed the tent open to rescue the English girl, and seized me because you thought I was her. I hit you and you let me go." She spoke English with a thick Norse accent, Shef noted, as bad as Brand's. But she did not speak it quite like him, nor like so many of the followers of the Way, edging towards a language common to both Norse and English. She was a Dane. A pure Dane, he guessed. Where had she come from?

"I brought her aboard," said Hund, finally able to command attention. "I hid her below decks. Shef, you were Thorvin's apprentice. I was Ingulf's apprentice. Now Svandis here is my apprentice. I ask you to protect her—as Thorvin protected you when the dogs of Ivar would have killed you."

"If she is your apprentice why is she not wearing an apple, for Ithun, for leech-craft?" said Shef.

"Women are not apprentices," growled Thorvin at the same moment.

"I can explain that," said Hund. "But there are other things I need to explain too. Privately," he added.

Shef nodded slowly. In all their experience he had never known Hund ask for anything for himself, not since the day Shef had pulled the slave-collar off his neck. Yet time and again he had done Shef service. He was owed a hearing. Silently Shef pointed forward to the closed space where they slung his hammock. He turned to Ordlaf, to Thorvin, to the watching crewmen and the dark-faced Arabs behind them.

"No more about stripping or putting over the side," he ordered. "Serve the food out, Ordlaf. And send some forward to Hund and me too. As for her, put her in the aft compartment with two of your mates to watch her. You are responsible for her safety.

"Lady," he added, "go where they show you."

For an instant she looked at him as if she were likely to strike him again. A fierce face, a familiar face. As she relaxed and dropped her eyes, Shef realized with death at his heart where he had seen it before. Glaring at him over a gang-plank. She was the female image of the Boneless One, whom he had killed and burned to ashes so his ghost would never walk again. What was it that Hund had brought back from the past? If she were a *draugr* or one of the twice-born, he would take Thorvin's advice after all. It would cheer the crew, dispersing sullenly now to their meal.

"Yes, she is Ivar's daughter," admitted Hund, in the dark, rocking privacy of the deck beneath the forward catapult-mount. "I realized that a while ago."

"But how could he have a daughter? or any child? He could do nothing with women, that's why they called him the Boneless One, he had no . . ."

"Oh yes he did," corrected Hund. "You should know. You killed him by crushing them in your hand."

Shef fell silent, remembering the last moments of his duel with Ivar.

"By the time we knew him," Hund went on, "I think you are right, he could have no relations with women. But when he was younger, he could— if he hurt them a great deal first. He was one of those men—there are more of them than there should be, even in your kingdom—who are aroused by pain and fear. In the end the pain and fear were all he valued, and I believe that no woman given over to him could hope to survive. You saved Godive from that, you know," he added with a penetrating stare. "He treated her well for a while, but from what I have heard that was only to get the keener enjoyment as her trust turned to fear: when the moment came.

"But it seems that in earlier years his demands were not so great. Women survived what he did to them. He may even have found one or two who co-operated with him, who had some deformity corresponding to his."

"What, enjoyed being hurt?" grunted Shef disbelievingly. He had been hurt often himself. The man he was talking to had burned out his right eye with a red-hot needle, to prevent worse happening. He could not imagine any faint association of pleasure with pain.

Hund nodded, carrying on. "I think in the case of Svandis's mother there may even have been some affection between them. Anyway, the woman conceived his child and lived to bear it. Though she died not long after, as Ivar's needs grew stronger. Now Ivar valued Svandis extremely, maybe for her mother, maybe because she was living proof of his manhood. He took her with him in the great attack on England. But after the surprise at Bedricsward all the Ragnarssons sent their women, their real women, not the slave-lemmans they picked up, back to safety at the Braethraborg.

"What you need to realize, Shef, is this, and I speak now as a leech." Hund gripped his apple-pendant to show his gravity. "That young woman has three times been hurt by fear. Once, at Bedricsward. Most of the women in that tent were killed, you know. You dragged Godive away. Svandis seized a weapon and crawled between tent-ropes where the warriors could not easily reach her. But most of them were cut down by men so blind with rage they could hardly see. She collected the bodies in the morning.

"Again, at the Braethraborg, after you stormed it. Again she had been living in safety, as a princess, her every command obeyed. Then it was blood and fire all over again, and at the end of it she was a beggarwoman. No one would take in a Ragnarsson's daughter. If she showed gold someone would take it from her. All her kin were dead. How do you think she lived after that? By the time she found her way to me she had been through many men's hands. Like a nun taken by a Viking band and passed round the camp-fires."

"And the third time?" Shef asked.

"When her mother died. Who knows how that came about? Who knows how much the child saw, or heard, or guessed?"

"Is she your lemman now?" inquired Shef, trying to get to some decision.

Hund threw his hands up in disgust. "What I'm trying to tell you, you brain-sick pissabed, is that of all the women in the world she is the least likely to be anyone's lemman. As far as she knows, if women lie with men they are likely to be disemboweled slowly, and the only good reason for doing so is in exchange for food or money."

Shef sat back on his bench. Though his face could not be seen in the dark unlit 'tween-deck, he was grinning faintly. Hund was talking to him as he had done when they were boys, thrall's child and bastard together. Besides, a faint excitement stirred within him at the thought that the new woman was *not* Hund's lover. A Ragnarsson's daughter, he reflected. Now her father and uncles and cousins were all safely dead, it might be no bad thing to ally with the Ragnarsson blood. All admitted that they were of the seed of gods and heroes, however much they hated them. The Snake-eye claimed descent from Völsi and from his own namesake the Fafnisbane. There was no doubt the Danes and the Swedes and the Norwegians would respect a child sprung from that stock: even if she was a female Boneless.

He brought himself back to the moment. "If she is not your lover, why did you hide her on board?"

Hund leaned forward again, his voice dropping low. "I tell you, that young woman has more brains than anyone you or I have ever met."

"What, more than Udd?" Shef meant the puny, slave-born stray who had risen to become Shef's steelmaster and the most respected smith among priests of the Way: though he would never leave the House of Wisdom in Stamford again, his nerve broken for ever by the terrors he had undergone in the North.

"In a way. But in a different way. She is no smith, no metal-beater or machine-minder. She thinks deeply. Somewhere after she fled from the Braethraborg, someone explained to her the doctrines of the Way. She knows the holy poems and stories as well as Thorvin, and can read and write them. That is why she has chosen to wear a quill, though I do not know what god she wears it for."

Hund's voice was a whisper now. "I think she explains the stories better than Thorvin does. Their inner meaning, the true tale of Völund or of King Frothi and the giant-maids, the truth behind all our fables of gods and giants, of Othin and Loki and Ragnarök. She preaches strange doctrines to those who will listen, tells them there is no Valhalla for the good and Naströnd for the bad, no monsters beneath the earth and in the sea, no Loki and no Hel . . ."

Shef cut him off. "She can stay, if you wish it," he said. "She can preach her strange doctrines too, for all I care. But you can tell her this: if she wants to persuade anyone that Loki does not exist, she can start with me. I would give heavy gold to anyone who could show me that. Or tell me his chains were sound."

Not far, as the raven flies, from the track of the war-fleet down the French Atlantic coast, the new Emperor of the Holy Roman Empire prepared with relish for an afternoon's sport.

Returned from his meeting at Salonae, the Emperor had embarked with his usual furious energy on the next task he had set himself, the counterpart of the naval actions that his general Agilulf and the Greek admiral of the Red Fleet were carrying out at sea. It was time, Bruno had declared, to deal finally with the Moslem strongholds established a generation before on the South Frankish coast, permanent menace to pilgrims and officials traveling to Rome, disgrace to Christendom and to the heir of Charlemagne. Easier said than done, some had muttered. But not many. Their Emperor did nothing without a plan.

Now Bruno stood, relaxed and genial, explaining what would happen to a group of wary, mistrustful, but deeply interested nobles: minor dukes and barons of the Pyrenean mountains, in their way the counterpart to the Moslem brigands about to be extirpated, their own strongholds hanging on the edge of Moslem Spain as the present one did on the coast of Christian France. From time to time a dart or arrow swept out of the sky, shot from the stronghold towering on its peak two hundred feet above them. The nobles noted the total lack of concern of the Emperor, who from time to time raised his shield to deflect or intercept a missile, without breaking the flow of his talk. This was no chair-warrior talking. He had been shot at more times than he had passed water.

"They build high up, as you can see," he explained. "That was safe enough for a long time. Can't get scaling ladders up easily, they have plenty of bowmen—good bowmen too," he added, lifting his shield once more. "Build on stone, so it's no good mining. Even our onagers can't be raised high enough to beat their doors down.

"But the Mohammedan rogues did not have to deal with my good *secretarius* here!" The Emperor waved an arm at a figure the Spanish barons had till then ignored: a small, scrawny man in the undistinguished black robe of a deacon, standing by the side of the great machine drawn forward by two hundred men. Looking again, the barons noted that two men stood always by the deacon, fully armored, with shields of double size. The Emperor might take risks with his own life, but none with those of this deacon.

"That is Erkenbert the Englishman, Erkenbert *arithmeticus.*" The barons nodded reflectively. Even they had heard of this man. All of Christendom had heard by now the story of how the great Emperor had traveled into the pagan lands and returned with the Holy Lance of Longinus. A major part of the story was the tale of how Erkenbert *arithmeticus* had destroyed the Kingdom Oak of the Swedes, the idol-worshipers.

The little deacon was calling shrill orders, had now a firebrand in his fist. He looked across at the Emperor, saw his nod, bent over his machine, straightened, and shouted a last word. An instant later, the Spaniards broke into a collective groan of amazement. The great arm of the machine had swept down, slowly, ponderously, dragged down by the huge bucket on its shorter arm. At the same instant the long arm had shot up, as fast as the short one was slow, and launched a trail of smoke into the air. But what had brought out the groan was the size of the missile it lobbed: bigger than any rock men could lift, bigger than a mule or a two-year-old bullock, it flew as if by magic up into the sky. Over the wall of the Moslem stronghold, vanishing deep inside. From high above they could hear yells of alarm and rage. Already the machine tenders were furiously busy round the bucket-arm, some of them jumping into it and hurling rock after rock out on to the dry ground.

"It's very slow," said Bruno conversationally, "but it can throw the weight of three men, oh, a hundred and fifty yards quite easily. And it throws it up, you see. Not flat like the onagers. So what we do with the villains is, first we set fire to the wooden buildings inside the holds—four hundred pounds of tarred straw is not put out by pissing on it—and then, well, you'll see. Once my *secretarius* has seen a shot or two, he will cut down the weight of the launcher—it is difficult, but he is the *arithmeticus*—and drop, not straw, but a boulder, right on top of the gateway there." He waved up at the iron-studded oak doorway.

"And then, as you can see—" Bruno waved again at the heavily-armed men waiting in ranks out of arrow-shot, "the heroes of the *Lanzenorden* stand ready to go in and finish the job."

"And us with them," said one of the Spanish barons, a scarred veteran.

"But certainly!" cried Bruno, "and me too! Why, it's all I come for!" He winked roguishly. "One decision we all have to make, though. My lads wear their mail, after all, they have to do this twice a week. But those of us who just have a chance now and then, why, we may think it better to go in light-armed. I only wear padded leather myself, it gives me a little more speed, and the Arabs wear no armor either. To tell the truth, I find it more like rat-catching than fighting a battle. But that is because we have found the trick of burning the rats out."

He beamed cheerfully at his *secretarius,* now supervising the winching up of the bucket-arm of his trebuchet, preparatory to filling it with its launch-weight once more.

"And do you take the Holy Lance into battle?" asked one of the Spaniards, greatly daring.

The Emperor nodded, the gold circlet welded to his plain steel helmet flashing in the sun. "It never leaves me. But I carry it in my shield-hand, and never strike a blow with it. What has once drunk the Holy Blood of our Savior cannot be polluted with the blood of some miscreant unbeliever. I defend it more than I do my own life."

The Spaniards stood silent. This assault, they knew perfectly well, was being staged as a demonstration to them as well as an extermination of the brigands. The Emperor meant to show them the futility of anything other than perfect alliance and obedience. Yet they relished it. For generations their ancestors had fought a losing struggle against the tide of Islam, seemingly forgotten by the Christians at their back. If now a strong king came with armies at his call, they were ready to show the way and share the profits. The relic in his hand was only one further proof of his power, yet a strong one. Finally one of the barons spoke, won over and ready to show his loyalty.

"All of us will follow the Lance," he said, in the mutilated Latin of the hill-folk. Murmurs of agreement came from his fellows. "It is in my mind that the holder of the Lance deserves to hold the other great relic of our Savior."

Bruno looked at him sharply, suspiciously. "What is that?"

The Spaniard smiled. "It is known to few. But in these hills, it is said, rests the third relic, besides Holy Cross and Holy Lance, known to have touched our Savior." He paused, pleased with the effect of his words.

"And that is?"

"The Holy Grail." In the border dialect the words came out as *santo graale.*

"And where and what is that?" Bruno asked very quietly.

"I cannot say. But somewhere in these hills, they say it is hidden. Has been hidden since the time of the long-haired kings."

The other barons looked at each other doubtfully, unsure of the wisdom of mentioning the old dynasty wiped out by the grandfather of Charlemagne. But Bruno cared nothing for the legitimacy or otherwise of the dynasty he had himself wiped out, his attention focused solely on what the baron was saying.

"Then who holds it, do we know that?"

"The heretics," the baron replied. "In these hills, they are everywhere. Not worshipers of Mohammed or Allah, worshipers, it is said, of the devil. The Grail fell into their hands many years ago, so men say, though no-one knows what such a thing may be. We do not know who the heretics are, they could be among us now. They preach, it is said, strange doctrine."

The machine behind them crashed again, a rock soared slowly into the air, fell ruinously upon the doorway behind which plumes of black smoke were rising. A hoarse cheer rose from the ranks of the *Lanzenorden* as they pressed forward to the breach. Their Emperor pulled his longsword free, turned to lead them, Holy Lance held with shield-grip in one brawny fist.

"Tell me more later," he shouted over the rising war-cries. "At dinner. Once the rats are dead."

CHAPTER SIX

The Caliph of Cordova, Abd er-Rahman, was troubled in his heart. He sat cross-legged on his favorite carpet in the smallest and most private courtyard of his palace, and allowed his mind to sort carefully through its troubles. Water ran continually from the fountain at his side, soothing his thoughts. In a hundred pots placed seemingly at random around the enclosed court, flowers bloomed. An awning defended him from the direct rays of the sun, already hot in the short Andalusia spring. All around, the word was passed in whispers, and servants fell silent, took their work elsewhere. On bare feet his bodyguards padded gently back into the shaded colonnades, watching but remaining unseen. A *mustarib* slave-girl of his harem, urgently summoned by his major-domo, began very gently to pluck out a faint tune on her zither, so low as to be almost inaudible, alert for the faintest sign of displeasure. None came, as the Caliph sank deeper and deeper into introspection.

The news from his traders was bad, he reflected. There was no question but that the Christians had seized every island that could conceivably be used as the base for a fleet: Malta, Sicily, Mallorca, Menorca, the other Balearics, even Formentera, all gone, and behind them—though this was none of his concern—the Greek islands of Crete and Cyprus. His traders reported that all ship movements even along the African shore were now subject to harassment from Christian raiders. It was strange that they had come so quickly, he mused.

There was a reason, though the Caliph did not know it. For all its size, the Mediterranean is in some ways more like a lake than an open sea. Because of its prevailing winds and the insistent current that pours in from the Atlantic to replace the constant evaporation of the almost land-locked sea, it is far easier in the Mediterranean to sail west to east than east to west; easier too to sail north to south than south to north. The first factor was to the Caliph's advantage, the second to that of his Christian foes. Once the block of the Arab fleets and bases in the north had been removed, the way was easy and open for every Christian village on the Mediterranean islands that could fit out a ship to send it south and try to reclaim their long losses from the traders of Egypt and Tunis, of Spain and Morocco.

No, thought the Caliph. The interruption of trade vexes me, but it is not the source of my trouble. Spain lacks for nothing. If trade is cut down, some men will become poor, others rich in their place as they supply what we used to buy from the Egyptians. As for the loss of fleets and men, that angers me, but it can be avenged. That is not what perturbs my soul.

The news from the Franks then? The Caliph had no personal feeling for the brigand strongholds that the new Emperor of the Franks was burning out. They paid him no taxes, contained none of his relatives. Many of them were men who had fled from his justice. Yet there was something there to irritate him, it was true. He could not forget the words of the prophet Muhammad: 'O believers, fight against the unbelievers who are nearest to you.' Could it be that he, Abd er-Rahman, had neglected his spiritual duty? Had not moved aggressively enough against the unbelievers on his northern border? Had not come to help of those of Islam who obeyed the Prophet? Abd er-Rahman knew why he had left the northern mountains alone: thin profits, heavy losses, and the removal of what was after all a screen between himself and the Franks the other side of the mountains. Christians, heretics, Jews, all mixed together, easier to tax than to rule, he had thought. Yet maybe he had done wrong.

No, the Caliph reflected again, this news angered him, and made him think of changing his policy in the future, but there was no danger in it. Leon and Navarre, Galicia and Roussillon and the other tiny kingdoms, they would fall whenever he put out his hand to them. Next year maybe. He must think deeper.

Could it be the reports passed to him by his Cadi, the mayor and chief justice of the city? There was indeed something in them that disturbed him deeply. For twenty years Cordova had been vexed by one foolish young man, or young woman, after another from the Christian minority. They thrust themselves forward. They abused the Prophet in the market-place, they came to the Cadi and declared that they had been followers of the Prophet and had now turned to the true God, they tried every trick they could to earn death beneath the executioner's sword. Then their friends revered them as saints and sold their bones—if the Cadi did not order and supervise total cremation—as holy relics. The Caliph had read the holy books of the Christians and was well aware of the parallel with their account of the death of the prophet Yeshua: how the *Rumi* Pilate had done his best not to condemn the man before him, but in the end had been provoked into ordering his death. A sorrow for the world that he had not been firmer. And they were at it again, so the Cadi reported, stirring up their Moslem fellow-citizens to fury and creating riots in the city.

Yet even that was not the heart of the matter, the Caliph thought. His predecessor had seen the cure for that problem. The Christians were quick enough to embrace death for the glory of martyrdom. They were slower to endure public humiliation. The way to deal with them was what Pilate himself had suggested: strip them and flog them in public, using the bastinado. Then send them contemptuously home. It appeased the Moslem mob, it created neither relics nor martyrs. Some took their beatings well, some badly. Few returned for more. The key was not to react to the provocation. A real believer in Islam who became a Christian: such a one must die. Those who merely declared their conversion to gain death, they should be ignored.

But there was the heart of the matter, the Caliph realized. He shifted uncomfortably on his carpet, and the tinkling of the zither instantly ceased. He settled back again and, very tentatively, the music began once more.

The core of Islam was the *shahada,* the profession of faith. He or she who once made it before witnesses was then for ever and irrevocably a Moslem. All that was necessary was to say the words: I testify, that there is no God but God, and Muhammad is the Prophet of God. *La illaha il Allah, Muhammad rasul Allah,* muttered the Caliph to himself for perhaps the hundred thousandth time. That witness was ordained by the Prophet himself. It could not be taken back.

Yet the Prophet, praised be his name, thought the Caliph to himself, had never had to deal with Christians hurling themselves to martyrdom! If he had, maybe he would have made the witness harder! The Caliph caught himself. There indeed was the heart of his trouble. He was on the point of criticizing the Prophet, of accepting change in Islam. He was becoming an unbeliever in his heart.

He raised a finger, made the gesture of one who unwinds a scroll. Bare minutes later the keeper of his library, the *katib* Ishaq, stood silently in front of him. The Caliph nodded to a cushion, to indicate that the *katib* should sit down, crooked a finger for sherbet and dates to be brought.

"Tell me," he said after a pause, "tell me of the Mu'tazilites."

Ishaq glanced at his master and employer warily, a chill at his heart. What suspicion prompted this question? How much did the Caliph want information, how much did he want reassurance? Information, he guessed. But unwise to neglect the appropriate disclaimers.

"The Mu'tazilites," he began, "were fostered by the unworthy followers of Abdullah, enemies of your house. Even in Baghdad, though, seat of the impure ones, they have now fallen into disgrace and been scattered."

A slight narrowing of the eyes told Ishaq to proceed more quickly to the information. "The seat of their belief," he went on, "was that faith should be subordinate, as the Greeks would have it, to reason. And the reason for their disgrace was that they argued that the teachings of the Koran were not eternal, but might be subject to change. Only Allah is eternal, they declared. Therefore the Koran is not."

Ishaq hesitated, unsure whether he dared press on. He himself, like so many of the learned of Cordova, sympathized heart and soul with those who offered free inquiry, a breaking of the chains of *hadith,* tradition. They had learned not to betray their sympathies. Yet he might venture to show the *dilemma,* as the wise thinkers of the Greeks, the *falasifah,* might put it.

"The Caliph will see that the Mu'tazilites provoke a hard choice," he continued. "For if we agree with them, we agree that the law of the *shari'a,* the clear path, may be altered. And then where is our clear path? But if we do not agree with them, we must believe that the Koran was there even before it was declared to the Prophet himself. And if we believe that, we take honor from the Prophet for finding it out and declaring it."

"What is your view, Ishaq? Speak freely. If I do not like what you say, I will not hear it nor ask you again."

The librarian drew a deep breath, sympathizing with that famous vizier of the Caliph Haroun, who said that every time he left the presence, he felt his own head to see if it were still on his shoulders. "I think the Mu'tazilites may have had some kernel of wisdom. The Prophet was a man, who lived and died as one. Some part of what he said was human, some part sent by God. It may be that the parts declared by his own human wisdom are subject to change, as are all the works of man."

"But we do not know which is which," summed up the Caliph. "And so the seed of doubt is sown."

Ishaq cast his eyes down, hearing the iron clang of finality, so often followed by the note of death. He had come to the end of toleration once again.

Outside the quiet courtyard there came a patter of feet, breaking the thin current of the slave-girl's song. The Caliph lifted his eyes, aware that he would not be disturbed save for something he had already indicated. The messenger who stood at the edge of the colonnade came forward, breathing deeply to show his diligence and the speed with which he had raced to his master. He bowed deeply.

"The deputation sent to the land of the *majus* has returned," he announced. "And not alone! They have come with the king of the *majus* and a fleet of strange ships."

"Where?"

"They have reached the mouth of the Guadalquivir, and are rowing up it in some of their ships, the smallest ones. They row swiftly, almost as swiftly as our horses. They will be here in Cordova in two days' time, in the morning.''

The Caliph nodded, flicked fingers to his vizier to have the messenger rewarded, murmured orders to have guest-quarters prepared.

"A king," he said finally. "A king of the barbarians. It means nothing, but let us take particular care to impress him. Find out what his tastes are: girls, boys, horses, gold, mechanical toys. There is always something the children of the north desire."

"I want a good display," said Shef to his chief advisers. He was crouching awkwardly on the bottom boards of one of Brand's five longships. The seven catapult-mounting two-masters had proved, to the surprise of the Arabs, too deep-keeled to pass far up the river, and had been left behind with full crews and guards. Shef had gone on up river with just the five boats and as many men as could be conveniently fitted in to them: just under two hundred all told. He had mixed his crews as well. Twenty men in each ship were Norsemen from their regular crews. The rest had been transferred to the catapult-ships, and replaced by a similar number of crossbowmen, all of them English. The English were taking their turn at rowing, amid much amusement. Nevertheless both sides were well aware of the extra protection the others gave them.

"How do we do that?" asked Brand. Like the others, he had been secretly shocked by the wealth and luxury visible all around them, and even more by the enormous numbers of people. From what they had been told, the city of Cordova alone contained as many people as the whole of Norway. All the way along the river they could see the roofs of mansions, water-wheels turning, villages and towns stretching out across the plains one after the other as far as the eye could see. "We can dress up, but it'll take more than a silk tunic to impress these people."

"Right. We don't try to look rich. They'll always beat us at that. We try to look strange. And frightening. I think we can do that. And it's not just look, right? It's sound . . ."

The quayside loungers drew back, muttering, as the Wayman fleet docked and began to unload its men. Shef's orders had been thoroughly digested, and his crews were playing their parts. First the Vikings poured off their boats, every man glittering in freshly-polished and sanded mail. Not a man was under six feet tall, spears bristled from behind the bright-painted shields, long-handled axes rested on shoulders. They had changed their seamen's goatskin shoes for heavy marching boots, studded with iron. They stamped heavily while Brand and his skippers roared orders in gale-force voices. Slowly they drew into a long line, four deep.

Another order, and the crossbowmen followed them: less impressive men physically, but more used to moving in unison. They ran to their places and also formed up, each one with his strange instrument sloped over his left shoulder. Shef saw them make their ranks, and then himself walked over the gangplank with careful ceremony. He too wore mail, a gold circlet on his head, as much gold as he could carry glinting from arm-rings and necklet. Brand followed him, with Thorvin and the two other Viking Way-priests who had joined the expedition, Skaldfinn the interpreter, priest of Heimdall, and Hagbarth the seaman, priest of Njörth. The four formed a rank at the head of the procession, immediately behind Shef himself, who walked alone. Behind them, and sheltered as much as possible by the bulk of Brand and Thorvin, walked Hund and his protégée Svandis. Under fierce orders from Shef, she had pulled a veil across her face, and was darting sharp looks from behind it.

Shef looked at the messenger who had been sent down to meet them, and gestured to him to lead on. As the man, puzzled and unsure at the odd behavior of the *ferengis,* began to walk away, continually glancing back, Shef gave a final wave. Cwicca, his most loyal companion and life-saver, stepped forward with three of his companions, crossbows slung across their backs. All four blew firmly into the bags of their bagpipes, reached full pressure, and began to march forward, blowing lustily in unison. The loungers fell back even further as the uncanny noise hit them.

The pipers marched forward behind the guide. Shef and his companions followed them, then the heavy-armed Vikings, their mail clashing, their boots stamping. Then came the crossbowmen, all stepping forward in time, a skill they had practiced on the new, level, hard stone roads of England. Every twenty paces the right-hand man of the front file raised his spear and the hundred Vikings behind him shouted together their approach-to-battle cry, which Shef had first heard rolling towards him from the army of Ivar the Boneless a decade before.

"*Ver thik,*" they shouted again and again, "*her ek kom,* guard yourself, here I come." The Arabs will not understand it, Shef had pointed out, they will not think we are challenging them. Let's shout something else anyway, suggested one skipper. Anything more complicated than that, Brand had replied, and your lot will forget the words.

The column moved on through the packed streets of the town with metal echoes clanging from the stone walls, preceded by wailing pipes and roaring voices. At the rear the crossbowmen had started to sing a song in praise of their own victories. As they moved on the excited crowds grew thicker so that the marching men began to mark time, stamping down on the spot with their hobnails. Out of the corner of his eye Shef saw a fascinated Arab watching Brand's enormous feet crashing up and down. First he looked down, at the boots half a yard long. Then he gaped up, trying to measure the seven-foot distance between them and the metal crest of Brand's helmet.

Good, Shef thought, stepping forward again as the crowd was thrust back by the Caliph's escorts. Good, we've got them thinking first. They're thinking, is he human? It's not even a bad question.

The Caliph heard the uproar of the crowd even within his shaded and enclosed hall of audience. He raised an eyebrow, listened while the news was poured into his ears by an attendant. As the noise came closer he could indeed distinguish the screeching of the *ferengis'* strange instruments, as lacking in beauty as the howling of so many cats. Could hear, too, the astonishing crash of metal on stone, the deep shouts of the barbarians. Are they trying to frighten me, he wondered, amazed. Or is that their custom at all times? I must speak to Ghaniya. If one does not understand the customs of the foreigner one cannot guess his thoughts.

The noise ceased abruptly as Shef gave the signal to halt and the right-hand marker, by arrangement, waved his spear in a circle. Shef's men, Vikings and English, stood rigid in their ranks in the outside courtyard.

"How many may enter for audience?" asked Shef. No more than ten besides yourself, came the answer. Shef nodded, pointed out those to come with him. Brand and Thorvin, Hagbarth and Skaldfinn. He hesitated over Hund. No-one in the North knew more of leech-craft, and Cordova was famous for it: he might be needed to judge or respond. Yet he would not be parted from the irritating, but still obediently veiled Svandis. Take them both, then. Finally he called forward two of the Viking skippers to flank Brand, both men who had fought their way to command in a score of single combats, nodded silently to his long-term companions Cwicca and Osmod, with their crossbows.

The Caliph, sitting high on his dais, observed the strangers enter, listening now to muttered commentary from Ghaniya, who had come forward while the *majus* assembled outside. The king was the one-eyed one. Strange for the *ferengis,* who respected strength and size so much. The king should be the giant beside him. Though the one-eye had indeed the bearing of command. Abd er-Rahman noted the way he strode forward confidently to stand directly in front of him, looked round for his translators.

He noted also the sweat by now pouring from under the hair and the gold circlet. What were these men wearing? Metal to hold the rays of the sun; leather underneath it to guard their skin; and beneath that, it seemed, sheep's wool? In the Andalusian summer men dressed like that would die of heat-stroke before noon. And yet the king and his men showed no awareness of it, felt no shame at the evidence of their own bodies' discomfort, did not even try to wipe their brows. My people think it dignified to withdraw from discomfort, the Caliph reflected. These think it dignified to ignore it, like a slave working in the sun.

The Caliph asked the first and vital question: "Ask, are any of these men Christians?"

He expected the question to go to Suleiman the Jew, who would speak in Latin, and be translated by some man of learning among the strangers. He was surprised to see, as Suleiman indeed began to translate, the king himself shake his head. He understood some Arabic, then. And the answer was already forthcoming. Skaldfinn had as his vocation the learning of languages and the understanding of peoples. He had spent the voyage learning from Suleiman, and teaching him Anglo-Norse in exchange. Shef too had sat listening much of the time. Skaldfinn spoke now in slow but passable Arabic, translating for his king.

"No. None of us are Christians. We allow Christians to follow their faith, but we follow a different Way, and a different book. We fight only against those who deny that right."

"Has it been explained to you that there is only one God, who is Allah, and that Muhammad is his Prophet? Believe that, and you can expect rich reward from me."

"It has been explained."

"You do not believe in Allah? You choose to believe in your own gods, whoever they are?"

Tension and the note of the executioner in the Caliph's voice. Brand shifted his grip slightly on the axe 'Battle-troll,' and marked the two men standing behind the Caliph, scimitars bared. Big men, he thought. Burnt blacker by the sun than I have ever seen before. But naked above the waist, no shields. Two blows and the third for the Arab in the chair.

Realizing that he could follow the Arabic that the Caliph spoke, Shef replied for the first time without a translator. Pitching his voice high, and speaking the simplest Arabic that he could, he called out: "I have not seen Allah. I have seen my own gods. Maybe if I had two eyes I would see Allah too. One eye cannot see everything."

A buzz of comment ran round the courtyard. The Arabs, used to metaphorical language and the art of indirect reproof, understood the last sentence. He means that those who believe in one thing alone are half-blind. Blasphemer, thought some. Wise for a *ferengi*, thought others.

This is not a man to fence with, thought the Caliph. Already he has shown he understands display. Now he is taking my own audience chamber away from me.

"Why have you come to Cordova?" he said.

Because you asked me, thought Shef, glancing slightly at Ghaniya standing between and to the side of both men. Aloud, he replied: "To fight your enemies. My enemies too. Ghaniya tells me the Franks have new weapons to fight on sea and on land. We men of the Way understand new

weapons. We have brought new weapons and new ships to see if our
enemies can stand against them."

The Caliph looked silently at Ghaniya, who began an excited account of
the ships and the catapults of the Wayman fleet. As they sailed south Shef
had several times encouraged the skippers to make raft-targets, drop them
over the side, and then destroy them at half a mile with hurled rocks. The
crews were skilled and practiced, and the results had amazed the envoy.
Indeed no ship known to him could take more than a blow or two from the
onagers: he had not seen the armored but virtually unsailable *Fearnought* of
the Braethraborg battle.

As Ghaniya came to an end, Abd er-Rahman looked thoughtfully once
more at the God-defier. He is still not impressed, he thought, watching the
grim impassive face. Nor his companions. He made a sign, and one of the
huge executioners walked forward, bringing his scimitar from his shoulder.
Another sign, and a slave-girl stepped out to join him. As she did so she
peeled away the long filmy scarf that covered her upper body and stood, still
veiled but with breasts bared before the men.

"I hear much of your new weapons," he said. "We have weapons too."

He flicked his hand. The girl tossed her scarf in the air. Slowly, gently,
the thin silk floated down. The executioner turned his scimitar edge up and
held it out beneath the drifting fabric. The scarf met the edge, divided,
settled in two pieces to the ground.

Brand grunted, muttered something to the skippers at his side. Now, the
Caliph thought, the king will tell that giant to split something with his great
clumsy axe.

Shef turned, looked at Cwicca and Osmod. Neither of them the best shot
in the world, he thought. Osmod is a bit more certain. He pointed silently at
a marble vase holding bright purple flowers in a niche above the Caliph's
head. Osmod gulped visibly, looked sideways at Cwicca, unslung his
crossbow. Cocked it with one heave on the goat's-foot lever. Dropped in the
short iron quarrel. Raised, aimed and pulled trigger.

Osmod had guessed right, aiming low to allow for the short-range rise.
The armor-piercing bolt smashed into the stone, shattering it into pieces.
Stone splinters hummed around the room, the bolt bounced back from the
wall and clanged on to the floor. The flowers fell in a decorative trail. Earth
from the shattered vase slowly pattered down.

The Caliph stroked his beard in the silence. I threatened him with my
executioners, he thought. But that Iblis-bolt would have split my heart before
I could move. Ghaniya did not warn me enough.

"You will fight our enemies," he said finally, "and you say that is what
you have come for. If our enemies are your enemies, that may be true. But
no-one works only for another's good. There must be something else that

has brought you here. Tell me what it is, and by Allah I shall do my best to see you have it."

For the third time the foreign king shocked him. In clear but simple Arabic he replied once more.

"We have come to see the flying man."

CHAPTER SEVEN

Shef pushed his way impatiently through the growing crowd, the pole-ladder emblem of his god dangling over his chest. As the days of waiting had gone by, he and his men had slowly discarded layers of clothing. First the mail armor. It had become clear that while Shef's two hundred men were indeed in the heart of a potentially hostile power, nevertheless they were so outnumbered as to make organized battle futile, while the streets of Cordova were guarded with such strictness that no man need fear private quarrel. Shef had put the Vikings' mail and the Englishmen's crossbows in a guardroom, less to keep them safe, he remarked, than to prevent them from selling their issued weapons for drink.

"There is no strong drink anywhere in Cordova," Hund had objected. "The orders of Muhammad forbid it."

"There's some somewhere," Shef had replied, and supervised the handover of weapons himself.

Then the jackets had gone. A couple of days wandering open-mouthed round the narrow, stone-walled streets of Cordova had convinced even the most conservative Northerners that leather was an encumbrance if not a risk to life. By now all the Waymen were down to hemp shirts and wool breeches, and those fortunate enough to retain a balance of their pay were sporting gaudy cotton. In the sun their silver pendants—no-one had yet been so rash or God-defying as to sell one—gleamed and jerked, marking their owners out yet again from the darker faces and gayer clothes around them.

Last, fear had gone. Shef had expected, given the importance of his mission, to be shown to the great bin-Firnas, the flying man, at once. It had taken days, not—so Suleiman the Jew assured them—out of desire for delay, still less deliberate insult, but because of the veneration here accorded to the wise. The Caliph might indeed have commanded an audience and a demonstration, but preferred instead to send messengers, present gifts, ask for the favor of the wise to be shown to the barbarians drawn from afar by rumor of him, and generally go through the established ritual of Andalusian diplomacy. Bin-Firnas too—Suleiman further assured them—was not making deliberate difficulties in his replies. He was anxious only not to disappoint, to be unable to live up to the doubtless exaggerated tales carried into far lands by hearsay; further, as messages traveled both ways, it transpired that he was waiting for a wind.

Shef and his men had spent the days of waiting wandering with increasing entrancement round the streets of Cordova, seeing for the first time for any of them the hundred thousand details of a developed commercial civilization: the carts coming in each dawn with produce, so many of them that those coming in had one side of the main streets, those going out the other, while there were men of the town Cadi who did nothing all day but ensure that such rules were maintained! The ever-turning water-wheels, or *norias*, which scooped water out of the river and transferred it to stone runnels, from which even the poor could fetch their water. The rigid regulations about sewage, which even the richest must obey. The houses for treatment of the sick; the public disputations where wise men spoke simultaneously of the Koran, the learning of the Jews, the wisdom of the Greeks; the surgeons, the mosques, the courts where the strict, even-handed justice of the *shari'a* was dispensed. Something there for everyone to stare at. In a while even the timidest lost their fear of the alien, even the fiercest and greediest ceased thinking of this world as merely another city to sack. If anything the feeling that had been created was one of awe: the word the Vikings used to mean, not fear, but a sense of being hopelessly outmatched. Could these people do everything?

Only a few rose above this to observe weaknesses, inadequacies. Shef, at least, strove to do so, conscious that it might be mere jealousy which drove him. And then the Caliph sent word that it was time to meet the impossible, the flying man.

This is going to be another disaster like the one with the hens'-feather man, Shef told himself as he neared the tower from which the launch had been promised, his companions shoving along behind him in the way they had grown used to in the continuous unbelievable swarm of the city. Probably another disaster. But it has to be said. There are two good things this time that were not so when King Alfred's man tried to fly from my tower. First, though there is this talk about the wind, as there was last time, no-one has mentioned birds or feathers.

And second: we have met men, truthful-seeming men if I and Skaldfinn can judge their words, who insist that they saw this man fly fifteen years ago.

Not heard about it, not been nearby. Saw it themselves. And their stories, if they do not tally on what they saw, agree on when and where.

The tower door was before him now, guarded against the pushing spectators by men in the yellow and green of the Caliph's guard. The spears pulled aside as the guards recognised the eye-patch and emblem of the *ferengi* king, and the holy-man white of those behind him. Shef found himself blinking in the cool and dark at the base of the tower.

As his eyes adjusted from the glare outside, he became aware that the owner of the tower was in front of him, bowing slightly and holding clasped hands to his heart. He began to respond, bowing in his turn, jerking out a greeting in simple Arabic. But as he did so he realized with a shock that the man in front of him was a cripple. He could stand upright for a few moments, but then his hands went back to the wooden frame in front of him. When he moved, he pushed the frame forward and then dragged himself after it.

"Your legs," Shef managed to say. "How were they hurt? With flying?"

The Arab smiled, apparently unoffended. "With flying," he agreed. "The flight went well, the coming to earth less so. You see, I had forgotten something. I had forgotten that all flying creatures have tails."

As bin-Firnas, the cripple, began to shuffle his slow way to the stairs leading up the tower, Shef looked round at Thorvin, Hund, and his priest-companions, an expression of doubt and disappointment on his face.

"Another birdman, after all," he muttered. "Wait till he shows us the cape of feathers."

But at the top of the tower, on the square airy platform overlooking the steep sides of the Guadalquivir, there was no sign of feathers, no preparation for a leap. Back in the bright daylight, Shef could see that bin-Firnas was flanked by aides and servants, among them the young man Mu'atiyah who had come on the embassy to the North and the ever-present factotum Suleiman. Some stood by what seemed to be a light winch or windlass, others held lengths of pole and canvas. Behind Shef mustered the priests of the Way, the only ones for whom he had been able to secure admission. Walking to the tower's lip, Shef looked down and saw most of his men in the crowd, staring up, the giant figure of Brand conspicuous even in the throng. The still-veiled Svandis was close by him, he noted, though neither turned to the other. Brand had accepted the charge of looking after her from his friend and curer Hund, but had refused to have more than absolutely necessary to do with her: the Ivar-face chilled him, he confided, right in his old belly-wound.

"The first thing we do is this," Shef realized bin-Firnas was saying. "If the king of the *ferengis* will condescend to notice? See—" he gave an order, the winchmen began to pay out cord. A kite lifted into the air, caught the wind, began to recede into the sky as the windlass handles span. Shef stared at it. It seemed a light box, four walls made of cloth between poles, open at both ends, with slats or vents cut here and there in the cloth.

"This of course is no more than a child's game," bin-Firnas continued. "The kite lifts no more than itself. See though that the cord keeps its open mouth pointing towards the wind. Control is much easier into the wind. Away from the wind, it seems easier to sail like a ship, but alas! then the wind is master, not the man. So I found. I would do it differently if I tried again."

Shef could hear the cries of the crowd from below as they saw the kite. They lined the riverbank, some of them almost on a level with the tower as the slope rose away towards the city's thousand minarets.

"You understand the kite, then?"

Shef nodded, waited for the word to haul in. Instead bin-Firnas hobbled two paces to the winch, produced a knife, laid edge to cord. The kite, released, leapt up, swooped, sailed away downwind in erratic spirals and flutterings. Two of the waiting servants jumped to their feet, raced down the stairs to pursue and recover it.

"Now we try a harder thing."

On a gesture four servants carried forward a different contrivance. Its shape was similar, the open-ended box of cloth between poles, but it was twice as large and clearly heavier in construction. Inside it, furthermore, was a sort of sling of rope and cloth. Short vanes projected from either side. Shef stared at it, puzzled.

A young boy wriggled between the other servants and stood serious-faced in front of the new kite. Bin-Firnas laid a hand on his head, spoke to him with a babble of Arabic too fast for Shef to follow. The boy replied, nodding. Quickly two of the big dark-colored servants lifted him up, dropped him into the mouth of the kite. Walking nearer, Shef saw that the sling was a harness into which the boy fitted. His head remained outside the box, his hands rested on handles. As he twisted them, the cloth vanes to either side of the box rotated.

Carefully, four servants lifted the box, held it up to the wind, walked to the edge of the tower. The winchmen heaved a trifle, took up a yard or two of slack. Shef heard a rising buzz of excitement from outside, which slowly stilled.

"Is this dangerous?" he said quietly to Suleiman, not trusting his own Arabic at this stage. "I do not want the boy killed on my account."

Suleiman spoke aside to bin-Firnas, while the serious-faced child remained poised on the edge of the tower, the wind tugging at him. He turned back. "Bin-Firnas says, of course, that all is at the will of Allah. But he says also that as long as the cord is retained, all may be safe enough. The danger would come if they released it, let the boy try to fly free."

Shef stepped back, nodding. Bin-Firnas saw the gesture, turned to feel the wind, and then in his turn made a gesture to his servants. With a grunt they heaved the box up to arm's length above their heads, felt the wind catch it, let go all together.

For an instant the kite sagged below the wall of the tower, then some updraft or eddy caught it and it rose again. The winchmen span their handles, let the cord out five fathoms, ten. Slowly the kite rose in the sky, the little face still framed in its open end. Shef saw the vanes twist and turn slightly, the box rotate upwards, turn, level off. It dipped and bucked in the wind, but the boy seemed able to control it, to keep the box facing the way he wanted. If it had swooped and plunged like the earlier one once they had cut it free, he might have been thrown out of his harness, Shef guessed. But no, it seemed to ride stably. No worse than a boat on a choppy sea.

Silently bin-Firnas passed to Shef a device like the one Mu'atiyah had demonstrated, a far-seer. Without words he showed that it was different from the last one: in two halves, one sliding over the other in a case of greased leather. It meant you could alter the length of the tube. Bin-Firnas made a squinting face, as he moved the bottom half in and out. Shef took the device from him, trained it on the kite and its flyer's face, gently moved the tube up and down till the image came into focus.

There it was. The boy's tongue stuck out between his teeth, he was concentrating grimly on managing his vanes, trying to hold the kite steadily into the wind. There was no doubt, anyway, that the kite could carry his weight.

"How far can you send him?" he asked.

"As far as the rope will run," reported Suleiman.

"And what if the rope is cut?"

"He says, does the *ferengi* king wish to see?"

Shef lowered the telescope from his eye, frowning. "No. If they've done it once already I'd like to hear about that."

He focused again as a long dialogue broke out. Finally Suleiman addressed him again.

"He says, fifteen years ago, first they let it fly free with a boy inside. When the boy survived he himself, bin-Firnas, risked the attempt. He says he learned three things. First, it is much easier to control flight into the wind than before it. Second, there is a skill in controlling the vanes which the boy had, from many trial flights on the tether, but which he himself had not had time to learn. He says you must react with the body before the mind has time to issue an order, and that is a skill that only time can bring. Third, he learnt that he should also have fitted a vane to control flight side to side, as well as up and down. He says the kite turned on its side as he flew down the valley of the river, and he could not turn it back. So, instead of landing gracefully like a water-bird, he turned end over end in the rocks. Since then he has not walked without support, for all the surgeons of Cordova could do. He says, his legs were his gift to Allah, for knowledge."

"Winch the boy in," said Shef. "Tell the master of the house how grateful I am to him for showing me this, and how much I respect his readiness to try for himself. Say we would like to make careful drawings of his contrivance. We may be able to find a better place to test it than the banks of the Guadalquivir. And tell him also that we are amazed by his tubes of glass, and would like to know how to make them for ourselves. We wonder how he came upon the idea."

"He says," the translation came back, "that the lens which makes small writing large has been known here for many years. After that, it was only a matter of mechanical skill and many tests."

"Making old knowledge new," said Shef with a beam of pleasure. "This is a wiser man than his pupil."

In one of the innumerable tiny tenements of the city, a man sat cross-legged in front of an open window. His hands moved continually as he stitched, the seam he worked on moving through his hands as if it were a living serpent. His eyes never looked down, never left the street. Everything that went by was observed. In the corner to one side of him sat another man, out of sight from outside.

"You got a close look at it?" asked the tailor.

"I did. They walk through the city all the time, gaping like monkeys. They wear no more than a tight tunic on their upper bodies, and many of them not even that. They would walk naked as apes in the sun if the Cadi allowed it. It is easy to see what they wear round their necks. And I have stood as close to the *ferengi* king as I am to you."

"What did you see, then? And what did you hear?"

"All the strangers wear a silver charm round their necks. Often it is a hammer, many times a horn, or a phallus, or a boat. There are some signs that only a few wear: an apple, a bow, a pair of strange sticks. Usually these are worn by the bigger strangers, the ones who entered the city wearing mail, but the apple is worn only by the very small one in white, whom they say is a leech."

"And what does the king wear?"

"He wears a *graduale*. There is no doubt of that. I have peered so close I could smell the sweat of his shirt. It is a *graduale*. It has three steps on the right and two steps on the left."

"Which is uppermost?"

"Two are level at the top, like a cross. Below that, the right as we see it."

The left as he wears it, the tailor reflected, still sewing.

"Tell me what you have found out about these signs."

The other man hitched his stool conspiratorially closer. "We found soon that all these men are very eager to find strong drink of the sort forbidden by the Prophet, more eager for it than for women or for music. We approached some of them, said that we were Christians for whom this was not forbidden, that we had a store of wine for the service of our God. We found then that the bigger ones were shocked, looked askance, wanted the drink but cared nothing for the Christ. Some of the smaller ones, though, said easily that they had been Christians too, knew all about the mass and the holy wine. These we drew aside."

"*Had been* Christians?" muttered the tailor. "So they are apostates now?"

"That is so. But they told a clear story, as far as our interpreters could follow. They said that their whole kingdom had been Christian once, but they spoke with horror of the practices of their Church. Some of them had been slaves to abbot or bishop, and showed us stripes to prove it. Then they had been freed by the one-eyed king, who had converted the land to what they call 'the Way.' It means much the same as *shari'a*. The sign of this is the pendant they wear, one sign for each of the many gods they have."

"And the *graduale*?"

"All agree that it too is the sign of a god, but none was very sure what god it might be. The name they gave was 'Rig,' which I think is one of their words for 'king.' It is like our word *rois,* or the Spaniards' *reje.* All say without exception that no other man wears it, except some of the slaves rescued by the one-eye, who wear it as a sign of their gratitude to him. If he did not wear it, the sign would never be used at all."

Both men fell into a reflective silence. Eventually the tailor, putting his pile of clothing aside, rose stiffly to his feet.

"I think we may have to return home, brother. This is news that we must share. A strange king, wearing a sign personal to him alone, the same as our holy *graduale,* though with rungs reversed, as a token of devotion to the King. Surely this must have some meaning."

The other man nodded, more doubtfully. "At least we can get the stink of the lowlands out of our nostrils, and breathe cool air again. And wake without the *salat* ringing in our ears."

He paused. "As they became drunk, the small Northerners said again and again that to them this man is not just their king. They call him 'the One King.'" He spat neatly through the window. "Whatever he may be, they are apostates and idolaters."

"To the Church," the tailor replied, "so are we."

Brand settled his massive shoulders back against the walls of the room with a contented sigh. He had been sure that the English, at least, had managed to get hold of strong drink somehow. But every time he had approached one of the pygmies, they had gone into their usual state of glassy-eyed denial. Finally, pocketing his pride, he had edged over to Cwicca and Osmod, and appealed to them as former companions, guests, and shipmates to let him in on the secret.

"Just you, then," Cwicca had finally said.

"And you can bring Skaldfinn," Osmod had added. "We have trouble understanding them most of the time. Maybe he can get a bit more out of them."

They had been guided deftly out of the crowd leaving the flying demonstration and taken into a little shabby room: where, Brand had to admit, they had been given, cheerfully and without a word of payment, surprising amounts of good red wine—good as far as Brand could tell, since he had not drunk wine a dozen times in his life. He emptied his pint pot and passed it forward for more.

"Aren't you supposed to be looking after that priestess-female?" inquired Cwicca.

Skaldfinn scowled. "Don't call her that. She just says she is. She hasn't been accepted."

Brand looked round as if surprised to note that Svandis was not present. "I suppose so," he muttered. "She makes me feel cold just looking at her. Daughter of the Boneless One! I knew she existed all right, there was a good deal of talk about it. I just hoped the whole Hel-spawn family was dead."

"But you are supposed to be looking after her," pressed on Cwicca. He and Hund, born and bred within twenty miles of each other, had a strong fellow-feeling. If Hund and his master Shef accepted the woman, the rules and rituals of the Way would not count for much with him.

"She's safe enough," said Osmod. "Find her own way back, I dare say." He too waved his mug at their smiling hosts for a refill. "In some towns, I know, woman wanders off, she'll end up raped in an alley with a sack over her head. Not here! Chop your hand off as soon as look at you, and other bits too. And the Cadi's men everywhere."

"Cursed noisy woman," grumbled Brand. "Not sure six drunken sailors isn't what she needs."

Skaldfinn retrieved Brand's mug and tipped half the contents of it into his own. "I don't like the woman," he said, "but you're wrong there. Six drunken sailors isn't a tenth of what she's met already. And it hasn't done her any good at all.

"But she'll make her own way back to our quarters right enough," he added pacifically. "She's got no choice. Doesn't speak a word of the language. Any language they speak here." He turned and called out to their hosts in the bastard Latin, studded with Arab words, which he had already recognised as their native dialect.

* * *

In a cool courtyard not far from the hot shut-in room where the men were sitting, Svandis sat on a bench eying the circle of women who sat with her, round the fountain. Slowly she put a hand up to her veil, pulled it away from her face, threw back her hood. Her copper hair spilled down, framing the pale ice-water eyes. Some of the women around her drew in deep breaths. Others did not.

"You speak English, then," said one of them. She too dropped her veil, as the others did. Svandis looked at the one who had spoken: realized she was almost as fair as herself, with hair the color of pale ash-wood and green eyes. Realized too that she was a woman of amazing beauty. Since she had grown past childhood Svandis had been used to being the center of all eyes. If this woman were in the room, she admitted to herself, that might not be so.

"Yes," she replied, in English also. "But not well. I am a Dane."

The women looked at each other. "Danes took many of us from our homes," said the first one. "Sold us to the harems of the powerful. Some of us did well—those who knew how to use their bodies. Others not so well. We have no reason to love Danes." As she spoke there was a continual patter of translation from English into Arabic. Svandis realized that those around her were of mixed race and language. All, though, young and beautiful.

"I know," she said. "My father was Ivar Ragnarsson."

This time the expressions moved from fear to rage. Hands moved inside the all-covering cloaks. The ash-blonde girl thoughtfully pulled a long steel needle from her hair.

"I know what my father was. I know what he did. It happened to me too—and worse to my mother."

"How could such a thing happen to you? A princess of the Danes? Of the Viking woman-stealers?"

"I will tell you. But let me make it a condition." Svandis looked round the circle of a dozen women, trying to estimate their age and race. Half of them Northerners, she could see, but some olive-skinned like the men of Cordova, one almost yellow-skinned, others—she could not tell. "The condition is that each of us shall tell the others what is the worst thing that has happened to her. Then we will all know we are on the same side. Not English, or Danes, or Arabs. All women."

The women looked sidelong at each other as the translation pattered out. "And I will begin. And I will tell you not of the day I lost my virginity for a crust of stale bread. Not of the day I buried all my friends at once, in one grave. No, I will tell you of the day my mother died . . ."

By the time the last woman had finished speaking, the sun had moved off the central courtyard and the shadows were lengthening. The ash-blonde girl wiped the tears from her face, not for the first time, and waved imperiously at the cloisters round the fountain. Silently slave-bodyguards appeared, setting out small tables with dishes of fruit, jars of cool water and sherbet, faded back into the shadows to watch their masters' property.

"Very well," she said. "So we are all the same. Even if you are a Dane and the daughter of a madman. But now, tell us what we want to know. What brought you here? Who is the one-eyed king? Are you his woman? And why do you wear the strange robes, like the priests they talk about? Have they made you a priestess, and of which God?"

"There is something I have to tell you first," said Svandis, her voice dropping even though she was sure none of the men in the shadows could understand her tongue.

"There is no God. Not even Allah."

For the first time the mutter of translation ceased. The women looked at each other, unsure how to put what she had said into other words. So close to the *shahada:* there is no God but God. So far apart. And if saying the *shahada* made man or woman irrevocably a Muslim, saying its opposite— that must mean death at the least.

"Let me explain."

CHAPTER EIGHT

What do you mean, you don't know where the Nithhögg-gnawed woman is? I told you not to let her out of your sight!"

Brand, never used to being spoken to in this way since the day his beard had first begun to grow, clenched his massive fists and started to rumble a reply. By his side, almost two feet shorter, stood Hund, his face anxious both at the disappearance of Svandis and at the growing confrontation between a guilty but unapologetic Brand and an angry, overburdened Shef.

All round them turmoil reigned. The Northerners had been assigned a whole courtyard, a kind of barracks by the banks of the Guadalquivir. Now men ran in and out of every door, the air was filled with shouts of rage and inquiry. Gear accumulated on the sanded courtyard floor, with men standing guard over it against comrades who might be inclined to remedy their deficiencies at the expense of someone more careless. Viking skippers and English captains of crossbow platoons counted their men and tried to work out who was missing.

"Look at the goats'-turd mess," Shef shouted on. "Twelve men missing, Skarthi says some bastard's sold half the oars for his ship—the oars, for Christ's sake, I mean Thor's sake—and the towel-heads screaming at me all the time to get moving, get back down river, the Christians are coming with a fleet and an army and Loki knows what. We'll get back to the ships and find they've already been burnt to the waterline without throwing a rock because everyone's asleep. And now I have to stop and look for some useless woman because *you couldn't keep your hands off the beer-bottle!*"

Brand's rumble turned into a growl, he thrust both hands firmly into his belt in an attempt to keep from strangling his king, lord and former crew-carl, Hund ludicrously stepped between the two much bigger men in an attempt to hold them back: Shef realized that the grinning faces watching the confrontation were now looking over his shoulder. He turned.

Through the gates of the courtyard, still in the early morning shadow, stepped Svandis. Her veil was still discreetly pulled across her face. As she met fifty hostile stares, set in a growing silence, she stripped the veil back. The pale icewater eyes glared out over a set jaw. Brand clutched his belly instinctively, with a low moan.

"Well, she's back," said Hund soothingly.

"Yes, but where has she been?"

"Out tomcatting," muttered Brand. "Out all night. Probably some Arab picked her up for his harem and then realized she wasn't worth the trouble. Don't blame him."

Shef considered the angry face in front of him, looked sideways at Hund. In his culture every woman was the property of some man, husband, master, father, brother. For one to stray sexually was above all a matter of disgrace for the man. In this case, as far as he could see, if Svandis had an owner it was the man who had taken her as apprentice, Hund. If he seemed unaffected, or undisgraced, then no harm was done. In any case, Shef reflected, he had a strong feeling that Svandis had not seized an unwatched moment to find herself a new lover, whatever Brand thought. She seemed far more angry than flirtatious, for all her beauty. From what Hund had told him, or hinted to him, that was only natural.

Svandis braced herself for a torrent of abuse, and probably blows, the normal consequence of what she had done. Instead Shef started to turn away, turned back and remarked, "well, as long as you're safe," seized Brand by the arm and began to drag him away towards the pile of stacked oars which Hagbarth was counting once more in an attempt to get a definite answer.

The fury she had been hatching as a protection burst out. "Don't you want to know where I've been?" she shrieked. "What I've been doing?"

Shef looked over his shoulder. "No. Talk to Hund about it. One thing, though. What language were you talking? Skaldfinn was dead sure you wouldn't find an interpreter except for Latin, which you don't know."

"English," Svandis hissed. "How many Englishwomen do you think there are in Cordova? In the harems?"

Shef let go of Brand, walked back to look at her more carefully. Svandis realized that his face had once more turned grim. When he spoke, it seemed to be to himself, though he addressed the words to Hund.

"We might have known, eh? I saw them in Hedeby market, Vikings selling Wendish girls to Arabs. The guard told me the price of girls had gone up since the English trade stopped producing. But they must have been selling girls down here for fifty years. Everywhere we go, Hund, we find them. In backwoods Norway, in turf huts on Shetland, here in Spain. There doesn't seem to be a place in the world without its slave from Norfolk or Lincoln. Or Yorkshire," he added, remembering the berserk Cuthred. "One day we must have a chat with an experienced slaver, I bet we have a few lying quiet in the ranks. Find out how they used to divide them up, price them for the market. Worn-out ones for the Swedish sacrifice, strong workers for the hill-farms. And the pretty ones down here, for gold not silver."

Shef's hands seemed to grope for a weapon, but as usual he was not carrying one, not even a sword at his belt.

"All right, Svandis, tell me about it sometime. I don't blame you for what your father did, and he's paid his price. Now, as you can see, we're moving. Get some breakfast, get your things together. Hund, see if we have any sick."

He moved off purposefully towards the oars, shouting for Skaldfinn to see if any could be ransomed from their new owners. Svandis glared uncertainly at his back. Brand too moved away, muttering into his beard. Hund looked up at his apprentice.

"Have you been talking to them about your beliefs?" he said quietly.

"The infidels are playing with their kites again," remarked the master of the Cordovan flagship to the captain of marines.

The captain, a Cordovan, spat neatly into the sea to show disgust and contempt. "They are trying to catch up with the learned man, bin-Firnas, Allah be merciful to him. As if the sons of dogs from the far end of Barbary could match the deeds of a true philosopher! See, their kite sinks already, and it has no man or boy in it. It is going down like an old sheik's penis. A far cry from bin-Firnas, I saw his kite fly like a bird with a stout boy in its beak. I wish the infidels may perish in torment, for their pride and their folly."

The master looked sideways at the captain, wondering if such fury was wise. "The curse of Allah on them," he said placatingly. "And on all deniers of the Prophet. But may it not fall on these ones till we have seen them use their stone-machines."

"Stone machines!" snarled the captain. "Better to meet the worshipers of Yeshua saber in hand, as we have always done before, and always defeated them."

So that's it, reflected the master. He sees his trade taken away from him. "As you say," he agreed again. "And if Allah wills we shall do so. But one thing, Osman, you will grant me. Let us keep these *majus,* these bookless pagans from the North, on our side at least until we have met the Greeks. Their stone machines can do what the bravest sabers can not. And I have no desire to meet the fire of the Greeks at sea."

He turned from the rail before the disgruntled soldier could frame a reply.

Half a mile away, across the clear blue water of the coastal Mediterranean, gazing through the far-seer the Arab philosopher had given him, Shef watched the kite slowly rocking down the sky. He felt no particular irritation. As soon as the combined fleet of the Way and the men of Andalusia had cleared for sea, after a racing passage down the Guadalquivir, he had begun to experiment, eagerly seconded by Cwicca, Osmod and the catapult crews of the *Fafnisbane*. Shef had made certain large quantities of the poles and cloth that bin-Firnas used for his devices had been taken with them. He and his men now set to construct kites after any fashion that seemed likely. "We don't know what holds the things up," Shef had told the eager attentive circle. "So we might as well try anything and see what works."

Today they were trying the effect of an unbroken box of sailcloth, without air-gaps or panels. It appeared to be a total failure. Did that mean the panels were necessary, after all, and against what seemed to be common sense? Or was it the two control lines they were also trying today? The two catapulteers holding them were trying gently to work the kite back into the sky, with limited success.

It didn't matter. For one thing it was keeping the men amused. Shef looked up at the masthead and saw, as he suspected, that the lookout was gaping steadily at the kite instead of attending to his duty. A shout, a wave, and the lookout turned guiltily to stare at the horizon once more.

For another, in Shef's experience a great deal of any technological breakthrough came from random fiddling, while the men who had to work the machine got used to it, discovered its problems, worked out how to counter them. Nothing ever worked absolutely right first time. He was quite happy now to let the men amuse themselves, see if they could at least reach the standard bin-Firnas had demonstrated to them, learn the skills they would need when the time came to improve. One thing bin-Firnas had not realized, with the curious playful reluctance to push a theory to its limits which Shef had already noted as characteristic of this culture: experimenting with manned flight, or boyed flight, would be a good deal safer over a calm sea than a rocky ravine. Shef had already checked to find out how many of Ordlaf's lightweights could swim.

The kite settled into the water, to a general groan of disappointment. One of the five Viking longships which they had taken up the Guadalquivir to Cordova cruised over towards it, oars sweeping in leisurely time, began to retrieve kite and rope and bring them back.

That was a weakness of the two-masters, one that no-one had ever noticed out in the Atlantic for which they had been designed. They were true sailing-craft, fast, sturdy, capable of mounting onagers and crossbows and carrying scores of tons of food and water. In British or Scandinavian waters, where the wind literally never ceased, and was more often too rough than too gentle, they had swept the seas against Frankish cogs or Viking longships, the first too slow, the second too fragile to contest with them.

But no-one had ever tried to row them for more than a few hundred yards working out of harbor, and that was done with massive four-man sweeps capable of reaching bare crawling pace. Here in the Inner Sea, as today, the wind often seemed to die away altogether. With both sails spread and what wind there was blowing directly from the sea, the *Fafnisbane* and her 'Hero' class consorts—*Grendelsbane, Sigemund, Wada, Theodric, Hagena* and *Hildebrand*—were barely making steerage way. By contrast the five Viking boats were keeping pace under oars at a mere paddling stroke on the placid sea, their crews happy to work off some surplus energy by fetching and carrying the kites. The Cordovan galleys, meanwhile, after repeated angry outbursts from their admiral, had seemingly accepted the situation. The routine now was for their main body to row on ahead during the morning, take their long siesta at midday, and then row on again as the sun declined to find a place to camp and water overnight. The infidels made up lost distance during the siesta, and caught up finally in the evening. Meanwhile contact was maintained between the advance body and the laggards by a string of intermediary ships. Seemingly out of courtesy—or more likely because he did not trust them—the admiral himself hung back in his own green-painted galley, with a double score of his larger ships: enough to board and envelop Shef's own fleet at need. There was no way of guarding against that other than making them keep their distance, to give time for the onagers to work. After thought, Shef had accepted the situation. If the Arabs had not overwhelmed him and his men in the streets of Cordova, they were unlikely to do so here and now, steering to meet a dangerous common enemy.

Hagbarth was preparing for the noon ceremony, at which he measured the height of the sun with his seaman's staff, and considered the results against a set of tables he was compiling. It was of little practical value. The answer might tell you—if Shef understood the theory—how far north or south you were, but all that meant in practice was that Hagbarth could say which spot on the Atlantic shore they were now level with. What would be more interesting would be to combine these results, one day, with a good map. Such information, Shef recognised, would have saved him and his companions much trouble during their long walk across the Keel of Norway from Atlantic shore to Jarnberaland.

Shef unrolled the map he had been given by his Arab hosts, one, he conceded, far better than any he had seen in his life before. They had watered the night before at Denia, a good protected harbor with smooth beaches either side for the shallow-draft ships to draw up on. There the commander of the local garrison had reported that the Christian warships, and in particular the feared Red Fleet of the Greeks, had made landings less than a hundred miles to the north within the last two weeks. They could, then, be just over the horizon at this moment.

At the thought, Shef raised his head and called to the lookout.

"Anything to see?"

"Nothing, lord. The admiral's spread his awnings and stopped rowing, dropping behind us now. A few fishing boats out to sea. All of them got those funny three-corner sails. The skyline's bare as a whore's—"

A yell from Hagbarth cut short the lookout's simile. For some reason Hagbarth had decided that the purity of their one female passenger had to be guarded from contamination. All the Vikings, Shef had noted, much as they might dislike her, were unable entirely to resist the awe they felt for the Ragnarsson blood.

Hagbarth sat down cross-legged on the deck next to Shef and the map, followed by Hund and Thorvin, who settled himself more deliberately on a canvas folding stool. Shef looked round for a moment, wondering who else might be invited to join the impromptu council. Brand was not aboard, had insisted on returning to his own ship, the *Narwhal,* built to replace the much-lamented *Walrus.* His excuse was that he felt impatient aboard the stately *Fafnisbane,* preferred the maneuverability of his own smaller ship. Shef suspected that he simply could not bear the presence of Svandis, for her father's sake or her own. Skaldfinn was standing in plain sight by the rail. Why did he not come over? Shef realized that Skaldfinn had with him Suleiman the Jew, did not want to abandon him, was not sure that Suleiman would be welcome at a conference which he could, by now, very well understand.

The Jew was a strange, dignified, withdrawn figure. For weeks Shef had been unable to imagine him as anything but a machine for translating. yet learning a language from someone gives many insights. Shef had begun to think that, for all his professed loyalty to Abd er-Rahman and his Muslim masters, Suleiman was—not quite to be trusted? Capable of being won over? One thing that had emerged was that in the Muslim world, Jews paid taxes, and Christians, while Muslims did not. That was bound to be a source of discontent, if not disaffection. Shef waved to Skaldfinn, indicated that Suleiman was welcome to join them too.

"Well," said Hagbarth. "Tell us again, lord, what's the plan? We launch kites into the air, steal Greek fire from the Christians, and rain it down from the sky."

Shef grinned. "Don't tell Mu'atiyah. He'll say his master thought of it first. All right. We're about here." He tapped the map with a grubby, nail-bitten finger. "The Christians can't be far away, and all we hear says they're coming for us just as we're going for them. We should expect a straight head-on clash. So that's what we won't get. They know something we don't know, we know something they don't know."

"So do the easy part," said Hagbarth, youngest and most careless of the Way-priests. "Tell us what we know."

Shef grinned again. "One thing we know is that none of these people, Christian or Arab, know how to fight a sea-battle."

Silence and looks exchanged. Finally Suleiman, looking round first to see if anyone else would take the bait, ventured the query. "Lord king? The fleets of Andalus have fought many battles. And so have the Greeks. Do you mean—they have not fought them correctly?"

"No. I mean they weren't sea-battles. It's obvious from the way old admiral what's-his-name works"—Shef jerked a thumb over his shoulder at the awning-rigged galleys taking their siesta two miles off upon the glassy sea. "His main idea is to fight a land-battle in which his ships form one wing. Ever since we made contact back wherever it was—Alicante?—he's just tried to keep pace with the land army marching up the coast. It's true our ships hold him back, but we could make better speed if we sailed all night, which is all right by us. But he camps every night in touch with his land-colleague. They expect to clash on the coast, army to army and fleet to fleet. They never go far from their water—they can't, with all those rowers on board in this heat—and they never go far from the army, horse and foot together."

"What advantage does that give us?" asked Thorvin carefully. What his one-time protégé said sounded very much like lunatic over-confidence, but no-one dared say that of the victor at Hastings and at the Braethraborg.

"What I'd like to do is locate the enemy, then swing out to sea on the land breeze we get every morning, come in on their flank and rear from the open sea in the afternoon. Then we could get the catapults to work in daylight with them trapped between us and the coast."

"You only have seven ships with—what do you call them?—mules," observed Suleiman delicately. "Are seven enough to determine a great battle?"

"The admiral here has hundreds of ships," Shef replied. "So, we're told, did the admirals of both fleets the Greeks have destroyed already. But those fleets were helpless against the Greek fire. We hope the Christian fleets will be helpless against our mule-stones."

"It will take a long time to sink hundreds of ships by shooting," said Thorvin sceptically.

"That's the point. I only want to hit the ships with the Greek fire. The red galleys, they say. Maybe twenty of them. In this battle, all that will count will be their twenty with the fire and our seven with the mules. The one of those that gets into action first will be the winner. All the other ships, once that's decided, will be porkers for the slaughter. Lambs for the slaughter, I mean," corrected Shef hastily, remembering the strange dietary customs of Muslim and Jew together.

"I see," said Skaldfinn. "Now, the other question: what do they know that we don't?"

"I don't know," said Shef quickly, before anyone else could make the obvious answer. All the Northerners laughed, while Suleiman watched them impassively, stroking his beard. They *were* like children, he thought, just as Abd er-Rahman had said. They would laugh at anything. Always mirth, always horseplay, the men hiding each other's food, tying each other's shoelaces together. The king himself would fly kites all day and never mind if they fell into the sea. They had no dignity. Or was it that they felt their dignity was so great that it could not be diminished by anything to which they consented? Mu'atiyah talked till he was hoarse about how stupid and untaught they were. Yet they learned with terrible speed, and Mu'atiyah would learn nothing that did not come to him on the authority of a great man or, better still, a great book. What, he wondered, did the one-eye really think?

"I'm hoping they don't know we're here," said Shef finally. "No-one in the southern sea has seen a mule shoot from a ship. They may be expecting to meet another over-confident Muslim fleet, all numbers and bravery. In that case we've probably got them. But if they do know we're here, I would expect them to try an attack at night. The exact opposite of what we want. We need light to shoot at a distance, and we want to spread out. They want to get up close and meet a packed enemy at close range, where light doesn't matter. In any case they'll make their own.

"The answer to that's pretty obvious."

"Right," agreed Hagbarth. "We lie inshore, with a screen of other ships. If they set light to them, we'll have light to shoot at them and time to wind the machines."

"Maybe there's something else we don't know," repeated Thorvin.

"I know. Could they have built a *Fearnought*, like we did?"

Hagbarth shook his head, still with a faint touch of sadness. The unwieldy, steel-plated, barely sailable *Fearnought* which had literally broken the back of the Ragnarsson fleet seven years before had once been his own *Aurvendill*, fastest sailer in the North, he had claimed, before her total rebuilding. But she too had had her back broken by catapult-stones, had never sailed again after the battle. Chopped up for firewood long since.

"They can't do it," he said flatly. "I've looked at these galleys of the Inner Sea, seen how they build them. They've been building them the same way for a thousand years, they say, and the Greek ships will be just the same. They lay the planks edge to edge, not clinker-fashion like we do. And they just fit plank to plank till it's ready, no frame to build on. Weak keel, very weak ribs. Strengthened fore and aft to take the ram, but even that's not much. Doesn't take much to punch a hole in one of these. I'm not saying their shipwrights are stupid, mind. Just that they build for a shallow sea with no tides and no swell. I am saying that you couldn't make a *Fearnought* out of any of these galleys. They haven't the strength in the frame. I'm sure about that.''

A long considering pause, broken only by yells and splashings from close at hand. The *Fafnisbane* was now at a complete halt in the midday heat, sails hanging limply, providing only welcome shade. The crew had seized the chance to strip and hurl themselves in to the welcome blue water. Shef noticed Svandis standing watching their nakedness by the rail, scratching absent-mindedly at her side under the long white wool dress. She looked as if she were about to strip and dive in too. That would cause some excitement at least, no matter what Brand might say about the wrath of the sea-hags and the marbendills of the deep. His authority on the subject had dwindled, paradoxically, once men knew that he was a quarter-marbendill himself.

"We'll stick to our plan, then," said Shef. "Hagbarth, you and Suleiman talk to the admiral tonight about night guardships. Tomorrow I will ask him to send light ships forward to find and fix the enemy, so we can outflank them. Our secret weapon, besides the mulestones, is that we do not fear the open sea nor running out of water for thirsty rowers. That's what we'll rely on.

"And there's one other good thing."

"What's that?" asked Hagbarth.

"Old yoke-shoulders Bruno isn't there. The Emperor, I mean."

"How do you know?"

Shef grinned yet again. "I'd have felt it if that bastard was nearby. Or had bad dreams about him."

Much less than a day's sail away, the two commanders of the joint Roman-Greek expeditionary force were also making their plan for battle. Only the two men sat in the rear cabin of the great Greek galley, in the hot cedar-smelling half-light. Neither believed in consulting subordinates. Like their masters before them, the emperors Bruno and Basil, they had discovered that they could communicate well enough in Latin, the language native to neither of them but understood, after a fashion, by both. Neither liked to talk it: Georgios the Greek had learnt the Italian form of it from Neapolitan sailors, whom he despised as effeminates and heretics. Agilulf the German had learnt the French form of it from his neighbors across the Rhine, whom he too hated as ancestral enemies and arrogant would-be cultural superiors. Yet both had learned to do what was necessary to co-operate. Each had begun even to have a certain wary respect for the skills of the other, brought into being by months of successful skirmishing and victory.

"They are a day to the south and coming on slowly?" inquired Agilulf. "How do you know?"

Georgios waved a hand at the scene outside the small port-holes fitted into the galley's sharp-ended stern. Among and around his own score of red-painted ships, each a hundred feet long, there lay a host of smaller craft of every size, the scourings of the Christian fishing villages of the northern Spanish coast and the islands, and of the borderlands between Spain and France.

"The Arabs are so used to the fishing boats that they take no notice of them. Nor can they tell Christian from Muslim, or from Jew. Our boats mix in with theirs. Every night one has steered out to sea and brought us a report. I have known exactly where every ship of theirs has been for days."

"Maybe they've been doing the same to us."

Georgios shook his head. "I am not as careless as the Arab admiral. No boat comes within fifty stadia of here without being boarded and inspected. If they are Muslims—" He chopped his hand down on the edge of the table.

"How come our spy boats are back here so long before their fleet. Are they faster?"

"Handier, certainly. You see the kind of sails they use?" Georgios waved a hand again at the cluster of boats alongside. One, slipping quietly across the water on some errand, had its sail up and rigged: a three-cornered sail on a sloping yard. "Round here they call it the Latin sail—*lateeno* in their language." Both men let out a simultaneous sharp bark of contemptuous amusement at the foreigners. "They use *lateeno* to mean—" Georgios hesitated for a word. "Something like *aptus,* handy. And it is a handy rig, fast and useful in light airs."

"Why don't you rig them, then?"

"If you were to look closely," the admiral explained, "you'd see that if you want to turn the ship from side to side—" neither his Latin nor Agilulf's ran to the word for 'tack'—"you can't do it by just turning the yard, the stick the sail is on. You have to lift the yard over the mast. Easy for a small boat. Harder and harder as the mast gets higher and the yard gets heavier. It's a rig for small boats. Or for ships full of seamen."

Agilulf grunted, not much interested. "So we know where they are but they don't know where we are. How does that help us?"

The Greek leaned back on his bench. "Well. Our weapon is fire. Theirs—as you have told me again and again—is stone. You tell me you have seen one ship of theirs, an iron one at that, sink a whole fleet in less time than it takes to say a Mass."

Agilulf nodded. He had been at the battle of the Braethraborg, had seen the Ragnarsson fleet battered into wrecks by Shef's own *Fearnought.* It had impressed him greatly.

"I believe you. So they will want to fight at a distance, we want to fight up close. They may expect us to try to attack at night. I have a better idea. You see, my men on the spy boats are all unanimous on one thing. These Northern ships, they say, are sailers. They have never seen anyone even try to row them, and they look heavy and round-bellied.

"But in these waters the wind always fades round noon, as earth and water reach the same heat. No wind either way. That's when I am going to hit them."

"They can shoot their stones without moving at all," objected Agilulf.

"Not over bow or stern. In any case my plan is to drive off or burn their support ships, the Arabs. And then to have a good look at the Northerners. When I can move and they cannot. If the worst comes to the worst—we just row away. If they show a weakness—we'll take it."

"So you drive off the fleet, leaving the Northerners becalmed if need be, and then come in with your marines and rowers, from the sea, on the rear of the Arab army. While I hold the Arab horse and foot from in front."

Georgios nodded silently. Both men knew there were many permutations possible within their overall plan. Each knew, now, how the other thought and what the other could do. They had never lost a battle or a skirmish yet, had swept the north-west Mediterranean from coast to coast.

Agilulf rose. "Good enough. My detachments for your ships are already told off. I'll have them by the shore an hour before dawn, fully provisioned. Just have the boats ready to take them off."

Georgios rose too. The two men shook hands. "I wish the emperor were here," said Agilulf suddenly. "My emperor, that is."

Georgios rolled his eyes with extravagant disbelief. "He is your emperor, not mine. Yet not even my emperor, not even the idiot before him, would go chasing relics at this stage of a war."

"It worked for him last time," said Agilulf, forcing as much loyalty into his voice as he could muster.

CHAPTER NINE

Tell me again about this God-damned—"

Bruno, Emperor of the Holy Roman Empire, Protector of the Faith, scourge of the heretics, apostates and false believers, paused. It had been a bad day. Another bad day. Here in the broken country where France joined Spain and both were separated by the high Pyrenees, every village had a fortress on a peak, most of them seemingly called 'Puigpunyent,' 'Sharp-point Peak.' That was why so many Muslim bandits had managed to establish themselves. No longer. He had cleared them out. But now, when he might have expected gratitude and co-operation from the Christians he had saved from their enemies, instead stubborn resistance, closed gates, flocks driven into the hills, people lodged in their high eyries. Not all of them. According to the barons who had come in and submitted to him, the people who were resisting him were now heretics, of some sect long established in the border country, with whom the Catholics had fought a bitter neighborly war in private for generations.

The trouble was, everyone agreed that it was the heretics who had the secret of the Holy Grail. If it existed—and Bruno believed passionately that it did, just as the Holy Lance on which his rule rested had existed, hidden among the pagans—it was in some mountain peak or other, hidden among the heretics.

And so he had set himself to reduce them, to burn, batter, frighten, bribe or wheedle them out of their mountain lairs. Sometimes it went well, sometimes badly. Today had been a bad day. Fierce resistance, the gate untouched by the heavy catapult rocks, and twenty good brothers of the *Lanzenorden* dead, along with many more of the troops levied from the barons of Southern France.

Even so, he had almost committed a mortal sin, in speaking ill of the precious relic. Bruno paused, looked round deliberately. He set his own penances. In time past he had taken a handful of wooden splinters, set them alight, and let them burn on his open palm. Yet the blisters had impeded him in battle. He had no right to disqualify himself from God's work merely for his own sin. And in any case it was not the hand which had sinned. No. Drawing a dagger, he held its tip over a candle, waited till he saw it glow. Then, deliberately once more he thrust out his almost-sinful tongue, laid the red-hot tip to it. Held it for long seconds. A tear slowly trickled down through the dust caked thick on each cheek, but his hatchet-face otherwise did not change. The smell of scorching flesh came to his nostrils, a familiar one now in these days of siege and skirmish.

He pulled the dagger away, looked critically at its tip to see if he had affected its temper. Seemingly not. He looked up and met the disapproving gaze of his confidant and spiritual adviser, the deacon Erkenbert. Erkenbert did not like these ascetic practices, felt they led to spiritual pride.

"If thine eye offend thee, pluck it out," said Bruno, answering the unspoken accusation.

"Better to attend to the instructions of your confessor," replied Erkenbert, "always assuming he has any." Erkenbert had a grudge against Bruno's confessor Felix as well, for Felix, being a priest, could hear confessions and give absolution as Erkenbert, still only a deacon, could not.

Bruno dismissed the incipient argument with a gesture. "Now," he repeated, "tell me again about the blessed Grail of Our Lord. My faith, alas, needs strengthening once more."

Erkenbert began the story, still with an air of reluctant disapproval. In a sense he, Erkenbert, was a man trapped by success. He had been with the Emperor, when the latter, a mere *Ritter* of the *Lanzenorden,* went into the waste places of the North, to return with the Holy Lance which had once more unified the collapsing Empire of Charlemagne. And because he had been with the Emperor all that time, had done the research which had enabled them in the end to identify the Lance, and had furthermore consoled the despondent Emperor when he felt his search might never end, now he was considered to be an expert on relics and on searches. But the Lance had been proposed and authenticated by the holy Saint Rimbert, Archbishop of Hamburg and Bremen. This story that the Emperor was now convinced of had a very different origin.

Nevertheless Erkenbert had studied what few documents could be brought to him: he knew the tale as well as anyone. Maybe it was best that it should be told by one who could not be in any way seduced by it.

"As you know," he began, "the four gospellers do not all tell the same tale of the Crucifixion of Our Lord. And this of course is proof of their truth, for how often do we not see that four men who have seen the same thing happen will nevertheless tell it in different ways? Yet where they do agree— as they agreed about the centurion who pierced Christ's side with his lance, and venerated him forthwith as the Son of God—we may be sure that something great and holy is meant by it, for all four were inspired by the Holy Ghost to see and write the same thing."

Bruno nodded, the satisfied expression on his bleak, hard face like that of a child who hears a well-known bedtime story unrolling.

"Yet there may also be great wisdom, or great knowledge, in something vouchsafed to only one witness. Now the Gospel of John tells us many things that are absent from the others. One thing he tells of is strange but not unlikely. I have read in other works that it was the custom of the Romans, a cruel and godless folk, when they crucified a man, to leave his body to be eaten by the birds."

Bruno, whose gallows groaned all over Europe with unburied dead, nodded again, perhaps with satisfaction, perhaps with imperial agreement on policy.

"But it was the law of the Jews that no dead thing might be exposed over their holy day of Passover. That is why men were sent to kill Christ and those crucified with him, not in mercy, but so that they might be taken down before sunset on Friday, when the Sabbath of the Jews begins.

"What happened then? Only John says this, but the story is not unlikely, nor need it have been known to all. He says that a rich Jew begged Pilate for the body, to have it wrapped in shroud and laid in a stone sepulcher—as is the custom in stony countries like this one, not laid in earth as we do. He gives the name of the Jew as Joseph of Arimathea. And then the story goes on to tell of the Resurrection, as all the gospellers in their different ways do.

"Now of this Joseph many other stories are told. My own people—not my Northumbrian people, but the English of the far West, have a story that this Joseph sailed from the shores of the Holy Land after the death of Jesus, and came in the end to England, not yet England but rather Britannia. And there, they say, he built a church at Glastonbury and performed many miracles. They say, too, that he brought with him the Holy Grail and that it still lies there."

"But we do not believe that?" queried Bruno, though he had heard the answer at least a dozen times.

"No. For a rich Jew to leave the Holy Land, if he had become an enemy of his own people, might be possible. But Britannia at the time of the death of Our Lord was not yet within the Empire. It must have been a wasteland inhabited by savage Welshmen. Who would wish to go there?"

"So why do we think there is a Holy Grail?"

Erkenbert managed to conceal a disapproving sniff. He at least did not think there was a Holy Grail; but he knew from experience that if he said as much, his pious but overbearing master would keep him arguing till he had confessed he might be wrong. "Mostly because so many people have believed it. Nevertheless," Erkenbert hurried on before his master could press for a better answer, "looked at correctly, the accounts of the death of Our Lord do leave room for wonder.

"I have already said that only the Gospel of the holy John tells the story of Joseph of Arimathea. Only that gospel also mentions the Jew Nicodemus, and it mentions him three times: at the end, when Nicodemus and Joseph arrange for Jesus to be laid to rest. In the temple of the Jews, where Nicodemus calls out for a fair trial. And when Nicodemus comes to Jesus by night to ask him a question.

"And yet there is another gospel I have read."

"Besides the four of the Bible?" prompted Bruno.

"Yes. It is the *Gospel of Nicodemus*. The fathers of the Church, in their wisdom, decided not to include it among those works called canonical. Yet it is clearly a work of great age. And what it tells us is the story of what happened after Christ died. And before he was resurrected."

"When he went down into Hell," breathed Bruno, face rapt.

"It is this gospel which allows us to have the words in the Creed, *descendit ad infernos,* he descended into Hell. So this Nicodemus saw Christ buried, knew of his Resurrection—and talked with those whom Christ released from Hell. How else could he know the story? He must have been a man far deep in the secrets of Our Lord. More so perhaps even than Joseph. Such men recognised Our Lord as the Son of God as soon, almost, as did the centurion Longinus, who kept his own lance as a relic. They had many chances to put by the things that the Son of God had touched, and one of them may have been the Grail. Some say it is the chalice of the last Supper, some the jar in which the Holy Blood was collected after the Lance had shed it."

"But that's because they're bloody French!" yelled Bruno suddenly, driving his dagger with his usual appalling speed and strength deep in and through the table in front of him. "They can't speak their own bloody language! Just gabble gabble Latin till it sounds like nothing on earth! Take *aqua,* turn it into *eau,* take *caballerus,* turn it into *chevalier.* I ask you. What might a *graal* have been before those miscegenated bastards got their tongues round it?"

Two bodyguards moved into the tent, weapons ready, saw their lord sitting unharmed by the table. Bruno grinned suddenly, waved at them, spoke in his usual familiar Low German. "All right, boys. Just saying what I think about the French." His men returned his grin, withdrew. *Brüder* of the *Lanzenorden,* they shared their master's opinion: especially after today, when there had been Frenchmen on both sides, and when they felt their own had fought less whole-heartedly than the enemy's.

"Well," said Erkenbert, trying to answer the question. "A *graal* can be a sort of flat plate or dish."

"Couldn't keep blood in it, could you?"

"Maybe it is blood. Maybe when these people say *sancto graale,* or *saint graal,* Holy Grail, whatever the pronunciation, their ancestors were trying to say *sang real,* royal blood. It would be much the same in Latin, too. The one is *sanctus graduale,* the other *sanguis regalis.* Maybe the Grail is just the Holy Blood."

For some time Bruno remained silent, meditatively touching the blister on his own tongue. Erkenbert watched his face with a growing interest. They had been over this ground several times, and what Erkenbert had not been able to understand was why Bruno seemed so sure of himself and his quest. There were indeed odd features in the Gospel of John and that of Nicodemus. There was nothing for the Grail, though, like the strong recent evidence there had been for the Holy Lance, possessed within living memory by Charlemagne. Nor was there anything like the centurion's letter that Erkenbert himself had seen. Erkenbert had suspected before that Bruno was hiding something.

"How do you get 'dish' or 'chalice' out of *graduale?*" asked Bruno finally.

"It is from *gradus,* a—a stage," replied Erkenbert. "So it comes to mean a course at dinner, and then what the course is served on."

"But *gradus* doesn't mean a bloody stage," snarled Bruno. "You're just saying that. It means a bloody step. It means something you step on. And a *graduale* is something with a lot of graduses on it. And you and I both call that the same thing, whether we talk my German or your English. Same word both languages. I checked. You know what it is! It's a bloody . . ."

"Ladder," completed Erkenbert, his voice low and cold. For the first time he saw where his master's thought was leading.

"Ladder it is. Like you-know-who wears round his neck."

"But how could that become a holy thing? Like the chalice of the Last Supper."

"Have you ever thought," inquired Bruno, leaning back in his camp-chair, "what happened after the Crucifixion?"

Erkenbert shook his head dumbly.

"Well, the Romans didn't take Our Lord, did they? I expect my ancestor Longinus"—Erkenbert noted silently the promotion of Longinus from predecessor to ancestor—"he marched off back to barracks, looking at his lance and wondering, I should think. But the body, the body of Our Lord— well, you just said it, it was handed over to the Jews. The friendly ones, that is, not the ones who had him crucified. But if you wanted to know what happened next, you'd have to ask the Jews. Not the Romans, they'd all marched off, not the Christians, they were all hiding. And what do you think was the first thing they'd do?''

Erkenbert shook his head mutely. He had a terrifying sensation that something was building up here, something stemming from the past, from Bruno's own past, with terrible ramifications for the future. He had no idea what it was.

Bruno poured two large goblets of wine from the handy pitcher and pushed one over to Erkenbert. "Thirsty work, talking," he remarked, his face taking on once more its unexpected glow of amiability and good fellowship.

"Now, have you ever really thought seriously about how to crucify someone? And how you de-crucify them? Eh?"

Shef lay in his hammock slung between the rail and the forward catapult mounting. A faint breeze moderated the heat still rising from the wooden decks, and the ship rocked gently on an almost motionless sea. Round him seventy men slept also, some in hammocks, some stretched out on deck. Above them the stars burned brightly in a clearer sky than any they had seen before.

In his dream, Shef knew he was far, far below earth, or sea, or sky. He was on some kind of gigantic stairway. A stairway so huge that he could only just reach the top of the next step with his fingertips. He might be able to jump, haul himself up, get a knee over the edge and scramble on to the next step. How often could he do that before weariness took him?

And there was something coming up the steps towards him. Something enormous, that dwarfed him as he would dwarf a mouse. He could feel vibrations through the cold wet stone, a thump—thump—thump of enormous feet climbing the stair. A waft of malice and malevolence crept up the stair ahead of the feet. If the thing that was climbing saw him it would stamp down on him as surely as he would crush a poison-spider. A faint light was beginning to glow from down below as well. The thing that was coming would see him.

Shef glanced around, already imagining his own flesh and blood spattered across the stone. No way up that did not lead to being overtaken. No point in going down. To the side. He sprang across, began to grope in the dim light across the side of the stairway. There was something there, a wooden strip or lining. And he was like a mouse. From years before Shef remembered his own vision of himself as Völund the lame smith, and Farman priest of Frey peering up at him from the floor like a mouse from the wainscoting. Now he was the mouse, and Farman— the thumping feet on the stair called Shef back from thoughts of the quiet Wisdom-House to his immediate reality.

A crack in the wood. Shef began to squeeze himself into it, first head first, then realizing that that might leave him unable to see the menace behind, pulling out and reversing in, careless of splinters tearing his tunic and digging into the skin.

He was back, covered at least from direct vision. He pulled his head back even further, knowing that nothing shows up so well in the dark as pale skin. There was still a line of sight. As the thump—thump—thump of feet became deafening, Shef saw a face cross his limited vision.

A set, cruel face, marked and pitted with poison. The face of Loki Baldersbane, free from his eternal prison, from the snake ever-dripping venom into his eyes when his loyal wife did not intercept it. The face of someone set on vengeance. Vengeance for unforgivable injustice.

The face passed by, the feet continued their steady climb. And then they stopped. Stopped level with Shef's head. He held his breath, conscious suddenly of the beating of his heart, that seemed to pound like a drum inside the echo-chamber of the little wooden crack. He remembered Brand's huge feet, stamping up and down while the baffled Arab watched. Loki could surely smash in his fragile hiding-place with a kick.

The feet moved on, began to climb once more up towards the light. As Shef breathed again, he heard a second noise. This time it was a slither. The slither of scales across stone. He remembered the awful sight he had seen of the great head striking at him, striking and falling short before it returned to its endless task of torment. Endlessly frustrated by the gods who had tethered it just out of fang-reach. The monster-viper that was climbing now after the one who had so long escaped it had had centuries in the dark to grow in rage. And its eyes were closer to the ground than a god's. And vipers had other senses than sight. Senses designed for catching mice in the dark. Shef remembered the blue swelling face of Ragnar Lothbrok, Ivar's father and Sigurth's too, as he died in the snake-pit, the orm-garth of York.

In panic he forced himself round to try to wriggle deeper into concealment. The crack was widening, he jerked his shoulder through, wondering what might be on the other side. All light had faded, but the slither behind him was coming closer and closer.

He was through. Through what he did not know, but now he was standing in a pit, and looking up. And there, far above him, was a full pale moon with markings on it like a ghastly skull. He could see a wall, a wall facing him, far lower than the cliff behind. But still far too high for him to jump and catch the edge, climb out as he might have done on to the next step of the stairway behind. In a panic now Shef began to run towards it, careless of what might see him. But as he moved there came from all around him, not just from behind, a piercing and universal hiss.

He stopped dead, aware of slithering all around him. He had escaped from Loki and the viper that pursued him. But now he was in a crawling carpet of snake-bodies. He was in the orm-garth of the gods. And there was no way to climb out.

As he stood stock-still he felt a thud striking his thigh, felt the first deep bite of the fangs, the poison spreading into his veins.

Shef sprang from his hammock in one convulsive movement, caught a foot in a cord and crashed to the deck. He was on his feet again instantly, ready to lash out in any direction, a great yell bubbling from his throat. As men around him cursed and scrambled also to their feet, groping for their weapons, he felt a brawny arm close round him, was swung momentarily off his feet.

"Easy, easy," muttered Thorvin. "All right, the rest of you, go back to sleep. Just a dream. Just a nightmare."

He propped Shef on the seaward rail, let him look round in the starlight and get his bearings.

"What did you see this time?"

Shef caught his breath, felt the sweat drying on him. His tunic was drenched, as wet as if he had been in the sea. The salt stung his empty eye-socket.

"I saw Loki. Loki loose. Then I was in the orm-garth, like Ragnar." Shef began to rub his thigh where he had felt the strike of the fangs.

"If you have seen Loki loose, the College must know," muttered Thorvin. "Maybe Farman in Stamford, or even Vigleik of the visions in Kaupang might have some counsel. For if Loki is loose we are that much closer to the doom of the gods and the coming of the Skuld-world. Maybe it is we who have stirred it up."

"Loki is not loose," came a cold angry voice from behind them. "There is no such thing as Loki. Or as the gods. The evil in the world comes from men alone."

In the starlight Shef pulled up the hem of his tunic, stared down at his bare thigh. On it, there, two purple marks. Puncture wounds. Svandis stared, reached out a hand, drew it back. For once found nothing to say.

Two hundred miles from the *Fafnisbane* floating on the placid sea, a group of other men sat huddled at the foot of another dark stairway, deep inside a mountain.

"He is likely to break in tomorrow," said one of them.

General nods, murmurs of agreement. "We caused them many casualties today. Tomorrow they will bring that great catapult up a little closer, start earlier with our outer defenses down, find the range. Then it will be a rock on top of the main gate and their stormers will come through. Of course we will make barricades inside, but . . ." A Gallic shrug, barely visible in the candlelight.

"If we surrender tomorrow at dawn they may give us terms, the Emperor

Bruno is said to be merciful, they will ask only for an oath which we can in conscience give falsely, then . . .''

The gabbling frightened voice was cut off by another fierce gesture. "What happens to us is of no moment," said the first voice. "We may get terms, we may live, we may die. What counts is the holy relics. And if the Emperor thinks they are here—and he already thinks they are here, that is why he is besieging us—anyone who lives tomorrow will be tortured till they tell all they know."

"Try to get them out? They have sentries. But in the crannies of the Puig, our mountain men could crawl out."

"With the books and the records, maybe. With the *graduale*"—the speaker's Occitan accent had turned the word to *graal*—"I don't think so."

"Get the other things out that way. Just drop the holy relic outside the wall. It has no gold on it, no marks of worship like the Catholics would give it. They won't know. Our brothers will pick it up later."

A long pause. "Too risky," said the first voice. "It could be lost in the rubble. Whoever we told to recognise it later might die, might be tortured, might confess.

"No. What we must do is leave it here, under the mountain. The entry to this place is known only to us, and to the *perfecti* among us outside the walls. The Emperor cannot tear down the mountain. He will never find the entrance—unless someone tells him."

"And none of us will tell him," answered one of his fellows.

A sudden flash in the candle-light, a thud, a choked-off gasp. Two men eased a body to the floor, that of the speaker who had suggested terms.

"Go to God, brother," said one of the killers. "I love you as a brother still. I would not have you put to a test you could not bear."

The first voice continued. "So that is clear. The relic must stay. All those of us who know the secret stair must die. For no-one can be sure what he will say at the last end of pain."

"Are we allowed to die in battle?" queried one of the dark shapes.

"No. A blow on the head, a crippled arm. Anyone may be captured without consenting to it. We would die later of the *endura,* but that might be too late. And alas, we have no time for the *endura.* One of us will go up the stair, and tell Marcabru the captain to make the best terms he can tomorrow morning for our poor brothers, the *imperfecti.* Then that brother will return. And we will take the holy draught together from the chalice of Joseph."

A hum of satisfaction and agreement, hands shaken across the table in the dark.

An hour later, as the silent perfect ones heard the step of their brother coming again down the stairs to share the poison draught with his brothers, a final voice in the dimness.

"Rejoice, brothers, for we are old. And what was the question that our founder Nicodemus asked of the Son of God?"

Voices answered him in chorus, garbling the Latin words in their own strange dialect. *"Quomodo potest homo nasci, cum senex sit?* How can a man be born when he is old? Or can he enter again into the womb of his mother?"

CHAPTER TEN

The enemy fleet was hull-up before Shef's lookout saw or recognised it. The Greek admiral had chosen his time perfectly: a little after noon, with the combined fleet of Arabs and Northerners split into its three habitual divisions. The advance guard and main body keeping pace with the cloud of dust which meant horse and foot advancing along the coastline, but already with oars shipped and prepared for siesta. The Northerners two long miles behind, awake but hopelessly becalmed, the sails acting only as awnings against the fierce heat. Another mile behind them, the admiral with his escort ships, dropped back to take their siesta, confident of their ability to catch up on the lumbering sailing ships later in the day.

In any case all attention was fixed on the land. Just dimly, from where they lay on the blue water, Shef could hear a faint sound of screaming trumpets, high and shrill in the Arab mode. Was that an answering bellow? The hoarse war-horns of Germans, or of Franks? Everyone on the ships was crowded on to the landward rails, listening intently, trying to make out what might or might not be happening there on the shore. A dust cloud? Pin-pricks of light? Weapons catching the sun, that was for sure.

Turning from the rail, Shef blinked his one eye, weary from straining across the dazzling water. Looked out to sea, into the noon haze. Fishing boats, creeping towards them, their three-cornered sails picking up what breaths of air there might be. A lot of them, Shef reflected. Had they found a school of tunny? They were using their oars as well, moving fast for fishermen in the heat. Too fast.

"Lookout!" he bellowed. "Out to sea. What can you see?"

"Fishing boats, lord," came the cry, a little puzzled. "A lot of them."
"How many?"

"I can see—twenty, thirty. No, there's more coming out of the haze, pulling hard."

"Do they have the grind here?" asked Thorvin, veteran of the journey to the far North. He meant the Halogaland custom of driving schools of whales ashore with a fleet of boats, to slaughter them in the shallows.

"That's no grind," snapped Shef. "Nor no fishermen either. That's the enemy fleet, and us all looking the wrong way. How long have those bastards been watching us, and us saying, 'oh, they're only fishing boats'."

His voice rose to a shout, as he tried to pierce the sunny lethargy, move the gaping faces turned towards him. "Cwicca, Osmod, man the mules! Everyone to the crossbows. Hagbarth, can you get any way on at all? Thorvin, blow the signal horn, alert the rest of the fleet. For Thor's sake, move, all of you. They're ready and we aren't!"

An incoherent yell from the lookout, and a pointing finger. No need for either. Out of the heat-haze, hull-up already, moving at terrifying speed, Shef saw the red-painted galleys of the Greeks sweeping down in a broad wedge. Their banks of white-painted oars flashed and swept in the sun, each ship had a bone in her teeth, a white bow-wave cresting over the menace of the ram. Shef could see the black-lashed female eyes painted incongruously on the high fore-quarters, could see the armor of their marines flashing as they waved their weapons in defiance.

"How far off are they?" It was Hund asking, his eyes were weak.

"A mile maybe. But they're not making for us. They're making for the Arabs. Going to take them from flank and rear."

The Andalusian advance-guard hardly stood a chance at any time. Deep in siesta, awnings rigged, it took precious moments to strike them and man the oars once more. The faster and more alert ships turned devotedly to try to ward off the attack sweeping towards them at twenty miles an hour. As they tried to engage Shef saw spears and arrows flashing across the water from both sides. As if in reply, a thin trail of smoke on the air, a far-off unearthly whistling.

And then the flame. The watchers on the *Fafnisbane* cried out as one man as the orange flame licked across, seemed suddenly to explode. Not like a fire catching in the hearth, not like a tree blazing in a forest fire: instead a sudden ball of flame that seemed to spread out, hang in the air, hold in its heart a ship already disintegrating. Shef thought he could see tiny black shapes struggling in it, plunging already alight into the sea. But then the rest were in action.

The red galleys slowed as they reached the main body of enemy ships, picking their targets, flame snorting first from one then from another. First to die were the bold ones who steered to engage, the feeble missiles that flew from them ignored like midges harassing so many great red bulls. Then the unprepared ships who remained still. Then, as the red galleys accelerated once more to ramming stroke, the cowards who had turned to flee. In one pass the Greek flotilla left behind them more than a hundred blazing shapes. In their wake the fishing boats from the Christian villages, packed with men with injuries to avenge, and stiffened by Agilulf's detachments, closed in on those who had dodged the flame, eager to board, slaughter and take plunder.

"Very well done," remarked Georgios to the captain of his own flagship. "That's them off the board. Now, let's see about the stone-throwers. Half-speed now, and watered wine to the rowers."

As the red galleys pulled round in a wide circle, Shef abandoned the attempt to make way under sail. Five minutes to furl the sails, prevent them from obstructing his catapult-crews. Then the giant sweeps over the side, only a dozen for each ship, each one pulled by four men, all that could be spared from the catapults. The men began to heave, drag their heavy, round-bellied ships through the water.

"If they don't want to fight they don't have to," said Hagbarth tensely. "They have five times our speed. Maybe ten."

Shef made no reply. He was watching for the range. Maybe the other side did not know what mule-stones could do. If they came on a little more— vital not to let them get close enough to use their fire-weapon. Its range a hundred yards at most. A mule-stone would fly true for half a mile. He might reach them now. Let them come on a little more—a little more yet. Better to get off a concerted volley. If all the ships shot at once they could sink half the fire-galleys in one shoot.

"Mule won't bear," shouted Cwicca from the forward catapult. An instant later Osmod echoed him from the rear. "Mule won't bear."

Shocked, Shef suddenly saw the trap. His ships were spread out in a long line ahead. None of them could shoot over the bow or the stern. A galley coming straight towards him could cover the distance from extreme mule-stone range to effective distance for their fire-weapon in—he did not know, maybe fifty strokes. And they were coming now. Or one of them was, picking up speed and leaving the others behind, oars threshing in perfect unison.

"Sweeps," he shouted, "starboard sweeps, start pulling, port sweeps back water."

Seconds of delay while the men at the sweeps worked out what was demanded, moved their cumbrous log-like oars into position. Then, slowly, the head of the *Fafnisbane* began to heave round, Cwicca, mule-captain on the bow catapult glaring tensely over its metal-plated shield, braced to lift his hand to show his sights were on.

As the bow of the *Fafnisbane* came round, so the galley heading towards them heeled over in the same direction. If that went on she would present her long fragile side to the waiting mule, no more than a quarter-mile off now, a certain hit and a certain sinking. But with beautiful speed and maneuverability she was keeping constantly in the *Fafnisbane*'s blind spot. They knew exactly what they were doing.

Maybe one of the other ships could get in a shot? Shef looked behind him, realized that the furious roaring he had tuned out in his tension was coming from the captain of the *Sigemund* close behind. The *Fafnisbane* had steered right across him, was blocking his complete broadside. And the Greek galley had completed her turn, was sweeping back to safety, her first plunge beaten off.

But even while he was watching the whole situation had changed yet again. The other Greek galleys had not lain on their oars while their consort darted in. They had split, swung in two wide arcs just neatly out of mule-stone distance—someone had been observing them very closely as they took their practice shots—and were forming a ring round the Northern ships. Already one was swinging round to try to get behind the stern of the *Hagena,* last ship in the line, and the captain of the *Hagena* did not seem to have noticed. It would only take one fire-galley to get within range, and she could then cruise up the long straggling line of the English two-masters, setting each one alight and using it as cover from the stones of the one next in line.

They had to cover each other. Each ship had to have bow and stern approaches covered by the mules of another ship. What was the formation they needed for that? And while he thought, he had to signal the *Hagena,* still floating motionless, sweeps not even out, lookout and skipper still staring fixedly in the wrong directions. Shef began to shout to the skipper of the *Sigemund,* to see the danger and pass on the message.

Brand had caught on quicker. As the shouted messages passed down the line, Shef saw the *Narwhal* suddenly streak past his line of vision, oars beating faster even than those of the Greeks. Another of the Viking longships followed him. Shef realized that all five had closed in, clustered to seaward of the seven bigger sailing-ships for protection against the Greek fire. But Brand had realized that there was a weak spot for all of them. He was moving to buy time.

Heart in mouth, Shef ran to the stern, climbed nimbly up, stood on the barely-moving dragon-tail that rose six feet above the deck. Suddenly remembering, he pulled the far-seer from his belt—if they had had a dozen like it lookouts might have given better warning! No time for regrets. He pulled it open, tried to adjust the length of the sliding tube so he could see clearly.

Through the smoky and discoloring lens he saw the three ships, one Greek and two Viking, closing on each other at prodigious speed, far faster than any horse could run. The Greek was twice the size of either of the other craft, could ram and run them down without troubling to use her fire. But she had to be delayed. Shef saw what Brand and his consort were trying to do. They were aiming to steer their bows along the whole line of the Greek's oars, snapping them and killing the rowers with the backlash. Then, maybe, board and see how the Greek marines would face Viking axes.

But the fire, the fire. For the first time Shef could see something of the strange device that burnt ships like tinder. A copper dome midships, men clustered round it, two sweating at handles which they worked up and down like a suction-pump in the East Anglian fields . . .

Suddenly the pumping men were whisked away as if by a broom, and those clustered round to shield them. Shef turned the far-seer frantically, trying to make out what was going on. There was Brand's ship, and he could see Brand in the prow, waving an axe. And a dozen crossbows lining the side, all simultaneously dropping in the quarrels and heaving on their goat's-foot cocking handles. The Greeks had not expected the heavy armor-piercing missiles at close range.

But their captain knew all about oar-snapping. As Brand's Narwhal cruised past the far side of the galley Shef saw a wood of oars leap into sight. The rowers had heaved them up in well-rehearsed display. As they did so Shef, in the round field of the far-seer, saw men scrambling again to the handles of the Greek fire weapon. Caught a glimpse of a gleaming nozzle as it trained round to bear on the second Viking ship, fifty yards behind Brand's and on the near side. A man standing by it pushing forward what looked like a lit cord . . .

Shef thrust the far-seer from him just too late to avoid seeing the flame leap out, the ball of fire at its tip. And, centered in the midst of it, the skipper of the Marsvin, Sumarrfugl, who had stormed the walls of York with Shef and Brand years before, hurling a spear and yelling defiance at the doom about to take him.

A great groan rose from the decks of the Fafnisbane as they saw the Marsvin go, fire rising higher than her mast, shapes again hurled into the water, some of them still thrashing on a burning sea. All men they had known and drunk with.

Shef looked round again, constricted with terror at the thought that everyone was looking in the same direction again, not watching for the death that might be coming up on them at racing speed from any direction. He realized that twice already he had heard the twang and crash of the mules, twang as the rope was released, crash as the throwing arm hit its padded bar, making the whole firm-braced ship shake. There in the sea, not so far off, wrecked timbers and men swimming. Not the great galleys though. Just fishing boats. The Greek commander was sending them in to draw attention and increase the number of targets. Like playing fox-and-hens with too many foxes for the hens to keep track of.

They're not frightened of us, Shef thought. That's why this is going badly. We are terrified of the flame, have seen our mates go up in it, there are some of them still there dying in the burning water—how can water burn? But they're just fencing with us. Those men out there on the wrecked ships. It's just a swim for them, a little wait till they're rescued. Got to make them worry. Make them afraid.

But first, make us safe. We must form a square. No, seven ships, four sides, there would always be a weak side, they might decide to come in on that, lose a ship or two to take all of us. Get into as near a circle as we can, that way any approach will face at least two broadsides. If there was just a breath of air, we could get some steerage way.

He seized Hagbarth by the shoulder, told him what he wanted, left him to shout over the side to the skipper of the *Sigemund* and the *Grendelsbane* beyond. Turned back to see what new disaster had come upon the scene.

This whole battle seemed to progress in a series of flashes, unlike any other he had been in. He had always known what was supposed to happen before. He had no idea, even, how long the shouted conversation with Hagbarth had lasted. Somehow, in the meantime, the *Hagena* had managed to get into action. Delayed for vital seconds by the *Narwhal* and the *Marsvin*, the Greek galley had been too slow in dipping oars again and keeping in the blind spot. The *Hagena* had veered round, come broadside on, and shot simultaneously with both catapults, each one sending a thirty-pound rock skimming over the water at a bare quarter-mile range. Viking longships, clinker-built and locked to the prow and the tail, simply fell to bits when struck square on. The galley, for all Hagbarth's contempt for the strength of her construction, lasted a little better. Keel broken in two places, she was going down, but leaving a mass of wreckage like a raft, with rowers and marines clinging to it. Fishing boats were already closing in, maneuvering to keep in shelter of the wreck, to pick up survivors.

Shef's eye was caught beyond the scene being played out a few hundred yards off by the now-familiar gouts of flame a mile beyond. With the fatalistic courage of his creed—and spurred on by thoughts of the impaling-post that waited for cowards—the Arab admiral had decided to venture forward to engage the Greeks. Half a score of galleys had turned to meet him, leaving the rest of their number to watch and circle the Northern ships like wolves round a bogged elk. Again and again the flames licked out like dragon-breath, a ship exploding at the end of each tongue. Yet the crowd of Arab ships seemed to be making some impact, steering through the embers of their comrades. Shef could just see—he pulled out the far-seer again to make sure—grappling irons flying as the rear ranks of the admiral's squadron managed to close with some of their enemies. Too close now for the fire. Now it would be saber and scimitar against pike and shield.

Shef felt his heart slow its frantic pounding for the first time since they had seen the fishing boats and realized they were hostile. He lowered the far-seer. Became conscious of a deep hum of satisfaction rising from the decks of the *Fafnisbane,* a hum that broke into growls and fierce shouting.

Brand's *Narwhal* was cruising gently past the wreck of the Greek galley, her crossbowmen pouring volley after volley into the defenseless men clinging to her planks. Some were crossing themselves, others holding out their hands in a plea for mercy. A few had even swum towards the *Narwhal,* were trying to catch hold of the sweeping oars. Shef saw Brand himself, easily recognisable even at a furlong's distance, leaning over the side, slashing downwards with his axe 'Battle-troll.' Where the water was not black with ash and embers it was turning red with blood. The *Hagena* was joining in too, its crew making uninterrupted target-practice with their heavy gunwale-mounted steel crossbows.

Shef became aware of hands clinging to his arm, looked down. It was Hund. "Stop them!" shouted the little leech. "Those men aren't dangerous any more. They can't fight. This is butchery!"

"Better be butchered than roasted," snarled a voice behind him. It was one of the ship's boys, Tolman, a small incongruous figure clutching an axe bigger than himself.

Shef looked over the side. The *Fafnisbane* had swung in a half-circle as Hagbarth formed the protective ring Shef had demanded. That, and some barely detectable set of the current along the coast, had swung the *Fafnisbane* into the patch of water where the *Marsvin* had been torched. Still floating in the water there were what looked like broiled sides of meat at an ox-roasting. Shef pointed. "Some of them may be still alive, Hund. Get the boat. Do what you can for them."

He turned away, heading for the foremast where he could scan the horizon and for the first time since the action began collect his thoughts. There was someone in his path, someone shrieking and clutching at him. Svandis. Everyone seemed to be shouting and shrieking today. He pushed her firmly aside and walked to the mast. A rule, he thought. There must be a rule. Don't speak to the man in charge until he speaks to you. Hagbarth, Skaldfinn and Thorvin were evidently of his mind. They had intercepted the still-shrieking woman, were hustling her away, waving others aside. To let him think.

Holding the mast as it swayed gently to the roll of the wavelets, he looked deliberately all round the further horizon. To the south: the Arab admiral's ships, burning, sinking, boarded, in flight. None still fighting. To seaward: four Greek galleys rowing in a gentle arc well outside his range. To the north: two more, and a great cluster of smaller boats, some of the latter sneaking casually closer, tacking to and fro with their strange, handy three-cornered sails.

To landward: three more galleys completing the circle. But beyond them?

Shef aimed the far-seer, scanned carefully along. A dust-cloud. Men moving. Moving south, and in a hurry. Impossible to say what kind of men were making the dust. But . . . a scan further, and there, cresting a small hill, caught by some trick in clear outline in the far-seer's blurry lens, he could see them. Stiff ranks of men in metal. Helmets, chain-armor, metal flashing in the sun as their feet moved. Feet moved together. A slow, steady, disciplined line of armored men moving forward. The *Lanzenorden* had won its land battle without hindrance from the sea. That was the situation. It was clear what should be done.

Shef raised his voice in what had now become silence. "Hagbarth. How long till the wind gets up again. Half an hour? When we have enough wind to make steering speed, we will head south down the coast. We'll go in a wedge, fifty yards apart. If the galleys try to take the last ships from behind, we all turn and sink them—it'll be easy once we're under sail again. We'll make as much distance as we can before it's dark and then anchor for the night in some cove we can block off—I don't want fireships coming up on us in the dark.

"Cwicca. See those boats trying to sneak up on us? When there are four within range, see if you and Osmod can sink them all. They're getting too cheerful out there.

"Thorvin. Call over Brand. When Cwicca and Osmod have sunk the fishing boats, he's to take two of his ships over there and kill all the crews. No swimmers, no survivors. Make certain the Christians see him do it."

Thorvin opened his mouth to protest, hesitated, held his tongue. Shef stared him full in the face. "They're not *frightened,* Thorvin. That gives them the advantage. We have to take it away, see?"

He turned and walked over to the seaward rail. Hund and a few helpers were struggling to lift a man over the side. As his face came level with the gunwale, eyeless, hairless, burned down to the gleaming skull and cheek-bones, Shef recognised him. Sumarrfugl, old comrade. He was whispering something, or husking it with what remained of his lungs.

"No hope for me, mates. It's in my lungs. If there's a mate there, give me the death. The warrior's death. If this goes on much longer, I shall scream. Let me go quiet, like a *drengr.* A mate there? Is there a mate there? I can't see."

Slowly Shef stepped over. He had seen Brand do this. He put an arm round Sumarrfugl's head, said firmly, "Shef here, *fraendi.* I'm your mate. Speak well of me in Valhalla." He drew his short knife, set the point behind what had been Sumarrfugl's ear, drove hard into the brain.

As the corpse fell to the floor he heard the woman behind him again. She must have got out from below-deck.

"Men! You men! The evil of the world is from men alone. Not gods. Men!"

Shef looked down at the charred skinless body at his feet, its genitals burned away. Over the side he could hear shouts and screaming as Brand's crew hunted another survivor from bits of wreckage, harpooned him in the water as they would have a seal.

"Men?" he replied, staring at her and through her with his one eye, as if to pierce down through the earth to the underworld. "Men, you think? Can you not feel Loki stirring?"

As the afternoon breeze off the sea strengthened, the Northern fleet picked up speed, the four remaining Viking ships swarming over the waves with their usual supple motion, the two-masters plowing through them, spray leaping up over the tall prows. The Greek galleys had feinted to bar their passage, then fallen back before the threat of the mules. Very soon they had given up their ominous shark-like pursuit and turned away into the haze. Fortunate for them, Shef remarked to Thorvin and Hagbarth. If they had held on longer he would have turned and tried to catch them, sink the entire fleet. Galleys held the advantage in a calm, sailing ships in the wind. Catapults trumped Greek fire in the light, and at distance. The other way round close up, and in the dark.

Well before the sun set Shef had marked a cove with high cliffs to either side and a narrow inlet, taken the whole fleet well inside. By the time the dark came he had taken every precaution he could think of. Brand's Vikings, experienced in the holding of beachheads, had set off immediately inland, reconnoitered the approaches, established a firm block on the one single footpath leading down. Four catapult ships were firmly moored broadside on to the cove entrance, so that any ship entering would face eight mules at a range well outside that of the fire projectors. Shef had sent two parties up to each of the cliffs on either side, with tar-soaked bundles of straw, and orders to light them and hurl them down at the first sign of any ship trying to enter. At the last moment one of the English crewmen detailed for the job had come over, asked uncertainly for some of the kite cloth. What for, Shef had demanded. Slowly the man, a stunted creature with a villainous squint, had fumbled out his idea. Attach some cloth, like a small sail, to each of the bundles. When they threw them over he thought the cloth would hold the air, like, like it did with the kites. Take longer for the bundles to fall. Shef stared, wondering if he had found another Udd. Clapped the man on the back, asked his name, told him to take the cloth and consider himself a kite-handler for the future.

It had all been done efficiently, under the driving force of the king's tongue and every single man's knowledge of what the Greek fire could do. Yet they had been slow, sluggish. Shef himself felt completely drained, exhausted, though he had not struck a blow or swung an oar. It was fear. The sense that he was for once facing a cleverer mind than his own, one that had made a plan and made him dance to it. Without Brand and Sumarr-fugl's intervention every single ship and man in the fleet might have been at the sea-bottom, or floating like a charred log on the water for the gulls to peck.

Shef had ordered one of the fleet's last barrels of ale broached, a quart served out to every man. What's that for, someone had asked. "It is to drink the *minni-öl*, the remembrance ale for the men of the *Marsvin,*" he replied. "Drink it and think where you would be without them."

Now, guarded, warmed by a fire, his belly full of pork and biscuit, cooked careless of the defeated stragglers who might be wandering the shore, Shef sat brooding over his last pint. After a while he saw the pale eyes of Svandis fixed on him from across the fire. She seemed, for once and unusually—not contrite, but as if she might listen to another voice for a change. Shef crooked a finger, beckoned her over, ignoring the routine flash of anger in her eyes.

"Time you told us," he said, pointing out a stone for her to sit on. "Why do you think there are no gods, only wicked men? If that's what you think, why this mummery with white robes and rowan-berries like a Way-priest? Don't waste my time being angry. Tell me the answers."

Weariness and strain gave Shef's voice a chill that brooked no defiance. In the firelight behind Svandis Shef saw Thorvin squatting on the sand, hammer in belt, and the other Way-priests with him, Suleiman the Jew next to his colleague Skaldfinn.

"Well. Do you need me to tell you why I think there are wicked men?"

"Don't be silly. I knew your father. I killed him, remember? The kindest thing you could say about him was that he was not of one skin, *eigi einhamr,* like a werewolf. Only he was a were-worm, I saw him on the other side. If you had to think of him as a man—well, what could you say? He cut women's living bowels out for pleasure, the only way he knew to put bone in his prick. Wicked?" Shef shook his head, without words. "No, tell us why you think there are no wicked gods. You're talking to a man who's seen them."

"In dreams! Only in dreams!"

Shef shrugged. "My mother saw one on a beach, like this, and felt him too, Thorvin says. Otherwise I wouldn't be here."

Svandis hesitated. She had explained her views often enough. Never in the face of such solid cast-iron certainty on the other side. Yet the fierce blood of Ragnar ran in her veins, only surging more strongly to opposition.

"Consider the gods that people believe in," she began. "The gods my father and his brothers sacrificed to, Othin god of the hanged, betrayer of warriors, prepared always for Ragnarök and the battle with Fenris-wolf. What are the words that Othin tells us in the holy *Havamal,* 'The Sayings of the High One.' Her voice broke suddenly into the chant of the Way-priest:

"Early shall he rise, who will reft another's
  Life or lands or woman."

"I know the sayings," said Shef. "What's the point?"

"The point is that the god is like the men who believed in him. He told them only what they wanted to know already. Othin—the High One as you call him—he is just a mouthpiece for the wisdom of a pirate, a murderer like my father.

"Think of another god. Think of the Christ-god—flogged, spat on, nailed to a cross and killed without a weapon in his hand. Who believes in him?"

"Those wicked bastards of monks," said an anonymous voice in the darkness. "Used to be my masters. They laid on the lash all right, but no one never flogged none of them."

"But where did the Christians start?" cried Svandis. "Among the slaves of the Rome-folk! They made a god in their own image, one who would rise again and bring them victory in another world, because they had no chance in this one."

"What about the monks?" said the skeptical voice again.

"Who did they preach their religion to? Their slaves! Did they believe it themselves, maybe, maybe not, but it was useful to them. What good would it have done them if their slaves had believed in Othin?

"And what of the followers of the Prophet here?" she went on, pressing an advantage. "They believe in the one clear way. Anyone can join it by saying a few words. No-one can leave it without facing death. Those who join pay no taxes, but their men-folk must forever fight the unbelievers. Two hundred years ago the Arabs were sand-rats, nobodies, feared by none! What is their religion but a way of gaining strength? They have made themselves a god who gives them power. As my uncles made a god who gave them courage and fearlessness, or the Christians one who gave obedience."

"Render to Caesar the things that are Caesar's," said the skeptical voice again, followed by a comprehensive hawk and spit into the fire. "True enough. I heard them say it."

Shef placed the voice finally. Not Cwicca, but Trimma, one of his mates. Strange that he should speak so freely. It must be the ale.

Another voice breaking in, the quiet one of Suleiman the Jew, by now speaking the fleet's common Anglo-Norse mixed speech with barely a trace of accent.

"An interesting view, young lady. I wonder what you will have to say of the Lord whose name is not spoken." He added, as ignorance remained complete, "the god of my people. The god of the Jews."

"The Jews live in a corridor," said Svandis flatly. "At the far end of this inner sea. All the armies of the world have marched up and down it, Arabs,

Greeks, Rome-folk, all of them. The Jews have been toads under the harrow since their history began, from what I have been told of it. Have you heard the toad shriek out as the harrow rakes it? It cries out, 'I will be revenged!' The Jews have made a god of total power, and total memory, who never forgets any injury to his people, and who will revenge it—sometime. When the Holy One comes. He has been a long time coming, and they say you crucified him when he did. But if you believe what you do, it does not matter that the Holy One never comes, because he is always coming. That is how the Jews live on."

Shef could see Suleiman's face in the firelight, watched it carefully for any grimace, any twist of anger. Nothing that he could see.

"An interesting view, young princess," said Suleiman carefully. "I see you have an answer for everything."

"Not for me," said Shef, draining his mug. "I have seen them, in dreams. And others have seen me in the same dreams, so it is not just my fantasy. They have shown me sights far off as well, and they have come true. As they have for Vigleik of the visions, for Farman priest of Frey, for others of the Way.

"And I tell you, those gods are not made in my image! What was it that bit me, Svandis, you saw the marks in my flesh? A pet of Loki's, a pet of Othin's? No pet of mine. I do not even like my father Rig, if he is my father. The world would be better with no gods, I say. If we all believed what we wanted, I would be a believer in Svandis. But I know better. It is the gods who are evil. Men are evil too, because they have to be. If it were a better world that the gods made, men would be better too."

"It will be a better world," rumbled Thorvin in his deep bass, "if we can escape the chains of Skuld."

"Keep thinking about it, Svandis," said Shef, standing up. He stopped as he walked towards his blanket on the sand. "I mean what I say, and not as a joke, nor an insult. You are wrong about the gods of the Way, or at least you have not explained to me what I know. Just the same, there may be new knowledge in there somewhere, knowledge of people if not of gods. That is what the Way is about. Knowledge, not preparing for Ragnarök."

Svandis dropped her eyes, for once silent, defenseless against praise.

CHAPTER ELEVEN

The small Northern fleet, only eleven ships now, mustered next morning the moment the highest lookout saw the first streak of light in the sky. Many men had dreamt of fire in the night, none wished to be trapped against a hostile shore by the red galleys of the Greeks.

Shef left the details of the withdrawal to be organized by Brand, who had rowed away from many a beachhead. The clumsier two-masters moved first, using their sweeps while they waited for the first puffs of the land breeze that blew from the cooled land towards the warmer sea every morning. The four remaining Viking longships lay on their oars close in, sterns just touching the beach. The party of sentries blocking the landward path ran down all together, their commander in the rear, shoved the boats out and scrambled aboard in the same moment, Brand counting carefully as they boarded. Ten strokes and the longships were out in the main channel, pulling easily past the *Fafnisbane*.

Two last groups to recover. On each of the headlands either side of the cove Shef had posted a dozen men, with their bundles of dried grass and pitch to illuminate any enemy trying to force the cove entrance. The Vikings had a routine for recovering such men too. On the hail, ropes appeared, men began to drop down like spiders on the end of their threads. The Vikings were lowering their more inexperienced English colleagues bodily, Shef realized. They touched ground, waded out into the water, seized outstretched oars, were hauled aboard.

Now the experts were doing it, at three times the speed, moving as if an enemy army were rushing up the other side of the hill. Ropes slung round firm-driven stakes, passed doubled round the waists, and the Vikings were walking swiftly backwards down the cliffs, bracing themselves against the pull. Into the water, the ropes jerked free.

And they'd left someone behind! As the last men scrambled for the waiting ships, Shef saw a head and a waving arm. He could even recognise the face, the squint. It was the innovator of the evening before, who had wanted to set kite-cloth to the flares. Shef knew his name now: Steffi, known familiarly as Cross-eye, said to be the worst shot with a crossbow in the whole fleet. He seemed unworried, was indeed grinning broadly. Shef caught the words floating down.

"I got a new way to come down! Watch this!"

Steffi moved to the highest point of the cliff, looked down into deep water, the boats moving gently across it a hundred feet below. He had something tied to him and trailing behind. Shef shut his eyes. Another one who thought he could fly. At least it was over water. If he didn't hit a rock. If he could stay afloat long enough to be rescued.

Steffi took a few steps backward, ran awkwardly forward again, and then leapt straight out. As he leapt, something billowed out behind him. Kitecloth. A square of it, eight feet across, fixed by cords to some kind of belt. As the small figure shot downwards it seemed to catch the air, form a kind of bell above him. For a few instants the figure slowed, hung marvelously in the air, Steffi's grin once again perfectly visible.

Then something seemed to go wrong, Steffi began to lurch from side to side in the air, his grin vanished, he hauled vainly on his cords, legs thrashing. A splash, barely twenty feet from the side. Two of Brand's men were in the water, swimming like seals. They resurfaced with Steffi between them, blood streaming from his nose, towed him to the *Fafnisbane,* heaved him up to waiting hands before stroking back to their own *Narwhal.*

"It was going fine," muttered Steffi. "Then the air started to spill, like. Like a mug that's too full. I've still got the cloth," he added, hauling on the lines attached to the belt now in his hands. "I didn't lose nothing."

Shef patted him on the back. "Tell us before you do it next time. Birdman."

He turned, waved to Hagbarth. Slowly the fleet rowed and swept its way out to sea, every lookout scanning the horizon with far-seers for any trace of the galleys, any threatening scout of a lateen sail.

No sign. Hagbarth coughed, asked the vital question. "Lord? Which direction now? South and back to base?"

Shef shook his head. "Take us straight out to sea, as far from land as we can get before noon. When the wind dies and we are helpless again I want us to be so far away that the furthest Christian scout cannot pick us up. They will be sweeping the shore in line abreast before long. We must be over the horizon by then.

"Conference at noon," he added. "Tell Brand to come aboard then." He turned to sling his hammock. A night on the sand with the sand-mites had left most men weary. Those not detailed to handle the sails or keep lookout followed his example.

Hours later, an awning shading them from the noonday sun, Shef and his council met on the high deck of the *Fafnisbane's* forward catapult mounting. Shef himself sat on the frame of the mule. Round him, sitting or squatting on the deck, were the four Way-priests, Thorvin, Hagbarth, Skaldfinn and Hund, with Brand resting his great back against the dragon-prow. After thought, Shef had once more called Suleiman the Jew over to listen to them. A few feet away, permitted to listen but not intervene unless asked, squatted Cwicca and Osmod to relay word to the crewmen once a decision was reached. Between them, a sullen expression on his face, was the young Arab Mu'atiyah. He would understand little or nothing of what was discussed in the Anglo-Norse patois of the Way, none of which he had troubled to learn in his weeks with the fleet. Yet he might be needed to answer questions.

"All right," said Shef without formality, "only one question, where do we go?"

"Back to Cordova," said Hagbarth promptly. "Or back to the mouth of the Guadalquivir anyway. Tell the Caliph what happened. He'll know before we get there, some stragglers must have got away, but at least we can tell him we didn't run."

"We'll have to tell him we failed, though," Shef replied. "These Mohammedans are not patient with failures. Especially as we'd told him we would succeed."

"Nowhere else to go," rumbled Brand. "Go north, they'll find out about us, send word to the galleys. Go out to sea like we're doing, well, they say there's islands out here but all in Christian hands. They'd catch up with us. But I agree, no point in going back to the Caliph. Why don't we just go home? Maybe pick up a little something on the way. Go back through the straits into the open ocean, sail home, see if we can't find a few bits and pieces to make a profit on the trip. From the Christians on the Frankish coast," he added, his eye on the listening figure of Suleiman. "If we decide we're still in alliance with the Caliph, that is."

Shef shook his head. "No. Even if we made a profit, we'd be going home without what we came for.

"Just in case you've all forgotten, we came for knowledge. At least I did. Knowledge of flight. And now, knowledge of fire. Don't forget, if the Empire of the Christians has learnt that, the next time we meet it may be in the English Channel. Home isn't safe any more."

"Nowhere else to go," insisted Brand doggedly. "Only safe thing to do is keep moving. There are no safe harbors left. Not here in the Inner Sea."

A long pause, while the ship rocked gently on the halcyon water. The sun burned down above them, crewmen stretched out on the decks, luxuriating in idleness and warmth, new experiences for almost all of them. The ships' holds were stuffed still with food and full water barrels. No need for care, or no immediate need. Yet the weight of decision pressed down. Home was many miles away for English and Vikings alike, and between it and them lay only hosts of enemies: enemies and uncertain friends.

Suleiman broke the silence. As he did so he began to unwind the turban that he had never been seen to shed before.

"It is possible that I can find you a safe harbor," he said. "As you know, there are many of my people, the Jews, who live under the rule of the Caliph of Cordova. What I have not yet told you is that there are some—many—who live, well, not entirely under it."

"At the other end of the Inner Sea?" queried Shef. "In the land where Christ was crucified, whatever they call it?"

Suleiman completed the unwinding of the turban, shook out the long hair it had bound in. On his head now there was only a small round cap, fixed on seemingly with hairpins. Out of the corner of his eye Shef noticed that the young Mu'atiyah had half-risen to his feet, been dragged down again by Cwicca and Osmod, was being restrained none too gently. Something was going on that he did not understand.

"No," said Suleiman. "At this end. To the north, between the kingdom of the Franks and the Caliphate of Cordova. There, in the mountains, my people have lived, along with others of different religions, for many years. They pay a tax to the Caliph, but they do not always obey him. I think you will be welcome there."

"If it's north," said Brand, "it will be the Christians we have to fear now, not the Caliph."

Suleiman shook his head. "The mountain passes are difficult, and we have many strongholds. In any case, as the fair princess said last night, my people have much experience in—being a corridor. The troops of the Emperor marched through by permission, never entering a town. It would be a major campaign for him to take our princedom. Septimania we call it, though the Franks among us say Roussillon. Come to Septimania. There you can judge a new faith."

"Why do you make us this offer?" asked Shef.

Suleiman looked across at Svandis, standing out of earshot by the rail. "For many years I have been a servant of the book, Torah or Talmud or even Koran. Now you—some of you—have shown me something different. Now I too share your desire for new knowledge. Knowledge outside the book."

Shef turned his one eye across to the still-struggling Mu'atiyah. "Let him go, Cwicca." He went on in his simple Arabic. "Mu'atiyah, what you have to say, say it. Say it with care."

The young man, released, rose instantly to his feet. One hand was on the hilt of the dagger in his belt, but both Cwicca and Osmod were crouched ready to drag him down again if he moved. Shef saw Thorvin slip the hammer he always carried in his belt free. But Mu'atiyah seemed too furious to care for threats. His voice shaking, he pointed to Suleiman.

"Dog of a Jew! For years you have eaten the bread of the Caliph, your people have taken his protection. Now you seek to break free, to leave the Shatt al-Islam, the path of submission to Allah. You will ally yourself with anyone, like some noseless whore in a kennel. Yet beware! If you seek to let the Christians into Andalusia, they will remember you for killing their god—may the curse of Allah rest on those who worship one born in a bed! And if you seek to ally with"—he swept an arm round—"with *these,* know that they are barbarians, who come and go as the wild sheep defecate, now in that place, now in this."

Faces turned to Shef and Skaldfinn, waiting for translation. "He's calling Suleiman a traitor," Shef observed. "He doesn't think much of us either."

"Why don't we just throw him overboard?" asked Brand.

Shef thought for a long minute before replying. Mu'atiyah, who had not understood the brief interchange, nevertheless sensed from Shef's immobile face and Brand's jerked thumb something of what was going on. His face paled, he began to speak, stopped and tried to draw himself up with an appearance of composure.

Finally Shef spoke. "He's certainly useless as regards knowledge. But I liked his master, bin-Firnas. We'll keep him. Maybe he can serve as an envoy one day. And he has done one thing for us." He looked round, met Skaldfinn's eyes. "He's confirmed that what Suleiman here said was true. Otherwise we'd have no reason to believe it. A Jewish city, in Spain! Who would believe it? But it seems it must be true. I say that we should sail there. Find a base. Try to frustrate the plans of the Christians. Not the Christians, we have no quarrel with them. Of the Church and the Holy Empire it supports and the Emperor who supports it."

"And see what we can learn about the Greek fire," amplified Thorvin.

"And give Steffi there another chance to fly," agreed Shef.

Round the listening circle heads nodded, there was a growl of agreement. Suleiman's dark eyes took it in, showed a gleam of pleasure.

From the mast-head there came a hail. "To the north there! A sail. Three-cornered one. Looks like a fishing boat, maybe four miles off. Steering west, might not have seen us yet."

Shef walked to the prow, clicked open his far-seer, tried to see if he could pick out the sail-tip nicking the horizon.

"Do you think *Narwhal* would catch her, Brand, oars against the lateen sail?"

"In this calm, easy."

"Go over there then, sink the boat, kill everyone aboard."

Brand hesitated. "I don't mind killing people, you know," he said. "But they could be just fishermen making a living."

"And they could be spies for the Greeks. Or both at once. We can't take any chances on that. Just go over and do it. Use the crossbows if you're feeling squeamish."

Shef turned and walked away, obviously heading for his hammock, the conference as far as he was concerned at an end. Brand stared after him, his face perplexed.

"That's the one who was always telling me to go easy on the looting, always fretting about the slaves."

"He still frets about slaves," remarked Thorvin.

"But he'll kill off innocent people for nothing, just because they might be a risk. Not even for amusement, like Ivar would have, or to make them talk, like old Hairy-Breeks."

"Maybe Loki is loose," said Thorvin. "Better go do what he says." He clutched his hammer pendant protectively.

The same day, the same time, and no longer so many miles away, Bruno Emperor of the Franks, the Germans, the Italians and the Burgundians, slowly and reluctantly raised his shield, to protect his face not from the arrows that had flown at him all day, their snapped-off points studding the leather facing of his shield. No, only from the heat that surged and crackled from the blazing tower in front of him. He did not want to lose sight of the tower, hoping against hope that some last cry would rise from it, some turn of fortune would come to save the day. Yet even for his ascetic frame, the heat was too much to be borne.

It had been a bad day all along, yet another bad day. He had been sure the fortress would fall this time, and fall it had. Yet he had hoped, expected, after the trials of the days before, that the defenders would see sense, take his offer, accept the mercy that they could hardly have expected. His system for razing these mountain fortresses had been worked out again and again against the Moslems of the coast, and his men understood it. The first thing was to get the great counterweight-catapult that Erkenbert had built close enough to throw its one titanic rock on to the top of the gate. Smash the gate, take the fortress. But the catapult had terrible limitations. Unlike the lighter onagers, or the dart-shooters or man-powered weapons, the counterweight-machine had to be set up on the flat. On the flat, and close to its target, no more than two hundred double paces.

Here, at Puigpunyent, there was no flat place anywhere near the gate, only a steep hillside. Grimly, the Brothers of the Order of the Holy Lance

had driven back the defenders inside their walls, grimly they had hacked out
a launch-platform from the living rock. The defenders had waited till all was
done, then rolled boulder after boulder leaping down the hillside, hurled
over the walls by the strength of twenty men at once. Grimly the brothers
had driven deep piles into the rock, strengthened them with timbers, made
a shelter for the precious catapult to cower behind. Hundreds of porters had
struggled up the hill with the machine, with the rocks that were its
counterweight. The great boulders it threw had been even more of a
problem, carried up in the end on wooden platforms by relays of sweating,
gasping men.

They had done it: set up the machine, hurled a first boulder skimming
over the top of the gate so that Erkenbert the deacon could make his strange
reckonings and say how much weight should be removed for the next
boulder to land exactly on top of the wooden structure. And then, the work
done and the threat displayed, Bruno had sent forward one of his best men,
Bruder Hartnit of Bremen, to make the offer. Life for all, and liberty. The
contents of the castle only to be surrendered. Bruno had been sure, almost
sure that they would take the offer, knowing as they must that once a breach
was made, all the laws of God and man said that there could then be no
mercy for man, woman or child who had put the attackers to so much toil
and risk. The other brothers, even of the *Lanzenorden,* had looked sideways
at their master as he had sent Hartnit forward, knowing the offer meant the
loss of their traditional privileges, hard-earned with the sweat of all and the
life-blood of too many: killing and plunder, vengeance and rape. The
brothers were sworn celibates, could never marry any more than monks.
Celibacy did not apply to what happened in a sack, however. After all, all
their partners would be dead before morning. The brothers needed the
outlet custom gave them.

Yet they had let Hartnit go forward, knowing their master had some
driving design. They had heard him shout his offer in the bastard Latin most
could understand. They had even, some of them, better aware of the
defenders' temper than Bruno, expected the flights of arrows that were the
traditional refusal of an offer to surrender. Hartnit, behind his oversized
shield or mantlet, had half-expected it too.

No-one had expected the great marble column that jerked over the wall
and came down like a bonding giant's club. One end of it had smashed the
mantlet and broken Hartnit almost in half before it plunged on and down
the hillside in a cloud of dust. Every man had heard the piteous whimper-
ings of Hartnit the bold, his splintered hip-bones driven through his
bladder, until the Emperor himself had stilled them with his *misericorde,* the
long thin dagger that gave final release.

Grimly, then, they had launched the next boulder from the counterweighted catapult, smashed the gate, fought their way in and over the barricade they had known would be set up in the inner courtyard, set themselves to winkle out every last defender from tower and attic and stair and cellar. Grimly the defenders had fought back, never leaving a man, killing their own wounded as they retreated, till they were penned into the one last tower. Only men inside. Bruno himself had seen, in the inner rooms of the fortress as they fought their way through, the ranks of women, old people, children, slumped over their benches or lying with arms crossed: poisoned, dead, not a survivor. Just the last twenty or so trapped in the last tower, which his men had fired.

He lowered the shield, cautiously, waiting for the instant arrow, stepped forward a hesitant pace. He risked looking foolish now, but it had to be done. Once again, he called out: "You in there! Heretics! If you feel the flame, come out, surrender. I give you my word, my word as a *Ritter,* as a *Kaiser,* you will not be harmed. No-one in the world could have fought better. You have done enough."

Only the crackle and stab of flame in reply, his brothers looking sideways at him once more, wondering if the Emperor was mad. And then, from the heart of the flame, a voice calling.

"Emperor, know this. I am Marcabru the captain, alas still an *imperfectus.* We care nothing for you, and nothing for the flame. Tonight, like the good thief, I will be with my master in Paradise. For God is kind. He will not let us burn both in this world and the next."

A crash from the tower as its roof-beams fell in, a waft of dust and smoke, and silence, long silence broken only by the slackening flames. None of the familiar dreadful sounds of sack, the screams and the tears and the deep shouts of release. Only the crackle of flame and the crash of falling stone.

Bruno backed away, shield still up. Erkenbert had appeared now that the fighting had died, his escorts standing a pace behind him. He saw, amazingly, a light of excitement and even good humor shining in the Emperor's bright blue eyes.

"Well, we know something now," he said to the scrawny Englishman.

"What's that?"

"The bastards must have had something to hide. All we have to do now is find it."

The *Fafnisbane* ghosted through the night, her consorts spread out behind her, sails carrying her on with barely a ripple. Shef sat near the prow, feet overboard, catching from time to time a faint spray from the bow. Like a pleasure-cruise, he thought. Nothing like the ice and hunger of his long voyage to the North. He remembered the burnt face and body of Sumarrfugl, the way the skin had crackled under his hand as he drove the dagger home.

A presence on his blind side. He whipped round, relaxed. Half-relaxed. It was Svandis in her white dress, settling herself beside him.

"Brand didn't kill those fishermen, you know," she began. "He sank their boat, but gave them time to make a raft and load water on it. They had a pair of oars. He said they should reach either the mainland or one of the islands in about a day and a half, time enough for us to be gone."

"Unless one of their friends picks them up," muttered Shef.

"Do you want to turn into a man like my father?" Svandis hesitated for a few moments. "After all, they say you too are *eigi einhamr,* not a man of one skin. Because of what you see in dreams. Will you tell me about them? What was it that gave you those marks on your thigh the other night? They looked like the bite of a poison-adder. But you did not swell up and die. And the marks have gone now."

Shef hitched his tunic, stared at the place on his own thigh in the faint starlight. There was nothing there now, nothing that could be seen anyway. Perhaps he should tell her. He could feel the warmth of her body, comforting in the cool of the night, could catch the faint scent of woman, making him wonder for an instant what it would be like to hold her, plunge his face between her breasts. Shef had never in his life known comfort from a woman, held at arm's length by his mother, deprived by fate of his one love Godive. He felt a temptation to relax into it. Shrugged the temptation aside immediately. Eyes watched them, to put his head down and appeal for an embrace like a crying child would not be *drengiligr,* warriorly. Still, he could talk.

Quietly he began to tell her the details of his last dream. The stair. Feeling like a mouse among humans. The giant coming up the stair, his boots stamping. The monstrous serpent that came up after him, following the god Loki, as he was sure the giant had been. The orm-garth of the gods, with the snakes underfoot and the one that struck at him.

"That is why I believe in the gods," he ended. "I have seen them, I have felt them. That is why I know Loki is loose and set on vengeance. As if I needed to know, after Sumarrfugl."

Svandis was silent a while, for which he was grateful. She seemed to be thinking about what he said, instead of merely shouting it down. "Tell me," she asked finally, "was there anything in the dream that reminded you of something you had seen before. Something you might have been thinking about before you slept. The boots, for instance. The boots of the god coming up the stair. You said you saw them."

"The boots? They were like Brand's boots." Shef laughed, told her how as they marched through Cordova he had seen an amazed Arab looking Brand up and down, from his enormous feet to the helmet on his head. How he had barely been able to believe that such feet belonged to a human.

"So you had a picture like that already in your head? What about the snakes? Have you seen an orm-garth."

Shef felt a prickle of doubt and suspicion once more. This was the daughter of Ivar, after all, the grand-daughter of Ragnar himself.

"I saw your grandfather die in the snake-pit," he said briefly. "Did no one ever tell you? I heard him sing his death-song."

"He used to hold me on his knee and sing to me," said Svandis.

"He used to grow his thumb-nail long to gouge men's eyes out with," replied Shef. "My friend Cuthred tore it out with pliers."

"So you have seen a snake-pit too," Svandis went on, "and seen a man die in it. Were you very frightened then? Did you imagine yourself in the pit?"

Shef thought for a while. "What you are trying to tell me," he said, "is that these visions of mine—I do not call them dreams—do not come from the gods at all. They are made up in my own head out of things I have seen, or been frightened by. They are like a story, a saga. One told by a fool, with no beginning or end and only bits of connections to each other. They do not feel like that. They feel—much bigger than that."

"Because you are asleep," said Svandis. "You are not thinking correctly."

"Anyway, the visions I see—they are visions of the gods! They tell the stories that I have heard from Thorvin, of Völund and Skirnir and Hermoth and Balder."

"Because you have heard them from Thorvin," said Svandis. "If you dreamt stories that Thorvin had not told you, that might mean something. Maybe only that you had made them up out of things you yourself have seen and felt. But do you not think that Arabs dream of Allah, Christians of their own stories of saints? Your visions are like the gods themselves. People make both of them up out of their own needs and beliefs. If we stopped believing—then we would be free."

Shef examined the idea with care and doubt. It seemed to him that sometimes he *had* seen the vision before he knew the story. Svandis would say that he had forgotten something, got the story backwards. Certainly he had no way of proving different. And she might be correct. Everyone knew that sometimes dreams were caused by the events of the day, or even by sounds that men heard in their sleep and turned into a story. The stoutest Viking had dreams of fear, often he had heard men muttering in their sleep.

"So there may be no Ragnarök," he wondered. "No Loki loose. I have been deceiving myself all along. If I could believe that, things would be much easier for me. And there would be no truth in visions."

"There is no truth in visions," Svandis said forcefully, determined to carry her point and make a convert. "Gods and visions are nothing but illusions, which we create to make ourselves slaves." She pressed closer in the cool night, leant forward to look up into Shef's one eye, her breast nudging against his arm.

Far to the north, at the Wisdom-House of Stamford in the English midlands, night had not yet fallen. Instead the stone tower with its many outbuildings lay in the long gray twilight of an English early summer. From the hedged fields nearby the heavy scent of flowering hawthorn drifted. Faint laughter came from the outskirts of the town where farm-churls and craftsmen, milking and ditching and trading done for the day, sat for the last hour before full dark with pint pots in their hands. Children played around their fathers in the dusk, and younger folk, men and women, exchanged glances and faded sometimes into the dark of the comforting fields.

At the Wisdom-House itself, the forges had fallen silent, though red light came still from banked fires. A priest strode across the central courtyard, intending to call on his friends, draw them out to drink mulled ale and discuss their experiments and their discoveries. As he turned the corner by the stone tower he stopped short.

On a bench in front of him sat Farman priest of Frey, most famous of the priests in England for the number of his god-visions, rivaled in the world only by Vigleik the Norwegian. Farman sat easily. His eyes were open, but he seemed unseeing. Cautiously the priest who had come upon him moved closer, saw that Farman's eyes did not move from their fixed unblinking stare. He stepped back quietly, went to the corner again, waved urgently for others to join him. After a while a score of Way-priests stood in a semi-circle round their unmoving colleague, apprentices and laymen chased away. They waited unspeaking for him to move.

His eyes blinked, he stirred on the bench, became aware of those around him.

"What did you see, brother?" asked one of them.

"At the end—at the end I saw a tree, and a serpent in it. Before the tree there stood a woman, one of great beauty. She was holding out an apple to a man, and he—he was stretching his hand out to it. And all the while the serpent watched, and its forked tongue flickered out and in."

No reaction from the Way-priests. None of them had read the Christian books, they knew nothing of Satan, of Adam and Eve and the Fall of Man.

"But before that, before that I saw something of more mark. Something the king must hear of."

"The One King is not here, brother," a priest reminded gently, knowing that those coming out of the vision needed time to recover themselves.

"His deputy. His partner."

"King Alfred is his partner. He presides over the council of aldermen. There is no deputy."

Farman rubbed his eyes. "I must write down what I saw before it fades, and then the news must go to the king."

"Can you tell us anything of what you saw?"

"Danger and destruction. Fire and venom—and the bane of Balder loose."

The priests stiffened, knowing who it was that Farman would not name, the god they remembered by the bale-fire in their holy circle.

"If the bane of Balder is loose," one of them asked slowly, "what is it that the English king Alfred can do? Council of aldermen or no?"

"He can turn out the fleet," replied Farman. "Send every man and every ship to the place of danger. And that is not the mouth of the Elbe now, no, nor the Dannevirke. The bane of Balder is loose everywhere, but he will show himself first in the south, where the sons of Muspell ride on the day of Ragnarök."

He stood up, like a man unutterably weary from an immense journey. "I did wrong, brothers. I should have gone with the One King when he went to seek his destiny. For his destiny affects us all."

CHAPTER TWELVE

From the hitherto barely-known rock of Puigpunyent the riders spurred in all directions. Some at the best speed their horses could make: they had little distance to travel, were under orders to go directly to every baron's hold and rock-based tower in the borderlands, to demand every man that could ride to join their Emperor. They would not get them, for in the complex local politics of the mountain marches, where Frank faced Spaniard and Christian faced heretic, where the Moors raided continually and Jewish levies watched the passes and the toll-roads, no baron, not even those whom Bruno's informants had selected for loyalty to Holy Church, would think of leaving himself defenseless. Nor would Bruno trust them if they did. But they would provide the first ring, till they were replaced by better men, at this moment when the Empire and the Emperor needed above all numbers.

Other messengers paced themselves more carefully, riding in small groups with a tail of spare horses behind them. They had further to go: some many hundreds of miles further, but all of them knowing that it would be days of riding before they reached the secure parts of the Empire, where remounts were to be had at the display of the Emperor's tokens. Those who had furthest to go were the ones selected to ride for the strongholds of the *Lanzenorden*, all of them in the German-speaking realms far to the east and north, through the mountains or across the Rhine: Freiburg and Worms, Trier and Zurich and even Bern high in the Alps. From there would come the men in whom Bruno had most trust, every last warrior-monk of the Order, the men he needed to fight his war and pursue his quest to the finish. There would be no hesitation or calculation there. But they could not come immediately, would never come in the numbers he needed.

In between were the riders heading for every bishop's seat in the marches of Southern France and Italy: Massilia and Vercelli, Lyons and Turin and Carcassonne and Dax. Their message was the simplest. Every man you can spare. No need for knights, no need for the heavy-armed and aristocratic, though they must come too, to officer the rest. Send every man who has a pair of eyes and a hunting bow. Send the poachers and the huntsmen, the falconers and the charcoal-burners. The confessors of every village must know who are the men who can find their way in the dark, who can chase the deer across the hills and into the *maquis*. Offer forgiveness and remission of sins to all who will take service now, for Church and Cross and Empire. Above all, Bruno had pointed out, I must have your *bacheliers*: the men who in proper Latin, if the Latin of the degenerating Empire, would have been *vaccalarii*, the men of the *vaches*. The cowboys, who rode the marshes of the Camargue on their rough horses, armed with the ten-foot ox-goads that were their trade-tool, strips of jerked beef wound round their hats, watchful at all times for the attacks of the stalking, furious-tempered wild bulls. Too flighty and light-armed for battle, but capable of scouring a countryside like a kitchen-maid sanding rust out of a kettle.

"I want this place sealed off tighter than an abbess's—tighter than a convent dormitory," Bruno had said, forgetting his usual careful respectfulness to every form of religious life. "We haven't the men now, but as soon as they start to come in, assign them and place them. Till then, Tasso," he added to his *Lanzenorden* guard-commander, "you can tell our lads that no one goes to sleep. Me neither. Get them out and watching every rock."

"What for?" said Tasso.

"You saw the way they all killed themselves. Why? Because they didn't want anyone to tell us something. Tell us where something was. So it must be here. And you can be sure someone will try to get it out. So we'll seal the place off."

"That won't find anything," said Tasso, an old comrade allowed to speak freely to a brother of the order, even if that brother was his Kaiser and commander.

Bruno seized him with both hands by the beard. "It won't lose anything either! And now we know it's here, once we're all sealed off, all we have to do is look."

"We've looked already."

"Not under every stone we haven't. And we're going to take every last stone of this hill down and throw it in the sea if we have to! Erkenbert!" Bruno shouted to his deacon, busily giving messengers their directions. "Tell the bishops to send pickaxes too! And men to use them."

Released, Tasso tramped off to survey the ground and set up his too-scanty sentry-posts. As the day wore on his expression grew more and more troubled. A Bavarian himself, from the vineyards of the south, he found the ravines and dense scrub of the sharp, steep Pyrenean foothills baffling. "Need a thousand men to do this job," he muttered to himself. "Two thousand. And where's the food coming from? Or the water? Still: *Befehl ist Befehl.* Helmbrecht, Siegnot, Hartmut, guard this path here. And remember, no one sleeps till reliefs are sent. *Kaiserbefehl,* understand?"

He tramped on in the heat, scattering detachments here and there. He did not know that keeping pace with him a quarter of a mile outside the ring he was setting up, sliding through the dense thorny scrub as low to the ground as a weasel, eyes watched his every move.

The shepherd lad had expected fear and strangeness as he came in to make his report, but even so he gulped and swallowed convulsively as his eyes adapted to the dim light. Facing him behind a rough table sat a semi-circle of men. At least, they might be men. Every figure was dressed in long grey robes, and each one had a cowl over his head, pulled so far forward that the faces could not be seen. If he had seen them, he might have recognised them. For no one could be sure who the *perfecti* might be, though among the heretic villages rumors and evaluations ran continually: he refused mutton the other day, maybe he eats no meat, his wife and he sleep together but speak to each other like brother and sister, she has not given birth for three years though her child was weaned last spring. All might be indicators of having passed into the central mystery. But in the heretic villages all strove to live like *perfecti* even though they might never reach that grade: so fasting or celibacy might indicate only ambition, not achievement. The cowled men could be anyone.

The shepherd boy knelt clumsily, straightened again. A voice came from the semi-circle, not from the middle. It might be that a spokesman had been selected because his voice would not be recognised. In any case he spoke in no more than a whisper.

"What did you see at Puigpunyent?"

The lad considered. "I went close up to the rock, from all sides except the east, where the road is. The gate is battered down, the towers are burnt and much of the stone has fallen in. The Emperor's men swarm over the castle as thick as fleas on an old dog."

"What of the outside?"

"The Christians have placed men all round the rock, as close to the base of it as they can get, in a ring on all sides. They are heavy men in armor, and walk about very little in the heat. Food and water is brought out to them. I cannot understand what they say to each other, but they do not sleep and they seem not to complain. Much of the time they sing their heathen hymns and prayers."

The *perfecti* ignored the lad's equation of Christian and heathen: it was what they thought themselves. The interrogating voice dropped even lower.

"Were you not afraid that they would catch you?"

The lad smiled. "Men in armor? Catch me on the hillside, or in the *maquis?* No, lords. If they saw me they could not catch me. But they have never seen me."

"Well then, tell us this. Could you—you and some of your fellows, it might be—could you pierce their ring and get over the wall and inside the castle? Perhaps take one of us with you. A mountain man, but not a swift boy such as yourself?"

The boy's face grew more hesitant. If he said yes, would they ask him to do it? He had no wish to join the corpses he had seen carried out and laid on the green plain below the castle entrance. Yet above all he wished for the good opinion of the men whom all respected, the men of honor.

"Their posts are badly placed, and the sentries start and shoot if so much as a fox rustles in the thickets. Yes, I could make my way through them. And maybe three or four of my friends. An older man . . . The spines on the scrub grow high, you see, maybe a foot, two feet from the ground. I do not walk, I slide on my belly, fast as another man walks. A heavier man, a man who does not stoop, who says 'oh, my back'—" for a moment the lad imitated the priest of his village, a heretic like the rest but one who remained in communion with the Church and the bishop, to throw off suspicion—"he could not get through. He would be caught."

The cowled heads nodded almost imperceptibly as they registered the finality of his statement.

"And caught he must not be," observed the whispering voice. "Thank you, lad, you have done us a service. Your village shall know of it. Our blessing to you, and may it grow as you grow older. Outside, talk to the men you will find there. Show them the sentry-posts as you have seen them."

After he had gone out, nothing was said for a while. "Bad news," said one of the cowls after a while. "He knows there is something there."

"It was the defiance of Marcabru that alerted him. If they had surrendered and walked out, he would have thought it was just another siege and gone his way. It is best not to attract attention. To surrender, to deny our faith, to vow obedience to the Pope as we have always done. Then return to what we know after they have gone."

"Marcabru fought to the last because he feared someone would talk. And who knows? They might have done. Maybe he had his orders. After all, we do not know what happened inside the castle. Maybe there were signs of treason."

The silence descended again. Another voice volunteered information. "They say that after the Emperor took the castle he had all the bodies inside it carried out on to the plain by the river, and there had them burnt. But before he did that his men stripped and searched all the dead. Searched their bellies with knives, even, to be sure they had hidden nothing. After they were burnt his men sifted the ash once more. And everything inside the castle, every stick of chair or table, was carried out and laid out to be inspected by the Emperor and his black deacon. He had them burnt too, before people of the nearby villages, while he watched their faces. He thought they would betray it if they saw a holy relic burnt."

"He does not know what he is looking for, then."

"No. Nor does he know how to find the entrance to the place of the Grail."

"But he is demolishing the castle stone by stone. How long will it take before some pick-stroke lays bare the door, or the staircase."

"Not for a long time," said one of the voices, with certainty in its tone.

"But if he digs down to very bedrock?"

For a third time the silence fell. At length, as the sun threw shadows further and further aslant across the dim-windowed room, the most certain of the voices spoke again.

"We cannot take the risk. We must recover our treasures. By war. By stealth. With a bribe. If we need help from outside we must find it."

"Outside?" came a query.

"The world is coming to us now. The Emperor, successor of Charlemagne, whom we drove off eighty years ago. But others too. Strange news from Cordova, as you know. We must guard above all against thinking like men, as if all that happens in this world were mere chance and mortal effort. For we know it is a battle-ground, between the One Above and the One Below. If all that happened, happened in this world, we know which one would win."

"And yet He is the *princeps huius mundi,* the Great Prince of the World."

"And so we must go outside. Outside our world, outside this world."

Slowly the *perfecti,* the men who believed the God of the Christians was indeed the Devil, to be overthrown when time came into its fullness, began to evolve their plan for bringing that fullness forward.

The old man who sat in the shade of the vine-trellis looked at the King of the North sitting opposite him with doubt. He did not look like a king, still less like the subject of prophecy. He was not dressed in Bozrah purple. His men did not bow down before him. He was sitting on a small stool, and following the custom of the Northerners, sitting in full sunlight, as if he could not get enough of it. Sweat ran from his brow, dripped steadily on to the flagstones of the balcony built out to overlook sea and harbor far below.

"You are sure he is a king?" the old man asked Suleiman again. They spoke in Hebrew, Shef listening patiently but without understanding to the alien syllables, which no Englishman had ever heard before in the history of the world.

"I have seen him in his homeland, in his own hall. He rules a wide realm."

"He was born a Christian, you tell me. He will understand this, then. Tell him . . ." The old man, Benjamin Prince of Septimania, Lion of Judah, Ruler of the Rock of Sion, spoke on. After a few moments Suleiman—or, in his own country, Solomon—began to interpret.

"My prince tells me that you will understand what it says in our holy book, which was your holy book also, in the days when you were of the Christian Church. In the Book of the Wisdom of ben-Shirach, which you call 'Ecclesiasticus,' it is said, 'The conies are a feeble folk, but they dwell in the rocks.' The Prince says that here—and I have told him what your strange woman said of the Jews—here the Jews are not a feeble folk. Yet still they dwell in the rocks, as you can see in all directions." He waved a hand at the mountains looming not far off, at the sheer stone walls guarding harbor and town.

Shef stared at him blankly. The Jewish prince's assumption that a Christian was bound to know Old and New Testaments was completely wide of the mark. Shef had never heard of 'Ecclesiasticus,' never read a Bible, had indeed never seen a Bible in his life till he attended the wedding of his love Godive and his partner Alfred in the great cathedral at Winchester. The priest of his fenland village had owned only a service book, with extracts from the Bible for the different services of the Church year. All that Father Andreas had ever even tried to teach was respect for authority, whether that were the Creed, the Lord's Prayer, the necessity for tithing, or social superiors. He had never seen a coney or rabbit either, though this did not matter since Solomon had translated the word as 'hare,' for want of a better.

"Hares don't live in the rocks," he said. "They live in the open field."

Solomon hesitated. "The point my prince wishes to make is that we have very strong natural and artificial defences."

Shef looked round. "Yes, I can see that."

"He did not understand my remark," cut in Benjamin.

"No. The fact is, prince, that these people receive almost no education, even if they are born Christians. Few of them can read and write. I believe the king here can, but he does not do so easily. I do not think he knows the Scriptures at all."

"They are not People of the Book, then."

Solomon hesitated. This was no time to explain the doctrines of the Way, its devotion to new knowledge. His prince and his people felt no loyalty to the Caliph, less to the Emperor, were ready for any new alliance that might bring change. There was no need to hinder their acceptance.

"I think they are trying to be," he suggested. "With difficulty and by themselves. I have seen their own writing. It is developed from a way of cutting signs with knives on bits of wood."

Slowly the prince pushed himself to his feet. "It is meritorious," he said, "to assist those who desire to learn. Come. Let us show the king here what a school is like. A school for those who are truly People of the Book, not like the followers of Mohammed, for ever remembering without understanding, nor those of Yeshua, for ever hiding behind languages no one but their priests is allowed to know."

Shef rose too, not unwilling to follow his hosts' demands, but increasingly bored with listening to conversations that no one troubled to translate. As Solomon explained the purpose of their visit his eye was drawn against his will to what was going on down in the crowded and sunlit harbor. By the outer mole, where the ships of the Northern fleet rode at anchor well away from shore and from the native craft, they were veering out the kites again. He glanced to see if the old prince was waiting for him, saw that he had gone a few steps inside into the cool dark. Pulled his far-seer from his belt and snatched a quick glance through it. The kite was lifting well in a fresh breeze, Steffi now confidently directing operations. And they'd got Tolman, smallest and lightest of the ships' boys, standing by the rail! Were the bastards going to try the next experiment without him? It was a good day for it, and Tolman, bred to a fisherman's family off Lowestoft, was known to be able to swim like a fish.

The Jews were waiting for him. Shef shut the far-seer up, followed Solomon, Skaldfinn, Prince Benjamin and the rest of the escorts and entourage glumly into the dark. To join the People of the Book.

As Shef was led firmly and unwaveringly round the stronghold of the Jewish enclave, planted long ago at the time of the fall of Rome, his sense of strangeness and oppression grew steadily. After the court of the Caliph, he had thought himself ready for any new experience, but the fortress town seemed arranged like no other he had seen in North or South. There was the same crowded and active life that he had grown familiar with in the streets and markets of Cordova, among people dressed in much the same way and talking languages in which he recognised the occasional snatch of Arabic or of some Latin tongue. Yet the sense of sprawl, of activities going on without license or control or physical boundary was missing. The prince led him first on a careful tour of the town's outer defences, a stone wall cunningly linking natural cliff and precipice so as to shut in completely the bay and the harbor like a three-quarter circle. The strange thing was that in every other fortress city Shef had seen, whether York or London or Cordova, there was always and as if immune to regulation a second city, an outer huddle beyond the walls of huts and shacks, the dwellings of those not rich enough to come inside the protection of the city yet drawn there all the same by the wealth it grew and slowly dripped from its boundaries. Alert guard-captains were continually tearing them down, driving the inhabitants further away, trying to keep themselves a clear field of view and dart. It never worked. Always the whores and the hucksters and the beggars crawled back and remade their outer village.

Not here. Nothing obstructed the walls, not so much as a kennel for dogs or a private latrine. Nothing grew in their crevices either—Shef saw a party of men on one stretch lowering some of their number over the parapets to grub out weeds from the stone. Though he could see tilled fields and groves in the distance, he could see not so much as a shed for a watchman. The parties he saw moving to and from fields to city carried their tools with them: in both directions, he noted. They did not even leave their heavy plows and grain-baskets outside the walls.

"I understand what you mean to do," he said finally to Solomon, still gravely interpreting the remarks of his ruler. "I do not see how you make people do it. I could not do that with my own people, even if they were slaves. There is always someone who will try to bend the rules, and ten more to follow him. Even if you flog and brand the way the black monks did, there will always be someone who does not understand what is he to do no matter how often you tell him. Those people out there, are they your slaves? Why do they obey so willingly."

"We do not keep slaves," replied Solomon. "Slavery is forbidden to us under our Law." He translated the rest of Shef's comments, listened to the long reply, spoke again.

"Benjamin ha-Nasi says that you are right to ask these questions, and that he sees you are a ruler in truth. He says you are right also to say that knowing the law is more wonderful than obeying the law, and declares that it is his belief that it is the unlearned alone who bring trouble into the world.

"What he wishes you to understand is that we Jews are different from your people, as from the Caliph's. It is our custom to permit open debate of any matter—your lady Svandis might stand up in our debating chamber and say all that she pleases, and no one would interrupt her. But it is our custom also that once a decision has been made, a rule passed, then all must obey it, even those who argued most strongly against it. We do not punish for disagreement. We punish for not obeying the will of the community. That is why people obey all the rules willingly. Because we are the People not only of the Book, but of the Law."

"And how do you all know the Law?"

"You will see."

Turning from the battlements, the party retraced its steps into the center of the crowded forty-acre site, full of houses of stone and plaster connected by alley ways no wider than two men, winding up and down flights of steps that sometimes seemed to reach the gradient of ladders.

"See there," said Solomon, pointing inside a narrow courtyard. There in the shade sat a man dressed in black, solemnly intoning a long unvarying drone to a dozen boys of different ages squatting on the ground. "That is one of the prince's *geonim*. The prince maintains a dozen such, scholars who instruct youth without pay, for the love of learning. See, he will not desist even though he sees the prince his master pass by. For learning is more important than princes."

"What is he teaching them?"

Solomon listened for a while to the steady drone, and then nodded. "He is reciting to them points of *halakhah*. That is, part of the Mishnah. The Mishnah is the law of our people, based first on our holy books, which the Christians call the Old Testament. But the Mishnah is all that has been thought and said on these books since we first made our Covenant with God. In the *halakhot* we learn particular decisions which have been made on particular points."

"Such as what?"

"At present the *gaon* is explaining why, though saving a man's life takes precedence over saving a woman's, it is proper to cover the nakedness of a woman before that of a man."

Shef nodded, walked on broodingly, following the Prince's unostentatious and unheralded tour. Another thing was beginning to catch his eye. Books in the crowd. He had seen several being carried, one man sitting short-sightedly with his nose almost buried between the covers of one. In one of the markets he thought he had caught a glimpse of a stall with a dozen or more laid out as if for sale. Shef had never heard of a book being sold. The Vikings stole them and ransomed them back, when they could, to their owners. The monks of Saint Benedict made them for themselves and their priest-dependents. No-one ever sold one. They were too valuable. Thorvin would have died in his boots before selling his collection of the holy songs, written down with difficulty in the jagged runic script. How many books did these people have? Where did they come from?

They paused again at what Shef identified as a church, if a Jewish one. In it men and women were praying, bending to the ground like Mohammedans, but somewhere in the dark interior Shef saw a candle burning, and in its light a man reading from another book, seemingly to two separated groups of men and women. Further on a square, and in it two men debating. Each listened impassively to the other, then, at intervals of perhaps five hundred words, spoke in his turn. From the ring of their voices it seemed to Shef that each would begin by quoting words not his own, and would then go on to explain them and fit them against the arguments of the other. A crowd surrounded them, intent and silent but for grunts of agreement, moans of rejection.

"The one says, 'Take thou no usury'," clarified Solomon. "The other replies, 'to a stranger thou mayest lend upon usury.' Now they are disputing as to the meaning of the word 'stranger'."

Shef nodded, reflecting. He knew of rule by the sword, like his own and that of the Viking rulers he had overthrown. He knew of rule by fear and slavery, like that of the monks and the Christian kings. It seemed that this was rule by book and by law, and by law which was put down in book form, not decided by the doom of king or jarl or alderman. The law of the book seemed, however, no wiser than that of the immediate judgment of his own courts. There was something he did not understand.

"Do your people study anything but law?" he asked.

Solomon translated, heard the reply from the prince still leading the way before them. "He says, all learning is either a code or a commentary." Solomon struggled to find expression for either idea in Shef's Anglo-Norse, fixing in the end on 'book of laws,' 'book of decisions.'

Shef nodded again, his face imperturbable. Was this new knowledge? Or just old knowledge continually chewed over, the thing he had set his face against in his own land and his own capital?

"See," Solomon said, pointing the way finally to a small building down almost by the harbor-front once again. In the background, between the alley-walls, Shef caught a momentary glimpse of a kite swooping in the air, gaped at it convulsively. They had flown off without him! And he was almost sure from the glimpse that they had sent Tolman aloft after all: the kite had not been moving freely in the air, had been under control.

"See," said Solomon again, more firmly. "This at least you will find new knowledge."

Reluctantly, still craning his neck upwards, Shef followed his hosts into the building. Inside, tables set round a central space. Men behind the tables, and from them a continuous scritch-scritch sound as their hands moved, seemingly all in time like the feet of the Emperor's marching soldiers or Shef's own troops. A man in the midst of them all, standing up, holding a book and reading from it. Reading, whatever the language, very slowly, a pause every few words.

They were copying, Shef realized. He had heard of such places even among the Christians. One man read slowly, the others wrote down his words, at the end, depending on how many copiers you had, six, even ten books where there had only been one. Impressive, and showing once again how the People of the Law knew their law. Yet this too was hardly new knowledge.

A word from the prince, and the reading stopped, the reader and the copiers turning to their ruler and bowing gravely. "It is not the copying that is new," said Solomon, "nor, the Holy One forbid, the copied. Rather that which they copy on to."

At a word the reader held his book, his master copy, out towards Shef. He took it clumsily, unsure for a moment at which side it might open. His hands were used to hammers and tongs, rope and wood, not these little thin sheets of skin.

Skin? If it was skin, he did not know what kind of a beast it came from. He raised the book, sniffed carefully. Felt the leaf between his fingers, twisting it as he would have a sheet of vellum. Not vellum. Not even the other thing, papyrus, made from strange reeds. The thin stuff parted, the reader stepped forward again with a look and cry of anger. Shef paused, held the book carefully, returned it, staring into the man's angry eyes without hint of expression or apology. Only a fool thinks everyone knows what he knows.

"I do not understand," he said to Solomon. "It is not the calf-skin we use. It has no flesh side, no hair side. Can it be bark?"

"Neither. But it is made from wood. The Latins call it *papyrium,* from some Egyptian plant or other. But we do not make our *papyrium* from that plant, only from wood, crushed and felted. We add other things to it, a kind of clay that prevents the ink from running. Knowledge of it came from very far away, from the other end of the Arabs' empire. There, at Samarkand, they fought a battle with soldiers from another empire far across the desert and mountain lands. The Arabs were victorious and brought back many captives from the land of Chin. They, it is said, taught the Arabs the secret of paper. But the Arabs put little value in it, preferring to teach their boys only enough for them to remember sections of the Koran by heart. It is we who have made the books. With new knowledge."

New knowledge to make the books, thought Shef. Not new knowledge— Solomon prayed to the Holy One to forbid it—not new knowledge *in* the books. Yet this explained something. It explained why there were so many books, so many readers. To make a book of vellum might take the skins of twenty calves, even more, for not the whole skin could be used. Not one man in a thousand could expect to own the skins of twenty calves.

"What is the price of a book?" he asked.

Solomon passed on the question to Benjamin, standing watching, his guards and scholars behind him.

"He says, the price of wisdom is above that of rubies."

"I didn't mean the price of the wisdom. I meant the price of the paper."

As Solomon translated again, the look of scorn on the face of the angry reader, still smoothing over his torn page, deepened into open contempt.

"I do not think there is much hope in them," said Shef to his counselors that evening, watching the sun go down behind the sharp and jagged mountains. Much the same, had he known it, was being said about him among the scholars and learned men who dominated the Jewish court. "They know a lot. But the knowledge is all about rules, either about their God or about themselves. Yet they collect what they need from far afield. They know some things that we do not, like this paper stuff. But when it comes to Greek fire . . ." He shook his head. "Solomon said we could enquire among the Arab and Christian merchants of the aliens' quarter. Tell me more about the flying. You should have waited for me."

"The men said they might be at sea again in a day's time, and the wind was just high enough without being a danger. So they put Tolman in the harness and let the wind lift him. But they did two things that bin-Firnas did not do . . ." Earnestly Thorvin went through the details of the day's launch, when the young boy, still moored but trying to maneuver his great box-kite, had flown out to the end of the longest rope they had been able to splice together, five hundred feet of it. At the far end of the ship Tolman was boasting of his prowess to the other boys and the crewmen, his treble pipe lifting from time to time over Thorvin's rumble. As the night came down the voices died, men turned to their hammocks or stretched out on the warm sun-retaining decks.

Usually, in his dreams, Shef knew that he was dreaming, could feel the presence of his instructor. This time he did not. Did not know, even, who he was.

He was lying on stone, he could feel the cold of it running into his back. There was pain all around him too, back and sides and feet, and something deep and tearing in his chest. He ignored it as if it were happening to someone else.

What frightened him, brought out the chill sweat racing down his face, was that he could not move. Not an arm, not a finger. He was wrapped round and round in folds of some stuff or other, binding arms to sides and legs together. Was it a shroud? Was he buried, still alive? If it were, he could struggle upward, would strike his head against the coffin. For long moments he lay afraid to make the trial. For if he were buried, he could not move, could not cry out. Surely he would go mad.

Convulsively he lunged upward, felt the tearing pain again near his heart. But there was nothing there. Why then could he not see? There was a band under his chin, binding his jaw up. He was buried. Or at least he had been taken for dead.

But he could see! Or at least there was a light, no, a patch of darkness less dark than the rest. Shef stared at it, willing it to increase. And there were movements coming towards him. In the terror of live burial, fear of other men had dissolved. Shef thought of nothing but attracting their attention, whoever they were, begging to be cut free. He opened his mouth, let out a faint croak.

But whoever it was had no fear of the dead, or the dead coming to life. There was a sharp point on his throat-ball, a face looking down at him. The face said, slowly and distinctly, "How shall a man be born when he is old? Or enter again into the womb of his mother?"

Shef gaped up, terrified. He did not know the answer.

* * *

He realized he was gaping up into a face, a face lit by starlight. In the same instant he knew once again who he was, and where he was: in his hammock, slung at the very bow of the *Fafnisbane* for the cool rising off the water. And the face above him was that of Svandis.

"Were you dreaming?" she asked quietly. "I heard you croaking as if your throat had dried up."

Shef nodded, relief flooding through him. He sat up carefully, feeling the cold sweat soaking his tunic. There was no one else nearby. The crew granted him the small privacy of the space beyond the catapult platform.

"What was it about?" she whispered. He could smell her hair very close to his face. "Tell me your dream."

Shef rolled soundlessly from his hammock, crouched face to face with the girl, the daughter of Ivar whom he had killed. He felt the awareness of her as a woman growing stronger every second, as if the years of sorrow and impotence had never visited him.

"I will tell you," he whispered with sudden confidence, "and you shall interpret it for me. But I will do it with my arms round you."

He embraced her gently, felt an instant resistance, continued to hold her as she felt the sweat of fear on him. Her rigid stance seemed to thaw, she let him draw her down on to the deck.

"I was lying on my back," he whispered, "wrapped in a shroud. And I thought that I had been buried somewhere and left. I was terrified . . ." As he spoke, Shef slowly drew up the hem of her dress, pulled her warm thigh close to his own cold body. She seemed to feel his need for comfort, began to co-operate, to press closer to him. He pulled the dress higher, the white dress of a priestess corded round with red berries, pulled it higher yet, still whispering.

CHAPTER THIRTEEN

From all directions the levies converged on the rock of Puigpunyent, where a tense and raging Emperor directed them as they came in, either to strengthening the ring upon ring of sentry-posts set in the ravines and thorny scrub all around, or to the ever-growing gangs of pickax-men who, stone by stone, were dismantling the towers and walls of the heretics' fortress.

A hundred miles to the south, admiral Georgios and general Agilulf stared puzzledly at each other as they digested the order to halt, return, cease the pressure on the Arab forces, abandon the search for the vanished Northern fleet: return at once with every man and every ship.

Little further to the south, the Caliph himself, taking the field in the service of the Prophet for the first time for many years, pressed forward at the head of the greatest army Cordova had sent out since the days when the forces of Islam had tried to conquer France and the lands beyond it, to be turned back by Charles whom the Franks called 'the Hammer,' Martel.

And crossing the Bay of Biscay came a force small in comparison with the others in numbers of ships and men, but their superior in the new qualities of range and weight of missile: the fleet of the One King, of England and the North, drawn from all its blockade stations against the Empire and sent south on the word of Farman the seer. Twenty mule-armed two-masters, thirty longships pacing them, packed with the unemployed and impatient warriors of the North, all laden as deep as they could be pressed with beef and beer and biscuit for the appetites of more than two thousand men. Alfred had accepted Farman's vision-warning, but refused the expedition command, saying England must not be left kingless: the fleet sailed under the orders of Gold-Guthmund, sub-king of the Swedes, once known (and still well-remembered) as Guthmund the Greedy.

Even in Rome, even in Byzantium, attention was falling on the remote borderlands where the Emperor of the Romans searched for the Grail-relic that would complete his empire, and where the Shatt al-Islam had suffered its first turning-back in more than a hundred years.

But the One King himself sat in the sunlight and linked fingers with his mistress, smiling foolishly.

"Completely slit-struck," snarled Brand to the rest of the king's council, watching the pair at their table by the harbor from a decent distance. "Always happens to him. Treats women as if they all had snakes up their skirts for years on end, then one of them does something or other to him, can't think how, and bang! You can't even get his attention. Behaves like a fourteen-year-old who's just been taken behind the barn by a milkmaid."

"There may be no harm in it," offered Thorvin. "After all, better that he has a woman than that he doesn't. Who knows, he may get her with child . . ."

"The way they're going on they should have triplets already, whole ship shakes half the night . . ."

". . . and if that were to happen, it might make the King—take his responsibilities more seriously. And she is who she is. Daughter of Ivar, granddaughter of Ragnar. She can trace her line back to Völsi himself, and through him to Othin." Thorvin pointed to the ship moored a furlong off on the still water. "Fafnisbane, Sigurth the dragon-slayer, his blood runs in her veins. No-one was more pleased than I when her father and uncles were killed. But there was no-one alive who did not in some way respect them. She is one of the god-born, and of a family favored by Othin. Maybe that will avert some of the anger of the god, which some of us have feared for him."

The council pondered his words. On the whole the Vikings among them, Hagbarth and Skaldfinn, even Brand despite himself, were impressed. Cwicca and Osmod looked at each other silently: their memories of Ivar the Boneless had not faded. Only Hund allowed trouble to show on his face. Brand, with the champion's sensitivity to matters of honor and precedence, noticed it.

"She was never your woman," he remarked with as near kindness as his voice could manage. "Do you feel he owes you a debt because she was your apprentice?"

"No," he said. "I wish them well, if they have chosen each other. But what is all this about the god-born and the blood of heroes?" Bitterness tinged his voice. "Look at them over there! Who are they? A pirate's bastard who spent most of his youth in a wattle hut. And a woman who has been a drab to half of Denmark. And that is the One King and the One Queen-to-be!"

He rose abruptly and stalked away across the bright and crowded quayside. The others watched him go.

"What he says is true," muttered Hagbarth.

"Yes, but he worked his way up, didn't he?" contradicted Cwicca, aflame with anger at any criticism of his master. "And I expect she only done what she had to, too. I think that's as important as kings' blood anyway. Me and Osmod should know: how many kings have we been at the death of, Osmod?"

"Six," said Osmod briefly. "If you count the Frankish king, that is, we didn't kill him but his men did it for us once we beat him."

"The trouble is," said Thorvin, "the more you kill, the more power goes into the hands of the ones you don't."

Only a few yards away from the Northerners on the crowded quayside, a different group watched the pair of lovers. They squatted in the shade of an awning where a tailor advertised his wares, the tailor himself crouched on a tiny stool, passing cloth through his hands while he stitched with the speed of a serpent. As his feigned customers felt material and from time to time called out the cries of surprise and outrage which were part of normal negotiation, tradesman and clients exchanged muttered comments.

"That is him for sure," said one in the thick and sweaty homespun of a mountain shepherd. "The one eye. The gold circlet. The charm round his neck."

"The *graduale*," corrected a better-dressed man, gray-haired and gray-bearded. The others looked sideways at him, corrected themselves and returned their eyes to the cloth.

"Two days ago he went all through the city with ha-Nasi," said the tailor, voice and eyes never rising. "At the *librarium* he tore a book and asked what was the price of wisdom. The *geonim* think him an idiot and have asked ha-Nasi to send him away. Yesterday and today he has been with the woman. His eyes never leave her. He cannot keep his hands from her body, or only with difficulty."

The gray-haired man looked first disbelieving, then sad. "It may be that he is still bound in service to the Evil One. But who is not, when he is born? It is from that that we have to climb. Thierry, do you think he would come freely, if we asked him?"

"No. He knows nothing of us."

"Can we bribe him?"

"He is a rich man. His clothes would disgrace an onion-grower, but see the gold he wears. They say . . ."

"What do they say?"

"They say he asks always for new knowledge. His men talk of the Greek fire in the taverns, say openly they seek a way to match it. Every day, when the wind rises, they fly strange kites with boys in them from the decks of their ships. If you could tell him how to make Greek fire he might go with you. Or send another."

"I know no way to make Greek fire," said the graybeard slowly.

The shepherd spoke again. "Then it will have to be the woman."

To cover the silence that fell, the tailor raised his voice in a cry of approval of his own wares and amazement at his prices.

"It will have to be the woman," said the graybeard heavily. "So it is with men. Their own desires lead them to danger and to death. Their loins urge them to give life. But every life they give is another hostage to the evil one. God the Father of the Christians."

"Jehovah of the Jews," added the shepherd.

"The Prince of this World," said all the men in the booth together. Ritualistically, each man spat briefly and secretly into his palm.

Shef, the object of so much hidden scrutiny, rose finally from the table where he had been sitting, throwing down a silver penny with his own head on it as payment for the strong resined wine: the Jews had no such prohibition as the Mohammedans against strong drink, though they did not consume it in the everyday fashion of the Latins or the determined drunkenness of the Way-folk.

"Let's go back to the ship," he said.

Svandis shook her head. "I want to walk round. Talk to people."

Shef's face showed surprise, dismay, alarm. "You did that before. In Cordova. You were away all night. You won't . . ."

She smiled. "I won't treat you the way I did poor Hund."

"There are no slaves here, you know. What language will you speak?"

"If I can't find anyone to talk to I'll come back."

Shef continued to stare down at her. Since they had mated on the deck of the *Fafnisbane* a bare day and a half before, he had thought of nothing but her. It seemed to be part of his nature that once he was attached to a woman, no other would do, no other thought could enter him. Except what had to be done. Now there was nothing to be done. Yet something told him that this was a woman who could not be held, who would rebel at the suggestion of it. And soon the wind would rise.

"Come soon," he said, and walked away, waving already for the boat and the rowers that would take him back to the *Fafnisbane*.

As the afternoon breeze began to rise, the kite-handlers prepared for yet another trial flight. A small elite of them had grown up. Cwicca and Osmod had places as of right: they had been companions of the One King in all his exploits. Even more important, both of them now had ground into them the deep belief that there was a technical solution to every problem. Technical solutions had raised both of them from slavery to wealth—first the catapult, then the crossbow, then case-hardened steel, then water-wheels, windmills, the cam, the trip-hammer and the mill-driven bellows. They were used to the immense difficulties of putting ideas into practice, turning imagination into technology. They knew it could be done. Perhaps most significantly, they knew it had to be done by trial and error, by combining the knowledge of many. Failure one day did not deter them the next. Their conviction was contagious.

Another member of the gang was Steffi, the squinter. He too had belief—belief enough, as the others recognised, to throw himself off a cliff and expect to live. Hama and Trimma were the line-handlers, Godrich and Balla cut and stitched the precious kite-cloth given by bin-Firnas. All the half-dozen ships' boys of the *Fafnisbane*, recruited originally by Ordlaf the skipper to man his yards, were eager contenders to be flown aloft, watched with bitter envy by their counterparts on the other six two-masters. All the kite-handlers were English, all except the boys were men rescued by the Way from slavery. The Vikings from Brand's ships showed a certain curiosity, and were ready enough to man their oars and act as retrieval or rescue ships. Their own sense of dignity, though, seemed to hold them back from the manic jostling try-it-and-see activity of the experimenters.

Most important member of the elite was the king himself, too often forced to worry about other matters, always returning like a hungry bee to the nectar of flight. Hagbarth, priest of Njörth, while half-disapproving of the whole project as a threat to seamanship, nevertheless saw it as his duty to the Way to record the experiments. He often found it difficult to get close enough to the apparatus to see what changes the stitchers or the line-handlers were making.

"See," said Cwicca finally as the preparations reached completion. "We think we got it rigged absolutely right now. And we had to make two changes that the Arab fellow in Cordova didn't know about."

"You took out all the hen-feathers," suggested Shef, remembering the total failure of the dive from Stamford tower.

"No feathers at all. Like the old Arab said, you got to fly like a man, not like a bird. And the old Arab was right about another thing. You got to stop thinking 'sail.' You don't want the wind to push you. You want it to hold you up. So you got to rig this kite here—" Cwicca struggled with the concept of 'asymmetry,' settled in the end for, "different at both ends. Wider upwind, narrower downwind.

"Right, now the two things we've figured out are these. First, he launched with the boy in the sling facing upwind. Good idea, for staying up. Not so good if you ever decide to try to fly free."

The twelve-year-old Tolman, most favored and practiced of the apprentice flyers, bounced on his feet with eagerness as Cwicca said the words, was immediately kidney-punched by a jealous rival. The king unwound the two boys with the ease of practice and held them apart at arm's length.

"Go on," he said.

"It's kind of—" Cwicca again struggled with an idea, this time what a later age would call 'counter-intuitive,' settled for "not the way you'd expect, but we've tried launching with the boy facing downwind. It means he doesn't keep his eye on the ship . . ."

"I watch the sea and the sky," shrieked Tolman. "I watch where they meet. As long as that's straight, and beneath my chin, I stay up."

"And the other thing we've found out," continued Cwicca determinedly, "pretty much like the Arab said, is you need two sets of controls. One for up and down. Those are the wing-things, that the boy works with his arms. But it stands to reason, you have to have left and right as well. So we fitted, like, a tail-vane, like they have on weather-cocks. He works that between his feet."

Hagbarth, watching, looked carefully at the double square of sail-cloth fitted now on the wider upwind mouth of the great kite. Hagbarth, skilled seaman as he was, had never seen a rudder. All Northern ships used the traditional steering-oar instead. Nevertheless, it was clear the idea could be adapted to water.

"And today's the day we're going to try free flight," remarked Shef. "Are any of the boys prepared to risk it?"

As the kidney-punching broke out again, the men of the kite-crew secured a boy each and held them firmly.

"We better stick with Tolman," said Cwicca. "He's skinniest and he's had most goes aloft."

"And he's worthless," added Osmod, Tolman's second cousin.

"Right. Now look, you men. Is there any risk in this? I don't want to lose even Tolman, even if he is worthless."

"Bound to be a bit of a risk," said Cwicca. "After all, he's going up five hundred feet. No-one can fall that far and just walk away. But it's over water. Warm sea. Recovery boats well downwind and watching. We've never had a kite just crash into the water. Worst they do is settle slowly."

"All right," said Shef. "Now show me the line release."

Cwicca showed him the single thick mooring-line, led forward to a place by the flyer's right hand. Showed him the dog-lead clip that held it, the neat contrivance that ensured a few inches slack even when the kite was tugged by the wind.

"When he hits the water he'll have to get out of the sling. Make sure he has a sharp knife. In a sheath, round his neck on a lanyard. All right, Tolman, you're going to be the first man from Norfolk to fly."

Struck by a sudden thought, Shef looked round. "That Arab, Mu'atiyah, where's he gone? I'd like him to see this, so he can tell his master."

"Him." Cwicca shrugged. "He used to hang around saying things. We never understood him, but we could guess. One of those 'it'll never work' people, you get them everywhere. Anyway, we got fed up with him, and Suleiman, Solomon, whatever we're supposed to call him, he took him on shore and locked him up. Said he didn't want him running off to Cordova too soon with some story about treacherous Jews."

Shef shrugged in his turn, went to stand by the rail while Hagbarth took command of the now-practiced routine of launch. The *Fafnisbane* tacking out against the on-shore breeze a good mile from the wall that guarded the outer harbor. Two of the fast and manageable Viking longships positioned close in, a mile downwind, ready to row for the point of splashdown. Two mule-armed consorts, the *Hagena* and the *Grendelsbane* a further half-mile out, spread wide north and south. Not to observe the launch. To watch and ward against red galleys sweeping out of the haze, sharp-eyed boys with far-seers at every masthead.

"They are playing their games again," said ha-Nasi the prince disapprovingly to the silent Solomon.

"It will never work," snarled Mu'atiyah to himself as he watched from a barred window overlooking the sea. "How can barbarians compete with my master, the glory of Cordova? They speak Arabic no better than monkeys even yet."

"The woman is by the well," reported Thierry the shepherd to Anselm, the gray-bearded *perfectus*. "She tries to talk to the women who come down to draw water, but in no language they know."

The ships cruised out across calm water, only ruffled by the rising breeze.

As the moment of launch approached, everyone aboard the *Fafnisbane* went into a now-practiced routine. Tolman wriggled into his sling. Four of the strongest men aboard lifted the whole frame of the kite to the rear larboard rail. Hagbarth, at the steering-oar, judged the breeze. At the right moment, the *Fafnisbane* moving at her best pace with the wind abeam, he yelled one order. Instantly the hands at the ropes hauled up both sails. The two-masted ship, still under way, swung bow into the breeze. The kite filled with air, started to lift from its handlers.

Cwicca nudged Shef. "Say the word, lord. This is the big moment, like."

"You say it. You know the right moment."

Cwicca, judging breeze and ship's movement, hesitated. Then called sharply, "Let her go!"

The kite lifted sharply away from the slowing ship. The handlers had begun by paying out line from a coil round palm and elbow. They knew now that that was too slow. Instead their lines ran almost freely from neat coils on the deck, slowed every now and then by horny palms closing. Just keeping enough tension to pull the kite back against the wind, gain another trifle of lift.

The box of cloth and cane soared gently into the sky, watched by a thousand eyes. "Line almost all out," called the handlers.

"What's the signal for him to release?"

"Two tugs."

"Give them."

High in the sky Tolman, son of a quern-slave by an eel-trapper, felt the two sudden checks on his rise. Felt for the dog-lead clip, jerked it free, dropped it carefully behind him. Another check while the metal clip struck the loop through which the line ran—they had carefully made that bigger so there would be no jam.

And now he was free, hanging in the sky on nothing but the wind. Slowly, with a caution belied by his normal behavior on the ground, Tolman began to test his controls. He was still rising. Could he level out? Alert to every shift of the frail frame, he tried the arm controls, to catch the wind and bring him down. Tolman had no theory about how anything worked. His decisions were based on trial and response. The lack of preconceptions of a twelve-year-old combined with quick responses to teach him basic aerodynamics.

Now he had the horizon level again. There was a moment to look down. Far ahead he could see the mountains, rising high out of the narrow coastal plain. Here and there his eye was even caught by movement, by flashes of light that must be metal. And far off to the north, in the distance, a smudge that must be burning. Where was the harbor?

With a slight catch at the heart Tolman realized that free flight had one major difference from dangling on a line. He was being blown steadily away from the *Fafnisbane* and from the recovery ships. Already the Viking boats were almost directly below him, a bare furlong from the land. He would be over the land himself in minutes, could see himself being carried miles away into the mountains.

He must turn back? But how? Could a kite turn into the wind? If a ship could . . . If he could make it point down, surely the speed of descent would counterbalance the tug of the wind. As long as he did not dive directly into the wind . . .

Gently, alert all the time for the first twinge of an unbalanced response, Tolman worked his foot controls, felt his craft heel away to the right, found himself automatically working the arm controls to lift the left side and lower the right.

A mile astern, Shef and Steffi and the rest of the watchers saw the seemingly runaway kite turn into a slow and gentle bank. Oars threshed as the recovery ships prepared to race after it, now that it was turning back towards the sea. Hagbarth prepared to shout orders, make sail, head in the same direction.

"Wait," said Shef, head fixed upwards. "I think he knows what he's doing. I think he's going to try to turn and come back to us."

"Well, one thing's sure," said Steffi with a defiant glare round for contradiction, made more defiant by his squint. "There ain't no doubt we can fly. And not with no feathers neither."

In the last moments of his flight, Tolman, like Steffi before him, seemed to lose control of his craft and come down hard and fast. He hit the water with a splash and a cracking of canes barely a hundred feet from the *Fafnisbane* itself, the recovery ships well astern of him. Shef, who had shed his gold circlet and bracelets minutes before, dived and swam over, knife trailing from his wrist, ready to cut the lad free if need be. In the warm water he and half-a-dozen other swimmers surged round the still-floating kite. But Tolman had wriggled loose already, was treading water like a frog, holding his craft protectively.

"Did you see?" he shouted. "Did you see?"

"I saw," Shef replied, kicking gleefully in the bright sunlight. The anxiety and depression that had grown on him with the years had vanished. Nothing so pleasurable as splashing in the warm Inner Sea, far from the freezing waters of England. And the problem of flight was solved, or at least well begun. And he was the lover of Svandis.

"I owe you a reward," he said. "The promised reward for new knowledge. But you will have to share it with Cwicca and Steffi and the gang. Maybe the other boys too."

"I should get most," shrilled Tolman. "I took it up and flew it!"

On the shore, by one of the gates out of the fortress-city of the Jews, Anselm the *perfectus* eyed the little convoy of mules and donkeys.

"You have her?" he asked.

"Wrapped up in a carpet, slung over the black mule. You can't see her because we've packed other bales round her. The gate-guards won't notice." Thierry the shepherd hesitated. "One bad thing, *mi dons.*"

"What's that?"

"We lost Guillem. She killed him."

"One woman against six of you?"

"We thought we had her. One each side of her, coming up from behind, grab the bottom of her dress, lift it right over her head like a bag. You'd expect a woman to start shrieking 'rape' and be too frightened to fight, arms trapped and her legs bare."

"So?"

"She had some kind of gutting knife in her belt. Slashed her own dress right open, stabbed Guillem right through the heart while he was trying to grab her arm. Then I hit her one and she went down. Kept on fighting, though, while we gagged her. We did it in an alley behind the well, only women around and I don't think anyone saw. I hope she has no brothers. I wouldn't want to have to fight one of them, if that's what the women are like."

"Guillem has earned his release," said the *perfectus*. "May we all leave the world as well, and earn the right to pass out of it. Go on, Thierry. I will leave the message and then follow."

The mule-train passed through the guarded gate, headed across the plain and up into the nearby mountains, Svandis slung bound, gagged, near-naked but conscious over the lead-beast.

CHAPTER FOURTEEN

As the dinghy approached the quayside, Shef realized that there was a considerable reception committee waiting for him. He could not see the prince himself, Benjamin ha-Nasi. But Solomon was there, and men he recognised as members of the prince's entourage, the captain of his guards. Their faces were grave. Trouble of some sort. Could it be that the flight that they must have seen went against one of their religious rules? Were they about to tell him to take the fleet and go? They seemed to have no aggressive intention. Shef composed his face into a mask of rigid severity. As the boat was pulled up to the steps he leapt nimbly out, straightened, marched up, Skaldfinn the interpreter at his heels.

Solomon did not waste words. "We have found a man dead in the city," he said.

"My men cannot have done it. They were at sea, or on their ships in harbor."

"Your woman might have done it. But she is gone."

Shef's face paled, for all his forced composure. "Gone?" he said. It came out as a croak. "Gone?" he repeated, more firmly. "If she has gone, it was not of her own free will."

Solomon nodded. "That may be. This letter was left with a boy from the Christian quarter. He was paid to deliver it to the captain of the city guard, and to say it was for the one-eyed foreign king."

Presentiment hanging over him, Shef took the paper—paper indeed, he noted—unfolded it. He could read Latin letters, with some difficulty, as a result of his childhood education, ineffective though that had been. Yet he could make little of what he read.

"*Nullum malum contra te nec contra mulierem tuam intendimus,*" he spelled out carefully. "Skaldfinn, what does this say?"

Skaldfinn also took the letter, read through it, brow furrowed. "It says, 'We mean no harm against you or your woman. But if you wish to have her back, come at the second hour of the day following this to the tenth milestone on the road to Razes. There we will tell you what we would have of you. Come alone.' It adds, in different writing—poor writing, it seems to me, and worse Latin—'She killed a man when we took her. Her blood is forfeit'."

Shef looked round at what seemed suddenly to be an immense crowd, all silent, all watching him. The hubbub of the market had ceased. His own men had come up from the dinghy and were close behind him. He knew, somehow, that the men on his ships lying at anchor had realized something was wrong and were lining the sides as well and watching him. Years ago he had decided on impulse to rescue one woman, Godive, from the slavers. But then no one had seen him do it, except Hund, and the thane Edrich, dead long since. He had no doubt in his mind that he had to rescue Svandis now. But this time he had to persuade people that what he was doing was right. He was less free as a king than he had been as a thrall.

Two things he was sure of. First, Brand and Thorvin and the others would not let him go alone. They had seen him vanish too often before. If he did not go alone, would the kidnappers kill their hostage? The other thing he was sure of was that there, in the crowd, there would be agents of the men who had taken her. What he said now would be reported. He had to make it look reasonable to them. Acceptable to Brand and Thorvin.

He turned, looked behind him. As he suspected, other boats had followed him over. Brand was climbing the steps, looking baleful and angry and bigger even than ever. Hund looking puny and anxious. Cwicca and Osmod too. They had cocked their crossbows, had the air of men picking their targets. Some he could rely on. Some to be swayed.

Shef aimed his voice at Brand, but pitched his voice high, to carry if it could even across the water to the watching ship-crews.

"You heard the letter Skaldfinn read, Brand?"

Brand twitched his silver-mounted axe 'Battle-troll' in reply.

"Years ago, Brand, you taught me the way of the *drengr,* when we marched to York and took it. Does the *drengr* abandon his comrades?"

Brand saw in an instant which way the questions were going, and who they were aimed at. He himself, Shef knew, would cheerfully have dropped Svandis overside as a sacrifice to Ran, goddess of the deeps. Nor did he consider her a comrade, but a stowaway. But once she was considered as a comrade, a shipmate, however junior, then public opinion among both Vikings and English alike was utterly solid against any desertion or sacrifice, and most solid among the most junior, the rank and file, the oar-pullers and shield-carriers.

Before Brand could frame a temporizing reply, Shef went on, "For how many comrades must an army march?"

Brand had no choice in answering this question. "One," he answered. An automatic pride straightened his shoulders, made him glare round at the watching southerners.

"And for that one must the leaders too risk their lives?"

"All right," he said. "You're going after her. But not alone! Take the fleet. And if these pigs' fry try to stop you . . ." He stepped forward, axe half-raised, anger at being out-maneuvered translated instantly to anger at any show of resistance. The guard captain's hand dropped to his hilt, spears snapped forward from the crowd.

Solomon lifted a hand and walked between the two groups. "We did not take the woman," he said. "The killing and the rape took place inside our city, and we too have an injury to avenge. If you have need of our assistance, it will be granted. But what do you intend to do?"

Shef knew by now. This time, as he raised his voice, it was aimed at the listener in the crowd who must be there, the one left behind to report on how the message was taken. He spoke in his simple Arabic, the lingua franca of this coast. It would be understood.

"I will go to the milestone, if someone will show me the way. But not alone! I will go one of thirteen."

As Skaldfinn translated, Shef realized Hund was at his elbow. "Who will you take?" asked the little leech, his voice strained.

Shef put an arm round him. "You, old friend. Cwicca and Osmod. Skaldfinn must come. I will leave Hagbarth and Thorvin to command the fleet. And Brand must stay too, he is too heavy on his feet for the mountain roads. But I will ask him and Cwicca to pick the best axemen and bowmen in the fleet."

Solomon too was close beside him. "If you are prepared to trust me, I would come too. I have at least an idea of what this may be about."

"I'm glad someone does," said Shef.

They filed out of the city the next morning, as the first streaks of light crept into the sky and the birds in the fields began their eager song. The men were at least well fed and rested, even Shef, though he had hardly slept at all the night before. The long weeks of sailing with hardly a hand needing to be raised, and with the burdens of rule necessarily far away, had left him a layer of endurance that had not yet been touched.

Solomon and Skaldfinn followed him, with Hund, who had hardly said a word since the news of Svandis's abduction, by his side. Behind the four of them came nine others, five of them crossbowmen selected from the English crews. Cwicca and Osmod led them, as was their right. As he checked the men's gear before the start Shef had been surprised to see the villainous squint of Steffi among the picked men.

"I said the best shots in the fleet," he snapped to Cwicca. "Steffi's the worst. Send him back and get another one."

Cwicca's face shifted to the glassy obstinacy he used when confronted by a direct order he did not like. "Steffi's all right," he muttered. "He was mad keen to come. He won't let you down."

"Crossbowman! He couldn't hit a cow's backside with the butt-end of one," snarled Shef. But he did not persist with his order. Loyalty worked both ways.

Shef was happier with the close-combat bodyguards picked by Brand: all Scandinavians, two Danes, a Swede and a Norwegian, all men with long records of success against men as big and strong as themselves. The Norwegian was a cousin of Brand himself. Looking at him, Shef could see the marbendill strain in him, the mark of the sea-troll, in his eyebrow-ridges and the flat-set teeth. He did not remark at it. Styrr, as he was called, had killed two men already in England for laughing at the way he ate, and been exonerated. One of the Danes acted as the leader of the little group, his experience showing in his expensive jewelry and the scars on his forearms. Shef had asked him his name.

"Bersi," he replied. "They call me Holmgang-Bersi. I've been out five times."

"I only one," said Shef.

"I know. I saw it."

"What did you think?"

Bersi rolled his eyes. Shef had won his holmgang outside the gates of York, and against two men, but hardly in classic style. "I have seen better contests."

"And I have killed greater champions," replied Shef, not ready to concede advantage. But Bersi and Styrr and their mates were a reassurance to him. There was no doubt of the courage of the warriors here in the southern lands, but Shef could not see the slightly-built, cotton- and linen-garbed Spaniards, whether Jew or Moor or Christian, holding their own for more than seconds against the barbed axes and iron-shod javelins tramping along behind him. He was safe at least from casual murder. And he bore with him at least a threat of revenge for Svandis.

By the end of the second hour the heat of the day was rising and Shef's troop looked less formidable than it had. The men were puffing, as they had been hurried along at a steady five miles an hour since dawn, taking turns to ride or trot alongside the overburdened mules that Solomon had provided. Sweat trickled from their hair and into the thick beards. Soon the sun would be shining directly on the mail of the Vikings. They would have to decide whether to shed it or roast. But at least the milestone was in sight, and not too far from the time set. Shef looked round. If there were to be an ambush, this was the most certain place for it. Cwicca and his men had dismounted and were walking more easily now, heads up, crossbows cocked, alert for the first flash of lance or arrow.

From the scrub came a trill of sound. Like a bird-call, but less artless. The sound of a flute. Hair rising on the back of his neck, Shef swiveled his one good eye to see where it came from. A boy standing there. He had not been there a moment before. Was this some creature of the mountains, some half-god, like the marbendills of the northern waste or the Finnish sorcerers from the snow? Five crossbows were covering the lad now. Three too many for security. Shef turned and looked deliberately in a circle. If the boy was a distraction, there would be an attack coming from some other point. Holmgang-Bersi had got the idea at least, had moved off the track, javelin poised.

But there was no-one else. The boy stood motionless till he was sure no-one would shoot from fear, then trilled his flute again, called out to Solomon. Shef understood not a word.

"He says, follow him."

"Where to?" Grimly, Solomon pointed up the side of the mountain.

Hours later, Shef began to wonder whether the boy with the oatstraw flute were not some particularly devilish trap sent to kill them slowly. They had abandoned the mules and set off up the hillside grumbling. Now, the sun directly overhead, not a word was spoken. It had been an unremitting climb up a slope as steep as the thatched roof of a house, but covered in thorn scrub and sliding stone. The thorns held you back, caught in every scrap of clothing, where the boy seemed to glide beneath them like an eel.

But they were not as bad as the stone. After a while Shef realized he and all his men were making detours, going out of their way to avoid the scorching heat of the stone in full sunlight, burning bare hands and starting to sting through leather shoe-soles.

Even the stone was not as bad as the slope. None of the Northerners were fit for walking after weeks at sea, but even a Finn from the moors would have struggled to keep climbing after the thigh muscles had long since gone past pain, after everyone had given up the thought of walking ever again, concentrating only on hauling themselves up the hillside with arms and legs together.

But it was thirst that would kill them. Thirst and heatstroke. Dust rose off the ground, into nostrils often only a foot from it, coated the mouth and choked the throat. All had carried skins of water at the start. The first halt had come after less than a mile. They had become steadily more frequent as the climb went on. At the third halt Shef, already croaking, had told the Vikings peremptorily to strip off their mail and leather, make bundles and carry it on their backs. Now he was carrying one man's for him. Styrr, he saw, Brand's cousin, had gone steadily redder and redder until he was the shade of bilberry-juice. But now he was death-pale. The water was gone. And still the wretched boy kept vanishing, returning, whistling them in this direction or that. Shef turned to Cwicca, keeping up a trifle better than the others, also carrying other men's gear besides his own.

"Next time that little bastard comes back," Shef rasped. "If he takes off again, shoot him. Solomon"—the Jewish interpreter seemed less troubled at least by heat and thirst than the others, though he too was gasping and staggering with fatigue. "Tell him. Rest and water. Or he's dead."

Solomon seemed to say something in reply, but Shef ignored him. The little bastard was back. Shef reached painfully to grab his one garment, but he twisted aside, swept an arm impatiently, started to scuttle forward. Cwicca had him in wavering sights. And there, just above, there seemed to be a crest with the boy disappearing fast over it.

With his last strength Shef struggled over it. Saw in front of him a small, mean village of a dozen houses, of stone that looked as if it had grown from the rock all around. More important than the houses, the flat green in front of it. By the side of it, trickling from the rock, a spring running into a stone cistern. Suddenly and clearly through the relentless noise of the cicadas in the scrub, Shef could hear the tinkle of water running.

He turned back, saw his men straggled out for a hundred yards down the hillside. He tried to call out to them, "Water!" found the word stick in his throat. The nearest saw it in his eyes, came on with renewed energy. Far down the slope Styrr and Bersi, Thorgils and Ogmund crawled hopelessly on.

Shef slid down the hill, seized the nearest, muttered "Water," in his ear, pointed him to the crest-line. Slid on to the next. Styrr had to be half-pulled the last fifty feet, and when he reached the top, even with Shef's shoulder under his arm he staggered like a drunk on the level ground.

They were making a bad show, Shef realized, whoever was watching. They looked less like a king and his bodyguard than they did a troop of beggars with a dancing bear. He heaved Styrr more firmly upright and snarled at him to pull himself together, look like a *drengr*. Styrr simply tottered towards the water, was met by Bersi with a bucket. He threw half of it over the gasping giant, thrust the rest into his hand.

"He will die if he swills cold water in that state," remarked Solomon, holding an empty dipper. Shef nodded, looked round. The rest had drunk, seemed able to think of something other than their thirst. He himself could smell the water, felt the urge to throw himself at it and into it as the others had clearly done.

They were being watched. If this had been a trap it would have worked. For long minutes there his men would have offered no resistance to sword or

spear or arrow, unless it had been between them and the water. Shef
stiffened himself pridefully, took the dipper full of water that Cwicca passed
him, forced himself to hold it without apparent awareness. He walked
towards the ring of watching men with his head up.

They had bows and axes, but they did not look formidable. Mere working
and hunting tools, and the men who held them, some thirty or so, looking
like shepherds or fowlers, not warriors. No signs of rank were visible, but
Shef had learnt to watch men's bearing. That one there, the graybeard with
no weapon: he was the chief.

He walked towards him, tried to speak sardonically, to say, "You brought
us by a weary road." The words would not come out. He lifted the dipper,
rinsed the dust from his mouth, felt it swirl across his throat. The urge to
swallow, constricting, almost overpowering. He would show them who was
master, of himself at least. He spat the water on the ground, spoke his piece.

No understanding. The eyes had widened when he spat out the water,
but just a furrowed brow when he spoke. He was speaking the wrong
language. Shef tried again in his simple Arabic.

"You took our woman."

The graybeard nodded.

"Now you must give her up."

"First you must tell me something. Do you not need water?"

Shef lifted the dipper, looked at the water in it, threw it on the ground. "I
drink when I choose. Not when my body chooses."

A slight ripple from the listening men. "Tell me then. What is that you
wear on your breast."

Shef looked down at the sign of his god, the pole-ladder of Rig. This was
like the scene he had undergone long ago when first he met Thorvin. More
was meant than was being said.

"In my language it is a ladder. In the language of my god and the Way I
follow, it is a *kraki*. I met a man once who called it a *graduale*."

They were listening now, very intently. Solomon was at his side, ready to
translate. Shef waved him back. He must not lose the intimate contact, even
if all the two could speak was mangled Arabic.

"Who called it that?"

"It was the emperor Bruno."

"You were close to him? He was your friend?"

"I was as close to him as I am to you. But he was not my friend. I have
had his sword at my throat. They tell me he is close to me again, now."

"He knows about the *graduale*." The graybeard seemed to be talking to
himself. He looked up again. "Stranger, do you know of the Lance he
carries?"

"I gave it to him. Or he took it from me."

"Maybe, then, you would take something from him?"

"Willingly."

The tension in the air seemed to drain. Shef turned and saw that his men were on their feet again, weapons raised, looking as if they might be able to resist attack, or even, as they reckoned the limited odds against them, begin one.

"We will return your woman. And feed you and your men. But before you return"—Shef's flesh shrank at the thought of retracing their steps, downhill or up, "—first you must pass a test. Or fail it. Either is the same to me. But to pass it might be good for you, and for the world. Tell me, your god, whose sign you bear: do you love him?"

Shef could not help the grin from spreading across his face. "Only an idiot would love the gods of my people. They are there, that is all I know. If I could escape them, I would." His grin faded. "There are some gods I hate and fear."

"Wise," said the graybeard. "Wiser than your woman. Wiser than the Jew at your side."

He called an order, men began to bring out bread, cheese, what looked like skins of wine. Slowly Shef's men sheathed or uncocked their weapons, looked questioningly at their lord. But Shef had seen Svandis coming limpingly towards him, wearing only the slashed and blood-stained tatters of her white dress.

To the Jewish scholars and counselors of the city-state of Septimania, the departure of their colleague Solomon—off in the mountains somewhere, escorting the king of the barbarians on some pointless chase—came as a relief. Doubt was already strong as to whether Solomon had been wise in bringing the strangers to them. Yet it could be represented as a service to the Caliph, their nominal overlord, to revictual and resupply men who had once been his allies, and who were at any rate enemies of the Christians now pressing so close. Nevertheless one matter at least was outstanding, a worry to both prince and council.

The affair of the young Arab Mu'atiyah. It was clear that he was a subject of the Caliph Abd er-Rahman: as indeed were they, the Jews of Septimania, at least in theory. Did they not pay to the Caliph the *kharaj* and the *jizya*, the land-tax and the poll-tax? And did they not guard their gates against his enemies and those of his Faith, the Christians and the Franks? It was true that that guard did not extend in any way to limiting trade with their near-neighbors, true too that the tax payments were made according to calculations done by the council itself, which would not have passed muster with the Caliph's own tax-collectors, none of whom any longer courted embarrassment by appearing in the city. Nevertheless—so said the majority on the council—there was no precedent for imprisoning the young man merely to prevent his return to his master.

As the council debated, the old prince watched his learned men, stroking his beard. He knew what Solomon would have said, had he been here. That the Arab would immediately flee to his master and report that the Jews had made common cause with the barbarians, the polytheists, that they were providing a base for a hostile fleet which had fled from contact with the Greeks and now planned its own attacks on the peaceful countryside. Little of that was true, but that was how it would be presented, and how it would be believed.

In any of the Christian dukedoms or princedoms of the border country, such a matter would have been the simplest thing in the world. Ten words, and the Arab would disappear. If he ever were inquired about, polite regret and ignorance would be expressed. And the baron or duke or prince would have thought no more about it than about pruning his roses.

In a Jewish community, that was not possible. Not even desirable. Benjamin ha-Nasi approved of what his wise men would decide, though he knew it would be a mistake. A mistake in the short-term. In the long term the fortress of the Jews, the place where they had kept their identity in the long centuries of flight and persecution, was the Torah and the Law. As long as they held to that, history had taught them, they would survive—as a people if not as individuals. If they abandoned it, they might thrive for a while. Then they would merge with the sea around them, become indistinguishable from the lawless, unprincipled, superstitious believers in Christ, their false Messiah.

Tranquilly the prince listened to the arguments, conducted as much to allow all members of the council to show their learning as to affect the final decision. Those who were putting the case for continued detention, in the way that Solomon might have done, were doing so passionately but insincerely, according to a convention understood by all. Against them was the deep reluctance of any Jewish community to order imprisonment as a punishment. Freedom to go as one pleased was one of the inheritances from the desert which they shared with the Arabs their cousins. It was the other side of the horror of exile from the community which was the council's ultimate threat against their own.

The learned Moishe was summing up, and preparing his final peroration. He was the Amoraim, the interpreter of the Mishnah. "And so," he said, looking round fiercely, "I will now speak of the Halakhah, which is the ultimate conclusion of this matter debated. First it was spoken and passed on from generation to generation, now it is written and fixed for ever. 'Treat the stranger within your gates as you would your brother, for this you will be thrice blessed'."

He ended, looking round. If his audience had not been constrained by the dignity of their place and cause, they would have applauded.

"Well spoken," said the prince finally. "Truly is it said that the learning of the wise is a wall to the city. And that it is the folly of the unlearned that brings woe upon it."

He paused. "And yet, alas, this young man is unlearned, is he not?"

Moishe spoke up. "By his own account, prince, he is the wonder of the world for learning. In his own way and his own country. And who should condemn the customs of another country, or its wisdom?"

Just what you were doing this morning, thought Benjamin to himself. When you gave us your opinions on the follies of the ship-barbarians, with their king who tears a book to find out what it is, and asks the price of the paper not of the contents. Nevertheless . . .

"I shall do as the feeling of the council directs," said Benjamin formally. He crooked a finger to his guard-captain. "Release the young man. Give him a mount and the food he needs to reach the Caliph, and escort him to our boundaries. Charge the cost against our next payment of the land-tax to his master."

The young Arab, who had squatted at the side of the room listening without understanding to the Hebrew exchanges that would determine his fate, recognised at last the tone and the gesture. He sprang to his feet, eyes blazing. Seemed for a moment as if he meant to burst out in complaint and accusation—as he had done fifty times already in his short captivity—but then thrusting it back in a transparent rush of policy. It was obvious what he meant to do: rush off to make every bitter denunciation to which he could lay his tongue. Revenge himself with words for every slight that had been put upon him, real or fancied, by the barbarians of whom he was so jealous. Jealous of their flying of kites.

The prince turned his attention to the next case. It was true about the learned, he reflected. They were a strength. And the unlearned were a plague. But worse than both, alas, were the class to whom both the Arab Mu'atiyah and Moishe the learned belonged.

The class of clever fools.

CHAPTER FIFTEEN

Inside the cool stone basement of the best house in the tiny village, the *perfecti* discussed what must be done, in whispers.

"He does not speak our language. How can we put him to the test?"

"He has some Arabic, as do we. That will have to do."

"It is irregular. The test must be given in the words of the test."

"It is we who make the rules and we who can change them."

A third voice broke in to the exchange. "After all, he has already passed the one test. And he passed it without knowing he took it."

"You mean the water?"

"I mean the water. You saw the way his men came over the hill. They were blind with weariness and mad with thirst. They are Northerners from cold lands, and seamen who never walk. The big one was near to death. And the king himself was so dry—we saw it—that he could not speak. Yet he threw the water on the ground."

Another voice corroborated the third. "And before that, he took it in his mouth. Then he spat it out. That is one of the tests. To refuse the man water till he can think of nothing else, then to give him it. To see if he can take it into his mouth and yet reject it, as a sign of victory over the body. The temple of the Evil One, prince of this world. That is what the one-eye did."

The first voice continued to complain. "He had not had long enough! In our test the man is kept without water for a night and a day."

"Sitting motionless in the shade," replied one of his antagonists. "Our rule says the candidate must be kept till he thinks of nothing else but water. I have seen candidates in better shape than that one when he came over the hill."

"In any case," said a voice that till now had not spoken, but now spoke with the tones of one who gave a decision, "we will proceed with the test. For as we speak, the Emperor's men are tearing stone from stone. Over our holy things and the bodies of our fellows."

The gray cowls nodded slowly, in the end without dissent.

Outside, his feet dangling over the edge of the near-precipice that shut off the little village to the north, Shef sat with his far-seer in his hand. Once he and his men had drunk their fill, it had been possible to look around, to understand the lie of the land. The village perched high on a slope, in what was a mere terrace in a sweep of baking stone and scrub. From high up, more terraces could be seen here and there, each with its little plot of trees and crops. Shef could see how people could live almost at ease up here. His far-seer had caught dozens of scrawny sheep browsing the grass on far hillsides. Sheep meant mutton, and milk and cheese. And one thing the villagers might count on, and that was that they would not be bothered by tax-collectors. Only very tough and determined ones, and such would find far easier pickings elsewhere.

Yes. It was clear that almost any kind of authority could be resisted up here. King or Emperor. Or Church and Emperor.

In the coldly objective way his mind worked when he was left alone, Shef set himself to considering the information he had been given. One thing he had come to understand about himself during the years of his rule was this. Good or bad, he did not believe all that was told him, even all that he himself saw. But his disbelief meant that he did not need to lie to himself, as so many people, he knew, did all or some of the time. They believed what they needed to. He did not need to believe anything, and could see things the way they were.

So he did not need to believe Svandis. She had greeted him, and his men, with tears of relief. Then, as he had seen, she had grown ashamed of herself and talked harshly and fiercely to cover what had been her fear. He did not blame her. He had known veteran warriors do the same. And when she told him what had happened, Shef, piecing together what he knew of her history, had understood both her fear and her shame.

A woman, taken from both sides with her dress whirled over her head. No woman wore anything beneath her dress, whatever she wore over it. A woman with her arms trapped, naked from breast down, could think of nothing but rape. That was why it was an offense in all the Northern codes of law to raise a woman's clothing above her knee. But Svandis had not needed legal prompting to think of rape. She knew all about that. Shef was proud, but not amazed, that she had slashed herself free and killed a man: he had seen her grandfather do the same, starting unarmed and half-drowned against two men who held his arms. She had the blood of Ragnar indeed.

But the fear had struck deep into her. What she said about her captors was tinged by it. And she said that they were savages, worse than the deepest heathens among the Swedes, cold and heartless. She had heard tales of them from the women in Cordova, she said—and that at least must be true. That in the mountains lived the sect where the men hated all women and the women all men. Where every joy and delight in the world was rejected. "And that is how they are," Svandis said again and again. "You can see it when they look at you! I stood there when they set me free with my legs bare and my body displayed like a dancing girl. And they looked at me. And then they looked away, all of them, even the mule-drivers. I would rather have heard your men shouting the things they do at women they see. They rape women, and hurt them, but that is because they need them, at least. Here you can see the hate in their eyes."

Fear talking, Shef reflected as he sat at ease looking out over the mountains and the passes beneath. Yet there might be something in it. It had a kind of relation to what Solomon had said, after he had consoled Svandis and she had gone to sleep under guard and in the sun. After he had told Solomon what they had said about the test. Solomon had thought for a long time and then approached him, keeping his distance even from his colleague Skaldfinn.

"Something you should understand," he said. "Something few know. You may have thought these people are Christians."

Shef had nodded. He could see a crucifix on the wall of what seemed a rude church. Folk who walked past it knelt, crossed their breasts.

"They are not. Or if they are it is of a kind that has no dealings with others. Few even with my people. You see—the followers of Mohammed, the followers of Christ, my people the Jews. They fight each other, they may persecute each other, but they share many things. To Islam, Christ was one of the prophets, to the Christians, their God is also our God, only they have given him a Son. The Mohammedans believe in one Allah as we believe in one Jehovah, like us they will not eat pork or meat which has not been bled. You see? We are—we began—on the same side.

"These people here are different. They do not believe in our God at all. Or if they do, they reject him."

"How can you reject God and reverence the crucifix?"

"I do not know. But they say—they say that to these people the God of Abraham is the devil, and that they make images of him only to defile them. And they say also"—Solomon's voice dropped even more—"that since to them God is the devil, that they have made the devil himself their God. They are devil-worshipers. That is the talk of the hills. I do not know how they worship him or with what rites."

Solomon could not be relied on, either, Shef reflected. It was the People of the Book again. At bottom the three great religions that had come out of the East were all religions of the Book. Different books, or the same book with different additions. They despised anyone who did not hold to their book. Called them devil-worshipers. They despised him for a start, he had seen the look in the eyes of the *geonim*, the scholars of the Law. If they despised him, and the Way, and they despised also this strange sect of the hills—then maybe he and they had something in common. Women-haters, said Svandis. Did he hate women? They had brought him no luck, and he had brought none to them.

His eye sweeping over far distances, as the haze cleared in the sun, and the far-seer let him probe out to the horizon, Shef saw again and again flashes of bright metal down on the roads, the roads through mountain passes. He remembered what Tolman had said of what he could see at the top of his flight. Metal moving, and on the edge of sight, Tolman said, a great pyre burning.

His mind emptied, his eye reaching far into space, Shef felt the strange blankness of the waking dream come over him: a better feeling than the last he had had, the dream of the shrouded corpse. This time his father was there.

"He's loose, you know." There was still the tone of mirth in his father's voice, of secret knowledge, of cleverness which he knew had no match. With it there was a new tone, of uncertainty, even of fear, as if the god Rig were realizing that he had set something in motion which even he with all his cleverness might not control.

Shef spoke back to his father, silently, in his mind alone. "I know. I saw you loose him. I saw him climbing the stair. He is mad. Thorvin says he is both father and mother of the monster-brood." In his new mood of disbelief and defiance, he did not bother to add the question, "Why did you do it?"

An image began to form before him, not with the usual fierce clarity, but blurred, as if through the poor glass and uneven lens of a far-seer. As it formed, his father's voice talked over it.

"The gods, you see, long long ago, in the time of your namesake, the first King Sheaf. That was when Balder was still in Asgarth. Balder the beautiful. So beautiful that all things on earth, except one, had taken the vow not to harm him. So what did the gods, my father and my brothers, what did they do to amuse themselves?"

Shef could see the answer. The god at the center, so bright-faced that it was impossible to look at him, a blaze of beauty. Tied to a stake. And around him, fierce shapes, mighty arms, hurling weapons at him with all their strength. An axe span away from the side of the god's head, a lance with deadly triangular point rebounded from his heart. And the gods laughed! Shef could see the familiar red-

bearded face of Thor turned up to the sky, mouth open in an ecstasy of mirth, as he hurled his deadly hammer again and again at his brother's skull.

"Yes," said Rig. "Till Loki showed them."

Another god being brought forward to the throwing line, a blind god, Loki at his elbow. A different Loki, Shef noted. Same face, but without the marks of poison and of rage. Without the look of bitter injustice. Clever and shifty, still, even amused. The brother of Rig, there was no doubt.

Loki put a spear in the blind god's hand, the spear of mistletoe, the plant so weak and so young that the strong gods had not bothered to ask it for its vow not to harm Balder their brother. The gods laughed even louder at the sight of the blind man with the feeble twig lining up to throw, Shef could see Heimdall, Frey, even the grim one-eyed Othin, calling to each other and slapping their thighs in merriment.

Till the dart struck. The god fell. The light of the world dimmed.

"You know what happened then," said Rig. "You saw Hermoth ride to try to bring Balder back from Hel. You saw what they did to Loki in revenge. They forgot something. They forgot to ask why. But I remembered. I remembered Utgarthar-Loki."

Utgarthar-Loki?, Shef wondered. He was used, now, to the vagaries of English and Norse, still so similar. That means 'outyard-Loki.' Where there is an outyard-Loki there should be an inyard-Loki.

"Utgarthar-Loki was the giant who challenged the gods to a contest. And they lost. Thor lost the wrestle against Old Age, failed to drink the ocean, failed to lift the Mithgarth-Serpent. His boy Thjalfi lost the race with Thought. Loki lost the eating-match with Fire."

In the background, as if through the far-seer again, Shef could see an immense hall, one greater even than Othin's Valhalla, and in it a table piled high with joints of beef and bear, man-meat and walrus: a table stocked from the smokehouse of Echegorgun. At one side of it a god sat gobbling, thrusting the food into his mouth with sweeping movements of the arms, not chewing but snapping like a wild wolf. Down the other side raced fire. Fast and deadly as the fire of the Greeks.

"Which Loki lost?" asked Shef.

"The god Loki. Not the giant Loki. You see, Loki was on our side once. Or at least half of him was. That was what I remembered and the gods forgot. But if you forget . . . he becomes the other Loki. The Loki outside the home-garth. The monster in the darkness."

I don't understand, thought Shef. If this all comes from my mind, as Svandis says, then it is some part I do not know. In-Loki and out-Loki? And Loki contesting with Fire? The word for 'fire' is logi, though Rig did not say it. Loki against Loki against Logi? In-Logi and out-Logi too? And who is this first King Sheaf?

*   *   *

He shook his head in a kind of exasperation, and as he did so the vision cleared, he saw the far-off mountains beginning to thrust their peaks through the tatters of his dream, of the scene in the giants' hall, devouring god and devouring flame. A hand on his shoulder, pulling him back from the near-precipitous drop in front of him.

"Are you all right?" Svandis's copper hair and bright eyes looking into his own. Shef blinked once and again.

"Yes. I saw something. From a god or from my own mind, I do not know. Whichever it is, I will work it out for myself."

Shef rose to his feet, stretched. The rest had done him good. The rest and the exhaustion of the morning. He felt as if he had sweated out the soft living and the mental strain of the years of rule. He felt like a *drengr* again, like a carl of what had been the Great Army: young, strong and cruel.

"Cwicca," he hailed. "See that barn door over there? Think you can hit it? You and your mates, put four quarrels each into the middle of it, as fast as you can shoot."

Shef watched impassively as the crossbowmen, not understanding but ready to show their paces, sent iron bolt after iron bolt thudding deep into the middle of the door. The villagers who had been quietly watching, their own bows and spears never far from hand, stared uncertainly.

"Styrr," Shef shouted when they had finished. "Take your axe. Go chop those bolts out and give them back."

Grinning, Styrr walked over, axe swinging loosely. He was glad of a chance to show his mettle after the near-collapse of the morning. The axe whirled and struck like the hammer of the gods, chunks of old oak flying with every blow. Shef could see the villagers staring uncertainly at each other. Styrr did not look like a man who could be brought down by a collection of half-armed shepherds. Professional warriors in armor would filter to the rear rather than face his axe.

"They are poor people," whispered Svandis, "and wood is scarce up here. You are destroying their door."

"I thought you said they were savages and devil-worshipers? Well, whatever they are, I know this. Time for them to worry about us. Not just us worry about them."

Shef turned from the demonstration as Styrr walked back to Cwicca with a score of bolts in his enormous Brand-like hand. He patted Svandis gently, still less than decent in her rags. "I am going to sleep now. Come lie next to me."

The sun was no more than a hand's breadth from the horizon when the guide came for him: a burly man in the sweaty woolens of a mountain shepherd. Svandis snarled at him as he came towards the northerners. "That is the one Thierry," she muttered. He looked down at Shef, sprawled on the grass, and said without expression, *"Viens."*

Shef rose, reached for his sword-belt standing propped against the barn wall. For this trip he had armed himself with one of the issue weapons of the *Fafnisbane,* a plain brass-hilted broadsword. The guide shook a finger from side to side. *"Non."* The rest of what he said made no sense to Shef, but the tone was unmistakable. Shef put the weapon back, straightened himself, made ready to follow. As the two men walked off, Shef heard a hail from Cwicca. The guide turned, alerted by the menace in the tone. Cwicca stared at him, pointed deliberately first at Shef, then with a sweeping gesture at the village around. He pointed again at Shef, jabbing a finger imperatively. Then swept his arm at the village, and drew the edge of his hand across his throat. "Bring him back," it meant. "Or else . . ."

The guide did not respond, but turned again and led Shef at a fast walk away across the little patch of land and immediately up a stony trail into the mountains. Shef followed, his legs stiff from the morning's climb, but working off their pain as he strode out to keep up.

The path, if it could be called a path, led them from stony outcrop to stony outcrop, climbing slightly, but mostly going across the side of the mountain, over patches of boulder, shifting scree, and again and again, round the head of craggy ravines. From time to time the mountain sheep, browsing everywhere as if they were goats, raised a head or bounded away at their passage. It reminded Shef of the path he had taken to the house of Echegorgun, years before. Only here the sun warmed the stone instead of merely casting a pale light on it, and the air was full of the scent of mountain thyme. The sun sank further, touched the horizon and crawled beneath it. Still there was light in the sky, but fading. If he were left alone on the slope, Shef decided, he would make no attempt to return. Find a flat stretch and wait for day. As he walked he began to mark possible resting-places near the path. Not a place for explorations in the dark.

His eye left Thierry the guide as he hurried on five or ten paces ahead. The path kinked abruptly left, round the side of yet another stony mass jutting out of the side of the mountain. Shef stepped round it. Found himself alone, on the edge of a steep fall down to dry rocks below. He halted, stood stiff and alert. Where had the man gone to? Was this a trap?

Too complex to be a trap. If Thierry had wanted to push him over an edge he had had a dozen chances already. And Thierry knew he had left hostages behind. Shef looked round carefully. A crack in the stone, a black line in the fading light. Of course, a cave-mouth. And Thierry standing just inside it, watching him. Shef walked over to him, gestured to him to lead on.

Inside the cave-mouth, a mere split in the rock barely three feet wide, someone had left a candle. Thierry struck sparks from flint, lit it, walked on, now moving more slowly. Shef followed the little patch of light. As he walked on he began to feel, through the worn leather soles of his shoes, that he was treading on loose rock. Loose rock with sharp-edges. He bent, picked one up, studied it in the faint light of the candle a few feet ahead. It was flint, sure enough. Shaped flint, stone chipped and flaked to produce a kind of point, like a spear-point. Echegorgun had done the same. Only his points and implements were four times the size, made for the race of trolls. Shef threw it down, walked on.

The cave led on and on, with every now and then the black line of some branching passage showing momentarily in the light. Shef began to feel more anxiety than he had done so far. If he were abandoned now, in the dark, the chances were he would never find his way out. Retracing his steps in the dark might seem easy, but he would be feeling his way. Easy, indeed unavoidable, to take a wrong turning. Then he would wander in the blackness till thirst took him. His lips dried at the thought, remembering what thirst had felt like only that morning. Better than the sword would have been a water-skin and tinder-box.

Thierry had paused to let him catch up. In the candle-light Shef saw something else on the walls, signed to Thierry to move the light closer.

Paintings. All over the one flat wall on the left of the passage, paintings of animals, done with perfect fidelity, not like the half-abstract dragon- and beast-shapes of the North. A bull, Shef could see. The sheep of the mountains, just like the ones wandering outside. And there, on its hind legs, what seemed to be a massive bear, a black bear as big as the white ones of the Arctic. A spear jutted from its chest, and round it pranced tiny stick-like man-figures.

"Pintura," said Thierry in an echoing rumble. "Pintura de los vechios. Nostros padres." His voice contained in it a note of pride. He walked on. Stopped, at the end of the gallery, at what seemed to be a blank unbroken wall. He pointed at himself, shook his finger negatively. Pointed at Shef, made pushing gestures. "I stop. You go on."

Shef looked at the blank wall carefully. At its base there was again a black crack, an opening. It did not seem deep enough for a man. But that must be the way through. A crawl, not a walk. As he realized what was meant Thierry began suddenly to walk away, took five paces with Shef beginning to reach out after him, then blew out the candle and vanished.

Instantly Shef stopped dead. If he ran after Thierry in the dark he would lose his bearings, perhaps never come back to the wall and the gap. Yet there must be a way through there. That was safety, or at least the way through to the test. And if there was a test, there was a way to pass it. Better do that than struggle in the dark.

Slowly Shef turned, careful to retrace his movements exactly as he remembered them, groped his way back to the wall, felt till he could touch the edges of the crack. Very faintly he could feel air blowing through. So there was something on the other side. Dropping on to his belly he began to squeeze forward under the lip of rock.

Halfway through, his groping hands met hard rock. He felt to either side. Rock as well, and no opening below. The edge of the rock lip under which he had crawled ground painfully into the small of his back. He did not think he could push himself back now, his ribs would catch. If he did not find a way through he would lie here under the mountain till he moldered away.

But he had been in this situation before. The makers of the old king's barrow from which he had rescued treasure and scepter, they had used the same trick. Maybe all treasure guardians used it. He was in a bend like the shape of the U-rune, and there would be a passageway above his head. Sure enough, the groping hand he could thrust a few inches above him met no resistance. Yet he could not crawl through the way he had begun, or his back would break. He should have gone through on his back, not his belly.

The sweat of fear had begin to break out on him, fear at the thought of lying here trapped for eternity. That was an advantage. And underneath him was not rock but sand or shale. Methodically, Shef began to scrape what he could from underneath his belly, making a little hollow in which to turn. He drew in his breath to reduce his mid-section every inch it would go, rolled, tried to force himself over. Stone dug into his sides, his leather belt seemed to catch on some projection. He twisted with panic force, felt the belt tear and give, felt himself roll over.

After a few seconds he found a purchase with his feet, began to force his back up the rock face behind him. A few painful inches, another moment of seeming immobility. Then he managed to get one knee under the lip of the crawl-ledge, found a better foothold, thrust his head up into the clear.

There was a ledge behind him, breast-high. He turned once more, pushed himself up, got a knee over and crawled out of the pit. As he did so, perfectly clear in the still black air, he heard a long hiss. The scratch of scales on stone. He could see nothing, but somewhere close to him in the blackness, he knew, there was a serpent.

He shuddered involuntarily. The dream of Loki, and the serpent pursuing up the staircase was still with him, and the moment when he found himself in the orm-garth of the gods. Yes, Svandis had explained it. The marks in his flesh where the snake had seemed to strike, they were his own mind playing tricks on him like women believing themselves pregnant. The dream of the climbing feet and the orm-garth, they came from a memory of Brand and a mixture of guilt and fear at the death of Ragnar.

But Shef had seen the death of Ragnar, had seen the adders strike him and the face turn blue and swollen. That had been no dream, and this was no dream either. There was a real snake somewhere in the blackness. Snakes had senses humans did not. It could detect him, could strike before he could raise a hand to defend himself.

There was someone in the blackness close to him as well. Some one, not some beast. Shef's sensitive ears could catch a faint scuff of sole on stone. At the same instant Shef felt around his neck an embrace of cold scales. A snake as thick as his arm had been dropped round his neck.

It was the faint reek of sweat that saved him. If it had not been for that he might have shrieked, clutched unavailingly for the neck of the thing round him, been bitten again and again by the angry rat-snake, and perhaps run fruitlessly into the darkness, there to die, not of poison—for the rat-snake held no more in its fangs than was needed for its rodent prey—but of thirst and despair. But the sweat-stink was that of Thierry. Shef realized in the same instant that Thierry must have come round the rock-wall which he had been made to climb under, had no doubt seen or sensed his progress all the way, was here to administer the next stage of his test. Was waiting for the stranger to flee in panic.

Shef stood stock-still, felt a forked tongue flicker across his face as the snake got its bearings, felt the scales rasp slowly across neck and body and leg as it determined which way to go and slithered down to the ground and off about its business. After it had gone Shef stood for a while motionless. Not from fear. He was beginning to grow angry at the way he was always held at disadvantage, at the thought of Thierry laughing silently in the dark. He mastered the anger, considered what he had already learned.

These people were testing him. They did not mean to kill him, so much was clear. If they had meant to kill him, he would be dead already. They were testing him. And they wanted him to pass the test. If he did, they would want something from him once he had passed. That did not mean that they would not kill him if he failed.

The sensible thing was to walk slowly forward, and to be alert for the next test. They would try to surprise him. Do not react instantly, whatever they do. He stepped forward, feeling carefully for footing with each step, arms spread wide for balance and warning.

Someone gripped him round the body. Again, he could not repress the jump, the shudder of fear. But this was no hostile attack. The arms that closed round him from in front were warm and naked, an embrace not a grapple. Lips kissed him suddenly on the chest. Automatically he closed his own arms round the person who held him. A woman. He could feel her breasts push against him. A naked woman. He dropped his hands, felt her buttocks, felt her immediately respond and push close against him, moving her groin up and down against his.

A week before, sunk in the doubt of his own impotence, Shef might not have responded. Since then there had been Svandis. She had roused him, had proved to him that the fear and horror that had lain on him since the death of Queen Ragnhild were not of the body, only of the mind. She had shown it to him half a score of times since, his body was roused and full of repressed youth. Before he could so much as think of it, Shef's manhood had responded, was rising urgently. The woman felt it, seized it in her hands with a throaty chuckle of triumph, began to sink backwards. He could roll with her on to the stone, take his fill of her here in the dark, clasp her deep and spurt the seed into her here where the sun never came.

A test. Don't respond. The thought of the dark and the lost passages everywhere around bit cold into Shef's heart. The woman could not escape him now he had hands on her, but once he was done, what then? She would slide into the darkness like the snake, and he would be left, alone and a failure. While the testers, whoever they were, watched and mocked.

Shef straightened, gently pulled the woman's hand from him. She came back, pressing herself to him and moaning with passion. She was lying. Her moans were pretense. He unwound the arms from his body, pushed her to arm's length. As she twisted he turned her round, slapped her sharply low down, pushed her away.

He heard her bare feet on the stone for a pace or two. And then, almost dazzling to eyes long groping in the black, a candle-flame. She had lifted a hood from a candle, and for an instant he saw her, naked, squat and middle-aged, vanishing into a cleft in the rock.

Shef turned back in the direction he had been going, and this time, leapt instantly two yards backwards.

A corpse-face had looked into his from no more than a foot away, yellow, rotten, its teeth bared, the eyeballs sunk to mere shreds of leather.

It was hanging from the roof, with half a dozen more. He had been meant to see them at the same moment as the woman vanished, Shef realized. But the closest was on his blind eye, he had not seen it till he turned. Maybe he had been spared the first shock. And now the shock was over: it was a test. Don't respond. At least he now had light to see. Shef walked over and picked up the candle before doing anything else.

The corpses. He did not think these would be their own folk, used in a trial. They buried their dead in stone up here, so he had been told. Every village had its secret sarcophagi somewhere, as every English village had its churchyard and every Norse one its barrows and burning-grounds. No, they did not look like villagers. One there had the face of a Moor, another still on him the leather, but not the mail, of a Frankish lancer. Wayfarers, maybe tax-collectors, ambushed in the mountains and kept here for use. The bodies swung on their ropes like the smoked corpses in the house of Echegorgun the troll. But these were dry, dry as tinder, mummified in the dry cold of the high mountain caves. Shef took a piece of cloth between his fingers, felt it crumble. Yes, dry as tinder. He could not bury these folk. But whoever they were, they did not deserve to hang here for ever. He could give them a sort of burial.

Stepping on from one corpse to another, Shef held the candle at the rags of clothing, watched them catch and flare, begin to work on the dry withered flesh beneath. As he walked forward a red glow filled the cave, showed him its full extent to either side, more paintings on the walls.

In front of him another rock face, but no more than eight feet high. Propped against it as if in invitation, a pole-ladder, for all the world like the one he carried on his own breast.

Nothing surprising there, he thought as he walked towards it. A true ladder, with two supports and rungs between it, that is work for a carpenter, fitting rung to drilled hole. But anyone can make a pole ladder, whether in the North or the South, the mountains or the fens. Take a tree, a fir-tree for choice. Take its trunk and trim off the branches, leaving only those which grow at either side, alternately, first one for the right foot then one for the left. It takes balance to walk up it, but no skill in the making. Once upon a time all ladders must have been like that. Like the stone tools we have grown out of.

Shef walked to the foot of the ladder, began deliberately to climb it as the corpses flared and blazed behind him.

CHAPTER SIXTEEN

The man who faced Shef at the top of the ladder, youngest of the *perfecti,* hesitated as he saw the head of the barbarian king reach the level of the rock floor on which he stood and then continue mounting, rung by rung. He knew what he was supposed to do, had seen it done a dozen times before. If the candidate for election entered the Womb, passed the trials of the Serpent, the Woman, and Death, and climbed the *graduale* out of the Pit, then he should be met by the most junior of the Council, the one who had passed the trial himself most recently. And the junior should put a drawn sword to his breast and ask him the ritual question: How may an old man be born again? And enter again into the womb of his mother?

But it was supposed to happen in the dark! The candidate should have only the tiny candle-flame, symbol of the secret knowledge, and should see nothing till the sword was at his heart! It was only ritual by that stage, for every candidate, whether he was prepared or not for the trials, knew the question and the answer. But they were not supposed to see the tester or his sword till they were face to face.

In the lurid glow of the dry and burning corpses, Shef could see the man facing him perfectly clearly, could see the needle-pointed sword in his hand, could see too that he had no intention of using it. Behind the man at the front of the rock ledge sat a dozen more men in gray cowls, in a ring facing him. They too were supposed to be invisible until they spoke. As they realized they could be seen, the cowls looked this way and that, men shifted position, broke out in undignified whispers. To the tester and his comrades behind him Shef himself, rising out of the Pit with every stride, looked larger and larger, his shadow reaching out in front of him with a menace in it, as if the men murdered to outfit the trial chamber had sent a representative to take their revenge. The gold circlet on Shef's head and the gold bracelets on his biceps caught the red glow and sent angry glints across the secret chamber.

"Why did you do that?" hissed the tester. "I mean . . ." the test had already gone wrong. He stretched the sword forward, found his wrist grasped easily by a man far his superior in strength.

"Try again," said Shef.

"How may a man be born again? And enter again into the womb of his mother?"

The question of his dream, Shef thought. He had not known the answer then. But he had just undergone a test, and passed it. The answer to this must have something to do with the form of the test. Something Christian, or half-Christian at least. How would Father Andreas have answered? Thoughtfully, using the Arabic in which he had been addressed, the common speech of the border, Shef replied, "Cast aside fear. And lust. And the fear of death. And so climb out of the grave."

"That is not the answer! Not in the true words."

"It's near enough," said Shef. The wrist he was holding was thin, that of a hunter or a shepherd, or even a priest, not a plowman. With a sudden exertion of his smithy-hardened muscles he bent it backwards, heard a gasp of pain, and the sword ring on the stone floor. He released the wrist, stopped and picked the sword up. Slight curve, one edge, needle-point. A back-stabber's weapon. Holding it in his right hand he stepped towards the seated half-circle, stood looking grimly down at them.

"Why did you set the—the men on fire?" asked the cowl in the center.

"Because they were men. Like you and me. I do not mind killing people, but I will not have them mocked in death. Among the men of the North burning is as good as burial.

"Now. You brought me here by stealing my woman. You gave me a test and I have passed it. You must have something to say to me. Say it. I expect there is an easier way out of here than the way I came. Say your piece and then let us all go home. And for the love of all the gods, light some candles! I have no wish to speak in darkness or by the flames of a funeral pyre."

The leader of the *perfecti* hesitated, aware that the initiative had gone from him. Yet that might be good. It showed at least that this man, this king, was no common man. It might be, might well be, that he was the one they sought. To gain a moment's time he pulled his cowl back, raised a hand, waved for the lamps to be brought out of their hiding-places in the stone and lit.

"What is it that you wear round your neck?" he asked.

"It is a ladder, which I am told you call a *graduale*. It was the Emperor of

Rome himself who told me that. Many years ago and many miles away. Sitting on a green hill, outside a city wall."

The *perfectus* licked his lips nervously. The conversation was getting away from him already. "It is the Holy Graduale," he insisted, "which we in our tongue call the *Seint Graal*. But before I tell you why it is that, you must swear to tell no one what is said here in this chamber. You must swear to be one of us. For if what I have to tell you were to come to the wrong ears, there would be in it . . ." He paused. "The death of Christianity.

"You must swear to silence! What will you swear by?"

Shef considered a moment. These people seemed to have no clear idea of how to deal with him. The death of Christianity—that was nothing to him. They should have understood that. Yet he did not believe in swearing false oaths. It might bring bad luck.

"I will swear by this," he said, laying his hand on his pendant. His father-in-heaven, or in his own mind, whichever it might be, would not worry about a false oath, or an oath honored only to the letter. "I swear by my own emblem and by your holy *graduale* to reveal nothing of what I am told in this chamber."

Tension began to drain out of the seated men, out of the one face he could now see: an elderly man with a face of shrewd cunning, the face of a successful trader among peasants.

"Good. The story has come to us that you gave the Emperor the Holy Lance he bears. You must know, then, why it is the Holy Lance. It was the weapon of the centurion who stabbed Our Lord on the Cross."

Shef nodded.

"Why should there be a ladder to go with a lance? I will tell you. After the centurion stabbed Our Lord, and the blood and water gushed over his hands, pious men prayed the Romans for Our Lord's body. They were Joseph of Arimathea and his cousin, Nicodemus."

At the last name all the seated men moved together, making a zig-zag sign across their bodies.

"They took the body down from the cross. And, of course, they used a ladder. That ladder is the *graduale*. They lashed the body to the ladder to carry it to the stone grave that Joseph had reserved for the man he accepted as a prophet.

"Now, king, I must ask you this. They tell me you were baptized, brought up as a follower of Christ. So, tell me this: what is it that the Christians offer to those who believe?"

Shef considered. This did not have the ring of ritual, seemed an honest question. He did not know the answer. As far as he remembered Father Andreas had said that Christians should be Christians or go to Hell with the heathen. Hell? Or heaven? Perhaps that was the answer.

"They offer life," he said. "Eternal life."

"And how can they offer it? How dare they offer it? They offer it because, they say, Christ Himself rose from the grave. But I can tell you. He did not rise from the grave of Joseph. Because he did not die on the cross! He lived."

The *perfectus* sank back on his chair, to see the effect of his words. Not what he expected. Shef shook his head emphatically.

"A German centurion stabbed him. He called himself Longinus. Stabbed him with an infantry issue javelin, a *pilum*. I have held the weapon, I saw the blow."

"The blow was struck. It went astray." The *perfectus* considered the strange certainty of the man who faced him, went on, "It may be that crucified men, men kept upright with their arms above their heads, that they stand oddly, their hearts shift. It is strange that water ran out of the wound. Maybe Longinus pierced some other vessel. But when Joseph and Nicodemus went after the Passover to the tomb they had made, to embalm the body: they found the Christ alive. Still wrapped in his shroud."

It was Shef's turn to think, to recognize a kind of truth. Ten nights before he had dreamed another dream, of the man waking from the dead with his arms bound to his sides and pain in his heart, a dream of horror. But it could have happened. He had known men to recover on the battlefield as their comrades prepared to throw them in the pit, it had happened to Brand himself. And Brand too had recovered from a deep belly wound. It did not happen often, but it could.

"What happened then?"

"They told a trusted few the truth. But soon the story spread that they find in the Gospels, that the tomb was empty, that an angel had appeared. That Christ had gone down to Hell to rescue the patriarchs and the prophets. The Christians say that story came from Nicodemus, for he was known to have had speech with Christ after his taking down from the cross. They read that story to this day in their false gospel of Nicodemus. But it is not true.

"The Christ did not die. Nor did he go back to his followers. They nursed him back to life, Joseph and Nicodemus and the woman they call Mary Magdalene. Then, secretly, Nicodemus the rich sold his goods, as did Joseph of Arimathea, and they and Jesus and Mary came here to this country. They left Palestine to the Jews and the Romans to fight over and came to the other end of the Inner Sea, but still within the old *imperium* of the Romans.

"Here they lived. Here they died. Here they bore their children, Jesus's children by Mary. And their seed is not yet dead. For we here, the people of the mountains, we can trace our blood back to him. And that is why we are the Sons of God!"

His voice rose in triumph on the last words, and the men sitting round him echoed them.

Yes, Shef thought. That is a tale the Christians would not like told. There is a great gap in it, for if the Jesus they claim descent from was merely another mortal, why should they call themselves the Sons of God, or believe in him? They have good reason not to. But they will have an explanation for that, just like Thorvin or Farman. Believers always do.

"What then do you want from me?" he asked quietly.

"The *Graal*. We kept it. It is in the deepest depths of Puigpunyent. But the Emperor knows it is there, has men digging for it every day. Soon, we fear, he will find it, and our holy treasures and testaments with it. And he will destroy them utterly, and the proof of our knowledge with them. We have to get them out. The Grail and the writings. Or drive the Emperor away. You— you came into our country with our holy sign around your neck, you passed the tests of our mystery without aid or prompting, some of us say that you are the holy Nicodemus risen again! We ask you to aid us."

Shef scratched his beard. It was an interesting story. More interesting would be the way out. He was still in the power of these fanatics. "I am no Nicodemus," he said. "But tell me. If I can do what you ask—and I see no way to—then what can you do for me? Your beliefs are not my beliefs, and your fear is not my fear. What is the price? And you must know that I am already a rich man."

"Rich in gold. They tell us though that you search continually for knowledge, that you and your men try continually to fly, to do what has never been done before. They tell us that you search for the secret of the Greek fire."

Shef straightened, his interest immediately caught.

"You know the secret of the Greek fire?"

"No. That is something we cannot claim. We believe that no one knows that save some few of the Greeks, and even they, it may be, only one small piece each. But we know something of fire, and what we know we will tell you. If you rescue for us our holy relics."

The red fires behind them had burned themselves out, the room was now lit only by the clear light of half a score of lamps, like any other room in which men might do business, apart from the stone walls all around.

"I will do what I can," said Shef.

The Emperor of the Romans was learning what so many harassed leaders have learnt throughout history: that the number of helpers in a large and difficult task increases the number of problems, unless those helpers are so disciplined that they never act for themselves or for their own interest. Those who knew him noticed the whitening knuckles and the tension in his neck. Those who did not noticed only his quiet voice and the care with which he appeared to listen.

The baron of Béziers was at odds, it seemed, with the bishop of Besançon. Both contingents were about the same size, a hundred men or six score, and both were rated as middling in loyalty and care. They were not locals, and so would contain no secret heretics in their ranks, but they were not men of Bruno's own blood either. Both contingents had been sent to the middle ring of the three that Bruno had drawn round Puigpunyent, there to patrol the near-impassable scrub in the days and spend their nights sweltering in the heat that baked up from the scorched ground. They were arguing about water, as was everyone in the army. The baron thought the bishop's men were calling off their patrols early in order to get there first with their horses and mules, and leave his men only foul water to drink. Not that there was any water for ten miles round that was not fouled by now.

And all the time, Bruno knew, his diggers and pick-axe men pressed closer and closer to the secret. Only this day they had opened up a secret passage within the stone wall they were demolishing, one that led from a hidden garderobe in the walls down to the very foundations of the castle, to emerge in the depth of a ravine—an escape-route when the castle might seem to be surrounded. Bruno was confident no one had taken it. If they had, the garrison would not have needed to fight to the last. But where there was one hidden way, there would be another. From time to time a great crash cut across the noise of the giant encampment, as another stone was lifted from its bed by a hundred men with a sheer-legs, and hurled into the choked gullies far below. Bruno's head hurt, and the sweat crawled down his neck, and he yearned furiously inside to return to the demolition, spur on the teams and gangs. Instead he had to listen to two fools arguing in a language he could barely follow.

The baron jumped to his feet suddenly, cursing in his own dialect. The bishop shrugged elaborately, affected to misunderstand the gesture, took it as a request to leave. Yawning, he stretched his hand across the table, the episcopal ring glinting upon his finger: kiss my ring and depart, he pantomimed.

The baron, furious, slapped the hand aside. The bishop, sprung like the baron from ten generations of warriors, leapt to his feet in his turn, hand groping for the weapon he did not carry. In an instant the baron had his own dagger out, the long *misericorde* designed for stabbing through armor-joint or eye-hole.

Far quicker than the baron, quicker than the eye could see, the Emperor's own hand shot out, seized the baron's wrist. The ape-like shoulders moved beneath the patched leather jacket the Emperor still wore, a twist, a snap of bone, and the baron was huddled against the flap of the tent. The guards drew their broadswords as a matter of form, but barely changed position. They knew from many battles and skirmishes that the

Emperor needed no protection. He was more dangerous with his bare hands than a skilled knight in full armor. Tasso the Bavarian raised an eyebrow inquiringly.

"Take him out," said the Emperor briefly. "He drew a weapon in the presence of his Emperor. Let him see a priest and hang him. Tell the Count of his county to recommend to me on the succession to Béziers. Send his men home."

He reflected a moment longer. "They will be rebellious. Take ten of them, cut off left hand and right foot, tell them it is the Emperor's mercy. You, your grace," he added to the bishop. "You provoked him. I fine you a year's income of your see. Till it is paid you have our permission to undergo the discipline which your hot blood needs. Ten strokes a day with a choirmaster's scourge. My chaplain will see to it."

He stared across the table at the whitening face, the face which after a very brief interval decided not to provoke the Emperor a moment further. The baron vanished, on his way to the already loaded gibbets on the edge of the camp. The bishop backed out, bowing and wondering how rapidly he could possibly raise a thousand solidi in gold.

"What's that noise?" asked the Emperor.

Tasso the *Lanzenbruder* looked carefully out across the lines of tents and pavilions.

"Agilulf," he replied. "Come at last."

The Emperor's face broke into its unexpected charming smile. "Agilulf! He took his time getting here. But that means a thousand men, good Germans with *Lanzenorden* officers to control them. We can pull out those rascals we have guarding the west face and put some reliable fellows in in their place. And I dare say Agilulf can find a couple of dozen good men with ropes' ends to keep those lazy devils on the rocks working. Ha, they have had a nice holiday by the sea, they will be ready for some real work."

Tasso nodded. The Emperor seemed to have cheered up, his moods swung a good deal these days. If the idiots in the tent had watched him carefully they would have seen it was no time to provoke him. Now, there might be a chance.

"Those men, you told me to cut their hands and feet off," he ventured. "Ten, did you say? Or five? Hands *and* feet, was it?"

The Emperor's smile vanished, he was across the tent before Tasso could blink or think of protecting himself. Not that he would have tried.

"I know what you're up to, Tasso," he said, looking up from his little more than average height to the eyes of his strapping captain. "You think I'm getting too tough with these bastards. Well, I'm getting tough because things are getting tough. There is no room for failure any more. Not with the devil loose. Not with the devil loose."

"Is the devil loose?" broke in another voice, the harsh and hostile one of

Erkenbert the deacon, reporting to his master from the ground where he labored continually at perfecting his siege catapults. "When that happens we can expect signs and wonders in the sky."

In the Caliph's camp too, the bodyguards were uneasy. Every dusk, as the army camped, the impaling-posts were set up, every night was made hideous by the shrieks of men who felt the spike driving up through their bowels, as they fought to keep their footing on the iron ring that held them from death. A brave man, it was said, could sink down and let the spike tear out his bowels and his liver from inside. It was a long way from rectum to heart, though: too long for any normal courage. The Caliph was in a black mood, perturbed by the continuous defeats to which the followers of the Prophet were little used. His navies burned, or fled, his armies were trampled underfoot, or hesitated, came on slowly and reluctantly as now. There would be more screams and deaths unless good news came soon. Maybe even among the bodyguards. As they spread out the leather carpet and poised their scimitars, they prayed for distraction.

The captain of the cavalry patrols approaching, dust matting his clothes. A young man dragged behind him by the wrists, struggling to get to his feet and shrieking imprecations. The bodyguards eyed each other with relief, waved the cavalryman through. A sacrifice for this evening already. Perhaps it would ease the master's mood.

Mu'atiyah did not notice the Caliph's baleful stare as he recovered his footing and angrily straightened his torn clothes.

"You are the pupil of bin-Firnas," he said slowly. "We sent you to escort and guide the *ferengis* of the North, the fleet with its strange machines that was to sink the red galleys of the Greeks. They did not sink the galleys, but fled, or so the survivors told me before they were led to execution. What story is it that *you* have to tell me?"

"Treachery," hissed Mu'atiyah. "My story is of treachery."

No word could better have suited the Caliph's mood. He settled back on his cushions as Mu'atiyah, fury chafed by days of silence and contempt at sea, days of idleness and imprisonment among the Jews, told his tale: the Northerners' abandonment of the Arab cause, their cowardly reluctance to close with the Greeks, their ignorant sporting with the secrets of the wise. Most of all, the betrayal of the Prophet and his servants by the treacherous Jews, protected against the Christians by the favor of the Caliph, repaying it only by making common cause with pork-eaters and wine-drinkers. Mu'atiyah's sincerity was patent. Unlike anyone the Caliph had heard speak for weeks, he gave not a thought to his own safety. His urge was only, so much was evident, to fall upon the enemies of the Shatt al-Islam and exterminate them. Again and again his words veered towards criticism of the Caliph: he had been too lenient, he had let his secret enemies gain courage from his forbearance. It was criticism the Caliph was prepared to hear. The words of an honest man.

"When did you last drink?" he said finally.

Mu'atiyah goggled, became aware through his rage of his own thirst. "Before noon," he said huskily. "I rode through the heat of the day."

The Caliph waved a hand. "Bring sherbet for this faithful one. And let others mark his zeal. When he has drunk, let his mouth be filled with gold and a dress of honor prepared. And now, send for my generals and my admirals and the keepers of my maps. Let all be prepared to turn our march against the Jews. First the Jews, then the Christians. The enemy within the gate and then the enemy without."

Marking the Caliph's good humor, those who held prisoners to be brought in and condemned to lighten the master's mood silently withdrew them. They would do, after all, for another day.

CHAPTER SEVENTEEN

The group on the deck of the *Fafnisbane* stared at Solomon with expressions ranging from doubt to horror.

"Tell us again," said Brand. "He wants us to dismantle the kite, take it and enough material for two more up into the hills, with a mile of rope, Tolman, and two more boys?"

Solomon bowed his head in agreement. "Such are the instructions of your master."

The eyes shifted to Steffi, standing a pace behind with an air of deep embarrassment. He shuffled his feet, unable to meet the concentrated gaze of his superiors with more than one eye at once. "That's what he said," he muttered in confirmation. "Enough for three kites and a guard, load 'em on mules, get it all up in the hills as fast as you can, only faster. That's what he said, right enough."

There was no doubt about Steffi's loyalty, though there might be about his sense. At least these orders were not a trap. The eyes switched to each other, looked back in the end to Solomon.

"We don't doubt that's what he said," offered Thorvin, "but things have happened here while he's been away. Things he doesn't know about."

Solomon bowed again. "Well I know it. After all, my own master has given orders that all our outlying people, our traders and our farmers on the hillsides, are to come in to the city at once, for safety. We have known for weeks that the Emperor of the Romans is too close for comfort, though he seemed completely occupied with his army across the border. But now the Caliph is barely two days' march away—less for a fast rider. And the Arabs can move fast when they are so inclined, however slow the Caliph himself may be. We could have light cavalry at our gates in the morning. They may be in the hills already."

"Light cavalry be buggered," commented Hagbarth. "What frightened me was those red galleys. Just turned up, no warning. Like the Ragnarssons used to do. There we were, flying the kites off, half a dozen ships out there, and they came out of the haze as if they'd planned it. Not even hurrying, just paddling along at twelve strokes a minute. Nearly cut us all off from the harbor just the same. If Tolman hadn't seen them first we could all have been fried."

"If we hadn't had to wind Tolman in and recover him we could have got out to the open sea and let them go by," grunted Brand, continuing a long argument.

"Either way. They came up to the harbor just after we got inside, had a look in, burned off a fishing boat that hadn't seen them—just deviltry that was, to show us they could do it, and kept on paddling north. But they aren't far away. Could be here before nightfall."

"We think it would be wiser," Thorvin concluded, speaking for all of them, "if the king returned here and made preparations for departure."

Solomon spread his arms wide. "I have given you his instructions. He is—or so you say—your king. I do not debate with my prince once he has said his word. Perhaps you Northerners are different."

A long silence. Brand broke it. "Will your prince let us leave the city?"

"He will let you leave the city. You are not under his protection. He will let me guide you. I am out of favor now. I spoke my mind concerning the release of the young Arab, and he is prepared to lose me. None of his other people may go."

"All right," said Brand. "We'll have to do it. Thorvin, hand over some silver to Solomon so he can buy the mules, Steffi, start getting the stuff together and work out how many mules you'll need. Pick the kite crews."

"Will you come with us, lord?" asked Steffi.

"No. I'm not very good at fast moving, and something tells me you're going to come down that mountain a great deal faster than you went up. If you're lucky. I'm going to stay here and think about how to guard this harbor. Against anything, flame included."

Miles further up the mountain, Shef was repeating an experiment, in his usual painstaking and skeptical way. He was familiar enough with the white residue that the head of the *perfecti* had shown him. So was anyone who had ever mucked out a cowshed or a pig-sty. A white earth, that condensed from the animals' urine, or so they said.

What Shef had not seen before was the crystalline form derived from it. How had they come upon that?, he had asked. The answer made a kind of sense. In English conditions, where earth was wet most of the time and earth from an animal-shed even more so, lighting a fire on the white earth was unlikely ever to happen. Here, in the cold, dry air of the mountain winter, where beasts were often stalled indoors, it was a natural event. Once the mountaineers had realized that the white earth made a blaze, someone, somewhere had put that knowledge together with the knowledge of the Arabs, familiar already with *al-kimi, al-kuhl, al-qili,* and other strange concepts. Now they knew that water trickled over the white earth from the animal sheds, the wood-ash from the fires, and the lime crushed from limestone, could be boiled to give these crystals.

Sal Petri, they called it, the salt of Saint Peter. Or did they mean rock-salt? Shef neither knew nor cared. He had realized soon enough that the Peter-salt could not be the secret of the Greek fire. But it was interesting just the same, as were the other ingredients that the Children of God had shown him. New knowledge once again.

He had built a pile of kindling, a sequence of piles, and poured the crystals over each one. Then to each he had made a separate addition from the materials the graybeard *perfectus* Anselm had given him. In normal life, each one would have to be lit painstakingly from kindling and blown into life with the care that children learnt from their parents. Some people could light fires, some people couldn't, so ran the folk wisdom: the former group were bound for Hell, where the devil would commandeer them. But these fires were not normal.

Shef whirled the half-rotted stick a few times round his head to make the punk glow brightly, leant forward and tossed the fire-brand a few feet on to the first pile of twigs. A soft 'whump,' a bright glare, and the fire was collapsing immediately into fierce embers.

He took another stick, stepped sideways three paces, repeated the process. This time the 'whump' was followed by an instant livid green. "Copper filings for green," he muttered to himself. "Now, what makes the yellow one?"

"We call it orpiment, the golden color," said Anselm at his side, the graybeard leader of the *perfecti.* "Though the Greeks give it some other name. Much of this our men learned from Greek traders. That is what made us think that it might be the secret of the Greek fire. Though the Arabs make colored flames like this too, when they light fires to honor their leaders and their Prophet. They have much learning in what they call *al-kimi.* The lore of burnings and distillations."

"It is not the Greek fire," replied Shef absently, working his way down the line of piles, and muttering a color and a substance for each one. "There is nothing pretty about that."

"But you will not go back on your word to help us?"

"I will not go back on my word to try. But you have set me a hard task."

"Our men saw you flying strange machines. We thought you might swoop down on Puigpunyent like an eagle and carry off our relics through the air.''

Shef lobbed the last torch, noted the result, turned and grinned down at the smaller, older man.

"Maybe one day we will know how to do that. But to land on a mountain? Not the kindly sea? And fly away again without the lines and the crew and the wind to lift you? Carrying Othin knows what as well as the boy? No, that would take the skill of Wayland the smith of the gods.''

"So what will you do instead?''

"That will take a great deal of work from all of us. From you, and from my men, once they come. Show me again, draw the map in the dirt, where the Christians' camp is and how they have their guard posts.''

Anselm whistled shrilly, and the shepherd boy who had been playing on his flute of oaten straw rushed over.

The next day, with the sun already beginning to sink, Shef called the whole of his party together—heretics, Northerners, and the kite-gangs brought hastily up by Solomon—and went over once again all the pieces of his plan.

The thirty men and three boys were on a grassy ledge on the last mountain slope looking out over the plains, the rock of Puigpunyent clearly visible, even without the far-seers. In the strong sun anyone could see, also, that the plain down there was alive with men: parties of riders moving one way and another, flashes of sunlight on weapons and armor from every gap in the scrub. It had been an uneasy ride to reach this place, with repeated halts and diversions: Anselm had turned out every man he could to act as a screen of scouts and spies. They were in their own country and close to their most secret fastnesses. Even so, reports had come back every few minutes of Christian riders out in the night, forcing Shef and Anselm and their men to fade from the paths into the rocks or the thorn scrub, till another soft call or whistle would lead them on again. They were safe enough where they were, or so Anselm thought. The ledge could be reached by only two paths, and both were by now heavily guarded. Just the same, it would be bad to attract attention. As he peered out all afternoon over the landscape, Shef had been careful to keep well back, to lie deep in the shadow of a bush.

He spoke, first, to the men of his own party, the snatchers as he thought of them. There were only seven including himself. The shepherd lad, whom Shef had privately dubbed 'Straw,' from his endless thin piping: he was to be the guide. Four young men chosen for their agility and speed: they were to be the carriers of the holy things. Richier, youngest of the *perfecti*. Shef had eyed him askance when Anselm had brought him forward. He was the man who had challenged Shef as he climbed out of the pit, and Shef had no high opinion of his presence of mind or even his courage. Nor was he even much of a lightweight like the others. Youngest of the *perfecti* he might be, but he was at least forty, an old man by the measure of the mountains or for that matter of the fens, not one who ranged the hills all day or eeled through the brush in pursuit of game. Yet Anselm had said it must be so. Only the *perfecti* knew the way into their innermost sanctum. No, another could not be told how to find it. Apart from the breach of their strongest rules of secrecy, the way in was not something that could be described. Only shown. So a *perfectus* must go with the company, and Richier it would have to be.

Finally, Shef himself. Shef had seen Straw looking at him with much the same expression that he used when he looked at Richier, and he knew why. Among the lightly-built people of the hills, Shef stood out like Styrr among ordinary folk. He was head and shoulders taller than any other man in the company, Richier included. He outweighed Richier by fifty pounds and every other man or boy by seventy at least. Could he keep up when it came to speed? Could he creep undetected below the cover? Straw obviously thought not. Shef himself was more confident. It was not so many years since he and Hund had stalked the wild pigs together in the marsh, or snaked on their bellies to take fish from some thane's private pond. He had grown bigger and stronger since then, but little of the weight, he knew, was fat. If anyone could elude the scouts and sentries, he could.

He had no fear, indeed, of being seen and killed in the night. He had a good chance, and death, if it came, would come cleanly, not as it had come to Sumarrfugl.

What did set a weight in his bowels and a chill at his heart was the thought of capture. For capture meant facing the Emperor. Shef had seen him close, drunk with him, felt no fear even when he stood with Bruno's sword-point at his throat. Something told him now, though, that if they met again the genial side of his old comrade would be gone, replaced by the fanatic. He would not spare a heathen and a rival a second time.

Shef looked round the small inner circle of seven. "Very well. We will start our ride as soon as I have finished speaking to the others. We work down into the plain behind our scouts, and at dusk we start to ride round in a wide circle. To come out on the other side of the rock, of Puigpunyent, to the north-west. Then we leave our horses and follow Straw here through the Emperor's guard-ring.

"You know that is asking a lot. But I promise you this. The Emperor's guards will all be looking at quite something else. If they are still there."

A mutter of assent, if not belief.

"Stand aside then and be ready to go."

Shef turned to the larger group standing further back, by their machines. Cwicca and his gang had brought light winches with them, mere cylinders of wood with a turning handle, and had spent a long hour slowly pegging them into the stony ground without noise of hammers. By each winch stood half a dozen of the ships' catapulteers now turned kitemen, with by them the bulkier figures of the Vikings sent along to act as close-quarter guards.

In front of each of the three groups stood a kiteboy, Tolman in the middle, to either side Ubba and—Helmi, that was his name, a small pale boy little more than a child. A cousin of some crew-member's, left orphaned and homeless by the wars. All three boys looked unusually serious and alert.

"You know what to do as well. Stay here, rest, light no fires. At midnight, Cwicca, you can read the stars, fly off the kites. There will be a wind coming down from the mountains behind, or so they tell us.

"Then you, boys. When you are at the end of your ropes and flying smoothly, bring out your fires. Light each of your baskets in turn and then drop them. Make sure the cloths are unfolded before you start lighting. Drop them one at a time, counting one hundred between each. Count slowly.

"Steffi, you count the baskets as they are lit. Once you have seen them all dropped, haul the boys in. Don't stop to unpeg the winches, just leave everything and follow Messer Anselm wherever he says to go. In the morning we meet up and all head back to the ships. Any questions?"

There were none. Shef moved over once more and looked carefully at the gear they had spent the day assembling. The basic idea was to put together Steffi's invention of the fall-delaying cloth with the thing that the heretics had shown him, the colored fires of the saltpeter and the Arab alchemy. Bundles of dry twigs, impregnated with saltpeter and sealed roughly with wax. A cloth tied by four corners to each one, each of them hanging from bent nails in the canework frames of the kites. Each cloth had a small hole in its center now: Steffi, experimenting continually, had discovered this prevented the trapped air from spilling sideways, gave a smoother and even a slower fall. The most difficult bit had been giving the boys fires to carry. There could be no striking tinder and steel in mid-air. In the end they had borrowed a sailor's trick from the Vikings, who made long crossings in their undecked boats and could not always find dry tinder: tarred rope, lit and set to smolder inside a stiff canvas case.

The idea was good. Shef realized, as he looked at the flame-baskets, at the flimsy construction of the kites, quite how much was being expected of three twelve-year-olds, bobbing at the end of ropes high in the air above unyielding mountain-side. No need to remind them of the reward. Boys did not think far enough ahead to value money. They would do this for the praise and admiration of the men. Maybe, a little, out of respect for him. He nodded at them all, patted Helmi gently on the shoulder, and turned away.

"Time to move," he said to his own party. As they filed away the English catapulteers and Viking guards looked after him with silent concern. Cwicca, at least, had seen this happen before, the One King going by himself to some uncertain fate. He had hoped not to see it happen again. From the place where she sat alone, arms wrapped round knees, Svandis too watched the retreating file. She could not go out, throw her arms round him, weep like a woman: her dignity forbade it. But she had seen many men go, few come back.

Hours later, as the sun finally crawled down to touch the flat horizon, the boy Straw led the seven horsemen into the rare shade of a clump of low and twisted trees. He whistled softly, and at the call figures appeared from the shadows to clutch bridles. Shef slowly levered himself off the horse's back and climbed stiffly to the ground, thigh muscles twinging and cramping.

It had been a hellish ride. At the very start Shef had been shocked to find not the tiny mountain ponies they had been using to come down from the heretics' stronghold, but bigger animals, and not with the usual blanket slung over them but strange high-pommeled leather saddles, with iron stirrups dangling either side. "Bruno's *baccalarii*," Richier explained briefly. "Cowboys from the country to the East. They are all over the place. Some of them rode too far and too few. From a distance, with these horses and this gear, we will seem just like some more of them. No-one asks where they go. They ride wherever they please."

Shef had clambered into the high saddle, appreciating immediately the help and support it gave even an inexperienced rider. Then he had realized that like the others he was meant to carry in his right hand the long ten-foot ox-goad that every cowboy brandished, control the beast with left hand on reins alone. As he kicked his heels and tried to force his unaccustomed seaman's legs to clamp the horse's barrel, they moved out into the sun and the dust.

No-one had challenged them, indeed. As they rode across the broken foothills and into the plain beyond, they had seen again and again other mounted men in the distance, but often, on every path or road, groups of infantry watching the crossings. Straw and his fellows waved their lances at the horsemen, but took care not to ride to meet or cross them, veering away when they could. To the groups of foot-soldiers they called out in what was evidently some imitation of the language of the Camargue, the cowboys' country, but kept riding, not waiting to engage in gossip. Shef was surprised that no-one acted, moved across to block their path, but it looked as if everyone expected the irregular riders to go where they liked, without orders or plan. Surely someone would notice the inept riding of Shef and Richier, at least, see that there were men there too old or too big for a cowboy patrol. But even the shouts that came towards them seemed good-natured or simply derisive. The Emperor had made a mistake, Shef concluded. He had put too many men out on watch, and too few of them knew each other. They were used to seeing strangers riding towards, or round, Puigpunyent. If the Emperor had ordered a complete ban on movement, patrolled by a few selected outfits, strangers would have been challenged instantly.

The break in the copse of twisted trees did not last long enough. Time to take the skins of heavily-watered wine and drain down first one quart and then another, drinking till the demand in the throat was gone, and then drinking steadily on, a gulp at a time, till the sweat began to break out again and the body felt it could hold no more. Then Straw was counting them in the deep shade and arranging them in the order he wanted: himself in the lead, another stripling in the rear, Richier next to last and Shef just before him. The other three heretic youths followed Straw, one directly behind him and the other two a little to left and right. A last mutter between the youths and a soft exchange of signal whistles. Then Straw led them into the depth of the tangled and ground-cloaking scrub. The *maquis* of Occitania.

Very soon Shef began to wonder if they would ever reach their goal. The idea had always been clear enough. The thorn-bushes were a total obstacle to movement on foot or on horseback, as long as one kept upright. But the thorns started their sideways growth a foot or two off the ground. Beneath them there was always a clear space, enough for an active man or boy to creep through, completely hidden from any sentry, as long as one could keep any sense of direction.

The trouble was the creeping. Straw and his mates, light and young, could wriggle forward at an immense pace, keeping their bodies off the ground and pushing forward on hands and toes. Shef managed the same movement for no more than a hundred yards. Then his overtasked arm-muscles gave out and he began instead to crawl, belly on the ground, pulling himself forward like a clumsy swimmer. Behind him grunts and gasps indicated that Richier was doing the same. In seconds the boy ahead of him had vanished, eeling along at three times Shef's speed. He ignored the disappearance and crawled on. Whistles from behind and then from in front, sounding like the calls of some night-bird. A shape wriggling back towards him, muttering some kind of appeal for more speed. It vanished again. Straw appeared, gabbling likewise. Shef ignored them all and continued to crawl through the roots, weaving from side to side to get round the thickest clumps, thorns catching in his hair, sticking in his fingers, dragging at his clothes. A hiss and a scurry on the bare ground brought him up short, jerking his hand away. One of the vipers of the plain, but hearing him coming long before his hand reached it. Shef's mouth began to clog with dust, his knees to bleed through the chafed wool trousers.

Straw had caught him by the shoulder, was pulling him to one side—out into a break in the cover, a path, only inches wide, but leading round the side of a hill. Shef climbed slowly on to his feet, feeling the relief in protesting thigh-muscles, wiped the hair out of his eye and looked at Straw

with doubt and enquiry. On their feet? In the open? Better to crawl on than
be seen.

"Too slow," hissed Straw in trade-Arabic. "Friends gone ahead. If hear
whistle, off path! Hide again!"

Slowly but relievedly Shef began to pad in the direction indicated, rustles
in the brush indicating the scouts ahead. He spared a moment to glance at
the stars, shining clear in the cloudless sky. Not too long to midnight.

He had gone maybe half a mile along the goat track as it wound through
the small hills when the whistles came again from the hillside. Straw was at
his side, gripping an arm and trying to force him back into the brush. Shef
looked at the apparently solid wall of thorns, ducked and crawled under. Ten
feet in and hardly a glimmer of light finding its way through, though more
gasping and grunting told him that the exhausted *perfectus* was being hauled
into safety too. Straw was still pulling at him to get further in, but Shef
resisted. He was a veteran of many marches, many spells of sentry duty.
Unlike Straw he could estimate a risk. In this kind of country, with no
alarms and no immediate danger at hand, he did not think the Emperor's
patrols would be at full alert. They would not see an eye peering from thick
cover in the middle of a featureless hillside. Carefully he edged to his feet,
held on to the base of a branch, carefully let it sink a few inches to give him a
spyhole.

There they were indeed, not twenty feet away, edging along the narrow
awkward path, too busy avoiding thorns to look around them. Shef caught a
low grumble of conversation, an angry bark of command from the man in
the lead. The grumbling did not stop. Low-grade troops, Shef thought. Local
levies like his own county *fyrds*. Reluctant to take trouble, thoughts simply
on getting home. Easy to avoid, as long as one did not actually fall over them
in the dark. It was the silent men who did not move who were the danger.

Back to the path, another half-mile on, then into the scrub and once
more the steady crawling round some obstacle or sentry-post. Another
hundred yards on a goat-path, and crawl again. On and on. Shef lost sense of
direction, ceased fatalistically to glance at the sky and reckon the time. The
gasping of Richier diminished as he too seemed to settle to their uneven
rhythm of movement. And then suddenly, they were at a halt, all seven of
them in a clump, looking from the shadows across a patch of bare ground at
glimmering fires. Behind them the great jagged mass of the peak, the Castle
of the Graduale, Puigpunyent itself.

Straw pointed very gently at the fires. "Them," he breathed. "Last men.
Last ring. *Los alemanos.*"

Germans they were. Shef could see the iron glinting as they moved on
their beats, shields and mail, helmets and gauntlets. In any case he would
have recognised the bearing of the *Lanzenbrüder,* whom he had seen
swarming to the assault in the battle of the Braethraborg years before. Then

they had been on his side. Now . . . There was no chance of creeping past them. They had cut down the scrub to make a bare belt, woven the debris into a rough thorn fence. The sentries were not fifty yards apart, and they moved continually. They were watching, too, not like the discontented levies further out.

Suddenly, from the bulk of Puigpunyent, there came a great crash and a thunder of rock. Shef started, noticed the sentries looking too, then turning back to their duties. A cloud of dust rose barely visible against the black and Shef could hear faint shouting. The Emperor's gangs were working on through the night, in shifts, tearing down the whole mountainside with pick and lever and crane, to rip out the heart of the heretics' faith. To find the Emperor his relic.

Shef looked again at the sky, the position of the moon, still some way off full. It was midnight now. But it would take time, he knew, time to rig the kites and winch them out. Maybe they would have to wait for a wind, even up there on the mountain. Straw was pulling at him again, anxious and wanting an instant answer. He was only a boy. In war, everything took longer than you wanted, except when the other side did it. Shef looked round, motioned them all to the ground. If there was nothing else to do, rest. If his plan succeeded, he would know soon enough.

Stretched out underneath the bushes, Shef put his head down on his forearms, felt the weariness come over him. There was no risk where they were, and the boys would stay awake. He let his eyelids close, fell slowly into the pit of sleep.

"He's not just loose now, he's out," said the voice, the familiar voice, his father's voice. "Out in the open."

Even in his dream Shef felt a surge of resentment, disbelief. "You're not there," he told himself, himself talking to himself. "Svandis explained all that. You're just a part of my mind, the same way all the gods are part of people's minds."

"All right, all right," the voice went on with weary tolerance. "Believe what you like. Believe what your girlfriend likes. But believe this. He's out. I have no hold over him. Things could go any way now. Ragnarök—that's what Othin wants, what Loki wants. What they think they want."

"You don't want it?"

"I don't want what would come after it. Church all-powerful, Way all-powerful, whichever. There's a better way—back to where we were before, before Sheaf became Shield. Maybe with something added, something new."

"What's that?"

"You're going to see. You're going to show them. The priests have it inside their holy circle, but they see it only as a warning, not a blessing. Can be either."

Shef had lost the thread, could not follow the hints. "What are you talking about?"

"What Loki lost to. What you are bringing back for him. His namesake, his near namesake. Logi."

"Fire," Shef translated automatically.

"Fire it is. Wake and see what you are bringing to the world."

Shef's head snapped upright, his eyes instantly wide open. He realized that he had already been half-woken by a rising babble of voices, from the ring of sentries in front of him. But all over the guarded plain were coming shouts and calls, the blast of a trumpet as some panicker decided to alert his men to what they had seen already. Fire drifting down out of the sky.

After a few seconds Shef's eye and mind adjusted to what he was seeing. Immediately before him, a white flare drifting down, as brilliant as a sun, throwing flickering shadows over the thorn below. Above it, a green one. Not far away, Shef could see a third and a fourth beginning to drift down, thought for a second he could even see the tiny glow of the slow-match. But any such light was killed instantly by the lurid colors spreading across the sky. Violet, yellow, red. More and more flares seemed to spring into life every moment, though Shef knew that could not be so. It was just that each one took moments for the mind to recognise it. By the time it had been taken in, there were others in being to focus on. All three kites must be aloft and working. The boy-flyers were doing their duty better than he could have believed.

To the troops on the ground, local levies, bishops' men, half-heretics and *Lanzenbrüder* alike, every man deeply superstitious and steeped from birth in a culture of demons and miracles, dragons and portents, the flares in the sky were even harder to take in. Men do not see what they see. They see the nearest fit between what they see and what they expect. All across the plain beneath the rock of Puigpunyent, cries rose up as men tried to fit a meaning to something that defied all experience.

"A comet! The tailed star! God's judgment on those who overthrew the long-haired kings," wailed a chaplain, starting an instant panic.

"Dragons in the sky," shouted a *Lanzenritter* from the Drachenberg country, where belief in dragons was ingrained. "Shoot for its soft spot! Shoot before the damned things get on the ground!" A rain of arrows poured into the air from those who heard him, relieved at hearing an order of any kind. The arrows landed among the horses of a cavalry unit corralled two hundred yards off, starting a stampede.

"It is Judgment Day and the dead rising to meet their God in the sky," lamented a bishop with much on his conscience which he had hoped to do timely penance for. His cry would have carried little conviction, since the lights were falling rather than rising, if falling more slowly than could possibly be natural. But as he called out some sharp-sighted man caught the vague shape of one of the gliding kites banking above the light it had just released, and shrieked hysterically, "Wings! I can see their wings! They are the angels of the Lord come to scourge sinners!"

Within moments a roar spread across the plain, of ten thousand men shouting their explanations. The cowboys of the Camargue, lightest of cavalry, reacted first, were in their saddles in moments and heading purposefully for safety. Panicked sentries abandoned their positions in the brush and began to draw together, hoping for comfort in numbers. As they saw the infection spreading, the disciplined Germans of the *Lanzenorden,* scattered here and there to officer and stiffen the more doubtful Frankish troops, began to seize the runners, knock men down with their lance-butts, try to drive them back to their posts.

Spying from the cover of the thorns, Shef watched intently for an opportunity. One thing he had forgotten. While the men down there, the inner ring of the Emperor's guard, had certainly been distracted—they were clumped together now, abandoning their set watch-pattern, pointing into the sky—the flares themselves were making the whole landscape almost as bright as day. If he tried to move forward now, across the bare strip that the guards had made, they would certainly see him. If not as he moved forward, then in the seconds it would take to force a way through the barricade of cut-down trees. He needed cover to reach that point. Then the time to cut a way through, and to crawl a hundred yards through the masking scrub on the other side. Then they would be on the edge of one of the deep ravines that led up to the rock and the castle itself, the ravine that Richier said they must follow. In the deep dark of that they might be safe. But how to reach it?

There was something else in the sky now, not the steady light of the flares with their mixed colors. A flickering light, a red light. A red that was growing, beginning to put out the competing white and yellow and green. Not flares but fire. Shef realized that the flares had burnt all the way to the ground, landed in the dense, thick, tinder-dry scrub through which he had crawled. Set it instantly aflame. The shouts coming from all around now had an added edge of fear. All those who lived in this land knew the dangers of fire during the *grande chaleur,* the great heat of the southern summer. Their own villages lived protected by fire-breaks, carefully cleared and renewed every spring. Now they were out in the open, fire spreading all around them. To the noise of shouting was added the drumming of hooves, the patter of running feet.

From the goat-path in the scrub, fifty yards from where Shef and the others lay, a dozen men burst out, running determinedly towards the bare rock of the castle, where nothing could burn. As they reached the ring, now a clump, of sentries, Shef saw spear-points flash, heard an angry shout. The head of the German sentries barring their way. Shouts in reply, arms waving, pointing behind them at the flames. More men running from different directions. Shef rose to a crouch beneath the bushes.

"Come on."

They gaped at him.

"Come on. Look like horse-boys who've got lost. Run as if you're frightened."

He writhed once more through the bushes, burst through a final tangle, and ran out on to the cleared space, looking round and shouting out in a gabble of Arabic mixed with Norse. The rest followed him, hesitant from the long hours of hiding. Shef seized Straw, lifted him in the air and shook him as if hysterical with fear, turned and ran the wrong way, not towards the gap where the other refugees clustered but round the side of the hill. German eyes saw him, saw only another damned local out of control.

Rounding a turn, Shef halted, pushed aside the youth who had cannoned into his back, stared at the tangle of thorn trees with which the Germans had made their abatis. A weak place, there. He stepped forward, drawing the short single-edged sword slung from the back of his belt. For a few seconds he cut and tugged, then plunged forward, disregarding the scratches that came through wool and hemp. The others followed him, Straw and his mates disappearing at once into the bushes on the other side, Richier gasping again and holding his side. Shef seized him, bent him by force to the ground, thrust him bodily in under the branches. Followed him, this time using all his hoarded strength in one last burst of lizard-like motion. Through to the ravine and the dark rocks below.

As the noise behind died and Shef saw at last the black unguarded cleft that led to the very base of the rock of Puigpunyent, something again made him look up.

There, in the sky, for the first time, he saw a kite wheeling above him and above the flares it had sown. It was silhouetted by flame. Flame running along the cloth of the square kite shape, along the vanes of the controls. In the middle, like a fat-bodied spider in its web, what must be the shape of the flyer, Tolman or Helmi or Ubba. His own match must have caught the cloth. Or perhaps a flare had not fallen properly from its release. But now the kite was swooping down, first in a crazy spiral, then as its lift surfaces burned away, seeming to fold its wings like a gannet and plunge towards the rocks, a meteor trailing flame.

Shef closed his eye, turned away. Thrust Richier to the fore.

"Someone died for your relic," he hissed. "Now take us to it! Or I will cut your throat in sacrifice to my boy's ghost."

The *perfectus* began to run clumsily across the dark rock to the entrance only he could find.

CHAPTER EIGHTEEN

His face tight-lipped with fury, the Emperor Bruno whirled his horse on the narrow flame-lit path, the great stallion rearing up and striking out automatically with its steel-shod hooves. A fleeing trooper struggling to get by took one of them on the temple and fell sideways into the brush, there to lie unnoticed till the fire took him. Behind their enraged Emperor his guards and officers lashed out with fist and whip, trying to force panicked soldiers to stand firm, obey their orders, begin to spread out and make a fire-break along the line of the path. Bruno himself ignored the struggle and the confusion.

"Agilulf," he bellowed. "Find one of these bastards who can speak a proper language. I have to know where that damned thing came down!"

Agilulf swung from his horse, obedient but doubtful. He seized the nearest man and began to shout into his face in the camp-Latin he used to the Greeks. The man he had seized, who spoke nothing but his native dialect of Occitan, and had never met anyone who spoke anything else, gaped at him uselessly.

Surveying the scene from his humble mule, Erkenbert the deacon intervened. In the swarm of runaways now being beaten into a standstill he caught the whisk of a priest's black robe. Some hedge-priest no doubt, called out with his parishioners. Erkenbert urged his mule towards him, extricated the man from the grip of one of Agilulf's yelling sergeants.

"*Presbyter es,*" he began. "*Nonne cognoscis linguam Latinam? Nobis fas est . . .*" Slowly the priest's fear died, he began to recognise Erkenbert's strange English pronunciation, he recovered himself enough to take in the sense of the question and to reply. Yes, they had seen the lights in the sky, they had taken them for signs of coming doom and the resurrection of the dead, the souls rising to meet their Master in the sky. Then someone had seen the flash of angel wings and his whole troop had fled in terror, urged on by the forest fire they could see beginning. And yes, he had seen the burning shape which had come swooping down.

"And what did it look like?" Erkenbert asked tensely.

"Certainly it was an angel flung from the sky in flames, no doubt for disobedience. It is a terrible thing that the Fall of the Angels should come again . . ."

"And where did the angel fall?" asked Erkenbert, before the man could start his lamentations again.

The priest pointed into the scrub to the north. "There," he said. "There, where a small flame has started."

Erkenbert looked round. The major fire was coming towards them out of the south. It looked as if the Emperor's men would be able to halt that along the line of the break they were cutting. They had hundreds of men at work already, and order was spreading out like oil on water. To the north, a small fire, blown on by the wind out of the south. It did not look dangerous, for it seemed to be on a barer patch of hillside. He nodded to the priest, turned his mule and rode it past the still-shouting Emperor, his sword now drawn.

"Follow me," he called over his shoulder.

After a hundred paces the Emperor realized what Erkenbert was making for and forced his warhorse past the mule, charging into the scrub careless of thorns and tangles. Erkenbert followed the trampled path at a more sedate speed. When he came to the source of the fire, the Emperor was dismounted, standing with the reins over one arm, looking down at something on the ground.

It was the body of a child, lying crumpled amid the stones. There was no doubt the child was dead. His skull was cracked, and leg-bones stuck out through the flesh of his thighs. Slowly the Emperor reached down, picked the child up in one hand by the front of his tunic. The body dangled like a bag of chicken bones.

"He must have broken every bone in his body," said Bruno.

Erkenbert spat in his palm and traced the sign of the cross on the split forehead in spittle. "It may have been a mercy," he said. "See, the fire had caught him before he died. There are the marks of the burning."

"But what set him on fire? And how did he fall? What did he fall from?" Bruno stared up into the sky as if to find an answer in the stars.

Erkenbert began to poke around amid the scraps and pieces lying on the ground, well lit by the fire now burning steadily away from them before the wind. Pieces of stick. Light stick, made from some kind of hollow plant, like an alder but tougher. And a few charred pieces of cloth. Erkenbert crumbled one in his hand. It was not wool, nor linen. The strange plant of the south, he thought. Cotton. Very fine-woven. Fine-woven to hold the wind, like a sail.

"It was some sort of machine," he concluded. "A machine to hold a man in the air. But not a man. A boy. A small boy. There is nothing supernatural about this, nothing of the *ars magica*. It was not even a very good machine. But it was a new machine.

"I will tell you something else," he went on, looking down again at the dead child, his fair hair, his eyes that might have been blue before the fire caught them. "That boy is one of my countrymen, I can tell from his face. Like a choirboy. It is an English face."

"An English child flying in a new machine," whispered Bruno. "That can only mean one man, and we both know who it is. But what has he done it for?"

Agilulf had caught up with them, heard the Emperor's question. "Who can tell?" he replied. "Who can fathom the plan of that fiend? I remember the strange ship at the battle in Denmark, I rowed past it at twenty feet and I still did not know what it was for till the battle was over."

"The simplest way to understand a plan," said Erkenbert, speaking now in the Emperor's native Low German so like his own Northumbrian English. "The simplest way to understand a plan is to assume that it's worked."

"What do you mean?" snapped the Emperor.

"Well, here is the Emperor of the Romans standing round in a dark thorn-wood at night, with his advisers, none of them knowing what is happening or what to do. Perhaps that is what our enemy intended. Just that we should be standing here."

The Emperor's anxious face cleared suddenly. He bent forward, gripped Erkenbert's scrawny shoulder with his usual delicate care, as if afraid to crush it.

"I will make you an Archbishop for this," he said. "I understand. This is a distraction, to make us look the wrong way. Like a night attack on the side away from the real one. And it has worked! And all the time the bastards are heading for what we had shut up tight as a mouse's larder a few hours ago."

He swung effortlessly back into the saddle. "Agilulf, as soon as the fire-break is made I want you to withdraw all the *Lanzenbrüder* from the line and send them back to the castle, at the double. And send six men round the inner ring to tell them to face about and watch both ways, inside and out."

He paused a further instant before driving in the spurs. "And send a man back to pick up this child's body. He died like a hero and he shall be buried like one."

The spurs drove home, the stallion crashed away down the rocky hillside. Agilulf followed to carry out his orders. Erkenbert, left alone, remounted his mule and trotted at a far slower pace in their wake.

Archbishop, he thought. The Emperor always fulfills his promises. And there is an Archbishopric free, in York. If the Church can once more extend her wing over the heretics and the apostates. Who would have thought that I would be the heir of Wulfhere, he of a great family and I the child of a country priest and his concubine? Strange what happened to Wulfhere. Dead of a stroke in his bath, they said. I wonder how long they had to hold him under. The Emperor is generous, and can pardon failure. Never idleness, though. All his dogs have to bark. And bite as well.

Light showed brightly along the edge of the rocky ravine along which Shef, Richier, Straw and the others were climbing, illuminating the forbidding mass of the stone castle above them. In the ravine, though, only black shadow. For a few moments they were shielded from sight. Shouts echoed into the darkness both from behind them, where the guards were still watching the lights in the sky, and from the castle walls above, where gaping sentries were being pushed and kicked back to their posts. Better be out of sight soon, Shef thought.

Richier pushed past him as they came up to the base of the wall, seeming to grow out of the native rock like a cliff. He turned, spoke harshly in his dialect. Shef saw Straw and the other youths turn their backs, hide their faces. Richier repeated his order, gesturing fiercely at Shef. Turn. Do not look. Slowly Shef obeyed.

For a few moments. He knew that Richier would look back once, twice, then carry on with whatever it was that he had to do. It was like playing the game they called 'Grandmother's Footsteps,' where the child approaching had to guess when the child being stalked would turn round to look. Shef turned his head alone, watched Richier in the blackness.

He seemed to have pulled something slung round his neck from under his tunic. Was scraping at the wall, fitting the object to it. A key, an iron key. Shef looked back at Straw and the others an instant before Richier began to turn, waited, looked again. This time he heard the click. Something engaging. Now Richier reached up, seemed to be counting stones. He fixed on one, got fingers over its rough edge, pulled. The stone came out of the wall, projecting a good foot from the surface.

Nothing happened. Interested, Shef padded gently over to within arm's reach, met Richier's blazing indignant eyes as he turned round again. Ignored them.

"What now?" he whispered softly.

Richier gulped, then whistled gently. The five youths crept stealthily up out of the gloom of the ravine. Richier looked in all directions, as if expecting sudden discovery, then made his mind up. Bent and pushed at one of the massive unyielding stones of the base of the wall.

With hardly a sound the stone moved outwards. Outwards and inwards at once. On a pivot, Shef realized. Prevented from pivoting by the stone

Richier had pulled out of the wall. That stone itself held in place by some contrivance the key had unlocked. And the keyhole? He looked at it more closely. Covered in moss, the moss just this moment scraped aside.

Richier had bent, was crawling through the gap. Shef followed immediately, twisting his broad shoulders to get through what could be only a two-foot gap. Inside, he put a foot down on stone, felt that he was on a narrow ledge. A ledge that narrowed in one direction. He stretched out a hand, felt stone wall ahead of him. He was on a staircase, a spiral staircase twisting down to the left. Carefully he edged past Richier in the dark, went up a step or two, heard the youths come rustling through. A heave, a grunt, and the stone slowly closing, cutting out even the faint glimmer of light from the ravine outside. In the dark, frightened breathing all around him, he could smell the stench of death, coming up from below. Coming up on a faint, barely perceptible current of air.

There were sparks in the blackness as Richier tried to strike a light, Straw holding out a bed of dried tinder for the sparks to fall on, one of the other boys clutching candles. Shef ignored them, began slowly and silently to climb the staircase. A call from below, first in dialect, then in Arabic. "Don't go up! We must go down." Shef ignored it.

As he climbed the steps, the draught increased, and so did the other thing his straining senses had noted: noise. Noise coming through the stone. Through the stone?

No. As he gripped the iron handrail Shef realized that he could see a faint something, not light but a paler darkness. And he could hear now, quite clearly. Voices shouting, the whack of a rope or a belt across someone's back. Order being restored. Yes, and there indeed was the hole in the stone, smaller than a man's hand, but there just the same. Shef put his eye to it, peered out.

He could see almost nothing, just a red glow in the sky, and in front of him legs scurrying. First bare ones, and then metal greaves over heavy leather boots. And that was German they were shouting, Shef could almost understand it. Out of the corner of his eye he saw and recognised something else. A pickax left lying on the ground. The Emperor's miners were through to the secret place. Only they had not realized yet, had been distracted just at the vital moment.

There was Richier at his elbow, candle lit. Shef reached out, ground out the flame between finger and smithy-calloused thumb. As Richier began to gabble he closed a hand over his mouth, pulled him forward, whispered, "Look. See the hole. See the pickax?"

As he took in the meaning of what he had seen Richier began to shake in Shef's fist. Shef whispered again, "Go down."

A few turns of the stair and the boys were there, candles lit but unmoving, waiting for orders.

"We have only a short time," Shef said in a more normal voice. "Lead on quickly."

Richier took a candle, began to hurry down what seemed almost an endless stair, winding down into the heart of the mountain. After two hundred counted steps he stopped, and Shef realized that he was at last standing on level floor. In front of him was a stout door, its top rounded, of oak reinforced with iron. Richier had another key out. Before he inserted it he turned to the youths behind him and muttered something. All of them fell to their knees, made the strange zig-zag sign of their sect.

"This is our holiest place," said Richier. "None but the *perfecti* may enter."

Shef shrugged. "Better go in, bring everything out then."

Richier looked at the forbidding figure of the man who had disarmed him, shook his head in exasperation. "Come in, you must. But remember this is holy."

Straw and the others seemed to need no reminder. They hung back, let Shef follow Richier through the door. Looking round in the candle-light, Shef reflected that they had reason for their shyness.

It was a place of death. The stench he had detected was stronger here. And yet he had known worse, much worse, on the battlefields of England. Here the dry air seemed to quell corruption. In front of him, round the circular table, a dozen men—a dozen corpses—sprawled in their seats, some face down with skulls on arms, some fallen to the floor. Richier made his zig-zag sign again, and childhood habit made Shef begin to make the sign of the cross. He corrected himself, turned it into a hammer. Thor, or Thunor, between me and evil.

"They died rather than take the chance of capture and torment," said Richier. "They took the poison together."

"It is for us to see they did not die in vain, then," prompted Shef.

Richier nodded, braced himself, walked across the room, skirting the fallen bodies, till he came to a further door on the other side. Unlocked it, pushed it open.

"The place of the *Graal,*" he said.

Moving into the last room, Richier took on a sudden assurance, like one who knew every detail of the place, and was anxious to show his mastery. Candle in hand, he moved round the small circular room, lighting candle after candle in turn as they stood in great candlesticks. Golden candlesticks, Shef saw immediately. The light that shone from them lit up more gold, on the walls and on the furnishings of what seemed a Christian chapel. But in the place of honor there was no altar.

Instead, a coffin, a sarcophagus of stone, placed almost next to the far wall. And rising out of it, incongruous in the gleam of wealth, a plain wooden pole-ladder, three rungs on one side and two the other, its ends untrimmed, bark still showing here and there on the pale peeled wood.

"That is it," said Richier. "The *graduale* on which our Lord was carried from Calvary. Rising from the coffin to show how we can rise again."

"I thought Anselm said that Christ had not risen. That he died like an ordinary man. Is his body not here?"

"Not here. Not anywhere! For we do not rise as the Christians say, by the favor of the Church, mother of iniquities. We rise by denying the body. By becoming spirit alone! 'How can an old man become young? And enter again into the womb of his mother?' There is only one way—"

A moan of superstitious fear came from behind Shef as the listening boys heard the great question of their faith emerge in Richier's clumsy Arabic, which they too only half-understood. Richier gazed angrily round, realized he had said too much before the uninitiate, realized too that in this holiest of holies, about to be defiled, mere words meant little.

"Do not enter into the womb! Do not spill the seed! Pay no more tribute to him, to the Father who sent his Son to die, to the Prince of this world, the God who is rightly a devil! Die and leave no child as hostage to the enemy."

No wonder Svandis wasn't raped, Shef thought, looking down at the working face, the angry eyes. Though it is not much of an answer. He glanced down into the empty coffin.

"Tell me. What is it we have to save? Besides the *graduale*."

Richier nodded, collected himself. "There is the gold, of course." He waved a hand round at the blaze of red metal surrounding them. "More important, much more important, are the books."

"The books?"

"The holy testimonies of our faith. The true gospels, written by men who had spoken with the Son of God face to face. The Son of God grown to wisdom, no longer in the folly of his youth."

Interesting books they must be, thought Shef. If they are not forgeries. "What do they weigh?" he asked.

"A few pounds, no more. And then . . . Then we must take with us the *graduale*."

Shef looked at the ladder rising out of the coffin more doubtfully, stepped across to handle it. Behind him, breath hissed in fear and muted anger that an unbeliever should touch the relic. But that was what they were here for. That was why the unbeliever had been sent. And he had passed the ordeal of the *perfecti,* Richier told himself, even if his faith was not sound.

No more than seven feet long, thought Shef. He lifted it gently. Old wood, dry wood, wood eight centuries old and more if what they said was true. Yet it had been seasoned to begin with, never exposed to the weather. In the old legionary buildings of York Shef had been shown stairs and galleries that men swore dated from the time of the ancient Romans. There was no reason to think the *graduale* was false just because it seemed still sound. No doubt it fitted the doctrines of the sect not to have adorned it with gold and jewels as the Christians did with all the many fragments of the True Cross. The thing was light enough, anyway, to lift one-handed. Awkward to carry up a spiral staircase. As for the thorns and the brush outside . . .

"Very well," said Shef, lifting the ladder from its place. "Richier, get your books, make a pack of them, you carry them. You boys, take the gold candlesticks, the plates, everything gold you can see, wrap each piece in cloth, divide them between you so you can carry them easily."

"Cloth, master?" asked Straw.

"The gentlemen next door will not grudge you their robes. Not for this purpose," added Shef, trying to shift the look of terror and awe. "If they were alive, they would tell you to do it. Their ghosts are with you."

Reluctantly the boys turned and went to their macabre task. Still holding the ladder, Shef went back through the antechamber of death and stood in the stairwell, listening. In the silence deep underground he could still hear shouting from above. Not a good sign.

As they scuffed heavy-laden up the stairs, the sound was still with them, coming louder and clearer over the deep breathing of tired men. Shef tramped up and up, in the lead, no longer aware of how far they had gone or where the exit of the pivoting stone might be. He held the holy ladder in his left hand, to keep it away from the central pillar. Every time he knocked it against a tread or the outside wall he could feel Richier wince behind him, sometimes hear a suppressed complaint. If there were light enough the man would be collecting together every splinter of bark that fell from it.

A hiss from below. Shef halted, realized he had gone past the stone. Richier, careless now of secrecy, was fumbling with a projecting knob of rock. He pulled it out, and the seemingly solid wall shifted slightly, pivoting freely again. Shef hesitated, stacked the ladder carefully against the wall on a higher tread, stepped three steps down. As Richier pushed the upper half of the stone outwards, Shef evaded the slow rise of the lower half inside the stairwell, and peered out into the dark.

A dark still light. Fires burning out there, though they were red now, not the strange colors of the Arab flares. Had anyone seen the stone move? There were no cries, no shouts of alarm. In fact, outside the castle, everything was still. Shef could see the circle of thorn through which they had struggled, could see the hillside beyond. There were no men running in panic, no visible sentries, no sign of movement at all. It was light out there, Shef told himself, though where he was he was still hidden in the shadow of the castle wall and the ravine below.

His skin prickled. He ducked back inside, put his shoulder under the stone, heaved up till the stone sighed its way back into place. In the glimmering light of the one candle he had allowed, Richier looked at him, appalled.

"Too quiet," said Shef briefly. "I've heard that quiet before. Means they're watching. Maybe both ways. Maybe they know we're inside."

"We cannot stay here."

"No. No." A voice Shef had not heard before broke in, one of the youths with the packs. He was gabbling in the local dialect which Shef could not understand, but he could catch the unmistakable note in his voice. The boy's nerve had cracked, from the secret crawl, the fear of the holy place, the horror of robbing the dead, the chill of dark stone.

"*Laissetz, laissetz me parti.*" He was pushing at the stone, swinging it open again, only part-way, enough to find a crack and wriggle through it like a weasel, pack still slung on his back. Shef grasped at him, caught only a rag of tunic which tore in his hand. Then the boy was out. Shef left the stone open half a foot, bent and peered one-eyed through the crack.

He could see nothing, hear only a faint whisk of bare feet on stone. That too died. Silence, and a faint smell of burning coming on the wind. And then, as Shef was almost ready to override his fears and lead the others forward, faint but clear, a crack like a stick breaking, a shrill shriek instantly muffled, a clang like a far-off gong being beaten. Metal bouncing on stone.

Shef heaved the stone shut once again, this time with total finality. "You heard," he said. "They got him. Now they know we're here."

"We're trapped," gasped Richier. "With the *graal* which our elders died to save."

"The stairway goes up as well as down," said Shef.

"We cannot break the wall down from inside, they would hear."

"But there must be a doorway up there, a secret one like the one by which we entered, only inside the castle."

Richier swallowed. "It comes out in an angle of the tower. The tower that was burnt, where Marcabru died."

"So we'll come out in a pile of rubble, that's good."

"It is across the courtyard from the main gate. I do not think there is any other way out. The courtyard is full of the Emperor's men, he has made it into a hospital for those wounded in fighting or injured in the work. We cannot just walk out. Not with a ladder over our shoulders! And besides . . . the boys might pass as workmen or helpers, and I too, but you . . ."

Too tall, he meant, like a German but without the armor. And too distinctive.

"Show me where the stair comes out," said Shef, a plan forming in his mind. "It cannot be far from where the pickax-men broke through."

Bruno, by the grace of God Emperor of the Romans, in his own mind vice-regent of God on earth, stood at the center of the main gateway of the castle of Puigpunyent and surveyed the scene in its milling courtyard. Everywhere his eye fell, men sprang to more frantic efforts. He took no pleasure in it. That was as it should be. Though his face was impassive, his body was filled with such furious excitement that it would barely obey him. Twice on his frantic gallop back from the scene by the crashed fire-machine his involuntary clenching on the reins had dragged his stallion back on its haunches, almost unseating him. But he had returned in time. He was sure of it. Sure too that the whole display of lights and flame and portents in the sky had been exactly what his puny deacon had said: a distraction. Certain proof that the treasure he sought was within his grasp. If only he could stretch out his hand to take it. As he stood there, clutching the new-shafted lance which never left him, the Emperor allowed himself to do something he did only in moments of greatest stress: he rested his cheek on the very metal that had drunk the blood of his Lord, to feel coming from it the power and the assurance that were his by right.

Inside the courtyard the turmoil was like the last square of the harvest, filled with trapped rats running in all directions to avoid the scythes and cudgels closing in on them. But only to the untrained eye. The Emperor could see order being reimposed on chaos. The men who worked day and night to dig down to the foundations of this heretics' nest were rushing back to work with their picks and barrows, reeving the ropes and pulleys once again to the great crane that lifted the stone blocks and hurled them into the gulleys outside. In one corner their overseer, who had allowed them to desert their toil as the lights in the sky appeared, was screaming at a triangle of pike-shafts while two of Bruno's *Lanzenbruder* sergeants methodically laid on the two hundred lashes which Bruno had ordered him. His deputy, new promoted, stood in the middle of the yard, pale with fear and shrieking orders.

What was causing the trouble was the hospital. Careful and solicitous of the welfare of those who served him properly, Bruno had ordered space made in the central courtyard for beds for the trickle of casualties who had come in from scuffles with the locals, and the greater trickle of men who had caught feet beneath blocks of stone or jammed their arms under moving ropes. Only in the castle was there pure water in abundance, from the well sunk deep into the living rock beneath. Water was what the sick needed more than anything. But now the fires and chaos outside were bringing in more than a trickle, a gush of casualties. Men burnt fire-fighting, men with broken bones from falls, fools who had tripped on their own weapons. He would have to countermand the order that injuries should be brought in, Bruno decided. Let them wait on the plain outside till daylight. They were beginning to impede the work-parties. There, in the angle, a stretcher-party rushing busily in entirely the wrong direction. He opened his mouth to hail them, then closed it, gestured grimly to Tasso to sort the fools out, turned and snarled his orders to the gasping Agilulf, who had finally caught up with him, to get the injured not already in their beds out of the way, and prevent any more entries.

As he turned back to watch the courtyard again, he saw a different group thrusting through the gateway. A group with a different look on their faces. Not fear, but glee and triumph. And as they entered, so too did the faithful Erkenbert, on foot, his mule abandoned at the base of the rock.

"What have you got there?" he asked.

"A rat," said the *Bruder* in the lead, eyes gleaming in the red light. Wolfram, Bruno saw, a good brother from holy Echternach. "He came running out of the castle, right into the arms of Dietrich here."

"*Out* of the castle? But you are posted out to the west, there is no gate there."

"No gate we can see, *herra*. But out he came, down the ravine to the west like a little mouse. He had not climbed down the wall, or we would have seen him. He was running full pelt like someone scared out of his wits."

"I tripped him with my lance-butt," added the burly Dietrich. "His leg broke and he tried to squawk, but I gagged him. He has given no warning to anyone still inside."

"And look, *herra*," said Wolfram the sergeant, his face shining with pleasure and anticipation. "See what the rat had for his hoard."

He tipped a makeshift sack out at the Emperor's feet. From it there rolled goblets and plates, a massive candlestick. The light of the fires still glowing out on the plain gave back glints of gold.

Bruno bent, picked up one of the plates, felt the unmistakable heft of it. Something engraved on it. He could not read it well. A letter 'N' in flowing script?

"What do you make of that?" he asked, passing it to Erkenbert.

"Little enough," said the deacon. "But this is no hedge-baron's hoard. More like the communion plate of the Holy Father in Rome. I fear we will have to ask the boy."

Eyes turned to the captive. Boy he was, face screwed up in pain, one leg lifted to keep it from touching the ground. Dark face, ragged clothes. A native. After the sight of the crashed kite and its dead pilot Bruno had half-expected to see another damned Englishman.

"Have you tried to talk to him?"

Wolfram nodded. "Can't understand a word he says. Nor he us."

"I will find an interpreter," said Erkenbert. "Then we will do what needs to be done. Take him outside the gate."

"One thing," said Bruno. "I know you will not be over-kind. Nor will you hold back in any way from what I must have from him. But my advice is this. Never begin by hurting anyone just a little, and then working up.

Courage grows with resistance. Hurt him very badly to begin with, more badly than he can bear. Then offer him the way out."

"As soon as I can find a local priest to interpret for us," promised Erkenbert.

The trapped youth looked from side to side. He had already seen what he needed to. What must he do now? Did he need to die like Marcabru and the garrison? He did not know.

A hundred yards down the path to safety, in a stream of evicted invalids and their helpers, Straw and his mates struggled with their burden: Shef, lashed firmly to the center-pole of the *graduale* itself, braced by the rungs that stuck out to either side as handholds for the bearers, his face with its betraying one eye covered like that of a burnt or dying man. Richier trotted behind them, face gray with fear, still clutching his precious pack of books. He had passed within twenty feet of the devil's incarnation on earth, the Emperor himself. Thank God, the true God whose power in this world had been usurped by the lying deity of the Christians, that all his attention had been on poor Maury. What would happen now to Maury—ah, that showed the power of the *princeps huius mundi,* whom even the true God could not entirely set aside in this his proper realm.

As they hurried down the hillside the terrible screams that began from behind them urged them on. Screams in a voice familiar to the other boys, even in its agony.

CHAPTER NINETEEN

S o we lost Maury," Richier concluded. A wail of grief broke from one of the women in the listening ring: his mother, it must be. Anselm made no reply, still staring uncertainly at the emblem and holiest relic of his faith, now displayed in the open for the lay-folk and the heathen to stare at. He seemed to have begun to realize that rescuing his *graduale* was only the start of his problems, Shef thought grimly. He slid with the familiar pain in his thigh-muscles from the back of the horse he had stolen.

"Who did you lose?" he asked, staring at Cwicca, at the front of the Wayman gang. "We saw someone go down."

"We lost two of them. Tolman got back, but he's hurt."

"Two? We only saw one go down."

"That were Ubba," broke in Steffi. "We don't know what happened, but before they gave Tolman the poppy to knock him out he said it was very hard lighting the flares and dropping them without them catching on something, with the kites pitching and all. Ubba must have set fire to himself. He didn't have a chance after that."

"And the other one, what was his name? Helmi?" Helmi the orphan, the small pale child.

"He came back well enough, but he was going too fast, much too fast. Slammed into the rock ledge below where we were. Kite broke up and he fell two hundred feet. We couldn't find the body."

Depression began to settle on Shef, together with weariness and delayed shock from fear too long suppressed. He had come to save Svandis, and save her he had—but from what? These people had had no intention of killing her. If he had not followed they would have turned her loose. And in saving one he had killed two. Two of his own. As for the *graduale* or the *graal* or whatever they wanted to call it, maybe Maury had died willingly to save it, but it seemed little enough to buy at such a price. Still clutching the old wooden pole, Shef tossed it absently to Anselm, who caught it automatically, and then stared as if he had clutched a viper. They had sought to bribe him with knowledge of the Greek fire too, but what had he learnt after all? That saltpeter made a fire burn more brightly, that flame could be colored. None of that was Greek fire.

"Tolman ain't too bad," put in Cwicca, seeing the look on his master's face. "He just came down a bit hard, rolled over and over on the rock. We put him to sleep till the cuts start to heal." He hesitated. "But he flew, master. Even over land and at night. No silly feathers nor nothing, either."

Shef nodded. It was an achievement of sorts.

"What do we do now?" Cwicca went on.

"I'll tell you." Shef looked round at the ring of listening people, Waymen and heretics mixed up together, in the tiny central square of the mountain village.

"First, Anselm. The Emperor is bound to have found out where Maury came from and even who he is. And what we took. You can be sure that his whole army will move from Puigpunyent and come after you."

"We are high in the mountains, they do not know the paths . . ."

Shef cut him off. "You do not know the Emperor. Whatever are your safest places, take everyone to them. You will lose your animals and your houses." He kicked one of the packs of gold lying ignored on the ground. "If I were you I would use these to replace them once the Emperor has left."

Anselm nodded reluctantly. "The caves, the bat caves, we can hide there for . . ."

"Start soon." Shef pointed at the wooden grail. "Take that. Your Grail was bought with a life, with three lives, I hope you find it worthwhile."

Shef changed direction, changed speech as well. "As for us, Cwicca, remember what Brand said about coming down the mountain faster than we went up? Get our animals together, load 'em up, don't forget Tolman, and we're heading back to the ships as fast as ever we can go. He'll have cavalry out already, and I want to outdistance them."

"And once we get to the ships?"

"Out to sea as fast as Hagbarth can rig sail."

The groups dissolved as Anselm and Cwicca began to call orders. Shef walked over, sat wearily by the edge of the village well, groping for the dipper he had thrown to the ground only two days before. After a few moments he found Svandis, her ragged white dress now stitched into respectability, by his side.

"So," she said. "What has the heretic God given you for the boys' lives?

A wooden ladder? Or have you and the old fool just thrown them away for nothing?"

Shef wondered dimly why people felt they were helping by asking that kind of question. As if he had not thought of it already. For if there was no such thing as a god, as Svandis insistently proclaimed, yes, the whole thing had been pointless. Anselm was approaching, having given his instructions. He knelt down before the younger man.

"You saved our relic and we should give you our thanks."

"I saved it because you stole her. I think you still owe me something."

Anselm hesitated. "Gold?"

Shef shook his head. "Knowledge."

"We have told you everything we know about fire."

"Besides the gold, and the Grail, we brought out books. The true gospels, Richier said. Why have you not given them to the world, as the Christians do with theirs?"

"We believe knowledge is only for the wise."

"Well, maybe I am wise enough. Give me one of your books. The Jews, and the Christians, and the Mohammedans, they all laugh at us Waymen and say we are not People of the Book. So give me one of your books, the one with the true teaching of Jesus in it. Maybe after that people will take us more seriously."

It is only for initiates, Anselm thought. The teaching not only must be read, it must be explained so that the ignorant do not understand it wrongly. We have only three copies, and are forbidden by our law to make any more. The barbarian king has thirty men here, armed with strange weapons. He could take them all and the *graal* as well, if he had a mind. We killed his boys. Best not to provoke him.

"I will bring you a copy," said Anselm reluctantly. "But will you be able to read it?"

"If I cannot, Solomon can. Or Skaldfinn." Shef thought of a saying in his own tongue. "Truth can make itself known."

What is truth? thought Anselm, remembering the saying of Pilate in the gospel of the Christians. But he did not dare to speak the words.

"So we lost the da—the holy thing, when it was right under our noses," snarled the Emperor. He had passed a tense night, disturbed not by the screaming from the tent where Erkenbert did his work, but by his own thoughts. All the morning after he had been pursued by reports of failure and desertion, his levies scattered half way across the county by fear and confusion.

"Yes," replied the black deacon. He did not fear the Emperor's moods. He knew that even in the worst of them the Emperor retained an ability to see things fairly. That was why his men loved him.

"All right. Tell me the worst."

"The thing, the holy *graal* as the boy calls it, was here, deep down. We had almost reached it. Your rival the One King was here as well. The boy described him unmistakably. The lights in the sky—they were as I said, a distraction only."

The Emperor nodded. "I have not forgotten my promise, and Wulfhere's see is still vacant. Go on."

"They worked. While the sentries were engaged with frightened Frenchmen they got in through some secret passage. Retrieved the relics of their heretic faith, including the *graduale*—and it is a ladder, just as you supposed. The boy does not know why it is holy."

"How did they get out?"

"The boy did not, of course. He panicked, was caught by our alerted sentries."

The Emperor nodded again, resolving internally not to punish Wolfram and his men, as he had originally intended. The distraction was not their fault, for it was not they who had responded to it, or at least no more than he had himself. And they had been alert enough on the return.

"He cannot say how the rest got out. But there was one thing he tried not to tell us. It came out in the end." Erkenbert hesitated. The Emperor was a fair man, but this was humiliation. "In the end the boy was persuaded to talk because he realized that his talking made no difference. The others were out already. *He saw them walk past us.*"

The Emperor blinked, straightened out of his cavalryman's slouch on the camp stool. "He didn't walk past me. No one-eyed man ever does without me having a very close look at him."

Erkenbert looked at the ground. "They had tied him to the *graduale,* so it looked like a stretcher. You told Tasso to kick them through the gate yourself."

A long silence. Eventually Erkenbert looked up. Was the Emperor meditating one of his own brutal self-imposed penances? He was staring at the point of his sword. "I had him there," he muttered. "On the end of it like a virgin about to squawk. All I had to do was push it home. And I didn't. I tell you, Erkenbert, this kind heart of mine will be the ruin of me yet, my mother always used to say so."

He grinned. "So they got past us. Up into the hills, no doubt. We shall just have to chase them. And all the damned cavalry deserted, or lost, or gone off to water their damned horses or something. But I'll have it yet. All right, Erkenbert, go find me someone with local knowledge."

The little deacon sat unmoving. "Your pardon, lord, but think again. The *graduale,* no doubt that is deep in the hills and it may take a deal of finding. But is that the most important thing now? Your countryman, the chaplain Arno, now in service with the Pope, he taught me always in a campaign to look for the *Schwerpunkt,* the vital point of attack or defense. I do not think it is in the mountains. I think it is where the One King is. Or where he will be."

He keeps using that title today, mused Bruno. Trying to needle me, I have no doubt. It's working too. "All right. Where is he, then, King Shef, the Victorious? As they call him. When they think I'm not listening."

Erkenbert shrugged. "Where all pirates always are. With his ships. In the port of Septimania. In the city of the Jews."

Bruno's eyes glittered a little more dangerously. "Heretics and Jews. Heathens and apostates. God sent his Son to bleed and die for them and they cannot so much as say 'thank you.' I prefer the damned Moors, at least they believe in something. And we know the ships are in Septimania, because Georgios saw them. Can we be sure they will stay there?"

"Georgios is on the watch."

"But if they have a wind he can't stop them, they'll just batter his galleys to pieces at long range, he said so himself."

Erkenbert looked down. "I have—taken certain steps to change that situation, lord. I gave the orders in your name, to save time. I was not asleep, after all, at the battle at the Braethraborg, against the heathen Danes."

The Emperor reached out, patted the little man on the shoulder with careful affection. "Don't do too much for me, comrade, or I shall have to make you Pope. And the damned Italian's not dead yet. Though that can be arranged."

Without seeming to move he was on his feet, yelling for his horse, his helmet, and Agilulf. In seconds he was outside, hand on the pommel of the high Frankish saddle of his war-horse. Without touching the stirrup he vaulted into the saddle, jerked his long sword into a more comfortable position, caught the helmet tossed to him and slung it over his saddle-bow.

"Where are you going?" shouted Erkenbert.

"To the funeral."

"Of the men who died last night?"

"No. Of the child who fell from the skies. He had a hammer round his neck, so he cannot go in a consecrated grave, but I have had one dug for him. And a stone cut in the night. It says, *Der erste Luftreiter,* 'first rider of the skies.' That is a great honor, is it not?"

He was away, in a shower of sparks where his horse's metal hooves struck the rock. The sergeant standing by the doorway of the tent, a stolid *Bruder* from Burgundy with a name like Jopp, smiled fondly after the departing figure, displaying a mouthful of broken teeth.

"He is a *Ritter,*" he said. "He honors courage even in his enemies."

The boy Maury was still alive, Erkenbert reflected. He might have recovered enough to talk a little more. Probably the mere sight of his questioner would do the trick by now.

Yet again Shef slid from a horse, this time feeling less stiff, sore and cramped, than certain that his legs would no longer support him. The level flagstones of the Septimania dock met him. After a few moments he straightened, looked past the heads of the crowd.

"The sea," he croaked.

Brand passed him a flask of the diluted wine they had fallen back on once the ale ran out, stood with thumbs in belt while his leader drained it down.

"What about the sea?"

"I love it. Because it's flat. All right." By now there were a hundred men gathered round, dockside loafers, Jewish traders, but most of them Waymen skippers and sailors. Tell them quick and the word would spread. No need for secrecy. "All right. We got Svandis back. I'm afraid we lost two of the boys, Ubba and Helmi. Tell you about that later. But the main thing is, we twisted the Emperor's nose. Twisted it very badly. He's looking for us and I bet he knows we're here. So clear for sea and let's get going. That's best for everyone, right, Solomon? He turns up, we've gone, everyone very sorry, no harm done. Why are you all still standing here? Clear for sea, I said, what's the matter . . ."

Brand put a vast arm round his leader's shoulder, lifted him companionably off his feet, and began to walk along the dock, the crowd parting to let them through, but showing no sign of wanting to follow.

"Come for a little walk along the staithe," he suggested. After a few paces he allowed Shef's feet to touch the ground again but did not release his grip. They walked carefully round the crowded harbor, on to the base of the long stone mole which sprang out from the very heart of the fortified city, began to walk along its hundred-yard extent, stepping over the iron rings to which the small craft were made fast, the larger ones lying out at anchor in the harbor, like the Wayman fleet. Half way along Brand stopped, gestured out to sea.

"What can you see out there?" He plucked the far-seer from Shef's belt, held it out to him.

Shef took it, put it to his eye, moved the lower half in and out on its sliding case as he had learned to, stared into the noonday haze. Nothing that he could see, the haze was difficult, scan round a bit. Oh.

"The galleys," he said. "The red galleys. Three of them out there, no, four."

"That's right. They were there at dawn, fried a couple of fishing boats, pulled back off shore. Just showing us they were watching."

"All right," said Shef, "it's noon now, no wind, they have the advantage. In a few hours, as the sun starts to sink, we'll get the breeze off the sea, regular as a mule's bowels. Then it's our turn. We'll put out, if any of them get in the way we'll sink them. And then have some harpoon practice, right, for Sumarrfugl," he added savagely.

"Keep looking," said Brand.

Puzzled, Shef took up the far-seer again. The haze was irritating, he could see almost nothing in some places, it was thickest down by the surface of the sea. There. There was something there, closer than he expected, closer than the galleys. But he could not make out what it was. It was gray, and low, barely projecting above the flat sea, not a ship at all, more like a long low island. He moved the far-seer in and out, trying to get the blurry image to become clearer.

"I can't see what it is."

"Nor could I. Try counting the ships in the harbor, you'll find that easier."

Shef looked round, a chill growing near his heart. The two-masters, they were still there, moored line astern, all seven of them. The longships of the Vikings, he had begun with five of them, they had lost Sumarrfugl's *Marsvin*, how many were there now? Three. He counted again. Three.

"When the galleys turned up later in the day they were towing that thing. I couldn't make it out either, so I sent Skarthi out in his *Sea-snake,* with a double crew of rowers. He said he could outdistance any Greek, wind or no wind. I told him to be very careful of the fire, and he said he'd make a point of it. But it wasn't the fire this time."

Shef was staring once more at the raft, at the humps he could now see rising from it. There was something familiar about them. Very familiar.

"Skarthi got out there," said Brand, "started rowing towards the raft. They let him get half way, and then—whack. Mule stones all in the air at once. The *Sea-snake* fell apart in the water, the Greeks came rushing in in the galleys . . ."

"How many did we lose?" said Shef tensely.

"No-one. All Skarthi's lot come from Gotland, swim like dolphins. And they swam hard, with the fire coming down on them! But Hagbarth was awake, he put a couple of rocks into the water ahead of the galleys, they sheered off."

Yes, even in the haze he could make out the mule-shapes, Shef realized. At least four of them. Maybe more. On a flat raft with no masts to get in the way, no ribs to fall apart from the recoil, you could put as many catapults as you liked. And he was not the inventor of the catapult, not of the mule-version anyway. Before it had been a mule it had been an onager: the work of the Rome-folk, brought back to life by the Emperor's deacon. Erkenbert. He had not forgotten them. And they had not forgotten him. And now Shef realized why he had not recognised them before, and why they were yet familiar.

They were armored. With steel plates like the ones he had put on the old *Fearnought*.

And there was something else familiar about what they were doing. Shef looked round the flat expanse of the mole, six feet above the water, should they just jump in the water and dignity be damned, was there a ladder to cling to . . .

A rushing noise in the air, a great crash of stone on stone, chips and splinters flying, Brand wiping blood from his forehead in amazement. A short, that had crashed into the far side of the stone wall. But aimed to kill, and aimed to kill them. And they had at least four in their battery.

Without ceremony Shef pushed Brand firmly off the mole and into the sheltered water of the harbor, jumped immediately after him. As they bobbed up and down in the warm sea, stones sighed over their heads, plumped among the scattered boats. Shouts from skippers, frantic attempts to man the sweeps, to come in closer under the protection of the wall.

"So we can't force our way out," said Shef. "We can shoot our way past the galleys, but the raft is like a *Fearnought* to us. It can't move, but we can't sink it. Now what are they doing that for? Brand, what's going on?"

"Well," said Brand. "I always thought you were supposed to be the clever one. But if you ask me, this looks uncommonly like what the Hel-spawn foreigners call a siege."

In the camp of the Caliph, moving slowly but inexorably towards confrontation with the traitorous Jews and the polytheistic rabble of Northern pirates, three women talked quietly, their faces together. One was English: ash-blonde, with green eyes, a beauty in her own land, a curiosity among the tents of the faithful. She had been taken by the Danes years before and sold as a virgin for a hundred dirhams in gold. Another was a Frank, from the border country: the child of a serf, she had been sold in infancy by a master anxious to raise capital. The third was a Circassian, from the far eastern border of Islam, from a nation which survived by the export of its women, famous for their beauty and their sexual skills. The women were talking in the strange argot of their multilingual harem, Arabic studded with words from many tongues. The women had invented it to keep some matters private from the ever-watchful eunuch slaves who guarded them.

All three women were discontented, and afraid. Discontented because they had been plucked from the comfort of Cordova and brought out on campaign, with barely half a score of others, to ease the tedium of their master. True, they were carried every step of the way in litters filled with silk and down. True, fans waved over them at night, continually worked by relays of slaves. Yet the hard hot ground of the camp could not be made into the

fountains and courtyards of Cordova. Their master might rejoice in the
hardships—the very modified hardships—of those who trod dusty ways to
fight the unbelievers, but they drew no consolation from that. One had been
brought up a Christian, one converted to Islam at the age of ten, one came
from a race whose beliefs were so strange that no outsider had ever troubled
to learn them. Nothing creates atheism as well as a profusion of contradicto-
ry beliefs.

There were two reasons why they were afraid. One, that none of them
had yet borne a child. Since it could not be the case that their master's
potency was waning, their barrenness must be their own defect, unless it
were the result of deliberate child-murder in the womb. The other reason
they were afraid was that the walls of no pavillion could keep out the
constant screaming of their master's victims, still ordered to the block, the
bastinado, or the impaling-post at the least whim or setback. They feared
the change of er-Rahman's moods, on which no-one alive was more expert.

"He listens still to that young fool, Mu'atiyah," said the Englishwoman.
"At his ear all the time, encouraging him. He is consumed with hate
himself, and jealousy."

"Could Mu'atiyah eat something that would disagree with him?"
suggested the Circassian.

"The Caliph would know it was poison," said the Frank. "Then who can
say where his anger would fall? We have no-one who would not betray us.
Not out here."

"Maybe it is best if he achieves his ends and we can all return home."

"Home?" said the Englishwoman. "You mean, to Cordova? Is that the
best we can hope for all our lives? Waiting for him to tire of us and send the
man with the strangling-cord? How many years have you got left, Berthe? Or
you, Ouled? I am twenty-three already."

"What else is there?" asked Berthe, wide-eyed.

The Englishwoman, Alfled, had taken part in many a harem plot. She did
not look round or change her expression, but laughed and jingled her
bracelets as if discussing some sexual exploit she had planned for the
Caliph. "We are out here in the heat and the dust of the campaign. Bad
news, and all we want is to return to comfort once the Caliph has won. But
what if the Caliph loses? His armies and his fleets have lost before, that is
why we are here. And in the confusion of a defeat . . ."

"We would be taken and raped by half an army if we were free."

"Maybe. It depends on the army. You heard what the Dane-woman told
us, in Cordova. One of the armies here does not take slaves, and it is led by
one of my countrymen. Even the Emperor of the Romans' army is full of
your countrymen, Berthe. If we made the cross sign and begged for release
from the worshipers of Allah, their priests would be delighted."

"But once you have turned your back on Allah, revoked the *shahada,* there is no mercy for you," pointed out the Circassian.

"We cannot afford to fail, that is so."

"So what must we do?"

"Press the Caliph to battle, but in such a way that he must lose."

"And how is that to be arranged? He has generals skilled in the art of war, to advise him much better than we ever could. We do not know even enough to say what is right and what would be wrong."

"We do not know war," said Alfled grimly, "but we know men. Pick the biggest fool, and urge on his advice. And the biggest fool in this camp is Mu'atiyah. Let us add our voices to his. Our voices from the pillow to add to the fool's from the divan. One thing we should add. Our wish to see our master conquer: the strongest of men, the most warlike, the most manly."

Silence greeted her sarcasm. Finally the Frankish girl spoke. "And we agree, then, if we escape, that whichever of us is in most favor among the conquerors will speak up for the others? If that is so, then I am with you. But one more thing I would counsel, and that is, delay. The spirit of the Caliph's soldiery diminishes day by day. Let him show his madness more, and the rot will spread. Among the secret eaters of pork, the Christian converts, the *mustaribs,* then among those who favor the house of Tulun, among the readers of Greek and those who wish to reword the Koran. All those who know in their hearts what the Dane-woman told us."

"That there is no God, not even Allah," said Alfled fiercely.

"No one god," contradicted the Circassian.

CHAPTER TWENTY

S lowly the siege of Septimania tightened, becoming first inevitable, then evident, then acute. The prince of the city, Benjamin ha-Nasi, had refused to believe in it at first, confident that this quarrel forced upon him by mere strangers within his gates could be averted. If not averted, at least deflected, if necessary by the capture of the strangers and their surrender to the enraged Christian Emperor, or else by their forced expulsion, to take their chances with the Greek and the Greek fire at sea.

He had been undeceived quickly. The Emperor, it became clear, in the grip of holy fury, would make no distinction between the Christian heretics who had hidden the Grail from him, the heathens who had helped them to steal it, and the Jews who had rejected Christ and crucified his Lord. The emissaries Benjamin sent were returned, their heads hurled over the wall one dawn. The rumor spread that they had been forcibly baptized before execution, to give the unbelieving dogs a last chance of salvation, or so the Emperor had said. A message shouted from a distance later that day announced the Emperor's terms: the Grail, first and foremost, the robbers of it led by their one-eyed king, second, and third, the surrender of all the garrison and the officers of the city, barefoot and in their shirts, with ropes round their necks, in token of their absolute submission to the will of God and of his viceroy.

But they had no Grail. Without it, the mercy of the Emperor would be nothing. Sadly, remembering Vespasian and the siege of Masada in their history long before, the Jews of Septimania prepared for desperate resistance. Messengers dropped down ropes or crept out along the seashore, to try to get word to their nominal overlord the Caliph of this Christian insurrection upon the *Dar al-Islam,* the house of Islam. Too often, shrieks and wailing in the night told that they had been intercepted. The Caliph would come, that was sure, in response to this provocation. How long he would take, how concerned he would be for those of his subjects not of his faith, what tales of treachery he might have been told already: that was another story.

With a better heart, the men of the Northern fleet bent themselves to assisting the defense. As soon as the watch-fires of the enemy began to twinkle in the night on the hills around, Cwicca set his mates to commandeering every scrap of cordage and balk of timber that could be taken from the city's stores or the scores of fishing-boats and larger vessels now lying blockaded in the harbor. With them, he set to making as many catapults as he could find material for or space for along the walls. The English and the Vikings now knew of three types.

First—though last to be used by them on the field of war—the mules, descendants of the Roman onagers, and reintroduced to the world by Erkenbert the deacon and his copy of Vegetius's *De re militari*. They threw stones, hard and flat, ship-destroyers, wall-breachers. Heavy and cumbersome, hard to make. Of little use against men, like trying to swat flies with a sledgehammer, as Brand remarked.

Second, what they called the twist-shooters. Torsion weapons, like the mules, and with torsion weapons' power, but shooting great darts or javelins, like giant crossbows. They would drive through almost any shield or mantlet, and had a terror effect out of proportion to the losses they caused. Hard to make also, and dangerous to use. No-one could tell for sure when such a weapon was likely to be overwound, and only those who had done it many times could even guess. Overwinding meant a snap, a sudden lash of broken rope and timber, a winder with no hand, no arm, or his ribs stove in. The English freed-slaves who had first been recruited to man them, years before, had learnt to put spring steel reinforcements on the wooden bow-arms, to save their own lives. There was no spring steel available in Septimania. But then, as Cwicca remarked under the cover of a language the inhabitants of Septimania could not follow, it ain't us that's going to wind them, is it? As long as they do more damage to the other bastards than they do to our lot, that's all right.

Third, the elementary and primitive weapons that Shef himself had invented personally, the pull-throwers as his men called them. Mere traction weapons, worked by a gang pulling in unison at one end of a beam, while the other end, the long arm, whipped up and whirled round a sling, to release its rock at the critical moment. Cheap to make, easy to build, capable of being worked by anyone with a minimum of instruction. Easy to aim for line, almost impossible to gauge for range. Throwing their stones up in the air and relying on gravity for their force, not the power of twisted rope. Used best against formed bodies of troops, who could not avoid them. Cwicca's gangs turned out dozens of them, sent them to every place they could think of along the walls, along with unlimited supplies of missiles dug out of the stony ground. After a while their operation was turned over to the women of the city, who could heave as well as men, and free men for the heavier work of close combat.

After the first few lunges by the Emperor's men, mere demonstrations or explorations—though each left its trail of casualties lying dead or broken on the stony ground—it became clear that the lie of the land would impose its own pattern on the fighting.

Like many towns along the coast, Septimania had sprung from a settlement along a *cala,* or creek-mouth, where a river ran down between high bluffs to the sea. The city had grown up on both hills and on the steep sides of the *cala* between, but as it had grown more and more populous the original single bridge across had multiplied, been made and remade in stone, so that in some stretches the river had become almost completely hidden. But in any case, in this, the growing heat of mid-summer, the river-bed was as good as dry. Where it ran was blocked now by a heavy iron grid or portcullis, lowered to the stony bed beneath.

Nevertheless the river-bed was a weak point, where men could enter under the walls, rather than over them. Brand, touring the defenses with Malachi, captain of the prince's guard, had said nothing when they reached it but told Cwicca to bring up his best twist-shooters and dig them in behind the iron grid.

Round the whole half-circuit towards the land ran the stone walls, beautifully made, fervently maintained and tended as Shef had seen. Assault on those was bound to be costly. At each end, where the walls met the sea, the road ran, the road along the coast that carried trade, and that carried it through the town where the traders must perforce pay toll. The gates at either end were as strong as could be made, of studded oak, with towers to protect them and cover the approaches with arrow-shot. Yet they too were a weak point.

And then the harbor itself. On the tideless Mediterranean there was no foreshore, and walls could be extended right down to the beach. Yet the sea was shallow. Anyone could wade or even paddle along it. As long as attackers faced nothing but wall, as forbidding as the landward one, no harm could be done. Yet as the sea-walls came into the harbor, there had to be a place of junction. To both the north and south of the harbor there ran long stone jetties, or moles, or staithes as the English and Norse called them, the northern one a good hundred yards long, the southern one half that length. They protected the mouth of the *cala* from the fierce sudden storms of the Inland Sea, had been built over the years as trade had increased and the size of the ships with it. Each jetty was six feet above the surface of the water—easy to reach from the deck of a ship, as they were intended to be.

Their defense caused Brand anxious concern. They're long, they're low, if we were to defend them with swords and spears we'd need five, six hundred men, he estimated. And they'd all have to be better than the opposition as well, he added.

"Yeah," Cwicca replied, "so we don't defend them with swords and spears, nor axes neither. They're long, they're low, there's no cover on them or coming up to them. Crossbows for short range and mules for long. Shoot the shit out of them."

"At night?" Brand asked, pulling his beard. He and Malachi fell into careful consultation, counting their numbers and trying to allocate the men and women they had as best they could.

The final problem was the sea. The harbor mouth, a hundred feet across from jetty to jetty, was guarded from shipborne entry by a boom of tree-trunks connected by massive bronze chains and rings. A galley sweeping in would smash its bow, tear its bottom out. Nevertheless, what men had made, men could unmake. No obstacle, as any veteran would know, seriously impedes assault unless it is backed by men and weapons, men with an advantage over the attacker. Brand carefully positioned the seven two-masters of the Wayman fleet where they could not be reached by flying stones from the raft offshore, but where they could bring their mules to bear on the sea approaches. Any ship or boat which tried to bring men to the attack would be sunk immediately. In theory. If everything went well. If no-one got distracted. If the other side didn't think of something clever too.

Brand had tried hard to think of something clever on his side, staring—from cover—at the raft offshore and the patrolling shapes of the fire-vessels usually further out. But nothing came to mind. He had considered unshipping the metal plates carried as ballast in all the ships, armoring the *Fafnisbane* or the *Hagena* like a second *Fearnought* and sending her out to battle the armored raft. But even armor would not protect against the fire of the Greeks: Beowulf, for whom the *Grendelsbane* was named, took an iron shield to protect himself against the dragon but then, as Brand pointed out when the story was told him, Beowulf didn't have a wooden hull. An armored catapult ship could of course sink a fire-galley from a distance, if the wind was right, but not do that and fight an equally armored and much less sinkable floating fort at the same time. We might have to try it one day, Brand concluded to himself, but only if the situation on land turns really nasty. A spear in the heart was one thing, being burnt alive like Sumarrfugl was another. The Greeks' brief demonstrations against small trading craft trying their luck rubbed the point home.

"It's all very tricky," Brand concluded in a bass rumble to his cousin Styrr, his skippers, and the priests of the Way gathered in informal conclave. "But you never know how tricky it looks for the other side as well. What we've got to do is not make any mistakes until, maybe, they've had a sickener or two. After all, they have to think of something or go away. We just have to sit here."

"Till something turns up," said Hagbarth sceptically.

"Yes."

"Like what?"

"Maybe the Caliph will arrive with a hundred thousand men. Maybe someone will bring him the damned ladder, whatever it is. Maybe the gods will intervene on our side."

Chill disapproval met the last remark. "I'll tell you one thing," Brand said in an effort to seem more cheerful.

"What's that?"

"He's making it easy for us right now."

The first moves of the siege might indeed almost have been planned to give the besieged confidence without exposing them to overmuch strain. Some two days after the watch-fires of the advanced cavalry appeared, and the heads of the emissaries were hurled over the wall, the Emperor—if it was he who had ordered it—launched a simple attempted escalade, simultaneously against a stretch of the land wall and a stretch of the wall running down to the beach. At each point a thousand men rose from cover at dawn and ran forward with ladders and grapnels.

They had made too much noise preparing. The defenders were ready and alert. As the ladders reached the top, crutches pushed them away again. The grapnel-ropes were cut. Arrows and catapult stones whirled into the mass of men huddled at the foot of the walls. After a few moments, when it became clear that all was well in hand, Brand dragged an enthusiastic Jewish guardsman away from a ladder he was about to thrust off, kicked aside an English crossbowman anxious to shoot the man climbing it, and stepped back, hunkered down behind the stone battlement, shield raised against the arrows pelting over the wall.

A head appeared, teeth bared in panic and rage, a man swung himself over the parapet, beside himself with the honor of success, desperate to make a lodgement on the walls. Brand measured him, lifted his axe 'Battle-troll,' and struck once, splitting helmet and skull. He stepped back, waving to the crossbowman and guardsman. One shot, the other pushed, the ladder fell with its load of heavy-armed men into the growing pile below. Brand looked at the man he had killed, his equipment, his armor, such of his face as the axe had left.

"A Frank," he muttered. "And a rich one." He removed the dead man's purse from his belt, and faced down the crossbowman's automatic glower. "Don't look like that, it all gets divided up in the end, fair shares, that's *hermannalög,* warriors' law. But I didn't let him up to take his money."

"What did you let him up for?" asked the surly crossbowman.

"I wanted to see who he was. And who he wasn't. And what he wasn't was one of those German monk bastards, never have a penny on them."

"What's that mean, then?"

"Means the Emperor isn't really trying. Just seeing if we're a pushover or not."

Ignoring the cheers of success from Jews and Northerners, guards and citizens alike seeing their enemies fall back in disorder, Brand shouldered his way along the walls, wondering where the real attack might come from.

Down the river bed, as he had expected. For a day and a half after the failure of the first, almost perfunctory assault, onagers had hurled stones unavailingly against the walls, sometimes skimming over to cause broken tiles and shattered windows in the houses of the city, but bringing no threat to the defenders. Then, as the pace of the bombardment increased, a watcher saw a wall of shields advancing slowly down the dried-up river bed that ran through the heart of Septimania. Not shields, in fact, but mantlets: heavy wooden frames that took two men to carry, proof against breast-bows, cross-bows, even lobbed stones. A mule stone would shatter one, and the men behind it, but there were no mules on the walls, too hard to train down. The mantlets inched forward, and after a while Brand, called from his command post, could see gangs furiously hurling stones and the rubble of the winter floods out of the center channel. Behind the mantlets, and following down the cleared center line, he could see another armored structure crawling. A wave ordered fire-arrows launched against it. They struck and fizzled on wet bull-hides. The structure crawled nearer.

"You see a thing like that before?" said Malachi to his giant colleague, in the fractured Arabic which was all that he could say and Brand understand.

"Yes."

"What is it?"

"A ram." Brand used the Norse word *murrbrjotr,* wall-breaker, backed with gestures.

"What we do?"

Carefully gauging the path of the approaching object with his eye, Brand ordered a gang to begin cutting away a section of stone from the bridgeway on the opposite side of the attack. They cut it away in one section, taking care not to break the mortar apart. An hour's work with chisels and picks and a mass of stone poised on the edge of the twenty-foot drop to the river-bed below. Thoughtfully, Brand supervised the setting of a massive iron ring into the top of the severed block, had men drag up the biggest iron chain the dockyard could supply. He noosed it, spread the noose wide with a wooden rod on a thin line. There was plenty of time. The mantlets crept closer, the ram followed them, both under a steady rain of rocks from the pull-throwers on the walls. Cheers rose as broken mantlets were withdrawn, from time to time an unwary or unlucky attacker caught stone or arrow, was left broken or bleeding in the channel. None of that made any difference. Behind the iron grid two of Cwicca's catapult gangs slowly trained round the sights of their twist-shooters, now facing the ram and the mantlets through the iron grid at unmissable range. Brand leaned over the rear battlement, careful not to touch the mass of stone swaying on the levers jammed beneath it, waved them into immobility.

Shouts from below, and the mantleteers fell thankfully back and to the sides, still holding their clumsy guards over their heads. Behind the ram, but well back out of shot, Brand could see what looked like heavy-armored infantry assembling for assault. They did look like the German monk-bastards. Maybe the Emperor was taking this move seriously. Pity he couldn't cut off a few of them and make them really pay for this one. But wisest not to take chances.

The ram, under its heavy protective frame, heaved on by a hundred men toiling at its ten massive cartwheels, edged into position. Its iron-shod head drew back, launched itself at the grill. A clang, a wrenching of iron. A hail of arrows suddenly sweeping inches over the top of the battlements, simultaneous double crash of onager stones from an unnoticed position further up the hillside. Brand grimaced, held his shield high, peered quickly and cautiously over. Arrows thudded into his shield, sprang back off the boss. One, hard-driven, broke through and gashed the back of his arm by the elbow-strap. Brand continued to wave his chain-men into position.

Another clang from below, Malachi staring worriedly at the twisting iron grid. Brand stepped back, raised a thumb. Four men in unison tossed the iron noose over. As they did so, the ram struck again. Through the noose.

Brand jerked the thin line, the rod fell away, the noose tightened with shrill iron screaming. Brand nodded once more to the men by the great mass of broken stone. They heaved in unison on the levers jammed into the base, the stone teetered on the edge of the drop into the river-bed below, they heaved again. Slowly at first, then all at once, the five-ton block swayed and disappeared over the edge in a cloud of stone-dust. The chain whirled after it, the noose tightened round the ram's iron head. Cwicca's twist-shooter gangs, poised underneath the bridge itself, only feet from the ram on the other side of the buckled iron grid, saw the ram jerked suddenly into the air by irresistible force, the whole protective structure going with it. Underneath, blinking like moles dragged into the light, or like snails whose shell had suddenly vanished, the haulers and ram-wielders gaped at their enemies, or at their machine now dangling from its iron chain feet above their heads.

"Shoot!" bellowed Brand. "Don't just stand there watching!"

The catapult-captains trained round the inches necessary to shoot through the grid, released their twisted ropes. One of the great darts, to a further bellow of rage from Brand, missed every man cleanly at a range of six feet, flew far on down the valley, buried itself in the ground at the feet of the waiting storming-party. The other, by luck far more than good management, drove its way into a whole file of wheel-pushers, spitting three in a row like larks on a stick, and driving on even to kill the man behind.

The ram-crew, Frankish knights and peasants alike, broke instantly and ran for the rear. Brand, waving forward Jewish bowmen and English crossbows, urged them on to shoot from the battlements, cursed as the arrows missed and the men ran on, swore discontentedly as he counted the bodies left sprawling.

"We turn them back," said Malachi to him in an attempt to conciliate the giant. "No good, kill men when no need."

Brand continued swearing in Norse, turned for an interpreter. "Tell him there is need. I don't want to drive them back, I want to sicken them. They have to know that every failure will be paid for in blood. Then they won't be so keen to come on."

He turned to organize the bringing up of buckets of pitch, to be lobbed out over the wreckage and set on fire with fire-arrows. Vital to leave no cover for a second assault, especially with the grid now buckled and damaged. The wet bullhides would dry soon in the sun. Meanwhile the wooden frames and wheels were exposed, would burn to ashes once started.

When all was done Skaldfinn, interpreting, spoke to him again. "The captain and I have been talking. He says you know a lot about sieges, and feels more confident of resistance than he did a few days ago."

Brand looked down below the jutting eyebrow-ridges he had inherited from his marbendill ancestor. "I have fought in the front for thirty years, Skaldfinn, you know that. I have seen a lot of battles, a lot of forts taken and defended. But you know, Skaldfinn, that up in the North there are few stone walls. I saw Hamburg taken and York, I was not there when Paris fought off old Hairy-breeks. What I know are only the obvious things—ladders and rams. What do we do if they bring up a siege-tower? No good asking me. And they may have many better ideas than that. No, sieges need more brain than brawn. I expect there are brains over there better than mine."

"He wants to know," said Skaldfinn after passing the message on, "if all that is true, why we do not see your master here on the walls, the one-eyed king. Is he not the wonder of the world for machines and inventions? So what do I tell him now?"

Brand shrugged massive shoulders. "You know the answer as well as I do, Skaldfinn. So tell him the truth. Tell him our master, whom we need more than ever before, is busy with something else. And you know what that is."

"I do," said Skaldfinn with resignation. "He's sitting down by the harbor with his girlfriend, reading a book."

* * *

Trying to read a book would have been nearer the truth. Shef himself was only barely literate. In his childhood he had the alphabet beaten into him by Father Andreas the village priest, more because he could not be parted from the education of his stepsister and half-brother than for any other reason. He could in the end spell out English written in Roman script, with difficulty, a difficulty that had not diminished much by what he had learnt as a king.

The book he had taken from the heretic sect caused him no difficulty as regards script. If Shef had known more, or indeed anything, about such things, he would have recognised it as written in Carolingian majuscule, handsomest of medieval scripts, as easy to read as print—and in itself proof positive that the book he held was a recent copy, no more than fifty or sixty years old. As it was, all that Shef realized was that he could read the handwriting well enough. Unfortunately he could not understand a word of the language it was written in: Latin, as it happened. Not good Latin, as Solomon the Jew saw instantly when the book was passed to him. The Latin of an uneducated person, far worse than the Latin of the Bible translated by Saint Jerome, and indeed, from the odd words scattered through it, the Latin of a native inhabitant of these hills. It had not been written in Latin to begin with, Solomon felt sure. Nor yet Greek or Hebrew. Some language he did not know.

Nevertheless Solomon could understand it well enough. At first he had simply read the book to Shef and the listening Svandis. But as the fascination of the story grew upon him, Shef had halted him, and with his usual fierce energy had organized a translating team. They clustered now, seven of them including auditors, in a shady courtyard close by the harbor. Wine and water stood in earthenware pitchers, wrapped in damp cloth to cool them by evaporation. If Shef stood up he could see over the white plastered wall to where the ships of his fleet swung at anchor, controlling their movement with ropes to the shore so as always to present their broadsides to the harbor mouth and the jetties. The catapult crews lay by their machines in the sun, lookouts watching for any sign of movement by the Greek galleys paddling up and down out of range, or from the floating fort which occasionally, and seemingly for practice, sent a rock skimming over the stone moles to splash harmlessly into the harbor. But Shef rarely stood up. His mind was intent on his task. A task, some inner calculator within him said, more vital even than the siege. Or the siege at this stage.

Solomon stood in the courtyard, book in hand. Slowly he translated the Latin he read, phrase by phrase, into the trade-Arabic that most of his hearers could follow. There the message broke into three separate strands. Shef himself translated Solomon's Arabic into the Anglo-Norse language of his fleet and court, to be written down by Thorvin in his own runic alphabet. A Christian priest whom Solomon had produced, and who had been defrocked by his bishop for some unknown crime, simultaneously translated the Arabic into the Latin-derived *patois* of the hills, which some called Catalan and some Occitan, or the language of Provence, and wrote it down in his own hand. With great difficulty, as he often complained, for whatever one called his native dialect it had never been written down before, and he had to decide continually how to spell each word. "The way to spell it is the way it's said," rumbled Thorvin, but was ignored by all. Finally, and with far more ease than the others, an apprentice of the learned Moishe translated the Arabic into Hebrew and wrote that down as well, in the complex vowel-less system of his native language. By the five men sat Svandis, listening intently and commenting on the story as it unfolded. In the shade, on a pallet, lay Tolman the kite-boy, still wrapped in bandages and staring out of swollen eyes. In the end one book would have become four, in four different languages, done with different levels of skill.

The master-copy itself was a strange work, whose weirdness caused Solomon increasingly to raise his eyebrows and pluck at his beard. It began with an introduction of a kind:

These are the words of Jesus ben-Joseph, once dead and now returned to life. Not returned to life in the spirit, as some say, but returned to life in the body. For what is the spirit? There are some who say, the letter killeth but the spirit giveth life. But I say to you, neither does the letter kill nor the spirit give life, but the spirit is life and the life is the body. For who can say that the spirit and the body and the life are three? For who has seen a spirit without a body? Or a body without a life but with a spirit? And so the three are one but the one is not three. I say this, I Jesus ben-Joseph who was dead but am alive . . .

The narrative went on in a kind of disorganized ramble. But through the ramble, and clearer as the translation team spelled through the many pages, came a sort of an account, and an account that agreed with what Anselm the heretic had told Shef, and—though he hesitated still to tell it to Svandis— with the visions he had had himself of the Crucifixion of Christ.

Whoever told the story declared that he had himself been crucified, nailed to a cross and drunk bitter drink on it, he said again and again. He had been killed and taken down. He had come again to life, and his friends had taken him away, away from the cross and away from his home. Now he lived in a place he did not know, and tried to draw some meaning from all that had happened. The moral that he drew seemed to be a kind of bitter resentment. Again and again he would refer to something or other he had said in a former life, and would deny it, call it folly, take it back. Sometimes he would answer what seemed to have been his own rhetorical questions.

Once I said, 'who among you, if a father and his child asked him for bread, would give the child a stone?' So I asked in my folly, and did not know that many a father has only stone to give, and many have bread but yet give only stones. So it was with my father, when I called out to him . . .

Solomon hesitated here as he translated, for he recognised the phrase he was translating. *Domne, domne, quare me tradidisti?,* it read in the barbarous Latin of the book. But in Aramaic it would have been *Eloi, eloi, lama sabachthani,* as it is given still in the Gospel of Mark. Solomon made no remark on the corroboration, but translated on, his voice as even as he could make it.

It seemed though that the teller of the story had turned against all fathers, or at least fathers in heaven. He insisted that there was such a father. But he insisted also that such a father could not possibly be good. If he were good, why was the world as it was, full of pain and fear and disease and suffering? If all these were the result of the sin of Adam and of Eve, as the narrator knew was argued, was this not a case again of the fathers and mothers sinning, and the punishment being visited on the children? What kind of parents would so condemn their children to slavery and to death? That slavery and death were what must be escaped, said the heretics' book. But the way to escape it was not by paying a price, nor a ransom, for the slavemaster-father would take no price for release. Rather it was to release oneself. And the key to that release was to believe in no afterlife, or not one under the control of the God of this world, *princeps huius mundi,* as the narrator continually called him. It was to live your life in such a way as to gain most pleasure from it, for pleasure was the gift of the true God beyond this world, and the foe of the devil-God who ruled the world, the betraying Father. It was to bring no more slaves into the world for that Father to rule and tyrannize over, but to control one's spirit and one's seed.

"What do you make of all this?" said Shef to Solomon as they paused to allow pens to be resharpened and throats to be moistened.

Solomon plucked at his beard, one eye on Elazar, the pupil and spy of Moishe, who blamed Solomon still for unleashing the Christians' fury on their city.

"It is badly told. That makes it the more interesting."

"Why so?"

"I have read my own holy books, the Torah of the Jews. I have read the Christian gospels also. And I have read the Koran of the followers of Mohammed. All are different. All tell us things their authors perhaps did not mean to."

Shef said nothing, let Solomon get round to the unspoken question.

"The Koran is said to be the word of God put into the mouth of

Mohammed. It seems to me to be the work of a great poet, and a man of inspiration. Nevertheless it tells us nothing that might not be known by— say, a well-traveled merchant of Arabia, who longed above all for religious zeal and an end to the hair-splitting of the Greeks."

"It is the work of a man, not a God, you mean," said Svandis, with a triumphant look at Shef.

"The gospels?" Shef prompted.

Solomon smiled. "They are, to say the least, confused. Even the Christians have noticed that they contradict each other in detail, and adduce this as proof that they must be true: either true in some spiritual sense about which, in the end, there can be no argument for there is no proof, or true as different accounts of the same event may still all be true. It is clear to me that all were written many years after the story they claim to tell, and by men who knew the holy books of the Jews in great detail. You cannot tell what happened from what the writers wanted to have happened. And yet . . ." he paused, with a glance at Elazar.

"And yet I have to say that they contain a kind of truth, if a human truth. All seem to tell the story of an uncomfortable man, a preacher who would not say what they asked him to. He would not condemn adultery. He would not allow divorce. He told people to pay their taxes. He liked Gentiles, even Romans. His hearers were trying to twist what he said even as he was saying it. It is an odd story, and odd stories are the likelier to be true."

"You have said nothing about your own holy books," remarked Shef again. Solomon looked at Elazar again. They were talking in the Anglo-Norse of the foreigners, which Elazar surely could not follow. Yet he was suspicious, ears ready for anything he might understand. He would have to put this carefully.

Solomon bowed respectfully. "The holy books of my faith are the word of God, and I say nothing against that. Yet it is an odd thing that sometimes God uses two words. For instance in the account of our forefather Adam and his wife Eve—" he used, as far as he could, the English pronunciations of the names "—the name of God is sometimes one thing and sometimes another. It is as if—as if, I say—there were a writer who said, so to speak, *metod* for God, as you sometimes do, and another who preferred to say *dryhten*. As if the two words testified to two writers with different versions of one story."

"What would that mean?" said Thorvin.

Solomon shrugged politely. "It is a difficult text."

"You said that all these holy books contain things their authors did not mean to say," Shef pressed on, "and I understand what you mean. Now what does this one, this one that we have here, tell us that its author did not mean to say?"

"In my opinion," said Solomon, "this is the work of someone who has been through great pain and grief and so cannot think of anything else. You have perhaps met men like that."

Shef thought of his former follower, the gelded berserk Cuthred, and nodded.

"You cannot expect such men to tell a clear story. They are mad, and the author of this text was in a sense mad. But it may be that he was mad because he saw clearly."

"I will tell you something about him," said Svandis with sudden definiteness, "and it is something those fools in the hills got wrong. Like Thierry, who kidnapped me but did not rape me."

Eyes turned towards her. To his surprise Shef saw the beginnings of a blush spreading across Svandis's tanned face. She looked uneasily at Tolman, plunged on.

"When men lie with women—in the North anyway, I have heard that these Arabs are wiser—they think of nothing but spilling their seed deep inside her. But there is another way . . ."

Shef gaped incredulously, wondering what she meant. And how she knew.

"To go on till almost the end, and then to—well, withdraw. Spill the seed outside the womb. It is as good for the woman, better if the act lasts longer. As good for the man too. It makes no children, no more hungry mouths. It is a pity more men cannot practice it. But of course it would mean they had to think of the woman, which no man ever does when he is intent on his pleasure alone!

"But anyway, that is what this book is talking about. The man who wrote it must have known something. But Thierry and Anselm and Richier, they think it means that you must leave woman alone, live like a monk! And yet all the time the book tells us to take pleasure in the world. If you cannot take pleasure from women—or from men either—then what pleasure is there? Men are such fools."

Shef was pleased to notice, sourly, that Thorvin and Solomon seemed as puzzled as himself. "So the book is a manual for pleasure in marriage," he remarked. "And we were thinking it was a lost gospel."

"Why can it not be both?" snapped Svandis.

CHAPTER TWENTY-ONE

The Emperor had had little hope of success from the scaling ladders: he had tried them out because he had plenty of men and one never knew the enemy's weaknesses. The ram had seemed more practicable. Watching from a distance he had made out the unmistakable figure of Brand on the ramparts, once his ally, never his friend. To lose to him had been galling. Now the time had come, he decided, for serious thought, and to help him he had called in the few men of his army he thought might be capable of it. Agilulf, his deputy, an experienced warrior. Georgios the admiral of the Greeks, with the proverbial subtlety of that race. Erkenbert the deacon, on whom he most relied. Once he and they had made their plan he would communicate it to the host of subordinate leaders who made up his army's contingents: none of them, in the Emperor's candid opinion, fit to lead anything more complicated than a charge or an ambush.

"Those in the city are not stupid," he concluded, "and their defenses are good. Also, we know the one-eye is there, and where he appears, strange things happen. Now, what can we do to puzzle them?"

Georgios replied, speaking slowly in his camp-Latin. "The harbor remains a weak point," he said. "I will not risk my galleys close in against their mule-stones, but at the same time we have proved that they dare not come out against the floating fort designed by the wise deacon here: I am glad to have seen it and will take careful note of it for my Emperor's uses in the future. Still, the stone jetties are only six feet above the water, and they run many stadia long. There is a chance there for an escalade, if we can get close enough."

"Many small boats, not a few large ones?" suggested Bruno.

"And, I would suggest, at night."

"What about the Greek fire? Can you not bring it close up to the jetties and burn all the defenders off as you did the Arab galleys?" asked Agilulf.

The admiral hesitated. He could not lie to Agilulf, who had seen the Greek fire used several times. Yet at the heart of the policy of the Byzantines was the need to keep their one great technical advantage secret. No barbarian—and barbarian included the servants of the Emperor of Rome, as far as the Greeks were concerned—was allowed to get too close to the projectors or the fuel tanks. The operators were the most highly paid men in the fleet, the admiral included, and all had moreover left hostages for their secrecy in Byzantium. Georgios felt that he had learnt much on this trip, including the details of the Roman and Northern catapults. He wanted to give nothing back in return. Yet he must answer.

"The Greek fire has certain limitations," he temporized. "It needs a large ship to carry it. I cannot put the devices into mere fishing boats. Nor can I take the risk of losing one to enemies who, as the Emperor says, are only too ready to learn new and strange devices. Yet at night, I might risk one galley close in." With trusted men aboard to burn and destroy the evidence if it might fall into the wrong hands, he did not say.

"We'll try it," said Bruno decisively. "Night after next, there'll be no more than a thin moon. Now, Erkenbert, where is the War-Wolf?"

'War-Wolf' was the name of the great engine that Erkenbert himself had designed, and that had battered down the gates of castle after castle in the Emperor's triumphant progress to Puigpunyent. It was, in a way, no more than a giant version of the simple traction catapults that Shef had designed and that even now were hurling rocks at every besieger who came within range of the city of Septimania. Yet it did not rely on mere feeble human muscles to give it power. Power came from the giant counterweight, the counterweight that was both its strength and its weakness: enabling massive boulders to be thrown, taking an age to empty and refill, demanding great weight and strength in its supporting timbers—timbers still crawling along the coast road to the siege.

"Two days' travel away still," Erkenbert replied.

"And where do you mean to use it once it has arrived?"

"We have little choice. It is coming down the coast road from the north. We cannot move it through the hills above the town, and if we were to load it on board ship we would need cranes and a stone jetty out into deep water. So we will have to attack the north gate of the town. It is a strong and stout gate, but only wooden. One boulder from 'War-Wolf' will beat it down."

"If it lands on the right place."

"Trust me for that," said Erkenbert definitely. "I am the *arithmeticus*."

The Emperor nodded. He knew that no-one in the world was more skilled than the puny deacon in the mind-numbing task of translating weight to distance in the number-system his world had inherited from the Romans.

"Harbour attack the night after next, then," he concluded. "If that fails, 'War-Wolf' breaks down the north gate the next morning."

"And if that fails?" enquired Georgios, always ready to disconcert his temporary allies.

The Emperor looked at him forbiddingly. "If that fails, we try again. Till the Holy *graduale* on which our Savior was borne is in my hands, along with the Lance by which he died. But I don't want to fail. Remember, all of you, we are dealing with clever heathens. Be alert for anything new. Expect the unexpected."

In silence, his advisers speculated on how this paradox might be achieved.

The bastards are too quiet, thought Brand, strolling along the harbor front in search of his master. There he was, still in the courtyard, all of them still reading, gabbling, scritch-scratching away with never a care in the world. He waited till Solomon noticed his looming presence and broke off his reading.

"Sorry to disturb you," he remarked ironically. "I thought I'd mention the siege."

"It's going well, isn't it?" asked Shef.

"Well enough. But I think it's time you did something."

"What?"

"What you're best at. Thinking. It's all gone quiet. But I've seen our friend Bruno through the far-seer. He won't give up. So—they're going to do something. I don't know what. You are the best person in the world for imagining new things. Time for you to do it again."

Slowly, bringing his mind back from the fascinating problems of the book, Shef realized the truth of what Brand had said. Realized too, with some subconscious calculation, that the breathing space he had counted on, and had been using on what he felt was the most vital if not the most urgent task, the task he alone could do—that that breathing-space was over. Besides, he was getting bored with sitting. And the book was nearly done.

"Find Skaldfinn to take my place here," he ordered. "He can translate from Solomon for Thorvin to write down. Tolman, you come along too."

He stepped out into the sunlight with the gigantic Brand and the limping kite-boy at his heels, followed by a glower from Svandis. She wanted to listen to the end of the strange book. At the same time she resented the way her lover could turn his attention instantly to something new. Something without her.

"I brought two people to talk to you," added Brand once they were in the open. "Steffi and a native."

Shef turned his attention first to the native, as Brand called him, another dark-faced man of clear Arab descent: there were still many non-Jews in the town, traders caught by the unexpected closure of roads.

"You speak Arabic?" he asked.

"Of course." A slight sneer at the question: Shef's Arabic was no more than serviceable, far removed from the pure tongue of Cordova or Toledo.

"What is your news?"

"The Christian Emperor, your enemy and the enemy of my master the Caliph, has destroyed many walls and forts this summer. He has killed many of the faithful too, all along the sea-coast they once controlled. Do you wish to know how he did it?"

"We will pay gold for it," Shef replied.

"I would tell you anyway, as a service against the Nazarenes. He has a machine. Only one machine, and it is many times bigger than anything you have here. He uses it for only one thing, and that is to hurl great boulders on to his enemy's gates. Some say that it needs flat ground, that it can shoot only very slowly."

"Have you ever seen it?"

"No, but I have spoken with men who escaped with their lives when strongholds were taken."

Bit by bit Shef drew from the Arab what little accurate information he could provide, and began to realize the use of the counterweight. Absently he dismissed the man, thinking already of the problems of a pivot, of retention and release: above all, the central problem of all the traction engines, of how to control range. It depended on weight. There must be some way to tell, if you knew how much was in the counterweight and how much in the launching-sling, what you needed to add or to take out in order to throw a set distance. But a three-element calculation was beyond Shef, or any other man in his realm. Even working out how many water-barrels you needed, or what share of loot went to each ship or each man, was a trial-and-error business with the Northern counting-system. Shef wished in frustration that he too, like Bruno, had in his service an *arithmeticus*. Even someone who knew what arithmetic might be. As he pounded a fist into his palm he became aware that Steffi was standing on one foot, eying him nervously from his usual wide angle.

"Why did Brand send you here?"

"I was thinking. About the flares we used from the kites. And that time I jumped off the cliff, you remember? I was thinking, how would it be, at night like, if we had some flares ready to light, and threw them from a pull-thrower? We could put some cloth on so they'd open out, see, and come down slowly, with a hole in, like we've learned how to do . . ."

After a few further moments explanation Shef sent Steffi off to find a gang and practice attaching the cloth.

"Don't light anything, mind," he warned him. "Just figure out how they have to be rigged to open properly. Go easy with the saltpeter crystals, it'll take time to make more."

As the squint-eyed ex-slave went off, Shef's mind went back to the counterweight machine no doubt already approaching. His eye fell on the still-bandaged Tolman. The lad had been silent and downcast ever since he came round from his long unconsciousness, not surprising with his two comrades dead. Could another boy be used? No, there was no doubt that Tolman was the most experienced flyer, the most likely to succeed. Yet he would have to be persuaded.

Shef's face took on the reasonable and friendly air that his closest associates had come to dread, the expression that showed he was about to use someone.

"Well, Tolman," he began. "Like to try a flight over nice soft water this time? Get your nerve back before it goes, eh?"

The boy's lip trembled, he blinked back tears. Dumbly, obediently, he nodded. Shef patted him carefully on his deep-grazed shoulder, led him away, shouting as he went for Cwicca, Osmod, and the most skillful of the kitemen and catapulteers.

As he had been during the long northern winter seven years before, Shef was amazed at the speed with which—sometimes—an idea could become reality. Before the day was out the materials for the new-style siege catapult had been assembled, including the massive beam that would be its throwing arm, stripped without complaint from the keel of a coasting vessel still on the stocks. It helped, of course, that there was no ordinary work to be done. The entire population of Septimania was idle, and when they thought of what a sack by Imperial troops would mean, anxious to assist in any way. Skilled carpenters and smiths abounded for every task: cost was not considered. It helped too that Shef had skilled taskmasters ready and willing to drive men beyond their normal habits—as he watched Cwicca swinging a rope's end at a sweating gang working on the iron rim of one of the six huge cartwheels that would shift the monster when it was done. Shef observed that having been a slave perhaps gave some men a taste for authority.

Like himself?, he wondered for an instant. No, he dismissed the thought. He did only what had to be done.

Besides, the critical thing, the thing that no other group in the world had in such abundance, was confidence. Confidence that to every problem, whether it was flying in the sky or launching huge boulders, there was a hard solution, if only one could work out all possible details. Cwicca and Osmod and even Steffi, like their now-missing comrade Udd, had seen kings collapse and armies break before them, all because of machines. They did nothing half-heartedly.

And that was all very well, but this time, this time they might be wrong! Shef plunged back into the problem that had preoccupied him ever since he had set the gangs working. He roved up and down the dock, muttering and counting, telling over the piles of white and black stones he had collected and stowed in every pocket he owned.

Cwicca, rope's end laid aside, nudged one of his mates. "He's getting in a rage," he muttered. "Someone'll cop it, you see."

"Us and all," his mate answered gloomily. "What's biting him?"

"Don't know. Something too clever for the likes of us."

Solomon the Jew, his translating labors completed, also saw the growing fury on the face of the strange king: the strange king he had grown to like, in spite of the dire fate he had brought to Septimania, for his constant curiosity. A mind more active than that of any Talmudist, he reflected. But in so many fields the mind of a child.

Rather more politely than Cwicca's mate, he moved to put the same question. "Something disturbs you, lord of the North?"

Shef glowered, caught his own fury and mastered it, made himself speak connectedly. Maybe, he thought, maybe saying the problem out loud would assist him. And after all, he had found out long ago, when you could not solve a problem, ask everybody. Someone always knew.

"It's like this," he said. "At some time or other I will need to know how far this thing will throw. Now, it ought to be easier with a machine of this sort than it is with the hand-pulled machines. For with them all you can say is 'pull hard,' or 'not so hard,' and 'not so hard' cannot be counted. But with this machine I can count everything! I have been thinking it out, what will happen when we try. Suppose I tell Cwicca to take ten hundred-pound bags and put them in the bucket, the bucket that drops the short arm. Now suppose I put a rock that weighs the same as three hundred-pound bags—if I could find one that would be so convenient, hah!—but suppose I did. Then suppose the ten hundred pounds threw the three hundred pounds one hundred paces. And I needed to make it throw one hundred and twenty paces. Then it is obvious, I would need more weight in the bucket. Or less weight to be thrown. And they have something to do with each other. But what?"

His voice rose to a strangled yell, he fought rage down again and continued with the thoughts that had buzzed round and round his head like weary bees. "Now, I am not a fool, Solomon. One hundred and twenty is to one hundred as six to five, is it not? So I must make the other things as six to five. Or is it five to six? No, lower the weight thrown. Lower the three hundred pounds as six to five. Or raise the weight throwing as five to six, the ten hundred pounds. Now how many fives are there in ten hundred? How many fives in ten, there are two. So two hundred, and then what do I do with that, I take six of them. Oh, I can find the answer, Solomon, in the end. But it takes me as long as it takes a slow ox to plow a furrow. And I end up doing it with these little stones for markers *because I forget what I'm doing!*"

Shef yelled with honest fury for a moment and hurled his handful of pebbles scattering into the blue water of the harbour. As if in answer, the fort floating almost a mile away beyond the stone jetties sent a rock at extreme range splashing into the dock. The laboring men averted their eyes, tried not to seem aware of what was happening.

"And all the time," Shef concluded, "I know that I am doing the whole thing with the simplest numbers. Because really any rock we use will weigh three hundred-pound bags and maybe twenty-seven over. And I will need to raise the range not twenty yards out of a hundred, but seventeen out of ninety-five."

He squatted by a patch of sand. "I wish I had learned the trick of numbers from some skilled Roman. See," he drew a V in the sand. "I know that is for five." He added a stroke to make a VI. "That is for six. Or the other side," he drew a IV, "that is for four. But how to make all this answer my question, that I do not know. Only the ancient folk of Rome were wise enough for that art."

Solomon pulled his beard, marveling internally. Fortunate that Moishe had not heard this. Or Elazar. Their remarks about barbarians would have become even more barbed. "I do not think," he said carefully, "I do not think it is the ancient Romans you should go to for an answer."

Shef looked up, eye gleaming. "You mean there is an answer?"

"Oh yes. They could have told you in Cordova, if you had asked. But even here, many men know the answer to what you seek. Every merchant, every astronomer. Even Mu'atiyah could have told you."

"What is the secret then?" Shef was on his feet.

"The secret?" Solomon had been speaking in Anglo-Norse, which he now spoke as familiarly as any man in the fleet. Now he shifted to Arabic. "The secret is *al-sifr.*"

"*Al-sifr?* That means empty. That means nothing. How can nothing be the secret, are you mocking me, longbeard . . . ?"

Solomon held up a hand. "There is no mockery. But look, this is not for prying eyes, see how everyone is staring. Come with me to the courtyard. I promise you, by the time men dowse their lamps you will be a greater *arithmeticus* than any Roman is or ever was. I will show you the devices of al-Khwarizmi the Great."

Solomon led a silent king towards the shaded court.

Little more than an hour later, Shef looked up from the table of fine white sand on which he and Solomon had been drawing. His one eye was wide with astonishment. Carefully he swept his hand over the sand-tray, obliterating all the markings on it except the column of ten signs which Solomon had showed him to begin with.

"Let's try it again," he said.

"Very well. Draw your lines."

Shef drew five vertical lines down the sand, making four columns. He drew two horizontal ones across the top, three more across the bottom.

"We will try to solve your range problem, only with harder numbers than the ones you told me. Let us say that you have thrown a boulder of two hundred and eighty pounds, and it has reached one hundred and twenty yards, six score in your language. But you need to reach one hundred and forty, seven score. Your throwing weight was eleven hundred and forty pounds. You must increase that in the proportion of seven to six. So, first, we must multiply eleven hundred and forty by seven and then divide by six."

Shef nodded: the words 'multiply' and 'divide' were strange to him, but he understood the ideas.

"First," Solomon went on, "write the numbers for eleven hundred and forty in their correct place."

Shef pondered for a moment. He had soon grasped the idea of a number-system based on position, but it still did not come easily to him.

"Try writing it the Roman way first," said Solomon gently. "Write it in the sand away from your table. The Romans wrote a thousand by 'M'."

Shef wrote a wavering 'M' in the sand, followed by a dot. Then a 'C' for one hundred. Then the familiar four 'X's for forty. His hand reached out to make the hole sign for *al-sifr*, nothing, but drew back. The Romans would have left such a number as M.C.XXXX.

"Now enter the Arabic signs at the head of your table," Solomon prompted. "Eleven hundred and forty at the top, seven at the bottom."

Shef hesitated again. This was the tricky part. Now. The right-most column was for numbers below ten. In the horizontal line one above the bottom, the line for the multiplier, he wrote the shaky hook of a '7': the multiplier. The topmost horizontal line was for the multiplied, as he could see from his Roman numerals, one thousand, one hundred and forty.

In the left-most column he wrote a '1,' corresponding to the 'M'. In the next, another one, corresponding to the 'C.' In the next, the more complex shape of a '4,' for the four 'X's. And finally, in the rightmost column, the column for the ten numbers below ten—ten, not nine, as Solomon had proved to him—he drew the *al-sifr* hole.

Now to do the sum. The first thing, the most vital thing, was that seven noughts were nought. *So write in the nought.* Deliberately, watched by four pairs of eyes, Shef began to work his way through the calculation on the sand-table, primitive ancestor of the abacus. For long moments he thought of nothing else, lost in a sensation no man of his race had ever before experienced: the fascination of number. In the end, hardly aware of how he had come by it, he stared with surprise and deep satisfaction at the result written in the sand. Seven thousand nine hundred and eighty. He had never seen a number like that before—not because it was too large, not when every part of his realm was counted in hides, thirty thousand for a province, a hundred thousand for what had once been a kingdom. No, because of its exactness. Over a thousand, numbers to him were counted in scores, or tens, or hundreds, or half-hundreds: not sixes and sevens and eights and fours.

"Now you are to divide seven thousand nine hundred and eighty by six," went on the quiet voice of Solomon. "Make your table for divisions."

Shef's hand brushed the sand away, began another table. Prompted again and again by Solomon, he worked his way doggedly through.

"And so in the end," said Solomon finally, "you know that you would need to increase your throwing weight to . . ."

"Thirteen hundred and thirty pounds," said Shef.

"So you would add to your original weight . . ."

"Two hundreds less ten. One hundred and ninety pounds. Exactly."

"But by the time you'd set up your sand table and done all this," objected Skaldfinn, "your enemy would have buried you under a hail of boulders. Because he'd have been shooting while you'd been drawing!"

"Not with the new machine," said Shef flatly. "I could have done all this while they were still taking the weights out to winch the arm back up again. Then I could just tell them to put the same weight back in with a measured one hundred and ninety on top. And besides: I can see this is just like the far-seer."

"Like the far-seer?" asked Solomon.

"Yes. You remember that fool Mu'atiyah. He could make the far-seer, he had been shown how the glass should be ground, something we might never have realized in a thousand years. But he never thought to go a step further. I swear, by the time we return to our own home my wise men will have learned more of glass and sight than Mu'atiyah, or even his master. Because they will not rest till they have! Now, this calculation you have shown me, this too I might never have learned for myself. But now I have learned it, I see it can be made quicker, much quicker. The sand table—it's not needed, nor the stones in my hand. I use them because I am not practiced. If I were, then I could put my counters on wire and carry it all with me, like a harp. Or I could do it without any columns at all. Ideas are hard to come by, easy to improve. I will improve this one yet. Improve it till—what was his name, Solomon, al-Khwarizmi?—till al-Khwarizmi himself would not recognise it. And I will use it for more than catapults! This is the anvil for a smith-craft on which the Way could beat out the world! Is that not right, Thorvin? Skaldfinn?"

Solomon fell silent, hand going up to his beard as if for comfort. He had forgotten the furious spirit of the Northerners, and of the One King in particular. Was it wise ever to tell them anything? Too late, now, to reconsider.

CHAPTER TWENTY-TWO

Dimitrios, senior *siphonistos* to the Greek fleet, listened to the orders of his admiral with doubt tinged with alarm. The orders were, of course, expressed with great care, somewhere between suggestion and persuasion. The *siphonistoi* were almost a law unto themselves, curators of the ultimate weapon of Byzantium, in their own opinion more important in the last resort even than emperors, let alone admirals. Dimitrios, if he chose, could make a fortune and live like a lord anywhere in the civilized world, Baghdad or Cordova or Rome, simply by selling the information in his head. A wife, a mistress, seven children and two thousand golden hyperpers in the banks of Byzantium stood forfeit to his treachery. But in any case the whole city knew that no *siphonistos* would ever reach mastery of his trade if there were the slightest doubt about his loyalty to the cause of Church and Empire: loyalty from principle, not compulsion.

That loyalty caused Dimitrios's doubt. One of his greatest compulsions was to preserving the secrecy of the fire. Better to lose a battle by destroying one's equipment, he had been told a thousand times, than to risk its capture for a purely temporary victory—all victories, for the beleaguered Empire of the Byzantines, had long been recognised as temporary. Now the admiral wanted him to risk a ship and a projector close inshore, in doubtful battle against Jews and strange heathens. Dimitrios was a brave man, who would take his chance of being sent to the bottom by the strange mule-stones, as the barbarians called them. Risking the fire and the secret were another thing.

"The small boats will go in first," repeated Georgios cajolingly. "Only if they make a lodgement will we bring up your galley."

"To do what?"

"If they can detach the booms you may be able to get into the harbor and burn out all the stone-thrower ships at once."

"They'd sink us as we came in."

"It will be black night, a thin moon, barely a hundred yards to row to the nearest. After that you can always keep an enemy ship between you and their catapults till you are close enough to pump the fire at them."

Dimitrios considered. He had indeed been enraged at the sinking of the galley and the butchery of its men in the inconclusive battle at sea weeks before: an act of defiance which had left him for the first time in his career feeling helpless. It would be a delight to avenge that shame by burning every enemy ship to the waterline, as all enemies of Byzantium deserved. To show the devil-worshipers the power of God and his Patriarch. And close range and at night were exactly the right conditions for the use of his weapon.

"What if they don't get the boom open?"

"You could pull along the stone jetty and sweep it of any resistance. That way you would have the jetty between you and the stone-throwers in the harbor. Clear the jetty and pull out to sea again in the darkness."

Dimitrios thought carefully. There were risks in this, he could see, but perhaps no more than were justifiable. He would take his own precautions, of course, as the admiral certainly knew he would. Men standing by to fire the tanks, boats in waiting to collect himself and his crew if they had to abandon ship. No need to repeat all that.

Seeing him waver, the admiral added a final dose of flattery to win his supposed subordinate over. "Of course we know that the most important thing in our fleet is yourself. You and the skill you have developed. We dare not lose that to any barbarian. I will myself stand by in the rescue boats, to come in for you if there is any sign of mischance."

Dimitrios smiled, a little mirthlessly. What the admiral said was true. But he had no idea how true. He himself, Dimitrios, knew the entire process of making the Greek fire from ground to nozzle, as the *siphonistoi* said. He had been beyond the Black Sea to far Tmutorakan, where the colored oils oozed from the ground. He had seen it in the winter, when the oil ran thin and clear, and in the stifling summer, when it came out like sludge from a foul farmyard. He knew how it was collected, he knew how it was stored. He himself had soldered the copper tanks with precious tin, to be sure there was no leak. He had built his own equipment with his own hands, tank and valves, brazier and bellows, pump and nozzle. Again and again, under the guidance of the old masters of the trade, he had fired up, pumped in the air, seen the flame flow. Three times his masters had made him pump on beyond the safe limit, using small and old devices and condemned criminals as pump-hands, so that he could hear the rising shrillness of the *niglaros,* the valved pressure-whistle, whose valve was opened to test the vapors within. He had looked with interest at the bodies of the condemned, to see what effect the bursting tanks had had upon them. Not one had ever survived, and Dimitrios thought they had chosen ill to take the *siphonistos* chance instead of sure but less painful death on the execution ground. He was acutely aware of every difficulty in the whole process, how much easier it was to have it go wrong than go right. Without him, he knew, mere knowledge would not be enough. It was his experience that was vital and precious. Good, at least, that the admiral had recognised it.

"With the proper safeguards, I consent," he said.

The admiral sank back in his chair with relief. While he knew how much less than biddable his corps of *siphonistoi* were, he would not have relished explaining the fact to the Emperor of the Romans: a man who, he thought, should be given a skilled Byzantine doctor as soon as possible, to ensure that he ate something that disagreed with him.

"Have one ship ready at nightfall," he said. "Take my own *Carbonopsina.*"

The Black-Eyed Beauty, thought Dimitrios. Pity that there were none such in this far land of strangers. Only thin Moorish women and the ugly descendants of Goths, with their pale skin and discolored eyes. Ugly as the revolting Germans, their allies, though these insisted that their barbarian enemies were even worse for pallor and bulk and the size of their feet. Certainly all should be swept from the sea, the Inner Sea, the Sea of the Middle of the World become once more a Greek and Christian lake. Dimitrios rose, bowed sketchily, withdrew to make his preparations.

The first sign of the sea-borne assault came only as the patrolling squad of city guardsmen marching along the longer jetty saw faint shapes crowding in out of the blackness. They stood, gaped for an instant to make sure, then began to blow the alarm on their ram's horn trumpets. By then the sixty fishing boats which Bruno had commandeered were bare yards from the stone wall, men in them already swinging their grapnels to pull the boats alongside, others raising the short boarding-ladders which were all they would need for the six-foot climb. The guardsmen bent their bows, the short breast-bows which were all they carried, shot, shot again at the targets pouring towards them. Then, as the first grapnels clinked on stone, they realized they were alone on a long stone causeway, about to be cut off. They ceased shooting and ran for the harbor end of the jetty, cut down as they fled by javelins and arrows flying out of the blackness. Bruno's first wave reached the jetty almost without resistance, divided immediately into two groups, one turning to their left and racing for the seaward end with hammers, saws and chisels, to try to cut the boom and open the entrance for

the reinforcements and the fire-ship. The other turned right and poured in
an armed mob for the landward end, seeking to reach and hold it till the rest
came up and drove either for the open harbor, or—just as disastrously for
the defense—to seize a stretch of the main wall and open it for escalade.

The rams' horns had done their work, though. While only a score of men
at a time marched along the jetties, open as they were to the unpredictable
shooting of the catapults on the offshore fort, many more stood to arms or
slept by them at the vulnerable points where jetties met shore. The attackers
charging along the stone strip, carried on with excitement at their easy
landing, met a sudden rain of arrows at close range, with behind them a
solid wall of spears and shields. Lightly-armed levies from the South, the
men Bruno habitually sent in first as most dispensable, many of them went
down even before the puny arrows of the breast-bows, shot at no more than
ten yards' range. Those who pressed on found themselves hacking at a
disciplined line behind a barricade. Slowly those who survived realized that
the pressure of comrades from behind was slackening, had gone. Unsure
why, or if they too were to be taken from behind in the darkness, they drew
back, at first step by step behind their shields, then as the arrows lashed at
their unprotected legs and sides, turning and running back into the
protective dark.

Shef had started from sleep at the first horn-blast. He slept naked in the
heat, seized tunic and boots, struggled into them in seconds, started for the
door. Svandis was there before him, naked also but barring his way. Even in
the almost pitch-black of the shuttered room Shef could feel the scowl on her
face, hear the lash in her voice.

"Don't run out like a fool! Mail, helmet, weapons! What good will you be
if the first stray slingstone cuts you down?"

Shef hesitated, full of counter-arguments, but Svandis carried on. "I am
the child of warriors, even if you are not. Better ready and slow than early
and dead. My father could have told you that. Who won the battle where I
first saw you? You, or he?"

Well, he did not, Shef thought to say. But it was no use arguing. Quicker
to obey than to try to thrust her aside. He turned to the mail-shirt which
hung ready from a hook, thrust his arms through the heavy sleeves. Svandis
was behind him, pulling the iron round, fastening it behind with the heavy
rawhide laces. It was true at any rate that she was the child of warriors. He
turned and embraced her, pulling her breasts on to the hard iron rings.

"If we live, when we return home I will make you a queen," he said.

She slapped his face sharply. "This is no time for love-whispers in the
dark. Helmet. Shield. Take your Swedish sword and try to live up to it."

Shef found himself thrust out into the courtyard, could hear her behind
him rummaging for her own clothes. Wherever the fighting was, she would

appear, he knew. He began to run, heavy under the weight of thirty pounds of wood and iron, towards the command post where he would find Brand. Across the water came a clangor of metal, war-cries and cries of pain. They had come by sea.

As Shef puffed up, he saw Brand towering in the midst of a squad of Vikings, his gigantic cousin Styrr standing next to him, almost his equal in size. Brand seemed in no great hurry or alarm, was busy counting his men.

"They landed on the jetty," he remarked. "I never thought that would give them much trouble. They've got to get off it if they're going to be a nuisance, and they'll have to do it fast."

Shef's ears had picked out different noises from the immediate ones of battle, already dying away: smithy noises, metal on metal, axe on wood.

"What's happening at the far end?"

"They're trying to cut the boom. Now that we don't want. We'll have to clear them off. All right, boys, got your boots laced up? Let's stroll along and shoo these Christians back into the water. You stay at the back," he added to Shef. "Organize some crossbows, make sure the catapults shoot at the opposition, not us. This would be easier if we could see what was going on."

In a solid mass the Vikings, perhaps forty of them, tramped round the harbor towards the point of contact, the hobnails on their boots crashing on the stone. A few lamps gleamed along the harbor-front, casting a dim light out over the water. In it, as his eyes adjusted, Shef could see the enemy massing for a second attack. There was something going on in the ships in the harbor too, he could hear rope creaking and catapult-captains shouting orders. If the Emperor's men did not fight their way off the jetty in the next few minutes, they would be swept by mule-stones. But there was something ominous happening out there, Shef could hear harsh voices taking command, metal clashing and ringing, could see the faint lamp-light reflected back on metal points and rings. A fierce cheer and a wall of metal coming forward, spear points in a line.

"Fall your men back," said Brand without haste to the city guard commander. "I think this is our trade now."

The light-armed guardsmen slipped back through the ranks behind, and the Vikings moved forward, forming their customary blunt wedge. The flimsy barricade at the end of the jetty had been torn down in the first assault, now offered no shelter. The steady line of *Lanzenbrüder*, picked men, armored from head to foot, tramped down on the Viking wedge, as heavily armed, for once their equals in size and strength. Neither side knew anything of defeat, both stood confident in their ability to batter down anything and anyone that stood before them.

Standing at the rear of the Viking formation, ten men wide but no more than four deep, Shef heard the simultaneous crash as shield met shield, the clang and thud of spears and axes meeting wood or iron. A heartbeat later, to his surprise and horror, the man in front of him stepped back, pushed almost off his feet by a surge from his own retreating line. Shef heard Brand's voice raised in a bull bellow as he called on his men to stand their ground. Vikings retreating?, he thought. They are falling back like the English used to, like they did the day my stepfather and I fought my father and his men on the causeway in Norfolk. That day I ran. But then I was only a nobody, little better than a thrall. Now I am a king, with gold on my arms and a sword of Swedish steel, made by my own steelmaster.

And still I am little more use than poor Karli. The line had steadied, was no longer falling back. From the front the clash of weapons was now continuous, both sides hacking and fencing rather than trying to force each off their feet. Shef sheathed his sword, turned abruptly and ran back along the harbor's edge, looking for something that would turn the tide.

The German warrior-monks had marched into the Viking line to try the tactics which had destroyed every Arab army that had come against them. Shield in one hand, shortened spear in the other. Ignore the man in front of you, stab at the man to your right as he lifts his arm for the sword-stroke. Rely on the comrade to your left to strike the man who threatens you. Stab with the right, strike out with the shield in your left, step forward with feet stamping. If the man in front goes down, trample him under foot, rely on the man behind to ensure he does not strike up from below. For an instant or two, the tactic worked.

But the men they now faced were not dressed in mere cotton or linen. Some spearpoints went home under the armpit, more skidded away from metal, were shrugged off brawny shoulders. The clubbing blows with the shields failed to knock heavy men off their balance. Some stepped back, shortened axe or sword, chopped at arms or helmets. Others saw the blows coming from their right-hand side, parried or blocked with their own blades, struck back at the unshielded sides of their enemies. Brand, having taken a pace back, to his own astonished rage, drove his axe 'Battle-Troll' through neck and shoulder, widened the gap with a thrust of his massive shield, and stepped into the German ranks, cutting to either side at the point of the wedge. His cousin Styrr swung an underhand blow that swept an enemy off his feet, broke the man's windpipe with a deliberate stamp from hobnailed feet, jumped forward to his cousin's side. Germans began to throw down their spears, draw swords, fill the air with steel as they hacked at heads and linden-shields.

Agilulf, watching from his position a few yards in the rear, pursed his lips as he recognised the giant figure of Brand. The big bastard from the Braethraborg, he thought to himself. Son of a sea-troll. Some rumor about him losing his nerve. He seems to have got it back again. Someone is going to have to take him out before he breaks our nerve, and I suppose it will have to be me. There don't seem to be very many of them. He began to work his way through the ranks of men thrusting with their shields at the backs of their comrades, trying to regain impetus.

As he trotted through the darkness Shef saw familiar figures closing round him: small men, with the rimmed metal caps of his own standard issue. Englishmen, crossbows ready, running down from their various stations or from sleep. He stopped, looked back at the barely-visible scrimmage at the jetty end, a frieze of weapons lifting and flashing over swaying bodies.

"I want to start shooting them up," he said.

"We can't see who to shoot at," came a voice in the darkness. "Nor we ain't got a clear shot neither."

As Shef hesitated, light suddenly spread over the whole harbor, bright white light like a summer noon. The fighting ceased for an instant, men screwed up their eyes to shield them, the working party struggling with the boom paused, caught like rabbits in torch-light. Shef looked up, saw the light drifting down from the sky, suspended under kite-cloth.

Steffi, dismissed by his master to work out the problem of flares on his own, had spent the afternoon with a gang, attempting to solve the problem of both throwing a flare in such a way that it would drift down, and then of lighting it. Two hours of experiments had solved the first problem: not an easy one, for anything put in the sling of a traction catapult was whirled violently round before launching. Some of the wooden bundles he had prepared tangled ignominiously in the sling, others had their cloths open as soon as they were released, crashing to the ground twenty yards off. In the end they discovered how to fold the cloths under the round bundle so that they flew straight, caught the air only at the top of their trajectory, drifted slowly down.

Lighting them was another matter yet, and Steffi had been forbidden to experiment with genuine flares for fear of enemy observers. When the attack came, Steffi was standing by one of the many traction catapults set up round the harbor and along the walls, waiting for a chance to shoot. In moments he had loaded the first of the saltpeter-impregnated bundles he had prepared, lit the short fuse he had devised, steadied the sling in his two hands, and given the order to throw. The missile had sailed out over the harbor, fuse glowing, and drifted, fuse still glowing, harmlessly into the sea. And the next. The third, its fuse cut ruthlessly back, had gone out.

"This is no good," called one of his crew. "Let's start throwing rocks down there at those boats. Even if we can't see we might hit something."

Steffi ignored him, mind racing in the panic of the failed inventor. "Get ready," he ordered. He thrust another bundle into the sling, ignored the useless fuse, instead gripped the torch with one hand and thrust it into the flammable bundle, hauling down on the sling with the other.

As the flare of flame sprang up he shouted "Pull," and let go himself as the team heaved with a will. The flare shot out like a comet, trailing sparks. The team gaped after it, wondering if the trailing kite-cloth would catch, if the flare would go out. At the top of its arc the flare seemed to steady, drop underneath its cloth support, began to drift gently down. From their vantage suddenly everything below them came clear: the fighting men on the jetty, the party clustered round the end of the boom, the boats grapnelled to the outer wall.

The great galley hanging on its oars a bare fifty yards from the harbor entrance, smoke rising from its center, a crackle of flame amidships with men moving purposefully round it.

The crew yelled and pointed at the galley, anxious to train round and shoot. Steffi shouted them down, prepared another flare. "We'll keep throwing these," he bawled. "'cos we're the only ones know how to do it. Let the others throw the rocks."

He thrust another flare into its place, ignoring the pain from already blistered fingers.

As he saw the flare drifting down, and remembered his own casual words earlier that day to Steffi, Shef's mind cleared from its near-panic. His voice dropped, he made himself breathe deeply and speak slowly, to spread calm and decision to those around him.

"Trimma," he said, recognising one of those crowding round him. "Take twenty men, put them in the dinghies there by the shore, row off till you're level with the fighting there. Then shoot carefully at the rear ranks of the Germans. Not the ones at the front, understand? You're too likely to hit our own lot. See Brand there, and Styrr with him? Make sure you don't hit them. Once the Germans break, start clearing the causeway. Take your time, stay out of range of their bows. Right, off you go.

"The rest of you, stand fast. How many boats are there left? All right, load them up. Now row out to our ships in the harbor, all the two-masters, two of you to each one. Tell the mule-crews to clear those men off from round the boom. But leave the *Fafnisbane* to me!"

He looked round, suddenly alone. Foolish! He should have held one man back. All the boats were gone, and . . .

Svandis appeared suddenly from behind him. She was staring up at the light, then looking round, trying to make sense of what was happening. It had taken her longer than he expected to find her clothes. Or else everything had happened more quickly than he knew. She pointed to the fighting men on the causeway, a grim struggle that had turned now into conventional battle, the play of swords over the war-linden of which poets sang.

"There," she shouted, "there, why are you hanging back, child of a whore and a churl, stand in the front like my father, like a sea-king . . ."

Shef turned his back on her. "Undo those laces."

The snap in his voice seemed to work, he felt fingers pulling at the rawhide knots they had so recently done up, but continually a flow of insults poured out, coward, runaway, skulker in the darkness, user of better men. He paid no attention. As the mail dropped free he dropped his sword, tossed his helmet after it and ran out, plunging from the harbor wall in a racing dive.

The lights were still filling the sky. As he looked up from the plunging overarm stroke he could see two in the air at once, one almost down to the water, the other still high up. Fifty strokes through the milk-warm water and he was clutching at the *Fafnisbane*'s anchor-cable, hauling himself up it arm over arm. A face gaped at him, recognised him, dragged him summarily inboard.

"How many men aboard, Ordlaf? Enough to man the sweeps? No? Enough to make sail? Do it. Cut the cable. Steer for the harbor entrance."

"But it's boomed closed, lord."

"Not now, it's not." Shef pointed out to sea. Just as the first mule-stones kicked up water round them or hummed ill-aimed overhead, the working parties round the far end of the jetty were scrambling back. They had battered their way through the stout iron rings holding chains and tree-trunks to the stone, or maybe sawed their way through the timber. But they had thrust the boom off, already its free end was floating inshore, opening the passage. And there was something out there, something beyond the harbor-wall. A flicker of motion told Shef it was a line of oars, dropping from the upright, the rest position, to the row. A galley coming in. And with the galley, the fire.

The *Fafnisbane* was moving now, on the faint breeze of night, just beginning to slip through the water. Too slowly, and coming bows on to the unseen menace out there. Bows on, where the mule could not bear. In ten seconds, Shef knew, he could be a burnt but living corpse like Sumarrfugl. He remembered the crisp feeling of the burnt skin crumbling under his hand as he had sent the merciful dagger home. Only there would be no merciful dagger for him. Faintly, he registered the snap of crossbows somewhere to one side low down on the water, the thud of quarrels striking home through flesh and armor, noted another flare burst into life directly overhead. He paid no attention. Voice still quiet, he spoke to Ordlaf: "Steer more to starboard. Let the forward mule bear on the harbor entrance. We may only get one shot."

Behind the clash of steel and the war-cries, Shef could make out another noise. A strange roaring, familiar but unexpected. For a moment he could not remember what it might be. Ordlaf had heard it too.

"What's that?" he called. "What are the devils up to out there? Is it a beast they have tamed, or a magic gale out of Hel? Or is it the sound of a windmill turning?"

Shef smiled, the sound coming back to him. "No beast, nor gale, nor windmill turning," he called back. "That is a great bellows blowing. But I hear no hammers with it."

A hundred yards away, Dimitrios the *siphonistos* had seen the signal from the men sawing and chiseling at the boom. A white flag swung furiously from side to side, just visible in the blackness. He had nodded his consent to the Greek captain. The oars swung down, the galley began its eager plunge towards prey. And then suddenly, light in the sky and everything as bright as day. The rowers had checked, the captain turned back for further instructions, robbed of the cover of dark.

But Dimitrios had already nodded his assent to the bellows-crew. They were heaving with a will, and as they did so the burning flax beneath the copper tank had sprung into flame. Dimitrios's first assistant had taken the first thrust down on the piston, the heavy one against resistance, was beginning to force it up and down with growing ease, counting to himself in an undertone as he did so: ". . . seven, eight . . ."

The count forced itself into Dimitrios's mind, ever aware of the danger of his own weapon. If the pressure got too great, the tank would explode and he too would burn like a wretched condemned criminal. If they stopped once they had started he would lose his inner sense of the heat and the pressure. But if they rowed on against catapults warned and manned, in this devil-light . . . And the long slim galley was still sliding forward, oars poised for the next heave, almost within the harbor-mouth with the boom floating away almost touching their ram . . .

They could be sunk in a moment. Or boarded and taken intact. As he hesitated a thin whistle began to rise from the top of the copper dome by which his men were pumping, a whistle that grew stronger every moment. The *niglaros* signaling danger. Dimitrios's nerve, stretched thin by the flares above and the menacing dark of the harbor-mouth, reached snapping-point.

"Turn to starboard," he yelled frantically. "Starboard! Turn along the harbor wall! Don't go inside!"

Shouts, a flailing of rope's ends, even on the shoulders of the paid and pampered Greek rowers. A heave from the port oars, a thrust back from the starboard bank. The galley was gliding swiftly along the stone wall, on the outside of the harbor, port oars tossed high to avoid the crash. Dimitrios could see frightened faces staring at him from hardly ten feet away, survivors of the first storming party, looking as if they meant to jump. As he looked across at them a group were hurled aside, falling into the sea in a confusion of staved ribs and broken bones: one of the barbarian catapults striking home.

The low galley was safe behind stone. And there ahead, not fifty yards away now, Dimitrios could see a target. Fighting men, men in armor struggling for the end of the jetty. He could row to the end, bear away at the last moment as the water shoaled, and launch the fire. Just in time, before the pressure built up. He could hear the whistle rising to one continuous shriek, could see out of the tail of his eye the two pump-men standing away from their handles, the bellows' crew looking fearfully up at him, all wondering when the dome would burst and the fire spring out at them.

But he, Dimitrios, was the master. He knew the strength of the pipes he had soldered with his own hands. He turned the gleaming brass nozzle, pushed forward the lit lamp to firing position. He would burn his own men as well as the enemy. But that was good tactics, and besides, they were Romans, Germans, heretics, schismatics. It would be a foretaste of the eternal fire they would all roast in. His lips drew back in a fierce grin.

Just behind him, the prow of the *Fafnisbane* nudged out beyond the harbor mouth. Shef had climbed out on to the very tip of the dragon-head, to see what was happening the instant his ship cleared the end of the jetty. He had seen the oars tossed up, had realized that the galley had turned away. His skin crawled for a moment as he wondered if the strange fire could be turned back upon him, then the thought vanished, dismissed by cold logic. Fire burnt everything, even Greek ships. They could not send it backwards over their own sterns. The zip of arrows plunging past him from the bowmen on the causeway meant nothing. His one eye strained for the target.

And there she was, stern on, gliding away, a lurid glow coming from somewhere amidships, by a strange red-gold dome, a high whistle trailing in her wake. They were going to shoot it, whatever it was. And Brand there was in their sights, he knew it. Would the mule never bear? Osmod was the catapult-captain, crouched behind his machine, swinging its trail round, round . . .

His hand flew up in the signal: sights on.

"Shoot!" Shef shouted.

The jerk of the lanyard, the vicious sweep and thwack of the arm, faster than a man could see, the even swifter lash of the sling, whirling round even before the ship could shudder from the smash of arm on padded crossbar. Shef's eye, almost in line with the flying rock, saw the familiar streak, rising and then falling . . .

No, too close to fall. The mule-stone missed its aim, the galley's curved stern, where it would have shattered stern-post and ribs and opened the entire ship like a gutted herring. Instead Shef's eye, half-blinded, caught only an after-image of the dark line flying straight into the mysterious red-gold dome, just as the dome itself released an ejaculation, a stream of glowing fire like the breath of Fafnir himself.

And then the fire was everywhere, exploding outwards with a thump that caught Shef fifty yards away like a blow in the chest. His dazzled eye for long moments could see nothing, then make sense of nothing it saw. Then he realized that the flaming mass was a ship rolling over, the torches in the water were men ablaze, the noise in his ears was tormented screaming.

He swung himself inboard. From the shore Steffi, hands now raw with pain, saw the *Fafnisbane* lit up in full view of the hostile offshore fort with its catapults, threw his torch aside, watched his last flare sing into the sea and go out. Darkness fell again on the harbor and the harbor wall, where dismayed combatants fell back groping, their only light the burning galley. His voice thick and fearful, Shef called to Ordlaf to turn the *Fafnisbane* and take her back.

And from his vantage point on the hillside a long half mile away, the Emperor Bruno grasped that his attack had failed, he knew not how. He turned to Erkenbert.

"Agilulf is gone, and the Greeks have let us down. It is up to you now."

"To me and to 'War-Wolf'," the Emperor's *arithmeticus* replied.

CHAPTER TWENTY-THREE

Shef looked down from the high seaward wall into the blue water below. The wreck of the Greek galley was there, he could see its outline maybe ten, maybe twenty feet below the surface, and no further out from the outer face of the jetty. He was sure that he himself could swim down, see what the fire and explosion had left, maybe attach ropes and drag what metal there was left into daylight. The floating fort was still there, still occasionally hurled a vindictive stone at any sign of movement, but he did not think they would hit a single man at that range.

No time, though. Not for mere curiosity. In any case he did not think that the wreckage would tell him very much more than he had worked out already. Most of the enemy storming party had got away in their boats before he could organize effective pursuit, but some had failed to find a place and remained in his hands: local levies for the most part, quite willing to talk out of fear or anger at being abandoned. They had confirmed much of what he had heard himself. Yes, the galley had had a fire amidships, a kind of brazier, fueled, one man had said very positively, by a kind of long match of burning flax. He himself had heard the bellows and others had seen it. So they had to burn, or maybe heat something before they could project it. Whatever it was, it was in the gleaming dome-shape which had exploded, and from its color that was almost certainly copper. Why copper, not iron or lead?

That was one clue. Another was the whistling noise. Shef had heard it himself, and so had many others. One of the Jewish levies closest to the Greek ship had also heard a voice counting, or so he had told Solomon. Counting in Greek numbers, for all the world, Shef reflected, like Cwicca's catapulteers in the old days counting the turns on a torsion catapult, counting carefully for fear of an overwind and a backlash. And finally there was the evidence from Brand's men. Two of his survivors had said with absolute certainty that at the very last moment they had seen a man point something at them, like a hose. The fire had come from that, come in a steady stream before the stone struck and everything blew up.

Brazier, match, bellows, dome, hose, whistle, and someone counting something. Shef felt sure that this would yet fall into place. Even the injured could tell him something. Or tell Hund something. Perhaps a dozen of the German *Lanzenbruder* had survived the crossbows, Brand's axes and the final flame turned on them by their own allies, though most of them were horribly wounded. The flame had reached into the ranks of Brand's men as well, if only for an instant. Five of them had felt a lash of it, were lying now in the makeshift hospital with terrible burns. Hund could maybe tell him something about what had caused the burns.

If he was prepared to talk to him at all. Since the start of Shef's dealings with Svandis, the little man had been quiet and sullen. When Shef had gone to visit the burned men, and had seen the one who had been blinded, flame across both eyes, he had tapped the hilt of his dagger and looked at Hund with a question. It was normal enough for the Vikings to kill their hopelessly wounded, and both Brand and Shef had done it before. But Hund had flown at him like a terrier, hurled him bodily out of the ward. A while later Thorvin had emerged and said apologetically, in the words of one of the sacred songs of the Way.

"He told me to remember life is sacred. As it is said:

A halt man can back a horse,
The one-hand herd sheep.
The deaf one duels and wins.
Better be blind than burnt.
    Now what good's a corpse?"

"Better blind than burnt," Shef had replied. "But blind *and* burnt?" But it was no good arguing with the little leech. He might have something to tell another day. More than would be gained from the surviving monk-bastards, as Brand called them. None had surrendered willingly, all been taken burnt, crippled, or unconscious. They refused to say anything at all for any fear or inducement. Brand would cut their throats as soon as the priests of the Way ceased to protect them.

With a last reluctant stare at the wreckage lying deep in the water—was that a gleam of copper he could see deep down?—Shef turned away. The mystery would wait. So would Hund. So would Svandis, who had said nothing to him since her bitter words on the quayside, was now sitting with one of the desperately hurt Greek sailors who had survived both fire and water. There were more urgent things to do. The enemy had tried a probing raid at the south gate already this morning, as if to show they were not dismayed. Time to anticipate them for a change.

On the deck of the *Fafnisbane* they were already making ready to stream a kite in the strong morning breeze. Tolman was already being fitted into his harness. Shef patted him encouragingly on the head which was all that could be seen sticking out of the sling—why did he seem to shrink away? Still sore from his fall, probably. Then he looked again at the rig. The top surface was seven feet wide and four feet long, each side four feet long again and three feet deep. Now, how much cloth was that? Think of it as so many squares a foot each way. Turning to the sand tray which two men now carried round behind him ready for instant use, Shef began to move the counters and write the signs, muttering to himself. All round, eighty square feet of cloth. And Tolman, he knew, weighed sixty-eight pounds. He himself weighed one hundred and eighty-five. If, then, you needed a foot of surface to lift a pound of weight . . .

"The wind makes a difference," Hagbarth cut in on his mutterings. "The stronger the wind, the better the lift."

"We can figure that in too," Shef replied. "See what have we now . . ."

"Fresh breeze, enough to drive us at four knots under full sail."

"Call that four then. And how many knots would we be going when you had to reduce sail."

"Maybe ten."

"Well that's ten. So if we multiply eighty by four we have a lift of . . . three hundred and twenty, but if we had a ten-knot breeze we would have a lift of . . . eight hundred."

"Enough to lift a walrus," countered Hagbarth sceptically. "Which it wouldn't."

"All right, we're allowing too much for the wind, but if you call a four-knot breeze one, and a ten-knot breeze two, or even one-and-a-half . . ."

Shef spoke eagerly, fascinated by the new experience of exact calculation. Ever since Solomon had shown him the basis of algorism, the methods of al-Khwarizmi, he had been seeking problems to turn it on. The answers might be wrong. To begin with. But he was sure this was the tool he had been searching for half his life.

A voice broke in, disapproving. Cwicca's. "He's up now. If you'd like to watch, that is. He is risking his neck." Cwicca growing sarcastic and Hund aggressive, Shef noted with a part of his attention. Time to think of that another day.

Tolman was high in the sky, not flying free but streaming on the end of his line, already two hundred, three hundred feet up, blown out across the harbor, higher than the topmost turret of the walled city. Like a watchtower in the sky. From the besiegers on the hillside someone shot an arrow, which looped hopelessly short. Shef licked his lips as he stared up at him. Now he had the basis of calculation, he was determined to make a kite with enough surface to lift him too. If it were a one-to-one relationship, he would need a kite maybe twelve foot by six by four. But how much did the kite itself weigh? There was an answer to everything.

Cwicca turned back from his place by the ropes. "He's pulled three times. He's seen something. And he's pointing north."

North. And the probing attack from the south. "Winch him in," Shef ordered. He had no doubt that this was the Emperor's famous machine approaching. The 'War-Wolf.'

The road which snaked along the coast towards the north wall of Septimania made its final turn some two hundred double paces short of the massive wooden gate, normally open for the passage of trade, now closed and barred, the towers either side of it bristling with breast-bows and cross-bows, traction catapults and torsion dart-throwers. None of that could save the defenders once their gate was battered down. And reinforced oak though it was, criss-crossed with iron, one blow from 'War-Wolf' would destroy it. This Erkenbert knew.

But the blow had to be in the right place. 'War-Wolf' lobbed its missiles, like all traction weapons. A shot which fell five paces short was of no value, just another obstacle to the final attack. One five paces over was as useless. The boulder had to come whirling from the sky and crash exactly into the center of the gate, ideally just a fraction short of central, so that it would burst oak and iron backwards. It had always done its work in the past, sometimes after repeated trials. Erkenbert was well aware that the little hornets'-nest strongholds of the Moslem bandit-lords, even the citadel of the heretics' Puigpunyent, had offered no serious resistance, had merely stood still for undisturbed target practice. One could not count on the apostate Englishman and his diabolic crew to be so passive. And so Erkenbert had given serious thought to the two great deficiencies of 'War-Wolf.'

First, its appallingly slow reload time. The great counterweight-chamber, the size of a peasant's dwelling, was filled with stones. Its crash to earth was what provided the mighty power for the missile slung from the long arm. How was the weight to be lifted twenty feet into the air? Till now, Erkenbert had used the slow way, the safe way. Raise the counterweight chamber by pulling down the long arm. Bolt down the long arm. Send fifty laborers to mount ladders and fill the chamber while it hung above their heads. Once it was full, load the missile, pull the retainer-bolt. After it had shot, empty the chamber once more, raise it up against the lessened resistance, send the laborers back again to pour in their stones.

Too slow, Erkenbert knew. He had decided to solve the problem. Stout iron rings sunk into the rims of the counterweight-chamber. Ropes lashed firmly to them, leading over a new and massive wooden roller at the very top of the whole contrivance. Now the laborers could simply haul the weight up again, slowly and with horrible effort for those who had to dead-lift half a ton and more twenty feet in the air. But it saved all the emptying and filling.

The second problem was the old one, so vital for this machine, of estimating the range. But this was partly solved by the now invariant quality of the throwing weight. All that needed to be changed was the weight thrown. Erkenbert had selected a pile of boulders of graded weight. The idle peasants complained bitterly about dragging them along too, in carts pulled by mule and human power, but Erkenbert gave no heed to that. He was confident that once he had shot his sighting shot—and who knew, it might be dead on target too—one calculation and he could select a stone to finish the job. Two shots and the gate would be down. Three at the very worst. All that remained was to maneuver the great machine into position, ignoring the inevitable harassing shots from the enemies' lighter weapons.

At noon Erkenbert, having surveyed the ground, gave the order to advance. It was obeyed gingerly by the sweating exhausted men of his catapult-gang, with disciplined readiness by the *Lanzenbruder,* as contemptuous as Erkenbert himself of the local noonday halts. With the Emperor himself at hand, there was no question of anyone disobeying.

Shef had had hours of warning from Tolman. Behind the barred gate, totally invisible to the besiegers, he had set up the answer of the Waymen to 'War-Wolf': a counterweight-machine based on what the Arab had told him and on what his own imagination and experience with traction weapons had suggested. Now, from the wall, he watched 'War-Wolf' creeping round the corner of the road with interest and alarm. It had been transported in pieces, assembled just short of its place of operation. It crept forward on twelve massive cartwheels. As it reached the flat place Erkenbert had selected, it stopped. Men began to set blocks under its frame, lever the wheels off. Why were they doing that, and how would they move the blocks once they were in place?

"Ready to shoot!" called a voice from the walls. Cwicca, crouched behind the sights of his favorite dart-thrower. He had a hundred men, two hundred, in front of him, clear targets. Shef waved impatiently for silence. Watching was more important than killing a few laborers. So the enemy must think too. More men were coming forward, staggering under the weight of giant mantlets, heavy wooden screens that would keep out a crossbow-bolt, even blunt the force of a torsion dart. The screens hid what he needed to see. But he had seen something. Something ominous.

"Shoot when you're ready," called Shef.

"Nothing to shoot at now," complained an anonymous voice. They began nonetheless to shoot at the mantlets, trying to aim for junction points. Something might get through. Some poor fool might be unnerved.

"What did you see?" asked Thorvin, the most interested of the Way-priests in mechanical contrivances.

"Theirs has two bracing timbers running out from the sides. Ours doesn't."

"What difference does that make?"

"We don't know. We've never shot ours."

The two men looked anxiously now at their machine, set up twenty paces behind the gate. It was nothing but a massively scaled-up version of their familiar old pull-thrower, the weapon that had won the Threefold Battle, as men now called it, the battle on two fronts against Mercians and against Ivar, Svandis's father. It had not won a battle since. Would its giant descendant work as simply as its ancestor?

"Start loading," said Shef. He too had seen the problem that Erkenbert had learnt from experience, could think with his more mechanical mind of two methods at least of solving it: had no time to make the necessary gears and ratchets, the great iron axle that would be needed for the better method. He too was thrown back on the simple way. Raise the bucket high and empty, then fill it while it was in the air. But his gang were not using stones. Each man had a stout sack full of sand, carefully and individually weighed. A hundred pounds a time. Thorvin counted the men off as they mounted the ladder, the burliest of Brand's Vikings, sweat pouring from them into their hemp shirts. Fifteen loads dumped in and the long arm bending visibly as it strained against its greased retainer bolt.

"Load the sling," Shef ordered. Another hard job. The sling itself lay along the ground like a gigantic empty scrotum. The boulder that went into it, Shef knew, weighed almost exactly a hundred and fifty pounds. A gang had dug it from the seashore, weighed it against sandbags over a steelyard, been told immediately to start chipping it round—and weigh the chips! Then they had been sent back to raise three more, carve them to a weight as near identical as care could make them. But now the first load had to be lifted into place. No great weight, for strong men, but round boulders are hard to lift from the ground. For a moment there was straining and cat-calls from the watchers, then as the two lifters turned angrily on their messmates, Brand and Styrr walked forward. They dug their fingers into the sand below the boulder, embraced it like two wrestlers, heaved it up and along into its double bullhide bag.

Now, when the weight dropped, the arm would rise. When the arm rose, the sling would whirl. When the sling whirled—the rock would come off and crash down on its own launcher and crew, unless the hook, the hook that was the free counterpart of the fixed ring on the sling's rope, unless that hook lifted off at precisely the right point. Shef stepped forward to check the angle of the nail it rested on. It was right.

As he stepped back, drawing a deep breath and looking at his old comrade Osmod, who had demanded the honor of first launch, he heard a great 'oh!' rise from the men on the walls, a gasp or groan of surprise that cut through the snapping of crossbows and twanging of ropes. Shef looked up, saw the moon coming down on him. Just as he had a decade before at the siege of York, he cringed, head sinking into shoulders like a turtle. Gigantic, weightless, the boulder sailed silently down from a point that seemed higher than ever Tolman had flown. Erkenbert and the Empire had shot first.

The boulder was almost a perfect hit first time. It cleared the top of the city gate by no more than six feet, shot past faster than eye could follow, crashed into the dry sandy ground almost equidistant between the foot of the gate and the place where Shef stood by the side of his own trebuchet. The earth shook beneath his feet, sand rose in a cloud. As it settled, in an awestruck silence, men stared at the rock that had appeared there, looking as if it had lain there since the dawn of time.

"It's bigger than ours," came a gloomy voice. Some friendly memory helped Shef to recognise it.

"Anything's bigger than yours, Odda," he replied. "What are you waiting for, Osmod? Pull the bolt."

As he saw Osmod turn, with a certain fear, to the bolt, Shef himself turned his back, ran up the stone steps to the parapet of the left-hand tower. Behind him he heard a squeak of protesting metal being drawn. Then a long scraping noise which ended in a great crash. He looked round just in time to see the sling release and the boulder that two mighty men had strained to lift fly into the sky like a pebble.

As it soared out on its long arc Shef followed it, ignoring the groans of protesting timber, the shouts and yells from the crew. The top of its arc, there, must be the midway point. He was sure it was on line for 'War-Wolf.' But the range?

Shef let the breath escape in a long sigh. He knew already it was going to be over, even well over. His shot had been far worse than the enemy's. The thump and cloud of dust had come down well over. How well over? He put down the far-seer with its cloudy lenses, strained his one eye to get a sure view. There were too many things in the way. At a guess he would say forty yards over. Consider. How many men, stretched head to foot, between what he could see of 'War-Wolf' and the already settling dust-cloud. Shef counted, nodding his head unconsciously to each imaginary six feet. Maybe not forty yards. More like thirty-five. Under rather than over. Say thirty-four.

Now how far was it from 'War-Wolf' to the gate. The guard captain Malachi was standing by him, saying nothing but looking anxious.

"Think carefully. You must have walked that road many times. How far is it from the gate to their machine? Think of it in double paces."

A long pause. "I would say one hundred and forty." And twenty, already paced out, from the center-line of his own machine to this side of the gate. A hundred and sixty, times five and a half feet, was the range he meant to shoot. That sum, plus thirty-four, times three, was what he had shot. He had to reduce the fifteen-hundred-pound throw weight in proportion to the reduced distance to get a hit with a boulder of the same weight. Two days ago he would have thrown his hands up, declared the sum impossible. Now . . .

Shef sprinted down the steps again to where his sand table waited. Osmod met him with a face of woe. "The machine. It's falling apart. The weight's too big for it. Needs side-braces, like what they've got . . ."

Shef pushed him aside. "Wedge everything back as best you can, use nails if you have to. It has to hold together for one more shot. Tell the men to unload, winch up, put in ten hundred pounds. Then wait."

He bent to his table, lines already drawn for the first of his sums. One hundred and sixty, times five, add on eighty—that was easy. Write '880' in the sand. Thirty-four, times three, add it on, write '982' in the sand.

Now, divide fifteen into 982 to find out how much distance to each hundred-pound bag. And then, divide *that* figure into the 880. Shef struggled on, absorbed. His own men watched him curiously. Solomon and Malachi exchanged glances. Either of them, they suspected, could have carried out the operation faster, as could any trader in the market. But then a market-trader would not have known what it was that the king of the barbarians was trying to do. He might be near-illiterate. But he had made the machine. The flares, the kites, the crossbows. Best to trust to what the Arabs would call his *iqbal*. The odor of success.

Shef straightened. He could not do quantities less than one, had had to double his numbers both sides to get a fair approximation, but he knew the answer.

"Ten hundred-pound bags in? Right, add three more. Open a fourth. Take half out. Exactly half."

Shef bent over the open bag. There should be fifty pounds in it. According to his figures he should now take out seven more. What difference could that possibly make to a boulder of the size they were throwing? Grimly he scrabbled out what seemed to him to be seven pounds of dirt, the same weight as two days' rations. He twisted the bag closed, stepped up the ladder, hurled it in on top of the pile.

"Ready to throw again? Have you checked the line?"

A shout from the parapet, where Thorvin had gone to watch. " 'War-Wolf' is ready! I can see the long arm raised!"

Shef looked at Osmod. There was no crash of metal here, no trumpets blaring and war-cries rising, but this was where the battle would be decided.

All 'War-Wolf' had to do was drop its range six feet. Unless they smashed it with this shot, the next act they would take would be to run for the harbor. To face the floating fort, the noon-day calm, and the Greek fire. In an hour they would all be burnt corpses floating in the sea.

Osmod shrugged like a farm-hand asked about the hay-making. "I checked her for line again. I can't say nothing about what happened to the timbers. You heard them start to come apart."

Shef took a deep breath, looked at the counterweight, the frame, the sling with its carefully-chipped boulder. It felt wrong. The figures said it was right.

"Stand by to shoot. Get back, everybody. All right, Osmod. Shoot!"

As he pulled back the bolt Shef was already in mid-leap for the steps and the parapet. Behind him he heard the scrape, the crash, and this time a chorus of yells of alarm as the hastily-wedged timber frame slowly, inexorably, sprang apart. The boulder was still in the air, still rising, as he reached his vantage-point. As he focused on his target he saw it, too, suddenly move. The great wooden counterweight-chamber dropped instantaneously behind the mantlets, he saw the long arm rise, the inconceivably powerful lash of the sling, like a giant's arm coming round. And then there were two boulders in the sky. One falling, one rising. For an instant he thought they would strike each other. Then all he could see out on the plain was dust. And out of the dust, the enemy's missile still climbing.

Erkenbert's weak eyes had not let him see the flight of his first missile. He had a *Lanzenbruder* standing beside him to act as his observer, but the man had said only, "Very close, just over the top, drop it just a cat's hair, *herra,* and we are through!" Encouraging, but hard to count a cat's hair.

Erkenbert did his best. One thing he knew was that his throw-weight would not change, not now that he had the system in place for hauling the counterweight up again by main force. As the men struggled with it, heaving at unyielding ropes, he reflected on his problem. It was three hundred yards from machine to gate, more or less. He needed to shoot just a trifle less. So use the next boulder up in his graduated pile. But would that then fall short? What was the difference? If a stone of some two hundred pounds were to be thrown three hundred yards by the weight he had, whatever that weight was, how heavy a stone would be needed to travel just two hundred and ninety-five? Erkenbert knew how to find the answer. He needed to multiply three hundred by two hundred, and divide the answer by two hundred and ninety-five.

But to Erkenbert, product of the great and famous school of Latin learning at York, the school that in its time had produced such men as Alcuin the deacon, the minister of Charlemagne, preserver of manuscripts, poet, editor and commentator on the Bible, the problem did not present itself like that. To him, three hundred was CCC, two hundred CC. III times II was VI, C by C—but there common sense would have to step in, not calculation, and give an answer as XM. Erkenbert had plenty of common sense, he could soon, if not immediately, deduce that CCC multiplied by CC must be VIXM. But VIXM—six-ten-thousand—was more like a word or a phrase than a number. What VIXM divided by CCXCV might be—that, hardly the wisest man could tell, and even he not on a battlefield.

Erkenbert considered, ordered forward the next size of boulder up from the one he had just hurled. According to the number painted on its side, it should be perhaps five, perhaps ten pounds heavier than the last one— more or less, like the three hundred yards Erkenbert had estimated for the range. *Arithmeticus* though he was, absolute precision in numbers was no part of his world-view, except perhaps for calculating rents, the symbolism of Bible numbers, and the date of Easter. And 'War-Wolf' had never before faced a reply. The stone that had crashed into the ground forty yards away had angered Erkenbert with its proof of hostile and inventive minds resisting him, and his Emperor, and their Savior's will. Its wild miss had cheered him as well: what better could one expect from illiterates imitating their betters, without so much as a copy of Vegetius to instruct them? Nor would they have had the ingenuity to match his roller and his ropes. Why were the laborers taking so long to haul the weight back into place? He waved forward the *Lanzenbrüder* to flog the idle levies on.

One of the men heaving at a rope, his feet slipping in the soft dust, dared to snarl a comment in the ear of the man next to him.

"I'm a sailor, I am. We shift our lateeno-yards over the mast all the time, just like this. But what we use is pulleys. Ain't this lot ever heard of pulleys?"

A slash of leather opened a weal across his back and shut his mouth at the same time. As the retainer-bolt finally slid home and the gasping men let go of their ropes, he looped his line unnoticed round the side frame, twisted it into a half-hitch, walked away. What it would do he did not know. He did not know what they were supposed to be doing, drafted here on the orders of his bishop and taken from his boat just as there was a chance of a successful voyage. But if there was anything he could do to obstruct, he would.

Erkenbert viewed the cocked and prepared machine with a grim pleasure, looked round at his Emperor watching from the hillside, within cover or out of range of the weapons still shooting from the wall. Behind him the two thousand stormers ready to pour through the gate, headed by Tasso the Bavarian and the Emperor's own elite guard.

He turned back. Saw with sudden incredulity the boulder already rising from behind the enemy's gate. In an immediate reflex of rage shrieked the order: "Shoot!" Saw his own missile drag along the ground in its sling, whirl round, climb into the sky almost into the very path of the other.

And then the great crash, the rending of timbers and ropes and iron all together.

Shef's exactly calculated rock came down precisely as intended, the various errors of calculation balancing out, as so often happens when each part is done as nearly as humanly possible. Range a little over-estimated, air-resistance never considered at all, the creep of strained timbers incalculable: but the answer correct. In one moment 'War-Wolf' sprang apart, struck just at the pivot point and square on, shattering arm and side-frame and rending out the side of the counterweight. The great machine lay in fragments, timbers slowly, creakily falling to the earth, like a stricken hero's limbs sinking in death. Gently, through the dust, earth began to patter out of the counterweight-chamber, falling on to the boulder that had shattered it as if to hide it from view, pretend that nothing had happened. Numbly, Erkenbert stalked forward to inspect the damage. Then caught himself, looked out across the plain to see where his shot had landed. Called on his eyes to report for him.

"Just short," reported Godschalk the *Bruder* with stolid unconcern. "Up just half a cat's hair and you've got it."

From the wall, Shef looked at the boulder lying now four feet short of the gate, looked across at the cloud of dust which marked where his shot had gone home, with surely an instant ago a glimpse of broken pieces whirling end over end out of it, and reflected on the value of calculation. A deep sense of satisfaction rose within him. He had the answer. Not just to this problem alone, but to many problems.

Not, perhaps, to his most pressing one. As the cries of glee and triumph began at last to die down, he turned into the exultant face of Brand, almost a foot above his own.

"We beat off the fire, we beat off the stones," shouted Brand.

"We have to do more than beat them off," replied Shef.

Brand sobered. "Right. We have to sicken them of it, I always said so. Now how are we going to do that?"

Shef hesitated. He had a feeling as of one who reaches out for a familiar tool, the hilt of a sword that has hung at his belt for ten years, and finds nothing there. He reached inside himself for a source of inspiration. Advice. The voice of his father-god.

Nothing there. He had the knowledge of al-Khwarizmi now. The wisdom of Rig had gone.

CHAPTER TWENTY-FOUR

The Emperor of the Romans sagged back on to his camp-stool, his face drawn and weary. "Total failure," he said. He reached out an arm, picked up the Holy Lance which never left him, cradled it to his cheek. After a few moments he put it reverently, but still wearily, back in its place.

"Even the Lance brings me no comfort," he went on. "The virtue has gone out of me. I have angered God."

The two bodyguards standing at the entrance to the tent, stifling at the end of the long Catalan summer's day, looked at each other uneasily, then at the fourth man in the room, the deacon Erkenbert, mixing wine and water with his face turned down.

"Angered God, *herra?*" asked Jopp uncertainly, the bolder and duller of the two. "You eat fish on Fridays. God knows—I mean we know you don't have no women in here, though if you wanted to there's plenty . . ."

His comrade trod firmly on his foot with a hobnailed boot, and Jopp's voice trailed into silence.

Bruno's face showed not even amusement, his voice continued wearily. "The Greek fire failed. Forty good brothers dead or missing, and Agilulf pulled out of the sea half-roasted." A spark of animation showed, he straightened for a moment. "It's my belief those Greek bastards flamed him with the rest, because he was in the way. But still," he sank back again, "we lost. The admiral won't try again, keeps wailing about his lost projector.

"And 'War-Wolf' smashed. The gate not down. I do not blame you, Erkenbert, but you have to admit, there was something devilish about the way they hit with the second shot. You would have thought God would send

His servants something. If they were His true servants. I fear I am not. Not any more."

Erkenbert did not look up, continued to pour one flask into another as if absorbed. "Are there any other signs, O *imperator,* that God has turned his back on you?"

"Too many. Deserters keep coming in. Men who say they were Christians, converted to the worship of Mohammed by force. We make them eat the bacon, then test what they say. They all say the same. The Arab army barely the other side of the hill, led by the Caliph in person, er-Rahman. Tens of thousands, they say. Hundreds of thousands, they say. All those who resist the will of the Caliph are impaled.

"And the worst of all you know, O deacon. No word of the Holy Grail, the ladder of life to go with the lance of the holy death. How many men have we sent to death in the search for it? Sometimes their screams come to me in my sleep. That boy, the one who had seen it, you tortured him till he died. And the child, the fair child who fell in flame from the skies. They should have lived many years yet, but they died. And for nothing. For nothing . . ."

The Emperor sagged back further, his long arms trailing on the ground, his eyes closed.

His metal gauntlets lay on the table in front of him. Moving carefully, Erkenbert the deacon stepped across, seized one of them, weighed it in his hand, and then swung it with all his scrawny force across the face of the defenseless Emperor. Blood spurted instantly from the broken nose. As the bodyguards reached reflexively for their hilts, Erkenbert found himself whirled off his feet, back stretched over the table, a forearm like oak and wire cutting off the breath in his throat, and a dagger-tip already poised an inch from his eyeball.

Slowly the pressure relaxed, the Emperor straightened up, hauling his counselor with him.

"Stay back, boys. Now, what the Hell did you do that for?"

No glimpse of fear showed in the pale face glaring up at him. "I struck you because you are a traitor to God. God has sent you to carry out His purposes. Whatever those purposes may be! And you, you fall into the sin of despair! You are no better than a suicide, who kills himself because he fears what God may send. Except in one way. You have time yet to make amends. Down on your knees, Emperor that should be, and beg forgiveness from the All-Highest!"

Slowly the Emperor sank down, dagger falling from his hand, and began to mutter the Lord's Prayer through the flow of blood from his nose. Erkenbert let him finish.

"Enough! For now. Confess this to your confessor. Now hold still." The deacon stepped forward, took careful hold of the broken septum, aligned it carefully, ran a finger along the top to check. The Emperor remained motionless, as he did under his own many private penances.

"Very well. You will look none the worse in a day or two. Here, drink." The deacon thrust forward an unspilled tankard.

"Now, listen to what I have to say. Yes, the Greek fire failed. Yes, 'War-Wolf' is destroyed. No, the Grail has not been found. But think: these deserters, these secret eaters of pork who have come to you. They are apostates and the children of apostates, traitors many times over. Would they have come to you if they had thought the Caliph of the Christ-rejecters were going to win? No. They fled in fear of his defeat. So, put them in the front rank of your army, remind them of the fate that comes to those who are captured having renounced the false prophet. But smite the Caliph as Samson smote the Philistines, strong in the Lord."

The Emperor rubbed a blood-stained chin. "It sounds as if we are well outnumbered . . ."

"Smite them in the mountain passes, then. Take revenge for the dead Roland. What is it the minstrels sing in his song, in the *Rolandslied*?"

Surprisingly, the stolid Jopp replied. "They say, the Franks, *Chrestiens unt dreit et paiens unt tort*. 'Christians are right and pagans are wrong.' I heard it sung back in Leuven market. That's what made me join up."

"'Christians are right and pagans are wrong.' That is all you need to know. But I will tell you another tale, to strengthen your faith. When the blessed Gregory, the Pope, sent his emissaries to England to bring my countrymen the holy gospel, they would not listen, just as they have turned heretic today. And Paulinus the Archbishop of that time, his heart failed him and he made ready to flee, to return to Rome in faintness of heart. But in his sleep the Apostle Peter, the first Pope, from whom all Popes take their power, he came to Paulinus in a dream and scourged him savagely with knotted cords, and told him to return to his post. And when the Archbishop woke the marks of the cords were still to be seen on his body where the holy Peter had flogged him. So Paulinus turned again, and conquered. Do you now likewise, Emperor! And as penance for your weakness, though I am not your confessor, I appoint you this: stand in the forefront, fight for the Holy Church."

The Emperor rose to his feet, stood looking down. "And what of your penance, little man? For you have struck the Lord's anointed."

The deacon stared up at him. "I will find you the Grail, or die."

A hand gripped his shoulder. "Find me the Grail, and I swear it. If I overthrow the infidels I will make you, not Archbishop, not Cardinal, but Pope. We have had too many Italian weaklings, who never pass the walls of Rome. We need a Gregory. A true descendant of Peter."

"The Papacy is not vacant," whispered Erkenbert, struck almost dumb by the immensity of the prospect suddenly revealed to him.

"That can be arranged," said Bruno. "As it has been before."

In the camp of the Caliph, the Successor of the Prophet, no such drama. As was the custom, the leaders of the divisions of the army came to make their reports at the hour of sunset, one by one entering the great pavilion, pitched hours before—its extent and the time needed for pitching it and striking it were a main reason for the army's slow progress across the northern peninsula. They came to stand before the divan of the Caliph, between it and them the notorious leather carpet, the executioners standing to either side of it, scimitars drawn, the strangling bowstrings twisted round their waists. At the side of the Caliph, as always now, his favorite counselor, the young savant Mu'atiyah. The generals let their eyes pass over him without sign. His advice was wild, his opinions foolish. One day the Caliph would tire of him. They looked also without expression at the curtains behind the Caliph's divan: by law and tradition the Caliph's women might not appear in formal audience, yet they had long been allowed to watch and listen unseen. Some said that they too had found favor with the Caliph, were leading him further down his present path of folly. No-one was going to report it.

"Tell me of the deserters," said the Caliph abruptly. "How many more secret eaters of pork have you allowed to escape us? How many have been in the army unseen for so many years, bringing us defeat and disgrace?"

The general of the cavalry replied. "Some have tried to escape, Caliph. My horsemen ride them down. They wait only for your sentence. None have escaped."

Only some fractions of this were true. The general had no idea how many fewer men the army had today than yesterday. He knew it was a good many, and many of that many from his own elite cavalry units. He would not confess it as he might have done once. In the first place he was the third commander of cavalry the army had had since it marched from Cordova, and the others had not died easily. In the second place, where once he might have been betrayed by an ambitious subordinate or rival, like the general of the infantry, they now made common cause: rivals could betray each other too easily, subordinates had no wish to come to prominence.

The Caliph turned to the general of the advance guard. "Is this true?"

Only a bow in assent. The Caliph pondered. Something was wrong, he knew. Someone was betraying him. But who? Mu'atiyah bent and whispered in his ear. The Caliph nodded.

"Those units which have sheltered the pork-eaters, the defiers of *shahada*. Let them be placed foremost in the battle." His tone sharpened. "Do not think I do not know which they are! My faithful associates have kept record. If my orders are not obeyed—I will know who still shelters traitors. The impaling poles are not yet tired. Go now, fill them again. Further off this time! The traitors' shrieks disturb my household.''

Dismissed, the generals withdrew. They did not look at each other as they dispersed. All knew the orders were foolish. Putting the unreliable units, the northerners, the converts and the *mustaribs* in the front was merely to blunt the attack. But even to hint as much was treason. All one could do now was trust in Allah, for some, prepare one's own way out, for others. The commander of the cavalry reflected on the speed of his favorite mare, wondered if he could transfer some part of his regimental pay-chest to his saddle-bags without remark. Decided, regretfully, that life was the only burden he might manage to carry.

Behind, in the *harem* behind the curtains, the three conspirators spoke quietly in their impenetrable woman's talk.

"We have two chances still. To reach the Franks, for Berthe, to reach the pagan sailors, for Alfled."

"A third," corrected the Circassian.

The others looked at her with surprise. No Circassian army existed in the West of the world.

"There must be a successor to the Successor."

"All successors are the same."

"Not if there is a change of faith."

"Cordova will eat pork and believe in Yeshua the son of the Bibi Miriam? Or learn Hebrew and reject the Prophet?"

"There is another way," corrected the Circassian quietly. "If the Successor of the Prophet himself is defeated in battle by the infidel, faith will be shaken. Those who say that reason is a surer guide will grow stronger. Ishaq, Keeper of the Scrolls, is one of them. So is bin-Firnas, in secret. His cousin, bin-Maymun, now commands the cavalry. They say that even al-Khwarizmi, the glory of Cordova, was of the Mu'tazilah: those who stand apart. Such men would listen even to the copper-haired princess of the North, if there was reason in her words. I would rather live with such men to rule in Cordova than go to live in furs and fleas in the north."

"If we could find such men," agreed Berthe.

"Any man would be a change from a tenth part of one," said Alfled. She stretched her long body discontentedly.

In a secluded court in the city of Septimania, faith and reason were also under discussion. For the first time in months, Thorvin had insisted that the priests of the Way should form their holy circle. There were only four of them, Thorvin for Thor, Skaldfinn for Tyr, Hagbarth for Njörth, and Hund the leech for Ithun. Nevertheless, with their holy oval drawn and marked out, the bale-fire burning at one end and the spear of Othin All-Father planted upright at the other, they could hope for divine guidance in their talk. For human guidance, as was their occasional custom, they had allowed both Brand the champion and Solomon the Jew to sit outside the oval as observers, to listen but only to speak if called on.

"He says his visions have gone," began Thorvin without preamble. "He says he can no longer feel his father within him. Isn't sure he ever had a father, or a god-father. He's talking about throwing his pendant away."

Skaldfinn the interpreter replied, speaking in tones of gentle reason. "There's a simple explanation, isn't there, Thorvin? It's the woman. Svandis. She's been telling him for weeks that there are no gods, that they're just some disorder of the brain. She explains his dreams to him and shows him how they're just warped memories of things that have happened, buried fears. Now he believes her. So the visions have gone."

"If you say that," cut in Hagbarth, "you're accepting that what she says is true. The visions come from inside. He's convinced inside that he shouldn't have any, so he doesn't. But we've always thought that the visions come from outside. And I've seen it proved. I've seen Vigleik the priest come out of a vision and tell us things he could not know. They've been proved later on. It's the same with Farman the Frey-priest, and many others. The woman's wrong! If she's wrong, then your simple explanation won't work."

"And there's another simple explanation," Thorvin went on. "That what he says and has been saying is all true. That Loki is loose and Ragnarök is upon us. His father, Rig, cannot speak to him because he has been— imprisoned? silenced? whatever happens to gods who are defeated. There is war in the sky. And our side has lost already."

A long silence, while the priests and their observers considered the options. Thorvin pulled his hammer from his belt, began to thump it gently and rhythmically into the palm of his left hand while he considered. At the center of his feeling was a deep belief that his considered opinion was right. The One King, Shef, whom he had first met as a runaway English thrall-boy, was the destined one: the One who would come from the North, in the deep belief of the Way. The peace-king who would replace the war-kings of old, who would set the world on its true path and away from the horrors of the Skuld-world of the Christians. Thorvin had not wanted to believe it in the beginning, had shared the prejudice of his people and his religion against the English, against all those who did not speak Norse. Slowly he had been brought round. The visions. The evidence of Farman. The old tale of King Sheaf. The overthrow of kings. He remembered the testimony of Olaf the Norwegian king, himself a seer and a prophet, who had accepted the death and displacement of his own bloodline as the will of the gods. He remembered the death of Valgrim the Wise, who had not been wise enough to cease his resistance to the truth, even when tests had proved it.

The thing that made Thorvin believe most strongly, in the end, was the unpredictable nature of it. The boy Shef, even when grown to a man, had not behaved like one sent by the gods. He had almost no interest in the will of the gods at all, had taken a pendant only with reluctance, and seemed most of the time on bad terms even with his own father and patron. He had no love for Othin, and little patience with sacred story. His interests were fixed on machines and devices. It was not what any wise priest of the Way would have expected. And yet again and again, it seemed to Thorvin, what the gods sent was what no man expected, and no woman either, for all that Svandis might say. What they sent, what they did, had about it a peculiar feeling—a *taste,* almost. It could not be missed once you were familiar with it. Thorvin had heard Solomon the Jew discourse on the peculiar quality of the Christians' gospels, how even in disagreement they seemed to bear witness to some real event. That was how he felt about Shef and his visions. They were awkward, often unhelpful, even unwanted. That was what proved them true.

Finally Thorvin summed up. "It is like this. If the visions are not true, then we have no witness for the existence of our gods. We might as well get rid of our clothes, our pendants, our holy emblems, and go back to working at our trades—as we do anyway. Either the visions are from inside, mere dreams, disorders of the brain and the belly. Or they are from outside, from a world where our gods exist, independent of us. But I see no way to test this."

A fourth voice came from inside the circle, a thin and tired one: the voice of Hund the leech. For weeks now, ever since the first joining of his friend Shef and his supposed-pupil Svandis, the little man had been withdrawn, sullen, even angry. Jealous, they all supposed, of the taking of the woman he loved by the one man who seemed least likely to. Now he spoke decisively.

"I can test it for you."

"How?" asked Hagbarth.

"I have known for a long time—since Shef and I drank the potion of the Finns—that I can create visions, with a potion. I think it likely that all his visions spring from the same root. Not a root, a fungus. You all know that if the rye gets wet when it is harvested, a kind of black spur grows on it. You Norsemen call it the *rugulfr,* the wolf in the rye. We all know to scrape it off, dry it out, not eat it. But it is hard to get rid of completely. It brings visions, brings madness in large doses. I think our friend is especially subject to it, as some are. His visions come on after eating rye-bread or rye-porridge. What have we been eating since we have been here, since we finished our own stores? Wheat-bread, from well-dried grain. But I have decoction of the ergot-fungus in my stores. I can bring on his visions at any time."

"But if you say that," said Hagbarth, "you are agreeing with Skaldfinn, and Svandis. The visions are just a disorder of the belly. Not a message from the gods. So there are no gods."

Hund looked round bleakly, without excitement or urge to make a point. "No. I have considered all this. You are all victims of a kind of thinking I know. Either this or that. Either inside or outside. Either truth or falsehood. It works with simple things. Not with the gods.

"I am a leech. I have learned to look at the whole of my patients before I decide what may be wrong with them. Sometimes it is not just one thing. So I look at the whole of our beliefs about the gods. If we—we priests of the Way—were to put our beliefs into words, we would say that the gods are somewhere outside us, somewhere in the sky, it may be, and that they were there before us. They made us. As for the gods of other people, like the Christians who brought me up, or the Jews we have met here, they are just mistakes, they do not exist at all. But they say the same of ours! Why should we be right and they wrong? Or they right and we wrong? Maybe we are all right.

"And all wrong. Right to think the gods exist. Wrong to think they made us. Maybe we made them. What I think is that our minds are strange, beyond our understanding. They work in ways we do not know and cannot reach. Maybe they work in places we cannot reach, places that are beyond our space and our time—for the visions of Vigleik, and Shef too, they reach where their bodies could not go. In those strange places I think the gods are made. From mind-stuff. From belief. They grow strong on belief. Wither on disbelief, or oblivion. So you see, Thorvin, Skaldfinn, Shef's visions could be a true guide to the gods. But sprung from rye-wolf, or from my potions, just the same. They need not be either/or."

Hagbarth licked his lips, spoke hesitantly, in face of the little man's certainty and composure. "Hund, I do not see how that can be true. If it were true that the gods spring from belief, think: how many Way-folk are there, how many Christians are there? If the Christ-god draws on the belief of thousands of thousands, our gods only on the belief of a tenth that number—surely our gods would be crushed like a nut under a war-hammer."

Hund laughed, mirthlessly. "I was a Christian once. How much do you think I believed? I believed that if I did not pay tithes to the Church my father's hut would be burned down. There are Christians in the world, I know. King Alfred is one of them. Shef told me once of the old woman he and Alfred met, grieving for her man. She was another. But Church-folk are not Christians. Nor do all those who say the *shahada* believe in Allah. They believe in nothing, or they believe in the *shari'a,* as your people, Solomon, believe in their books. I do not think that kind of belief will do. For if the gods are our creation, then they cannot be deceived, as we deceive ourselves."

"And if the One King has ceased to believe in his gods?" asked Thorvin.

"That need not mean they have ceased to believe in him. For they come from other minds besides his. Let me try my potion. But one thing first. The woman—keep her out of the way. It comes to me that she too has power on the other side, like her father, the boneless one, the were-dragon."

The priests looked at each other, looked at the dying fire, nodded in wordless agreement.

Shef took the cup that Hund handed to him, looked not at its contents but into the eyes of his friend—his childhood friend, now perhaps his rival or his enemy.

"This will make me dream of my father?"

"It will make you dream the way you used to."

"What if my father has no message for me?"

"Then you will know that, at least!"

Shef hesitated, drained the cup. It tasted musty, old. "Now I am not sure I want to sleep."

"Stay awake then. The visions will come either way."

Hund took the cup, walked away without another word. Shef felt deserted, alone. Svandis had vanished, no-one knew where. Brand and the others were avoiding him. He sat in a small room by the dock-side, hearing dim whoops and cheering as the catapult crews celebrated their victory over the Greeks and over the 'War-Wolf.' He wished he could join them.

After a while the room faded from his eyes, began to be overlaid with strange sweeps and spirals of color. He found himself examining them with manic attention: as if, by doing so, he could prevent himself from being pulled on to what he knew was waiting.

As if his eyes had cleared, Shef found himself staring into an enormous face. The nose alone was bigger than he was, the eyes were like black pools, the lips curled back to reveal monstrous teeth. The face was laughing at him. With a crash sound came to his ears, and he staggered beneath the gale of laughter that blew towards him. He was like a mouse, Shef felt. Like a mouse caught on a table-top when the owner of the kitchen returned. He span round, crouched, looked for a point of hiding, began to move.

A slam, and something was over him. A hand. Light gleamed at the bottom of it, and as he moved towards the opening, two fingers came through, a thumb and finger, and picked him off the table-top as if he had been a cherry. The thumb and finger closed round him, not forcefully, not yet. They only had to squeeze, he knew, and his guts would force their way out of his mouth and anus like a man crushed between a launched longship and its rollers.

The face was looking at him, still with manic glee. Shef could see, even from this terrible vantage, that the face was mad. Not mad, but crazy. It was the face of the man he had seen staked out for the serpent to spit its venom on. The man his father had loosed, and whom he had avoided on the giant stairway by the gods' orm-garth. It was the face of Loki. Loki unbound. Loki as the gods had made him.

"My brother's little favorite," teased the voice in a bass rumble so low he could barely hear it. "He loosed me, but I do not think he meant me to catch you. Shall I squeeze you now and end his plans? You do not believe in me, I know, but you will die in your sleep just the same. And some part of you will stay here with me, for ever."

Shef could make no reply, kept looking round. His father Rig? The other gods? Surely Loki had many enemies.

"Or I could throw you to my pets," the voice went on. The hand tipped Shef so he could see down, to what lay beneath the table. A crawling mass of serpents, that twined round the mad god's legs. From time to time they struck at him, he could see the fangs bared, smell the poison. "I have swallowed so much venom I feel it no more," laughed the voice. "And there are my other pets, you have seen some of them before."

A tilt, and Shef could see out into the open sea, where backs rose and fell. Some of them were the orcas, the killer whales who had nearly taken Cuthred and himself, had destroyed Valgrim the Wise and all his men at Hrafnsey. But they were warm-blooded beasts, almost human in their cunning and their converse. Shef could see others, mere cold eyes above monstrous teeth, and worse things below. The fear of being dragged down, of ending his life in the jaws of a thing that did not even know what it was doing came over him. He could feel the cold sweat break out on his body.

"Good, very good. Now you are afraid. But you need be less so than some. Because I can use you, mannikin. You have brought me much service already. The Greeks burn men alive, the Arabs thrust poles up them till they die. But you have brought them fear from a distance. You have brought them fear from the sky.

"And you can bring them more yet. You with your strange salts and your strange machines. There is more there than you will ever learn. But you could set men on the right path. My path. And if you do, you can have my favor. I could not help my favorite whom you killed in the water, Ivar Bane-of-Women, for I was bound. But now I am free. Is there no revenge you wish for, like Ivar, like me?"

"No," said Shef, his voice like a thin bird's piping, a mouse's squeak in the cat's paw. He was not conscious of any courage. Loki had asked him a question. He knew the answer. It would do no good to lie.

The crazy face stared down at him. Shef found himself trying to imagine what it would have been like without the scars and pits of poison, the bitter marks of resentment. Like looking at a scarred and defeated old warrior, and wondering what he might have been like if his life had gone aright. The finger and thumb were pressing tight around him, but they had not squeezed yet.

"See there." Shef found himself staring up an immense bridge, a bridge that was at the same time a rainbow, and at the end of it a cold glitter of blades. "The gods, my father and my brothers, they have gone back over Bifrost bridge, and Othin has called out his Einheriar to man it. They expect me to storm it, with my allies the giants and my children the monster-brood. Why should I not?"

"It was your home once, lord. Before you slew Balder."

This time the thumb and finger were tightening, he could feel his ribs groan, ready to snap and send splinters through his heart.

"I did not mean to slay Balder. I meant them to see themselves for what they were."

"I know that, lord. So does my father Rig. It was why he loosed you."

The face had gone quiet, and a kind of reason was coming back into it.

"Are you trying to bargain with me, mannikin?"

"Yes, lord."

"Then what is your offer?"

"I do not know yet, lord. To give you a footing again in Asgarth?"

"You cannot give me that," said the voice of Loki. "But maybe you can give me something. Listen then to my offer. Do my wishes. Make more fire, make more machines, be my follower and not Rig's, turn your back on the Way and bring terror to the world. And in exchange I will give you more than my father Othin ever offered. He gives his favorites success till he chooses different, like Sigurth Snake-eye, whom you gave to death when his shoelace tripped him. I would give you success till you died, old and terrible. Think of the men at your command. Think of the women you can take. All that can be yours.

"Now here is my token. Above all else you want the fire. I will send it to you, and with it a hope beyond your hope. When it comes to you, say to the Greek: 'it is best on a winter morning.' See him grovel.

"Go now. But do not think you can escape me now I am loose. Or that your father can protect you, locked at the end of Bifrost bridge."

Shef found himself suddenly tossed in the air, going up and further up like a stone from a catapult. He turned in the air, trying to get his feet under him, possessed with fear of where he might land, in the sea with the cold eyes and the teeth, on the land where the serpents crawled and struck.

There was a bed beneath his back, he was struggling to his feet, trying to draw his legs up from the fangs. Arms were pressing him down, he felt a soft breast on his naked skin. Svandis. For long moments he clung to her, shaking.

"Do you know what you were saying," she said to him at last.

"No."

"You called it out again and again, in Norse. *Skal ek that eigi, skal ek that eigi, that skal ek eigi gera.*"

Shef translated automatically, "I shall not that, I shall not that, that shall I not do."

"What is 'that'?" asked Svandis.

Shef realized he was clutching his pendant protectively. "Give up this," he said, looking down at it. "Give up this and worship Loki in exchange for his favor. What is that noise outside?"

CHAPTER TWENTY-FIVE

The sun was already above the horizon—a night had passed by while Shef struggled in his dream with the god of chaos—and the noise was the noise of frenzied cheering. Ship after ship was nosing its way into the harbor, the first one challenged from a distance and then covered by alarmed and wary mule-crews. But as the ships' build became obvious even to the naked eye, and as shouts were exchanged backwards and forwards between the oncoming armada and the catapult crews, the tension vanished. The hastily-repaired boom was cast off, the covering artillery ceased to swing its trails round, tight-wound ropes were slacked off. As the news spread through the town all those who could be released from sentry-go ran down to the dockside, waving and shouting with the relief of tension.

The fleet that Alfred had fitted out and sent to the rescue, warned by Farman's vision, had gathered slowly from its various stations in the Northern seas, and then probed its way cautiously south. Fishermen had often seen Shef's smaller fleet making its way down across Biscay and along the coast of Spain: no seaman who had seen them ever forgot the strange two-master design, and it was easy in any language to ask, "Have you seen ships like ours?" Information became harder to gather, or to understand, once they had rounded the narrow straits of Jeb el-Tarik and made their way into the Inland Sea, urged on by the steady current from the Atlantic. The ships of the *majus* had gone to Cordova. No, they had sailed against the Nazarenes. They were in alliance with the Caliph. No, the Caliph had denounced them as treacherous dogs. All ships fled from the spirits of the *majus*, who threw great stones at the order of their sorcerer-king. On the contrary, it was the Nazarenes who ruled the Inland Sea, with their tame dragons which burned the very sea with fire.

Hardred, the English fleet-commander appointed by Alfred, did his best to pick sense out of all he was told, assisted by Farman priest of Frey, the visionary who had brought them all on this expedition, and by Gold-Guthmund, once Shef's comrade, now king (under the One King) of Sveariki, land of the Swedes. One thing all three had grasped. The Greek galleys were everywhere feared, for reasons no-one was sure of: "Proves no-one's lived to report," remarked Guthmund. As they probed up the coast, opinion also hardened on the fact that the Northerners were in harbor, and unable to escape.

Hardred had at bottom little fear of an encounter with any fleet. Twenty catapult-armed two-masters of the 'Hero' class—every ship named for a hero of Northern legend—followed his flag, and round them skimmed a score and a half of conventional Viking longships, manned by the best that Guthmund's Swedes and the mercenary-market of London could provide. Yet the rumors gave him a little caution. He had spent the night his king had passed in dream lying well offshore, all lights dowsed, the two-masters grapnelled together, the longships rowing cautious, quiet patrol. With the sudden Mediterranean dawn he had come in on the harbor of Septimania, on a long slanting tack against the dawn breeze, all catapults wound and loaded, scouting ships out well ahead.

The first thing Guthmund had seen had been the floating fort: a formidable obstacle if attacked from the direction of the harbor it was meant to block. Attacked from the opposite direction it could offer no resistance. The first fifty Vikings scrambling on to it, axes in hand, met only raised hands and scared faces. Even the twenty *Lanzenbruder* there to keep an eye on the Frankish levies, caught without warning in the midst of a peaceful breakfast, could do no more than eye their stacked armor, and join the surrender.

The Greek commander of the galley on standing patrol, who had done no more for many days than incinerate careless fishing boats, tried a little harder. He saw the strange vessels approaching, manned his oars, and screamed at his *siphonistoi* to make ready. It took time. The flax to be lit, the bellows manned, the pump to be shipped, the safety-checks of oil vessel and connecting pipes scrambled through. As the *siphonistoi* scrambled to their places, the commander manned his oars and tried to outrun pursuit. Two longships were already ahead of him, curving round under oars alone to take him from either side. As he shrieked at his fire-crew to make ready to shoot, regardless of their preparations, a mule-stone from the leading two-master knocked away his stern-post. The galley sank back in the water, the oarsmen immediately quitting their posts. As the *siphonistoi* gave up their impossible task, the commander, remembering his prime directive not to let the secret of the Greek fire fall to any enemy, ran towards the pressure tank with an axe, determined to hole it and let the oil run on to the blazing flax. One of the oarsmen, highly paid and valued as he was, had nevertheless seen too many fishermen screaming in agony in blazing water to accept the same fate for himself—regardless of the fate of Constantinople and the Empire. He tripped his commander, brained him with his own axe, and swept the uncertain *siphonistoi* aside. The longships closed, crews scrambling aboard and eyeing the copper dome and nozzles nervously. Hurriedly the Greek oarsmen and marines were thrust overboard, to cling to ropes and planking in the warm sea. Grapnelled between her two capturers, the Greek galley wallowed half-sinking in the water. As the two-masters came up, Hardred sent his most skilled men aboard to rope the shattered stern together, cover the gaping hole with tarred sailcloth, and drag the water-filled wreck to beach on the shore a bare half-mile away.

Fort and galley seized, the thirty-odd ships remaining sailed for the harbor wall behind which they could see already the distinctive masts of their fellow Northerners. Doubt and suspicion—were they in enemy hands? was there some trap laid behind the stone walls of the city?—dissolved as both sides saw identical catapults training round, as men recognised comrades and relatives, as hails of greeting began to echo back and forth. By the time Shef, rubbing his eyes, still gaping from his dream, had been forced into his clothes by Svandis, the relieving fleet was already squeezing into the crammed harbor in a storm of shouting in English, Norse, and both together.

Cwicca met him at the door of his lodging, gap teeth grinning broadly.

"It's that Hardred," he announced. "Fellow who left you stuck on the Ditmarsh, I never trusted him. But he's come at the right time this time. Cleared them right off that old fort before they even saw him coming. And he's taken a galley too, they say, fire-machine and all."

He waited, face alive with cheer, to see his gloomy king brighten at the news. Shef stared at the thronging harbor, and slowly Cwicca realized that yet again his expectations would be disappointed.

"Above all else you want the fire," he remembered the voice saying. "I will send it to you. Tell the Greek—" what was it he said to tell the Greek?

"Did Hardred capture the Greek operators too?" Shef asked, almost absently.

"I don't know," Cwicca replied. "I don't see why not."

Shef turned to Svandis at his side. "You will have trouble explaining this last dream of mine," he said. "For already I can see it has come true."

The Emperor of the Romans had very little fear for the outcome of the battle he had provoked against the army of the Caliph. It was true that he was heavily outnumbered. True also that the Arabs had a centuries-long record of success against the Christians of the peninsula and the border mountains—sure proof, in the Emperor's view, of the heresy that had taken deep roots among them, for otherwise how would God allow His believers to be worsted? But against that, Bruno was well aware of the rotten state of morale among the enemy, if even a tenth of what the deserters said was true—and the fact that there were so many deserters was a proof in itself. His own troops, whether the reliable *Lanzenbruder* on whom he depended, or the Frankish and German knights he had called from all over his Empire, or even the normally fickle and evasive local levies from the borderlands, were by contrast in good heart and accustomed to success, gained in the many small sieges and skirmishes he had fought to clear the Moslem bandits from his dominions. Some of the gloss had been taken off them by the failed siege of Septimania: but even that was not entirely a bad thing. He had noticed a definite lift in spirits as they had marched away, and broodingly put it down to the superstitious fear that some of them had gained of the man they called—if no superior officer was in hearing—the One King. They would have to be reassured when he turned back to deal with his real enemy. But fighting the Caliph seemed to some of them a virtual holiday by comparison. Less resistance, and a great deal more loot.

In any case there were two other factors the Emperor relied on. One was his faith in God. From time to time he still touched the tender but healing bridge of his nose, and smiled inwardly. A penance he had not inflicted on himself, he welcomed it. In his heart was a growing determination to set his trusty deacon, in minor orders alone though he might be, on the throne of Saint Peter. He was a little man, and a foreigner. But if he had had a confidant the Emperor would have confessed that the little man's heart was bigger than his own. And if he was not a German he was the next best thing. Not for the first time he had given the Emperor back his faith.

And faith or no faith, as the Emperor made a final survey of his dispositions, there was something he could count on even if he had been a mere devil-worshiper like the Waymen-Norse and their apostate English fellows. Constant warfare among the descendants of Pippin the Great and Charles Martel had made all Christian European armies, apart from the backward Anglo-Saxons, into modern fighting forces. On his flanks were planted the siege implements and catapults, both his own design and those copied from their Wayman enemies. Behind him waited the main striking force of five hundred heavy-armed and armored lancers, dismounted and in the shade. Platoons of the *Lanzenbruder* dotted the hill slopes, ready to be bugled forward to form their irresistible infantry line. Really, the Emperor could see only one problem, and that was the penance Erkenbert had imposed on him. Not to fight in the front—he would have done that anyway. But to do so in the company of the most unreliable people in his army, the Christian or pseudo-Christian deserters.

And even that could be turned to account. The Emperor strolled up and down the nervous-looking ranks, still wearing no more than cotton or linen, equipped like the army from which they had deserted with only spears, scimitars and wicker shields. They could not understand a word he said, but they understood that he was there among them. Interpreters had pointed out to them the rewards of success, the impossibility of deserting back now that they had renounced Allah; the penalty of failure was vividly present in the memory of all of them, in bastinado and impaling-post. They would fight all right. And he had taken steps to see that they fought in good heart and even good humor. As the priests passed among them, extending the cups of wine and the wafers of the communion, Bruno set an example by kneeling himself and taking bread and wine humbly. Then he turned his attention to the fires set up in front of his position along the valley-bottom.

"Take communion fasting, then time to feast," he called. "Translate that," he added in an undertone. He stepped forward to the nearest fire, drew his belt-knife, cut away a long rasher, chewed it with exaggerated relish, waved the doubtful deserters forward to join in, to take meat, bread and watered wine from the barrels. Make a party of it, he thought. Cheer them up. Half of them look as if they outran their supplies a week ago. Or their officers steal it from them.

Further up the valley, Mu'atiyah looked through his own far-seer across the advancing cloud of Arab infantry. Proud though he was of his master, he had rejected the use of the sliding tube. What Allah had sent him, that he would retain.

"What are the infidels doing?" asked the Caliph behind him. He stood still in the shade of the awning of his great pavilion, which he had had erected on the very verge of battle, to show his confidence.

Mu'atiyah turned to him, allowing the indignation he felt to show in his face: rage was the safest emotion to have in the vicinity of the Caliph, as long as it was directed outwards. "Caliph, Successor of the Quraysh, the infidels are mocking God. They have set up fires in front of their line, and on each they have roasted a pig. Now those who deserted from our army, those who turned their back on the shahada, they are eating the unclean in the face of you and of the faithful."

From inside the pavilion, unseen, there came a chorus of horror. Then female cries of encouragement. "Smite them, master. Let them feel your wrath." Greatly daring, a voice called out the Caliph's own favorite saying, " 'You believers, fight those of the unbelievers who are nearest to you.' Now they are near enough! Smite them! Oh, that I were a man."

The Caliph nodded slowly, pulled from his belt the jewel-hilted scimitar that could slice drifting silk. Threw aside its scabbard. He walked ceremoniously forward, while his guards closed in around him and the trumpets blew for the advance. On the scrub-covered hillside the dozens of cavalry skirmishes going on between the Islamic cavalry and the goad-wielding *bacheliers* of the Camargue halted while both sides weighed the situation. Then the commander of the Caliph's cavalry, bin-Maymun, cousin of bin-Firnas, waved his men on while edging in the direction of the pavilion itself. The *bacheliers* began their practiced custom of feigning flight while remaining ready to turn it into real flight at a moment's notice. Bruno cut himself a last chop with a steaming kidney attached, used it to wave his men with elaborate unconcern into their rough and barely-disciplined line. The Arab infantry, looking over their shoulders for encouragement, found it in the spears of the Caliph's bodyguard, and broke into the chaotic charge that was their only tactic. At the front ran the *ghazis* among them, calling on Allah to witness their martyrdom and their faith.

Their martyrdom came quickly. As they ran forward over the quarter-mile between them and the deserters who faced them, the forgotten of God, the stones and arrows began to rain down. Bruno had a dozen traction catapults placed to either side of the valley in which he had made his stand, inaccurate weapons, but capable of doing great execution against a crowd. The breast-bows which made no impact on mailed men sent their arrows sleeting through cotton and wicker. Standing unafraid in the center of his own line, Bruno reflected that only ultimate belief and a religion which exalted suicide would have driven men on through the storm they faced. It did not drive them all on, he noticed. His experienced and professional eye saw men slowing to a walk, men drawing to one side, men who did not seem to have been touched throwing themselves to the ground and remaining there. There was a disciplined body following up, he observed, but too few and in too short a line. The disaffected could leak away to one flank or the other. A hundred breaths, he reflected, the time it would take a slovenly clerk to gabble a Mass. Then his penance would be over. He hoped God would grant it to him to shed his blood for the faith, in expiation of his fault.

He would not shed it needlessly. As a knot of *ghazis* drove for the mail-clad *ferengi* beneath the eagle banner of Rome, Bruno kissed once more the Lance which he held secure behind his shield, ducked under the first sweep of a scimitar and neatly thrust his man through the breast-bone. Four inches, no more, twist and recover and ready to parry the next slash with his blade. For fifty of his hundred breaths Bruno stood firm amid the whirling single combats between desperate *ghazi* and confident deserters, Jopp, Tasso, and the rest of his bodyguard protecting his back. Like a machine he parried high, cut low, twisted his shield to deflect a point or curled it to take a blade flat across its face. Every few seconds the snake-tongue blade licked out and another enemy fell back. Then, as one man desperate for glory swung a clumsy blow directly downwards, Bruno parried it automatically, thick edge against blade-tip. The scimitar snapped, the point flew on, its razor edge gashing open the Emperor's left eyebrow. As he saw the blood flow down, and felt it half-blind him, Bruno relaxed. He thrust the man off with his shield, split his skull with a backhand twist, and took his first pace backwards into the protecting line behind him.

"Sound the trumpet," he remarked.

The platoons of *Lanzenbrüder* on foot were moving even before they heard the signal, clumping down the hillside, forming into two lines that converged from either side of the confused battle in front of them. As they met resistance they started their harsh mechanical shouting, trying to keep in step on the stony hillside, always thrusting to the right and guarding to the left. There were no *ghazis* left, only the demoralized. As he saw the battle clear, the commander of the mounted knights eased his men forward in a careful trot, trying to work his way round his own infantry and get space for the one climactic charge which would carry all before it.

The Caliph, striding forward at the head of his personal guard, saw the shredding away of his attack with incredulity. Never before had his wishes been ignored. But all over the valley men were slinking to the flank or rear, getting up from the ground and retreating, ignoring the battle as if they were so many secret Christians. He looked round, not so much to find space for flight as to see if there were further supports he could call up. Behind him there was only his pavilion. Between it and him, the figure of his commander of cavalry, mounted on his famous mare. Er-Rahman cleared a throat to call to him, to wave him indignantly to the battle. Bin-Maymun saw him first. Across the battlefield he too waved, an insolent gesture of farewell. And then he too was off, accompanied by a cloud of his men withdrawn from their pointless skirmishing with the Christian light horse. The Caliph saw suddenly the eagle-banner of the *Rumi* in front of him, with beneath it the one who must be the Caliph of the Christians. He raised his scimitar and ran forward, bounding over the rocks with a cry, "Cursed be those who add gods to God!"

Jopp, who had made his way into the front rank to shield his Emperor while they patched his eye, took the scimitar slash on the flat of his shield— the matchless blade cut through wood and leather till the shield hung only by its iron rim—and stabbed the unarmored man neatly through ribs and heart, the triangular blade driving on till it snapped the spine. As he dropped his point the Caliph, Falcon of the Quraysh, rolled off it to lie on the hillside. The delicate blade of Cordova snapped beneath a hobnailed boot.

With the fall of the Caliph and the precipitate retreat even of his bodyguard, the battle focused suddenly on the Caliph's pavilion of green silk, most obvious piece of loot on the hillside. The *bacheliers* of the Camargue reached it first, on their half-wild ponies. Eunuch guards were speared on tên-foot goads, the wild cowherds sprang from their barebacked ponies, ran screeching inside.

"Tell them, Berthe," snarled Alfled, crouched behind the inner curtain. "They must be Franks."

"*On est français,*" began Berthe uncertainly, her Frankish rusty after ten years of captivity. The cowboys spoke only their native Occitan, saw in front of them only half a score of veiled but bare-legged women, the trulls and whores of the Prophet-worshipers who had oppressed them so long. Calling to each other, they strode greasily forward.

Alfled elbowed her fool of a comrade aside, dropped on her knees, tore away her veil and made the sign of the cross. The cowboys checked, uncertain. As they did so bigger shapes blocked the light. Armored men, the *Ritters* of the *Lanzenorden.*

"*We beoth cristene,*" tried Alfled, fear edging her voice. "*Theowenne on ellorlande.*"

"*Ellorland,*" repeated the leading *Ritter,* himself a man of Alsace, in his Germanic tongue *Ellorsetz.* "Good. Guard the women well. Let the Emperor decide their guilt. And guard the loot too," he added, looking round at silk and finery with a professional eye. "Go on, kick those cowboys out of here."

A hundred paces behind him the Emperor, still on foot, his eye roughly stitched together, strode across the battlefield, noting the small number of corpses. Few had stayed to fight, he noted. He hoped no army he commanded would ever shred away like that. What it showed was how few people had faith, true faith, in their cause and in their god. But faith that was only mouth-deep could have no value. He must put the matter to the wise and learned Erkenbert.

The mouth of Richier the junior *perfectus* was completely dry as the soldiers marched him up to the long black shed in which, only days before, Tartarin the wool-merchant had stored his fells and fleeces. No longer was it just a part of the local economy. In less than half a month it had become part of the local mythology. Those who went in did not come out, unless they were servants of the Emperor. Even the servants of the Emperor, however much wine was poured into them, said nothing of what had become of the others. The most that any of them would say was, "Ask the deacon." But no-one dared even to approach the small black-robed man who pored over his papers, called man after man, and woman after woman, and child after child, to answer his questions. There had never been any doubt that he was in league with the devil, since he proclaimed himself the servant of God, whom all the heretic believers knew was the devil. But if there had been any doubt, it would have vanished as the little man, who knew nothing of the country, spoke not a word of their language, nevertheless detected falsehood after falsehood, punishing each one immediately and mercilessly with whip or brand, block or rope, according to the sex and age of the offender. Richier still did not know what answer had condemned him to the final walk, the walk that none returned from. He could not even guess what kind of lie would serve. And the black deacon had not even bothered to accompany him to the shed—The Shed, as it was now pronounced. In his dreams he had often been permitted to endure martyrdom for his faith: but the martyrdom had been gallant, public, a profession of faith, or done in company like the deaths of the suicides of Puigpunyent. This, this seemed more like the sheep trooping into the slaughterhouse, with as little concern. He tried again to moisten his lips with a cracked tongue as the two soldier-monks jerked on the rope that held him and guided him to the very door of the windowless building.

In his search for the Holy *graduale* Erkenbert was following the principle that had led him in the end to the Holy Lance, or at least to its last human owner. Somebody knew. The number of those somebodies could be narrowed down. It was somebody within, say twenty miles from south-east to south-west of Puigpunyent. True, the inhabitants of the mountain villages were hard to catch. The least hard, though, were the most senior and most important, and most likely to know. Begin with them.

But before beginning the actual questioning of the major targets, build up the background. Write the lists. Erkenbert began to list the villages. Then the people in them, their trades, spouses, children and relations. Proven heresy was of interest, but not the major matter. Erkenbert assumed that all were heretics, including the village priests, if there were any. What was important was to determine the truth, so that any deviation from it, any lie, stood out and proved the speaker a liar. So, one with something to lie about.

It had taken time, but Erkenbert had noticed before too long that his answers corroborated each other and came freely for some areas. Contradicted each other in others. Then the business was to find someone from a reliable area who could give reliable information about the unreliable areas. Then find out the core, the center, of the unreliability. Even the names of the villages had helped him. Once he knew the name of every village in the area, furnished where possible by outsiders such as wandering peddlers and muleteers, it was striking how often three of them were omitted by people who must have known them well: the Hidden Villages, he called them privately. Then within the villages, when he called the roll of their inhabitants, how often were prominent men strangely forgotten, sometimes by their close kin. They were the men he could not find or hunt down. But the attempts to deny their existence by the amateur liars of their kin, they told him whom he should hunt down. Even when their lies were unimportant, liars were punished, to deter further lying. Those who came under Erkenbert's suspicion, they went, in the end, to the Shed. Erkenbert did not believe in torture except where, as with the boy Maury, you knew the victim knew something and you knew what he knew. It was too time-consuming, and the tortured invented too much that might be true but could not be checked. The Shed was a better answer.

Richier's self-control broke as the two soldiers heaved the door open. "What is inside?" he croaked.

"Come see," replied the *Lanzenbruder.*

The secret was very simple, and Richier took it in at a glance. Along the whole length of the building ran a central timber. Over the timber ran a line of a dozen thin cords. From every cord dangled one of the men who had been taken inside, noose round the neck, hands tied, toes sometimes almost brushing the floor. Some of the corpses, in the stifling heat of the closed room, were swollen and unrecognisable. Others, there only a day or two, showed the terror and pain of their deaths on their faces. There were two *perfecti* among them that Richier could recognise. The last and most recent man on the line was one whom Richier knew to be a fierce enemy of the heretics, a devout Catholic, though of a heretic family. He too dangled from the strangling cord.

The monks had produced a three-legged stool, lifted Richier, hands tied, on to it. Seconds later the thin rope was round his neck. Richier could feel it cutting already into his flesh, could imagine all too vividly how it would cut further. And there would be no neck-break. He would die slowly, and alone.

One of the monks had turned to him, the face of the big man almost on a level with Richier's even though he stood on the stool.

"Listen," he said. "Listen good." The German could hardly be understood, his accent was so thick. There was something terrifying in the fact that the Christians had not even sent an interpreter, as if they did not really mind whether anyone spoke or not. The German did not care whether Richier lived or died. He was following his orders, and would turn the key on the shed and walk into the sunshine without a thought.

"You know where this *graal* is, you tell me, I bring deacon. You don't tell me, I kick the stool away. You don't know, I kick the stool away. Someone tell me in the end. We got plenty rope, plenty space on timber."

The man grinned. "Only need one stool."

His mate guffawed, said something incomprehensible in their own language. They both laughed again. Deciding that he had spent enough time on this chore, the first one drew back his foot for the kick as the second began to walk already towards the door. He did not mean even to wait while his victim strangled.

"I know," gasped Richier.

The German paused in mid-kick. "You know?" He called something over his shoulder. His mate returned. A brief colloquy.

"You know where *graal* is?"

"I know where *graal* is. I tell."

The two executioners, for the first time, seemed uncertain, as if they had not been briefed for this eventuality, or as if they had forgotten the briefing.

"We get deacon," said the first eventually. "You. You stay here."

The humor of the remark struck him as he turned away, and he repeated it to his mate with a second roar of laughter. Richier stood on the stool, trying to keep his legs from fainting under him, in the dark, in the stinking shed. By the time the light came back, and he saw the implacable face of the little deacon staring up into his own, even the deacon could see that his nerve had cracked for ever.

"Lift him down," ordered Erkenbert. "Give him water. Now, you. Tell me at once what you know."

The story babbled out. Location. Need for a guide, a guide, himself, if he were dead they would never find it. How he had rescued the precious thing. The one-eyed man they thought a new Messiah. His falsity, his treachery. Erkenbert let it all pour out, confident that a man so broken would never try to go back on his ignoble bargain. At the end Richier risked a word that was not relevant.

"The men you killed here," he husked. "Some were of us, some were not. Will you not answer to your God—to the true God—for the Catholics you have killed?"

Erkenbert looked at him strangely. "What can it matter?" he asked. "God granted it to them to die in His service, and their reward is sure. Do you think God will not know His own?"

CHAPTER TWENTY-SIX

Erkenbert looked with doubt and suspicion at the aged wood held out to him. He had seen many relics: the bones of Saint Wilfrid and Saint Guthlac, of Saint Cuthbert and of the Venerable Bede, even, once, a fragment of the True Cross itself when it was exposed for adoration. He had never seen one entirely unadorned. This looked like something a peasant had left behind his wood-stack for twenty years, and never got round to burning. It was old, he conceded. It looked exactly like the device the one-eyed pagan wore round his neck.

"Are you sure this is it?" he demanded.

Richier the traitor began to babble pleas of assurance.

"Not you. You, Sieghart. Is this the holy thing itself that the Emperor seeks."

"It was well-hidden," said Sieghart stolidly. "Deep inside the mountain, traps all the way. Ambushes too. Lost a few men. But I kept the rat here on his leash, and had plenty of torches burning. We found it in the end. Strange place. Lot of burnt bones."

"Answer my question!"

Sieghart screwed his face up with the effort of decision. "Yes, I think it is. I think *they* think it is, anyway. We found a lot of other stuff with it."

He jerked a thumb and four men came forward. At another gesture they opened their sacks, tipped the contents on to the mud floor of the hovel Erkenbert had made his base. He drew in his breath at the sight of the gold plate, the cups, the incense burners, objects that he could see were there for divine service. No, service of idols, he corrected himself. But it was no secular hoard, not even a king's hoard. An idea began to stir. As it did so his eye caught unexpected objects amid the loot. Books. Two of them.

He picked one up, opened it. "What is this?" he demanded of the despairing Richier.

"They are the holy books of our—of the heretic faith. There are only two copies of them." Richier had meant to say "two copies left," but some mistaken instinct of self-preservation warned him.

"And what is holy about them?"

"They tell the story—they claim to tell the story of what happened after . . . after Christ was taken down from the Cross."

"But that story is in the Gospel of Nicodemus. Not a work that the Church has admitted into the canon of the Bible, but a work worthy of reverence. There are many copies of it in the libraries of Christendom."

"This tells a different story," whispered Richier. He did not dare even to hint at what the story might be.

His face set, Erkenbert began to skim the book's pages. The Latin it was written in caused him no difficulty, though for an instant or two his lip curled in contempt of its barbaric style. Then his face seemed to set even harder and grimmer. He had come to the claim that Christ survived. Did not die. Did not rise again. Fled, married, raised children. Abjured his faith.

Abjured his faith.

"Have you read this book?" asked Erkenbert quietly.

"No. Never."

"You are lying. You knew it told a different story. Sieghart! What have you done with the men who were hanged in the shed."

"Dug a grave. Waiting for a priest to say the burial service over them. Some might have been good Catholics."

"There will be no burial service. Some were assuredly heretics. Heretics so vile they deserve no burial, if it were not for the stench they leave in the nostrils. But the stench of these books is greater. Before you fill in the grave, Sieghart, throw these in. Let them not go to clean flame, but lie and corrupt with the corruption of their authors. And Sieghart . . ."

The two men's eyes met, a faint nod. Sieghart freed his dagger noiselessly, mouthed the word "Now?" Another nod. Catching some hint of what was meant, Richier struggled forward to the knees of the deacon, babbling still, "I brought you the *graal,* I deserve a reward . . ."

The dagger sank from behind into the base of his skull. "You have your reward," said Erkenbert to the face-down sprawling figure. "I released you from fear. You did not deserve shrift and salvation. Worse than Pelagius, worse than Arius. They brought false belief, but you . . . you would have left Christians with no belief at all. Do not open that book, Sieghart, on your soul's salvation."

"That's all right, *magister,*" said Sieghart amiably. "I can't read."

"Reading is for the wise alone," confirmed Erkenbert.

* * *

Two days later and thirty miles to the south across the mountain passes, Erkenbert timed his entry to the Emperor's banquet with precision. For three successive nights the Emperor had remained on the field of battle, resting his men, burying the dead, dividing the loot of the Caliph's baggage train, and hearing the priests of his army sing the *Te Deum laudamus* from behind an altar built of captured weapons. Now, inside the great pavilion, its inner hangings torn away so that all could banquet where once the Caliph's *harem* had been kept, he sat at the head of the high table.

Erkenbert walked slowly in to face him, six *Lanzenritter* pacing gravely behind him, their armor polished to an unearthly gleam. The Emperor's minstrels ceased their playing, the servers and wine-pourers, recognising the gravity of the scene, stood back against the silken walls. The Emperor too caught the signs of ceremonial, of vital portent. His face paled as hope seized his heart. He rose to his feet, and all speech stopped instantly.

Erkenbert said nothing, continued walking forward. Then he stopped, turned away as if self-effacingly, an icon of Christian humility with his slight frame and dull black robe. He raised a hand to Sieghart.

Swelling with pride, the *Ritter* drew aside the elaborate altar-cloth with which he had hidden the *graduale,* passed it to his second-in-command. Silently he held the wooden pole-ladder at arm's length above his head, like a battle-standard.

"Is that it, is that the . . ." the Emperor began.

"It is the ladder of Joseph of Arimathea, on which our Lord's body was carried to the Holy Sepulchre," cried out Erkenbert at the full force of his lungs. "From which He rose again the third day, *according to the Scriptures!* According to the Apostles' Creed! Let all see it and know their faith confirmed."

The Emperor dropped instantly to one knee, followed in moments by every other man and woman in the pavilion, except for Sieghart, standing like a resplendent statue.

Finally Sieghart lowered the *graduale* gently to the earth, and as if by compensating machinery, the Emperor and his following rose. Bruno held out a hand. Sieghart stepped forward and placed the Grail in it. With his other hand Bruno brought Grail and Lance together.

"Death and life," he muttered, tears running from his eyes. "Life in death. But Erkenbert . . . It is bare wood."

Erkenbert waved to the four other *Ritters,* and as they had done before, they spilled the contents of their sacks on to the pavilion floor.

"The holy vessels of the heretics," said Erkenbert. "Captured to the glory of God."

"And God shall have them all," said Bruno. "I swear that no man shall receive a pennyweight of what you have taken. I will compensate the army and the *Lanzenorden* from my own private purse. But every ounce of what you have taken shall be made into the greatest reliquarium of the West, to enshrine this relic for ever and ever.

"And I swear this too," shouted Bruno, drawing his sword and holding it up like a cross in front of him. "In gratitude for the favor that God has sent me, I swear to conquer the whole of Spain for the Catholic Church, or die in the attempt. More! I will leave no-one alive within the old Empire who does not accept the sole authority of Saint Peter. Whether in Hispania or Mauretania or Dacia."

"Or Anglia," said Erkenbert.

"Or Anglia," repeated Bruno. "And I further swear this. In gratitude for the faith that the deacon Erkenbert has brought me, the faith that I weakly doubted, not only will I bring his country back to the Church from its apostates, but I will make him the heir of Saint Peter, and set him on the Papal throne. And he and I will rule Church and Empire together. From Rome!"

The audience stirred slightly, did not dare to mutter. They had no doubt the Emperor had power to make a Pope. Had he the right? Some at least had no objections. Better an Englishman that they saw campaigning with them than some unknown Italian who never left the city walls.

"Now, Erkenbert," Bruno's voice sank to its normal pitch. "Put the Grail in a place of honor, and tell me the story of how you won it. And I need your advice. I captured one of your countrywomen amid a batch of others, there she is, acting as a wine-bearer. Whores of the Caliph, God rot their faithless marriageless ways. Not her fault, though. What am I to do with her, with all of them?"

Erkenbert shot a glance at the beautiful woman listening intently to the conversation in the half-familiar Low German. A disapproving glance.

"Let her expiate her sin," he rasped. "Her and the others. Found an order of the Grail, an order of nuns. A strict order, for penitents." He thought of the evil wickedness in the books he had had destroyed, their accursed fable of Christ's marriage to the Magdalen. "Call it the Order of Saint Mary Magdalen. God knows there are enough whores in the world to fill it."

Alfled's hands did not shake as she filled the cup. She had had long training in self-control.

Shef had spent long days in trying to make his entire fleet once more fit for sea: transferring supplies from the new arrivals to the old, reprovisioning all the ships with water and such preserved food as could be had in Septimania, organizing squads to find and chip replacement mule-stones from the shore, remounting those machines that had been taken from ships to battlements.

The work had got easier as time passed. Indeed it seemed to him sometimes as if some kind of watershed had been crossed with the unexpected arrival of reinforcements. Either that or—and this was what he feared in his heart—some new favor had been granted him by the gods. By a freed god.

The Emperor's forces, much weakened as soon as the Emperor himself had left to fight the Caliph, raised even their token siege one night and disappeared. Soon food and news began to trickle in as the mountaineers of the interior realized the roads were once more open. The kites flew gaily as Tolman and his fellows delightedly displayed their prowess to the new arrivals. In exchange Farman had produced a dozen far-seers made by glass-blowers in Stamford: the lenses inferior in clarity, and scratched by grinding even with the finest sand and chalk, but proof that Arab skills could be matched in time. Cwicca and his gang had carefully and leisurely built a replacement giant catapult, with proper side-bracing, and shot it in till they were confident of dismantling, storing and re-erecting it at any time. Steffi's flares illuminated day and night as he too practiced unhurried and unhindered. Solomon had found in the market-place a device of wires and beads which much improved on Shef's lines and columns in the sand.

Shef himself had closely examined every part of the Greek fire contriv-ance in the captured galley, noted its tank of fuel, sniffed and tried to taste the strange stuff inside it, examined slow-match, brazier and bellows, worked the handle of the strange pressure-pump that seemed to be vital for its operation. He had not ventured to test the device. I will send you fire, Loki had said, and he had. That did not mean Shef had to use it, or to pay Loki's price.

One day, perhaps, he would bend his energies to the task of forcing the skilled Greeks to break their oath of silence. Just now he was content to know that he had the strongest naval force on the Inner Sea, capable of driving off the Greek fleet even in a flat calm, and of bringing it to battle and sinking it at any other time. Besides, he reflected, the very sight of the copper dome on one of his ships, and the Greeks would hesitate to close. He had, once more, the technological lead which for a while had been threatened. In short, while the Emperor ruled the land, he ruled the sea. His escape-route was clear. Should he choose to take it.

It was other matters, now, which occupied him. Matters which seemed without urgency, mere questions for philosophers, but which his instinct told him must now be settled. Settled before he found himself taking the bait of Loki. He had thought long about the scene Rig had shown him, of Loki and Logi, of Loki the giant and Loki the god. In the priest-conclaves of the Way, the bale-fire always burned inside the circle. Should the fire-god not be inside the circle too?

He had called, then, a conclave, in the shaded court where he had had translated the heretics' book. To it were bidden the priests of the Way, the four who had sailed with him, Thorvin, Skaldfinn, Hagbarth and Hund, and with them Farman the visionary who had seen the need for the new fleet and brought it with him. His executive officers, Brand and Hardred, Guthmund and Ordlaf, two English and two Norse. And in addition Solomon the Jew, and Svandis, once again in the provocative display of Way-priest white. Of the eleven men and one woman present, all but two wore the pendants of the Way: Solomon the Jew, and Hardred, who like his master Alfred had never given up the Christianity in which he had been raised. With deliberate purpose, then, Shef had made the table at which they sat an oval one, like the oval in which Way-priests held their conclave. He had not ringed it round with the holy cords and the rowan-berries of life, nor had he lit the bale-fire by which the priests timed their meetings. But behind him, in the sand, he had planted a seven-foot battle-spear, in conscious appeal to the Othinic symbol of the Way. He saw the priests looking at each other as they caught the imitation—was it mockery, or challenge?—of their own ceremonial.

He rapped the table with a knuckle. "I have called you here to consider our future plans. But before we do that, we must draw some lessons from what has happened already."

He looked round the table, fixed his eye on Svandis. "One thing we know now is that Svandis was wrong. She told me, she told us all, that there were no gods, that they were created by men out of the wickedness of their hearts, or their own weakness. And that the visions they have sent me were mere dreams, created by my own brain as a hungry man dreams of food, or a frightened one of what he fears. Now we know that the last, at least, is not true. Farman, thousands of miles away, saw our trouble and came to help us. His vision was true. But it was a frightening one. For what he saw was what I have seen, seen now three times. Loki loose. Loki unbound from his chains. Ready to loose Fenris-wolf from the bond of Greipnir and bring Ragnarök on the world.

"So we must think again about the gods. They do exist. And yet Svandis may not be wholly wrong. For the gods and their worshipers do have something to do with each other. I turn to Hund. Tell us all, Hund, not only those you have told already, what is your view of the gods."

"I would say that Svandis is part right," said Hund. He did not look up, did not look at her. "The gods are created by men. But once they are created, they become real. They are mind-creatures, born of our belief, but once they are born they have power even over those who do not believe. I too think they are evil, created from wickedness."

"Even Ithun?" said Thorvin harshly, staring at Hund's apple-pendant, sign of the healer-goddess. Hund did not reply.

"But if Hund is right," Shef went on, "then we have to accept another thing. That there are gods besides those of the Way. The Christian God. The God of the Jews. The Allah of the Arabs."

"So why have they not blasted us?" asked Hagbarth. "Their worshipers hate us enough to wish it, to believe in it."

"Hund has given a good answer to that. He reminds us how many of us there were—he and I among them—who were brought up as cradle-Christians, and had no faith at all. Only habit. It may be that the mind-stuff of which the gods are made is delicate and tricky, like the Greek fire. Perhaps some minds, most minds, do not produce it. And remember, the Christians have their saints and visionaries too.

"Besides, if the gods come from us, then they have our strengths, our weaknesses. Just as Svandis said. The Christian God does not act in this world. He takes his followers to another." Shef remembered the awful vision he had seen once of King Edmund, martyred by the heathen, passing beyond him to some fate he could not even glimpse. "Our gods, the gods of the Way, work in the world, as do their priests and their worshipers. They believe in things made with hands."

Brand laughed as he saw the strained faces round the table. "I am a man of the Way," he called out. "I bearded the damned Ragnarssons for the Way, did I not? But the more I see and the more I hear, the less I believe in anything except three things. My ship, my gold, and 'Battle-Troll' here." He lifted his silver-inlaid axe from where it lay beside him, flourished it, and drank again from the quart pitcher of beer that the new fleet had brought with it.

"So far we can follow you," said Thorvin. "I do not like what you say about the Christian God, but I can accept it. After all, we have always said—you have always said, and you have proved it by your deeds, see Hardred here—that our quarrel is not with Christ nor with Christians, but with the Church that comes from Rome. Because while we listen to what you say, and consider it, if you said it to the Emperor and you were in his power, you would be lucky to earn death alone. The Christian Church brooks no rivals! Will not share power or the claim to truth. That is what our founder Duke Radbod saw and foresaw. That is why we preach the Way. So that everyone may choose their own way."

"Everyone may choose their own way," Shef repeated. "That is why we are here." He drew a deep breath, for this was the moment of decision. "I think it is time for new ways."

"New ways?"

"New pendants. New knowledge. Svandis has made a start, with her quill-pendant. It stands for the study of our minds, the writing down of all that has seemed to us most fleeting. Mind-study, and mind-stuff. Who is the god that you have taken as your patron, Svandis?"

"No god," Ivar's daughter replied. "No goddess either. A name in our myths. I wear the quill for Edda, that is to say 'great-grandmother,' for old tales and traditions."

"*Edo* means 'I write,' in the Latin tongue," observed Skaldfinn. "Svandis did not know that. It is the kind of accident the gods send. I think this is new knowledge we should accept."

"Another pendant we need," said Shef. "The *sifr* sign of the Arabs, the round hole that means 'nothing.' The powerful nothing. If I did not have my own sign I would take that one. It should be the sign for those who can reckon, and its god should be Forseti, who settles disputes and brings certainty.

"A third, the wings of Völund. For Tolman, and the fliers." Shef looked round with his one eye, gauging support, trying to bend the uncertain to his will. So far they were with him. Völund-priests, priests of Forseti, they would be new but welcome. Way-priests always liked new trades, whether flying or lens-grinding or calculation. Now for the hard one.

"I say we need a fourth. For the likes of Steffi, who burned his hands to bring us light. We need men to wear a fire-sign. For Loki."

Thorvin was on his feet immediately, hammer sliding from belt to hand, and there were looks of horror on the faces of Skaldfinn and Hagbarth, and Farman too.

"No man can take that sign! We let his fire burn, to remind us of what we face. We do not worship it, or him. Even if all that you said is true, about men creating gods, why should we create a god like him? The trickster, the father of monsters. The bane of Balder."

"Why should we? *We already have.*" Shef looked round the room to see his words sink in. "If Hund is right, and he exists, then we made him. Made him out of fear and hatred. Made him kill the good and beautiful because we are jealous of it. Chained him so we did not need to blame ourselves. Drove him mad.

"He is loose now. I fear him more than you do. But what I am saying is this. Freedom for Loki as well as for Thor. For the bad as well as the good. If he attacks us, we will destroy him. But fire can be for us as well as against us."

Thorvin looked round as if expecting thunder and a lightning-bolt for the cloudless sky. "Freedom for Loki as well as for Thor!" he repeated. "But he is the father of the monster-brood, you have seen them. You have met them." His eye rested uncertainly on Svandis, as if unsure how far he could continue. Thorvin was convinced, Shef knew, that Ivar the Boneless, Svandis's father, had been a creature of Loki with a non-human shape in the other world of the gods. If it came to that, Shef believed it too. But then Loki was bound and crazed with pain.

"Freedom is not the same as lawlessness," he said. "If a follower of Loki were to come and say that his worship forced him to sacrifice slaves at his barrow, or to cut women to pieces for his pleasure, we would tell him the penalty for *morth*-deeds is death. Under Wayman-law that is already true. It is what makes us different from the pagans. Now I do not know what made Loki kill Balder, what made men imagine a Loki and a Balder and imagine the one killing the other. But I do know that if we are to cure the maim of the world and bring back Balder, then we must believe in something other than eternal enmity."

Farman stirred in his seat, and spoke in his quiet voice. He was an unimpressive man: the first time Shef had seen him, it had been in a Völund-vision, and there Shef had been the lame but mighty smith of the gods, Farman no more than a mouse-shape peeping up from the wainscoting. Shef still saw and heard him sometimes as a mouse, squeaking and peeping. Yet he was greatly respected. His visions, all agreed, were true ones. He and Vigleik were the far-seers of the Way.

"Tell us the story of the weeping for Balder," he said, his eyes on Thorvin.

Thorvin looked uncertain, suspicious, sure that in some way his narrative would be challenged. Yet by the conventions of the Way he could not refuse to speak. "You know," he began, "that after the death of Balder through the machinations of Loki Laufeyjarson, Othin built a pyre for his son and laid him on it. But before the fire was lit Othin sent his servant Hermoth, greatest hero of the Einheriar, into Hel to ask if there was any way by which Balder could be released. And Hermoth rode down over the Giallar bridge, and came to the gates of Hel, and leapt his horse over them."

Shef too stirred in his seat, for though this was a story he had heard, it was not the one he had seen.

"He went on, and begged the goddess Hel to release Balder, but she refused, saying that Balder could only leave Hel if everything in the world, alive or dead, would weep for him. If any creature refused, then he must stay.

"So Hermoth rode back, and the gods instructed every creature in the world to weep for what had been lost, and so they did, people and animals and earth and stone and trees. But in the end the gods' messengers came upon a giantess sitting in a cave, and she said"—Thorvin's voice turned to the deep chant he reserved for holy song:

"No tears will Thökk trail on her cheeks
 for Balder's burial. Bane alone got she
 from the one-eyed one, wise though he be.
   Let Hel hold what she has.

"And so the demand of Hel was not fulfilled, and Balder was not released, Instead he was burnt on the pyre, and with him his wife Nanna, who died of sorrow. Most men think that the giantess was Loki Laufeyjarson in another shape."

"Well and truly told, Thorvin," said Farman softly, "but there are questions to ask. You know that the spittle that runs from the mouth of Fenris-wolf is called Vön, which is to say Hope, and that is to show us that to trust in hope, as the Christians do, and cease to struggle when there is no hope, is below the dignity of a warrior. But what then is the meaning of the giantess's name, Thökk—which means 'thanks' just as Vön means 'hope'?"

Thorvin shook his head.

"Could it not mean that the price of Balder back is no more than thanks?"

"Thanks for what?" rumbled Thorvin.

"Thanks for whatever Loki may have done in time past."

"The stories say that he was a good comrade when Thor went to Utgarth-Loki, to wrestle with Old Age and try to lift the Mithgarth-Serpent," Hagbarth corroborated.

"Loki was a good comrade against Loki, then," said Farman. "But when that comradeship was not recognised, and thanks given for it, he became what we have made him. Is the king's proposal not to thank and recognise the good Loki? To enlist him against the mad one?"

"Hermoth did not get into Hel," Shef added with the crushing certainty that came from vision. "He was stopped by the gates. He cut a cock's head off and threw it over Grind-gate, and rode back. But before he rode back he heard the cock crowing on the other side."

"So there is life even in the place of death," concluded Farman. "Even where Balder is. So there is a chance . . . A chance of curing the world's maim and bringing back beauty to it." He looked at Shef, aiming his words at him alone. "And that is how the old become young. Not like dragons, by clinging on to what is theirs. Like adders, by shedding their skin. The skin of worn-out belief. Old knowledge gone dead."

He has shared more than one of my visions, Shef thought, even if I did not know it.

Thorvin looked round the table, conscious that the argument was slipping away from him, seeing faces that ranged from Hardred's stupor to Skaldfinn's dawning interest, angry conviction from Svandis.

"It would have to go to the full Council of priests," he temporized.

"In the end," Farman agreed.

"But how does this affect our plans? Our plans for here and now?"

"I will tell you that," said Shef. "It seems to me that there are many things we could do. We could go home, brushing the Greeks out of our way."

"Perhaps making a little profit as we go," suggested Guthmund.

"We could sail our ships to the Guadalquivir and march on Cordova. It has no Caliph now, if what we hear is true. Our support might make a difference to the next one. It is in my mind that we might demand the right to preach the Way. It would have been denied by the last Caliph, by any Caliph securely in power. Just now—well, who knows?"

"We could make quite a *big* profit out of Cordova," Brand said to Guthmund. "You haven't seen the place, but I'm telling you, that raid by the Ragnarssons fifteen years ago can't have scratched the surface."

"But if what we have been saying is true," Shef went on, "I think we should do something else. For what we have been saying, what Hund and Svandis and even Farman have been saying, is that strength in this world comes from belief. So we must strengthen ours, and that of those who are friendly to us, or at least tolerant of us.

"And we must destroy the faith of those who give no space to others. Who allow freedom neither to Loki nor to Thor. Nor to any other than their own One God."

"And how is that to be done?" asked Solomon the Jew, with deliberate politeness.

"With paper on the one hand. And with emissaries on the other. I will explain . . ."

CHAPTER TWENTY-SEVEN

From Hlithskjalf, the vantage-point of the gods, the Aesir deities looked down on earth. Far below they could see points of flame like spear-points on fire, could see the wolves and ravens gathering. Heimdall, who can hear the grass growing and the thoughts inside a man's head, or a god's, cocked his head and lifted an eyebrow towards his brother Rig. The thought inside the head of Othin was: "This is getting out of hand." But All-Father would not speak his thought, and Heimdall kept silence.

"I wish I knew who broke his bonds," said Othin finally.

Not even Heimdall knew that Rig had done so, for Rig could keep even his thoughts secret when he chose.

"All things weaken in time," observed Rig.

It was not a tactful thought to express to one who admitted no limits to his power—though in truth those limits were clear enough. Rig tried the other half of the observation. "But seeds can grow in time as well."

"What are you talking about?" snarled Othin. "Loki is loose, Heimdall is ready to blow his horn, the Last Battle of gods and men may begin at any moment, with weapons of fire and creatures in the air, and now our own followers are turning to Loki. Your follower is."

"He has not changed his pendant yet," said Rig. "I ask you, All-father. Think back a few lifetimes. What were we then? Weak. The creatures of a few wood-runners and sea-thieves. Dwindling to being mere kobbolds or nixe. Now, we have grown strong. Not from the sacrifices at Uppsala, that terrified thousands for the belief of a score. From belief and devotion."

"How is that helped by Loki loose? And men prepared to worship him?"

"Loki was not always bad."

Othin turned on Rig a terrible eye. "He killed my son. He took the light out of the world and left it pale."

Rig was not afraid, but the eye of Othin is hard to face. He turned his own eyes down, but spoke on. "He was a comrade once. If that had been recognised, he would not have felt the jealousy, the envy that made him use the mistletoe and betray Hod."

"He said many ill things to us in our own hall," said Heimdall. "Me he called 'mudback,' said I was the slave of the gods, never allowed to sleep."

"You never do sleep," replied Rig.

"This has to do with your own son," said Othin. "Your own son and follower, whom you have made me spare once, twice. He is the one who has loosed Loki, is calling him back to the world. Though he does not seem to want what Loki wants. Say now, though, why I should spare him the third time." He raised his spear Gungnir, pointed it down to the far blue Inner Sea.

"I do not ask for him to be spared," said Rig.

All the gods, the dozen assembled, looked at their brother doubtfully.

"Take him if you wish. He will be an uneasy recruit for your Einheriar, Othin. Before Heithrun's mead-vat has been emptied ten times the heroes will be smithying new weapons to fight each other from a distance, and the weakest will be the strongest. But take him if you will. I say only this: wait and see. It may be that if he has his way, gods that are strong will grow weak, gods that once were weak—as we were, a few lifetimes ago, as I was, almost forgotten—they may grow strong."

It was true, Heimdall reflected, that barely a lifetime ago, less than a lifetime ago as men count, Rig had been a mere shadow on the fringe of the gods' feasting, not important enough to be taunted by Loki or consulted by Othin. Now many wore his pendant, and his brothers made way for him. And how had that come about?

"Who do you think will grow weak?" asked Heimdall in the end.

"Those gods who cannot share power, or win the hearts of men without compulsion."

"Do you mean me?" asked Othin threateningly.

"No, father. Say what Loki will about you, he cannot say some things with any truth. No-one has ever called you a jealous god."

The Aesir reflected on the meaning of their brother's words. Some looked again at the scene below, at the broad Middle-earth on which their worshipers were a mere scattered fringe. Their faces set immobile like the faces of horse-copers who have seen an unnoticed bargain.

"But your son will not bring my son back."

"The prophecy is that after Ragnarök, those who are spared will see a new age and the rebirth of Balder in a fairer world. But you will not be spared, father. Fenris-Wolf waits for you, as Surt for Frey. But if there is no Ragnarök, if there is no *Ragnarök, can we say that Balder cannot just the same be reborn? Once even Loki is prepared to weep for him? If you wish to see your son again outside the halls of Hel, then you must take another turning.*"

This time it was the face of Othin that changed to that of a man who sees advantage far off.

"How did you get away?" asked Svandis. Facing her sat the woman she had met and wept with in the fountain-court of the Caliph, Alfled the fair, once her enemy, now her colleague.

Alfled shrugged disdainfully, swept the hair back from a face that was reddened with sun. "The little black bastard told the bastard with the wide shoulders to turn us into nuns. Berthe—the Frankish girl you met, you remember—she was happy with the idea, she has never had much use for men. But Ouled has no mind to be a Christian, and I, I have no mind to be a nun. I saw little enough of men, or of any man, while I was in the *harem* of the Caliph. I have time to make up!"

"So, how?"

"Oh, men are easy to handle, you know. In the convoy that was taking us to some Allah-forsaken spot, I talked to one of the guards. Told him how unfair it was to be locked up half your life and then taken away to be locked up again. Looked at him till he looked at me, and then looked a second more before I dropped my eyes. Made him think I admired him. They are so vain, so weak.

"When he came to me in the night I let him loose the door-chain and sweep me into the bushes. He did not see Ouled behind him with the hair-pin." She laughed suddenly. "He was a brisk lover, I will say that for him. It may be that he died happy. Then Ouled and I made our way from one village to another, exchanging this and that for what we needed. You told me you had done it too."

Svandis nodded. "And now, what do you want?"

"They say the king here is an Englishman, and a freer of slaves. Even the men here say they are freed slaves, those that speak English. Surely he will free me too, give me passage home."

"Your kin will not be pleased to see you," observed Svandis. "A dishonored woman. You have no husband, but you have not the right to wear your hair loose like a virgin."

"I am a widow," said Alfled firmly. "Widows have the right to remarry. And no husband can blame them if they know more about some things than a virgin. Ouled and I know a lot more than any virgin, or any wife in Christendom. I think I can find myself a man, here or in London or in Winchester. As for Ouled, she wants only passage to Cordova, for she thinks the same of herself as I do."

"What do you think of the men here?" asked Svandis.

"Not much. The ones who speak English are the sons of slaves. When I was captured by the raiders no thane would speak to such without a whip in his hand. I cannot understand why they should have been freed. There is not one who looks like an atheling."

"That one does," said Svandis, pointing out of the window at Styrr walking by sucking an orange with his great horse-teeth.

"He looks like a warrior, at least. But those are the Norse-folk. Like you. Your people captured me, sold me down here. I could not live easily with one of you."

"There are still plenty of thanes and thanes' sons in England," said Svandis, "and I dare say you could capture one of them easily enough. You are your own dowry, and after a wedding-night with one of your experience, I expect you could ask whatever morning-gift you wished."

Ouled the Circassian, sitting listening to a conversation in a language she could not follow, shifted and looked up at the unmistakable sound of two women beginning to scorn each other. In one of the private signs of the *harem,* she spread her fingers, looked at the nails. Don't fight, it said. Sheathe your claws. Alfled choked down a scornful answer, tried to look amused.

"I think you could do the One King a service," said Svandis. "The One King, who has said he will make me his queen."

Men say all sorts of things to get what they want, reflected Alfled, but did not say the words, only lifting her eyebrows in polite enquiry.

"He needs information about the state of things in Cordova now the Caliph is dead. He may need an emissary, too, one who speaks better Arabic than we do. One thing you can be sure of, he is a generous payer, a true ring-giver to those who serve him. And you are right, he has a soft spot in his heart for those who have been slaves, like you."

I will see if he has not a hard spot for me somewhere else, reflected Alfled grimly. Copper hair, blue eyes, complexion like a Moorish laborer's. In the *harem* you would have been called once, out of curiosity, and never again. "I am at your mercy," she replied, eyes prudently downcast. "What is the king's particular interest?"

"At the moment," Svandis replied, "he is interested in the making of holy books, and how they come to be."

Whips, poetry, little boys, scented oils, now holy books, thought Alfled. God, or Allah, or Jesus, send me a man one day with simple interests.

In a room deep within the Prince's private palace, Shef confronted a quadruple row of benches. In front of each bench ran a long table, on each bench sat six scribes. Their quills were in hand, pots of ink stood by each one, each one had a fresh sheet of the strange Oriental paper in front of him. The scratching of pen-knives had died away, the two dozen faces looked expectantly at the barbarian king who had driven off the Emperor of the Nazarenes.

Solomon addressed the scribes. "The king here," he said, "has discovered a document. It is one which casts great doubt on the faith of the Christians, would tell them—if they knew of it—that their Messiah is as we well know already, a false one, a foreshadower of one who is yet to come. He wishes to have many copies made, to spread the knowledge widely in the Christian world. So we have called you together. He will dictate a version of what he has read to me, I will translate it into the trade-talk of Spain, the Arabic that we all know, and you will write it down. Later we will make more copies, and more, both in this language and in the Roman tongue of the south. Maybe also in Latin. But this is the beginning of it."

A hand raised, a skeptical voice spoke. "How long will this account be, Solomon?"

"The king says, it must cover no more than a single page."

"How long was the first document?"

"As long as the Book of Judith."

"It will take skill, then, to reduce it to one folium."

"The king knows his mind," said Solomon firmly.

Shef listened without understanding to the interchange in Hebrew, waited for the rustling and gentle mirth to die down. Solomon nodded, to show that the scribes were ready. Shef stepped forward, the heretics' book, in its Anglo-Norse translation, open in his hand—not for him to read, for his grip on the runes was still shaky, but as a prompt.

As he looked at the rows of faces, at the blank sheets in front of them, his mind seemed to dowse itself, like a fire which has had a wet blanket dropped over it. There was nothing there. A few moments before he had been ready to speak, to tell the story of the rescue and escape of Jesus from the Cross in words that any man or woman might understand. Now there was nothing there. Stray phrases wandered through his mind: "They call me Jesus . . . What you have been told is not true . . . Have you ever thought about death?" None of them seemed to lead anywhere. He realized his mouth was hanging open, in what must seem an idiot's gape, became aware of the slight sneers, the dawnings of contempt on the faces that looked up at him.

He cast his eye down. He was trying, he told himself, to instruct these men at their own speciality, which was books and the making of books. How would they fare if they came into his camp and told Cwicca how to wind a catapult? The thought of the furious bawdry with which a learned scribe would be received round the camp-fires amused him momentarily, seemed to break a hole in the barrier of silence. Remember, he told himself again. What you have to do is to take a story, the story that was written down, and make it into an appeal. You have to change it from an I-story into a you-story. Start with that. If you do not know where to start, start with the beginning.

He raised his head and his one eye again, stared at the room full of men, beginning to exchange glances and pass remarks at the immobility of the barbarian. As the glare passed over them, the glare of a man who had stood face to face with Ivar, Champion of the North, and killed Kjallak the Strong on the King's Stone of the Swedes, the scribes fell silent again. Shef began to speak in a tone of suppressed fury. As he spoke, phrase by phrase and sentence by sentence, Solomon's voice pattered out the quiet accompaniment, and the scratch of many quills on paper followed it.

"Followers of Christ," Shef declaimed, "you have heard of the joys of Heaven and the fires of Hell. In hope of one and in fear of the other, you give your children to be baptized, you confess your sins, you pay the tithe. You wear the Cross. On Easter Sunday you crawl to the Cross on your knees, the priest holds it in front of your dying eyes.

"Why? Because it is the sign of life, of life after death. You hope to live in Paradise after you are dead because there was One who once came back and declared He had power over death and after death. On the Cross, and on the Resurrection, all your hope rests.

"What if there was no Resurrection? Where is your hope then, and what good are your tithes? What need have you then of a priest? Now who has told you the story of the Resurrection? Was it a priest? Would you buy a horse on the word of the man who took your money? If you never saw the horse? Listen to this story instead.

"There was a man called Jesus, and many years ago Pontius Pilate crucified him. But the hangmen bungled in haste, and he did not die. *He did not die.* Instead, his friends came and took away the body on a ladder, and brought it back to life. When he was strong again, he fled and made a new life, and in that new life he took back many of the things he had said. Heaven is in this world, he said, and men should make it for themselves. Women too.

"Do you live in Heaven? Or in Hell? Ask your priest, ask him how he knows what he knows. Ask him, where is the Cross? Where is the ladder? Look in his eyes when you ask him, and think of selling the horse. If you do not believe him, think what you can do."

"It was an interesting account," remarked Moishe the scribe to Solomon as they walked away together, for the moment on friendly terms again. "Inept, of course."

Solomon raised an eyebrow, but did not challenge the view. "I had trouble," he agreed, "in translating some of it. His words for 'baptize' and 'Resurrection' are very simple, and I had to do the best I could. In what lies its ineptitude?"

"Oh, seven rhetorical questions in a row, like a schoolboy who has not felt the rod. Constant repetition, horses and hangmen and ladders and tithes all mixed in with life and death and the mysteries of faith. No grandeur. No idea of style. I would blush to have it known that I had written such a thing. But to your One King I am just the part of a machine, a machine for making many copies."

I will pass that on, reflected Solomon. The thought of a machine for making many copies. And what does not please Moishe may nevertheless affect people of whom the learned Moishe knows nothing. The unlearned, to begin with. There are many of them, and not all are stupid.

"Where are you from?" asked Shef.

"I was taken from Kent," the woman replied. She was dressed still in what remained of an all-enveloping Arab *burqa,* but she wore no veil, and the hood was thrown back to reveal fair hair and blue eyes. She spoke English—old-fashioned English, Shef realized with a slight shock, better English in a way than his own, used as he now was to studding his language with words and tricks of speech that he had picked up from the Wayman Norse. Twice already he had seen her frown as she struggled to follow him.

"Kent. That is within the realm of my co-king, Alfred."

"The king in my time was Ethelred. Before him, Ethelbert. I think I had heard of Alfred as their younger brother. There have been many changes. Still, I would like to go back. If I could. If I could find my kin, and if they would have me back, a disgraced woman."

The woman sank her eyes, feigned to dab at them with the corner of her sleeve. She is playing for sympathy, Shef realized. Trying to look attractive while she does it, too. A long time since a woman has bothered to do that for me. But in her position, what else can she do?

"There will be a place for you in Kent, if that is where you wish to go," said Shef. "King Alfred is a generous lord, and one of your beauty will never lack suitors. I can see to it that you have wealth enough to please your kin. England is a rich land now, you know. Nor is it afflicted by pirates any more, so you will be safe."

He reacts to weakness, Solomon reflected, watching them, by trying to take the weakness away, not by exploiting it, as the woman expects him to. It is a good quality in a king, but I wonder if the woman understands it.

Shef patted Alfled's hand. His voice turned business-like. "There is something, though, that you can do for us, I believe, for you are one who knew many or all the secrets of the Caliph's court. Tell me, what is your belief in Allah?"

"I have made the *shahada*. The profession of faith," Alfled added. "It goes *La illaha il Allah, Muhammad rasul Allah,* which is to say, 'There is no God but Allah, and Mohammed is his Prophet.' But what could I do? It was that or die, or be one of the lowest slaves in a laborers' brothel."

"You do not believe it?"

She shrugged. "As much as I believe anything. I was brought up to believe in God. He never helped me against the pagans who caught me, though I prayed to Him many a time. The only difference between the Christians' God and the Arabs' Allah that I can see is that the Arabs believe in Mohammed and in their Koran."

"Different books, different faiths. Tell me, are there any in Cordova who take an interest in how books are made?"

Here it comes, thought Alfled. Perhaps he will ask me to whip him with a quill, or drain him on to parchment. There must be something his woman will not do for him. There always is. "There are shops that sell books," she replied, "where copies are made to the order of the buyers. The love-poetry of bin-Firnas, say. Or the Book of a Thousand Pleasures, it might be."

"That is not the kind of book the king meant," cut in Svandis, observing watchfully. "He means, where do holy books, books of faith come from. Where does the Koran come from. Or the Bible come from. Because someone, some person, must have made them at some time, holy though they are. Made them with fingers and pen and ink." She tapped the quill-pendant that hung now over her breast.

"The Koran was dictated by God to Mohammed," said Alfled. "Or so they say. But there are some . . . yes. The Mu'tazilites, as they are called. Ishaq the Keeper of the Scrolls was one such."

"And what do they believe?" The king's one eye was trained on her with fierce interest.

"They believe . . . They believe that the Koran is not eternal, even if it is the word of Allah. They say that it is the word of Allah as heard by Mohammed, but that there may be other words. They say that it is not enough merely to collect *hadith,* that is to say tradition, but that one must also apply to it one's reason, which is the gift of Allah."

Moishe would not like to hear that, Solomon thought again. He thinks it is the first duty of a scholar to preserve the Torah, and the last to collect commentary on it. To reason from it, not reason about it.

Shef was nodding slowly. "They do not want to destroy books. That is good. But they are ready to think about them. That is better. If I could see a Mu'tazilite Caliph in Cordova, and a Pope in Rome without an army, then, I think, Ragnarök would be averted, and Loki put at rest. But at the root of it all is to have books in many hands. I do not suppose all the booksellers in Cordova, nor all the scribes in Septimania, could make as many books as we need. What was it you said, Solomon, that we need a machine to make many copies, faster than a man can write? I know no way to hitch up a millwheel to a scribe's arm, alas, though it may do the work of a smith."

"The Caliph often had more documents to sign than his arm could manage," ventured Alfled.

"What did he do?"

"He had a block made, of gold, with a handle of ivory. But on the base of the block was a copper plate, with his name on it standing out the depth of a finger-paring. The rest had been eaten away by cunning acids, I do not know how. He would put the plate on to cork with ink in it, and then stamp the block down on documents as fast as Ishaq could present them. Some said Ishaq would put documents in there that the Caliph never read, for a price. It was like putting a brand on cattle."

"Like a brand," Shef repeated. "Like a brand. But no-one can brand paper, or parchment."

"And the end of it all is a false paper," said Svandis, face twisted with disgust. "One that no-one read and no-one signed."

"That is one way books might be made," agreed Solomon.

CHAPTER TWENTY-EIGHT

The news of the disaster for Islam ran south faster, seemingly, than any horse could carry it. Than any single horse or horseman, certainly. As the first reports arrived in any town, carried by the cavalrymen who had fled first from the battle, each man was helped from his horse, carried to drink sherbet in the cool, pressed for further information. Meanwhile such information as could be gleaned was carried on by trusted messengers to those whom the local governor of a province or cadi of a city regarded as most in need of it. By the time the survivors rode on, their stories growing more elaborate and self-justifying each time they were repeated, the news was often ahead of them.

As the news was received, those in power under the Caliph-who-had-been thought carefully about their positions. Who was to succeed the Caliph? It was known that he had many children, but none designated, and none old and strong enough to survive the civil war that threatened. He had had many brothers, or half-brothers. Most dead, gone to the leather carpet or the bowstring. Many unacceptable, children of the *mustaribs*. Or were they, now, so unacceptable? Those who had been considered so, governors of the north for the most part, began to reflect on their own strength and on their alliances. Horsemen rode, troops were gathered, governors wondered how many of the levies they had sent north would return. As they trickled in, surprisingly many of them for a battle that according to the first runaways had been fought with great valor, governors reckoned their strength again. Almost all of them came to the same conclusion. Too soon to strike, or to give up hope. Do what is obviously right and you cannot come to harm. Protest loyalty to the Faith. Surround one's own person with every armed man that can be raised. And meanwhile, since the men are there and must be paid, there are private squabbles that may as well be taken care of. Old enmities between Alcala and Alicante, the coast and the mountains, disputes over water and land, flared into conflict.

In Cordova itself, as the news arrived, there was shock and horror. No alarm, since clearly the unbelievers could offer no threat to the established civilization of the south and of Andalusia, but fear at the judgment of Allah. The question of succession struck every listener at once. Within days the carts of market stuff and poultry, the herds of sheep and beef cattle, had ceased to stream through the gates, the peasants of the Guadalquivir valley fearing to enter what might be bloody civil war. The few half-Berber half-brothers of the Caliph vanished into their own strongholds, were known to be calling for men, for help from the kinsfolk of North Africa. At any moment a fleet might arrive from Algiers or Morocco, to sail up the river. Or, said the pessimists, the Tulunids of Egypt may take a hand: mere Turks from the steppe.

At that thought, the Christians of the city, and the Jews of the Juderia, the ghetto established for them, also began to reckon their strength. The rule of the previous Caliph had been cruel to those who renounced the *shahada* or who sought for martyrdom. It would be like a caress compared with the random and profitless cruelties of the Turks or the Berbers, anxious to show their loyalty to the faith because of their recent and doubtful conversion to it.

Better any Caliph than no Caliph, said the wiser heads of the city to each other. Best of all, a Caliph acceptable to all. But who? The young man, Mu'atiyah, pupil of bin-Firnas, had appeared from the wreck and ruin, ridden without ceasing all the way from the moment the Caliph fell back in his arms—or so he said. He called for Ghaniya, the Caliph's oldest half-brother and trusted emissary to the North, to succeed to the cushion. Ghaniya, he shouted in a score of market-places, Ghaniya could be trusted to take up the war. And not only the war against the Christians. Against the *majus* also, the heathen fire-worshipers who had deluded the Caliph into war and disaster. But most of all, the war against the faithless, the secret traitors. Had he not with his own eyes (and the invention of his master) seen men of the Caliph's army arrayed against him, eating roast pig between the battle-lines? How many more secret devourers of swine hid in the streets of Cordova? To be rooted out! Along with the Christians who sheltered them, under the mistaken kindness of the former Caliph. Enslave them, send them into exile, impale those who renounced their faith . . .

"Too much impaling already," remarked bin-Maymun, once commander of the cavalry in the army of the Prophet, to his cousin bin-Firnas, as they ate grapes in the cool of the latter's riverbank mansion. "You can't expect men to fight if some of them are dragged off every day and heard screaming to their comrades every night. He is your pupil of course, son of my mother's brother . . ."

"But not a ready learner," his cousin replied. "It seems to me—eager though I am for *shari'a*—that a little relaxation may be in order? Other learned men are with me on this, Ishaq, Keeper of the Caliph's Scrolls for one. Without wishing to go as far as the sect of the Sufi, he remembers that a House of Wisdom was once established in Baghdad, and flourished under the rule of Mu'tazilites. Why should Baghdad have had what Cordova cannot?"

"There are other reports, too, of what happened after the battle, after I and my men had been driven from the field," his cousin replied. "Some of the Caliph's women escaped from the Christians who seized them and found their way by ship and horse to Cordova. One a Christian by birth, so her loyalty cannot be doubted if she turned her back on her fathers' faith. I have taken another into my own *harem,* a delightful woman from Circassia. They too say that the Caliph's rigor was too great—a compensation, they say, for certain . . . inadequacies. They say also that he put too much faith in your pupil." Bin-Maymun cast a glance sideways to see how his hint was taken.

"He is my pupil no longer," declared bin-Firnas firmly. "I withdraw my protection from him." As bin-Maymun sank back, remembering threats and insults and considering which of his men to send to put a stop to Mu'atiyah's babble, bin-Firnas pressed on. "And will you join Ishaq and my learned friends later on, for song and poetry, and perhaps, a little discussion?"

"I will," said bin-Maymun, paying the price for the freedom just granted to deal with Mu'atiyah. "And I will bring my friend the Cadi with me," he added, to show he was throwing his full weight into the struggle. "He is concerned about the state of the city. Your poetry will relax him. Within the walls, of course, only he has any great force of armed men."

With perfect understanding the two men listened to the song of a slave-girl and considered, the one revenge and power, the other freedom for reason and learning from illiterates and zealots.

In Rome the news of the battle was received with joy, the ringing of bells and singing of *Te Deum*. The news, a little after, of the Emperor's recovery of the holy relic of the *graduale* and his vow to elevate his personal adviser to the throne of Saint Peter, was taken differently. If all had gone well, the current Pope, John VIII, weak child of a powerful Tuscan family, would never have heard the news at all, his own fate outrunning it. But somewhere between the Emperor's camp and the Vatican Hill, word spread to someone still loyal. The Pope was informed, hurried immediately to gather his entourage and retire from the dangerous city to the estates of his family. When Gunther, once Archbishop of Cologne and now Cardinal in Rome, heard the news and moved instantly with his one-time chaplain Arno and a

dozen German swordsmen of his own guard to reassure the Pope, and hold
him incommunicado till the Emperor's wish became clearer, he found
himself facing more than his own number of Italian nobles, relatives and
adherents of John. The two sides exchanged polite greetings and arguments,
while the guard commanders weighed each other up. Stilettos and perfumed
hair, thought the German: back-stair back-stabbers. But we have no mail
nor shields. Great blunt chopping-swords and onion-stinking breath,
thought the Italian: but ready to use them. The two sides backed off from
each other, protesting friendship and concern.

Despite the pleas not to desert his flock, the Pope made his way
determinedly from minster and hill, from Rome itself. Despite the assur-
ances of joy and congratulations at the Emperor's victory, Gunther seized
control of the Curia, evicted Cardinals not of his own nation or faction,
prepared for a disputed election. He would have gone further, but the news
that the Emperor had fixed on the English deacon Erkenbert dismayed him
even in his loyalty to Emperor and *Lanzenorden,* his own creation. Erkenbert
had been a good comrade, he knew. But Pope? Gunther had had another
and a more suitable candidate in mind for that office next time it should fall
vacant, one who was already a Prince of the Church and no deacon. Yet a
vacancy was definitely desirable, so much at least could be agreed . . .

It would take an army, now, to create one. Though the army of the
Emperor was at least approaching, marching across the borderlands of
southern France and northern Italy, hot-foot for Rome. Or so they said.

In the cool underground cave which had once been an olive-press, Shef
examined carefully the rows and rows of tiny lead blocks wedged tightly into
their steel frame. He made no attempt to read them. Still a poor reader of
any script, the complexity of reading mirror-image letters, in blocks facing
different ways, which were in any case in a language he did not understand,
would have been far beyond him. Anything like that was entrusted to
Solomon. All Shef was looking for was technical perfection. Letters fixed
tight, none of uneven size, all letters of the same height. Shef finally nodded
with satisfaction, passed them over.

With Alfled's image of a brand in their minds, the idea of branding on to
paper had been fairly clear. But all a brand needs to convey is ownership.
One sign is enough. It was soon evident that something like a brand with
two hundred words on it would take years to make and be invalidated by a
single change. Make a stamp, or a brand, or whatever it was to be called, for
each word, suggested Solomon, as the Caliph er-Rahman used to. That too
was soon seen to be a false trail, as the amount of work needed to make
individual words, some of them in large numbers, became apparent. It was
Shef who suggested making tiny dies for each letter, and once that was seen
the job became easy. Deft jewelers had carved the individual letters from

brass, pressed these into clay to make a mold. Baked the clay molds then filled them with molten lead. Over and over again until there were filled trays of the leaden letters.

Short trials pointed out the necessity of making the marks mirror-image instead of right-way round. Then came the problem of fitting them together. Of making the ink adhesive enough to stick to the lead and not run once pressed on to the paper. The easiest thing of all was finding a device that would fit the letters now locked into a chase, something that would hold the entire page-sized mass of type rather than the mere signature which er-Rahman had used. Presses were familiar objects to the whole Mediterranean seaboard, with their diet heavily dependent on wine and on olive oil, both of them needing to be pressed out. Shef had simply taken over an olive-press, inserted a flat steel bed for the letters to rest on.

Now for the full-scale trial. The carefully-set blocks of lead letters rested on the bed of the press. A cloth pad soaked in ink was patted over their surface, a sheet of white paper placed gently on top of them. Shef nodded to Solomon, who had claimed the honor of first trial. Solomon put the block on top of the paper, then pulled on the arm that exerted pressure on the block. Shef held up a warning hand. Too much weight pressed the blanks down on to the paper as well, smearing the result. He cut his hand through the air, Solomon released the pressure and removed the pressure block and Svandis slid the printed sheet out. Shef ignored the cries of wonder, thrust another sheet in, signed to Solomon again. And again. And again. And again. Only after ten trials did he stop, and turn to Svandis.

"We don't need to know, does it work?" he said. "We need to know, does it work faster? If it isn't faster than a team of scribes, then there's no point to all this. It isn't faster so far, when you think of all the time we've wasted."

Svandis passed him the sheet. He looked at it, passed it to Solomon, who examined it carefully. "It seems correct," said the Jew thoughtfully. "As for speed . . . We have just printed ten pages in a hundred heartbeats. A practiced scribe can write, maybe, forty pages in a day. A hundred heartbeats, and three people, and we have two hours' work from a skilled scribe. I cannot say . . ."

"I can," said Shef, turning to the apparatus of beads and wire which stood not far away. He flicked beads this way and that with the skill of continuous practice. "Three thousand heartbeats in an hour," he muttered. "Say twenty-five thousand in a day's work. Twenty-five thousand divided by one hundred multiplied by ten . . ." He straightened. "Three people can do the work of sixty scribes. Once the blocks have been set up. The blocks, is that the word?"

"Call it the press," said Svandis.

"Sixty scribes," repeated Solomon, marveling. "It will mean, at the very least, that every child can have his own Talmud. Who would have believed it?"

More Talmuds may not mean more faith, thought Shef, but he did not say it.

As he walked through the streets of Septimania later that day, a mule laden with printed paper following him, Solomon met Moishe the learned. Anything like a book could not escape Moishe's eye. He pulled one copy out, scanned it suspiciously. "This is not Hebrew writing," he said. "And whoever wrote it was a bungler. The letters are ill-formed and straggle from each other like a schoolboy's." He sniffed the paper. "It smells of lamp-black too."

Needed for adhesion, thought Solomon, but he made no reply.

"It is in the Romance tongue," added Moishe accusingly. "I can make out the Roman script, but this is not even Latin!" Ingrained respect for the written word prevented him from throwing the offending object to the ground, but he waved it contemptuously. "What does it say?"

"It is a longer version of what the One King dictated to you and the others some weeks ago. The attack on the Nazarenes' faith. I have five hundred of them here. Tomorrow I shall have five hundred more, in Latin, for the more educated believers."

Moishe snorted, torn between agreeing with attacks on Christianity and disapproving of attacks on faith. In his heart he believed that all should stay in the faith of their births, those who held the correct one reaping their destined reward, those who held false ones taking the punishment due to them and to their ancestors. "Five hundred?" he replied. "There are not scribes enough in Septimania to write all those."

"Nevertheless it shall be done," said Solomon. "The One King will take many of them, to spread them round the Christian islands on which he means to cruise—his men are pirates by trade, I fear, and anxious to earn their living now the Christian army has withdrawn."

"And the rest?"

"Those fall to me. To give where I think they will do most good." Or most harm, he did not say. For these are books, but they are also anti-books, books to turn People of the Book from their Bible, which is their word for 'book.' I do not think I had better tell Moishe the learned that. It is a use of learning he will not learn to accept.

The One King, at sea already and heading for the island of Mallorca, his entire fleet spread out around him in cruising formation, was watching the kite-men struggle with the immensely unwieldy contraption he had had designed. Tolman stood to one side with an expression of deep disapproval on his face.

"Tell me again," said Shef to the child, "what are the things to remember."

"To begin with, keep the open end, the larger open end, pointed into the wind. Feel the wind in your eyes. If it shifts, you must shift with it." The boy took the king's hands with an air of authority. "If the wind is above you, roll the hands this way. If it is below, that way. The tail-flap moves like a rudder, that you will understand. The first thing is, if you think anything is going wrong, it is already too late. You have to move all the time, never stay still. Like a bird. It takes time to learn," the boy added condescendingly. "I crashed into the sea time after time."

Cwicca, listening, reflected to himself that a sixty-pound child crashed much lighter than a hundred-and-ninety-pound warrior. Long experience had taught him that the One King paid no attention to probabilities. At least he was a strong swimmer. Cwicca himself had sharpened the One King's belt-knife to a more than razor edge, in case he needed to cut himself free in the water. Brand had selected a dozen of the strongest swimmers in the fleet, himself included, and put them in pairs round the rescue boats.

The experiment still seemed impossible. Guided by his abacus, Shef had ordered a new kite with four times the surface area of Tolman's. So enormous was it that it overhung the deck of the *Fafnisbane* on all sides and over the stern as well. A first difficulty had been that the weight of the One King himself would snap the fragile struts suspended between the gunwales. Shef had ordered up trestles for him to lie on till, he hoped, the wind should take him.

At least there was plenty of wind. All the ships in the fleet, more than sixty of them now, were tearing along as fast as a man could run, or a horse canter, the wind on their port beam. The familiar cloudless blue of the sky was as cloudless as ever, but with a darker tinge. Ordlaf predicted a storm, though all agreed that a storm in this millpond of a sea could hardly be compared with a North Sea widow-maker. The One King had figured the strength of the wind into his calculations as well.

"Ready," he said. He climbed up the short step-ladder—a proper ladder this, not a wretched *graduale* or *kraki*—slid feet-first into the holding leather sling. Wood creaked and flexed. Handlers looked anxiously at the stitching, linesmen tested their holds. The kite, which had strained at its ropes, took on an ominous immobility, lay there as if made of lead.

Shef gripped the controls, turned them this way and that. He too felt the kite's lack of motion, wondered for a moment what would happen. Would he just lie there like bacon on a slab? Would they cast him over the side and see him simply go down like the fool who had leapt from the tower of the Wisdom-House in his Völund-suit months before?

Shef looked round at the anxious faces surrounding him. One thing he could be sure of. Success or failure, the idea that men could fly had at least been firmly planted. Round half of the necks of the kite-crews, half at least, dangled the new wing-pendants of Völund, or Wayland as the English called him. Men who were proud to call themselves fliers. They would not forget. He had created a new trade. More than one new trade.

"Ready," he said.

The eight tallest men in the ship stepped to their places, each of them crouched on a block, gripping a part of the frame in two hands. Now Cwicca took over, as launchmaster.

"Lift," he shouted.

The eight men simultaneously straightened and thrust their arms high over their heads: no great weight, indeed two strong men might have done it, or Brand or Styrr on their own. But it was important to have even balance. Cwicca glanced at his linesmen standing by the windward rail, almost crowded overboard by the immense spread of canvas facing into the wind, but each maintaining tension and ready to pay out line. He waited with the skill of much practice till he could see the wind beginning to catch the canvas, belly it out from underneath.

"Launch!"

The eight men swayed backwards like a catapult-arm bending, and then threw the kite forward and up, into the wind. Shef felt the shock, immediately felt the kite sweeping backwards as if from under him. The wind had caught him, but it was taking him down, down under the side of the *Fafnisbane,* to be trampled deep into the sea and drown there in a mess of broken cordage. He twirled a hand control at random, felt the kite dip alarmingly, faces on the leeward rail staring at him open-mouthed. Turn the other.

The side-vanes turned, the wind caught the great expanse of waxed cotton more fully, began to blow across the top. Struggling against the dead weight of its rider, the huge contrivance began to lift. The linesmen felt the tug, paid out line gently, carefully, each man striving to keep resistance without drag. They had had much practice.

Above, Shef tried to remember what Tolman had said, tried even more to put it into effect. The wind was below his eyes, turn that way. No, above, turn back. And all the time he was skidding sideways, work the tail-flap between his knees, no, no, other way.

For a brief instant all seemed to be in balance, and Shef could glance down. Below him the ships were strung out like children's toys on a pond, all of them lined with faces staring up. He could make the faces out clearly, could recognize Brand there in one of the rescue boats out to windward. Could he wave, shout to him?

The moment's loss of concentration was all that the wind needed. The kite began to turn up, the two linesmen controlling that began to try to edge the top frame down, at the same instant Shef worked his own correction.

The watchers saw the kite tip nose-down, bank suddenly to the right, seem to lose the wind and the lift altogether, and drop into the sea like a loose bundle of rags. The *Fafnisbane* slanted gently across, linesmen reeling in as she did so. Brand's *Narwhal* was already in front of them, swimmers diving over the side and threshing towards the bobbing contraption.

Shef met them in the water. "I didn't need to cut myself free," he said. "Just slid out. Haul her out," he shouted to Ordlaf in the approaching *Fafnisbane*, "and check her over for breaks."

"Then what?" asked Cwicca, as the dripping king scrambled over the side.

"Then we'll try again, of course. How long did it take Tolman to learn the trick of it?"

"If Tolman has learnt the trick of it," protested Cwicca, "why do you need to? Is this just for fun?"

Shef looked down at him. "Oh no," he said. "We have to do the very best we can to get better. Better at everything. Because there are people over there who are also doing their very best. And not to make life easy for us, either."

The Emperor looked carefully at the paper which Erkenbert had produced for him. It meant nothing to him. Skilled in the instant evaluation of land, river-lines, armor, the good and bad points of a horse or its harness, Bruno had never learned to translate lines on paper into reality.

"What does it do?" he asked.

"It cuts the reloading time of our new catapults by more than half. You see," Erkenbert tapped the paper, "the difficulty was always dragging down the short arm, the arm which holds the counterweight. If we had been quicker—" He did not complete the sentence. If he had been quicker outside the wall of Septimania, he might have shot three times and smashed the gate down before the enemy could reply. Then the greatest of their troubles would have been over.

"Well," he went on, "we tried different ways, and in the end I tried dragging the arm down by ropes over a roller. Now, what I have designed are two wheels, one each side of the frame. Men stand inside each one. They tread down with their feet, and the wheel turns, turns so that there is always another tread under their feet. The wheel that they turn operates a cog-wheel, and the two cogs drag down an iron chain. That chain pulls down the counterweight."

"Does it work?"

"I cannot tell while we march every day. I need time to find smiths and make the wheels, both the cogs and the tread-wheels. But it will work. There is a picture in Vegetius, to give us authority." Though they were speaking German, he used the Latin word *auctoritatem,* that which comes from an author, a written work, a book accredited.

Bruno nodded. "The march will stop one day. Then I will need your new device. Not just one next time. Six, a dozen. I have to beat some sense into these Italian heads. Maybe some others too. Come now and see what Agilulf has devised for us."

The two men left the tent and went out into the sprawling camp, tents pitched for the night but not yet at rest. Outside the marshal Agilulf waited. Erkenbert looked again with professional interest at the crusted blisters and dead skin that ran like the mark of a broad belt across his neck and the side of his face—the track of the Greek fire. Agilulf had lain in pain and fever for weeks after they had pulled him from the sea. A surprise that he had lived. No surprise that he had become even more taciturn than ever before.

"What is our strength now?" asked Bruno.

"Much the same. Four thousand rabble." By rabble Agilulf meant the levies called up from the districts Bruno was marching through, first the Spanish borderlands, then the coastline of southern France, then the plains of northern Italy. As the army moved towards Rome and the seat of Saint Peter, there was a constant stream of desertions, replaced by new levies. Few of them had any military value in a serious clash, and some Bruno had dismissed, like the half-Arab deserters, sent back to loot and cause dissension in their own countries.

"About five hundred of the cowboys. They stick around as long as they're allowed to loot and rape away from home."

"Hang some of the rapists," said Bruno without heat. "I'll hang them all when their use is over."

"Five hundred Frankish knights, with a hundred *Lanzenritter* as stiffening. Seven hundred *Lanzenbrüder* on foot. A dozen onagers in the battering-train, with a *Lanzenbruder* attached to each one to stop the crews running away. More to come when the Holy Father has time to make the designs."

The 'Holy Father' was Agilulf's only joke. He was one of those who most whole-heartedly approved the coming elevation of Erkenbert to the throne of Saint Peter. The little deacon had dressed his wound, given him feverfew for the fever. He was never far from the fighting, never showed fear. In the tight world of the Emperor's army, it was coming about that no one outside it, German, Italian or Frank, had any weight. Nationality was less important than comradeship.

"Are they good enough to beat the heathen, this time?" asked Bruno.

"I do not think anyone can stand against the charge of the *Lanzenritter.* But they can be shot down by machines from a distance. For close work—

the *Lanzenbrüder* are stout kerls. But those damned Danes—they are stout kerls too.''

"Better equipped?"

"Our shield-and-spear tactic does not work against them. They are too strong, they learn too quickly. No shield can keep out their axes if they use them. All we can do is keep a steady line, hope to use our horsemen."

"And our machines," said Erkenbert.

"Everything," said Bruno. "All at once. To put down our enemies, to make Christendom one, without rival."

CHAPTER TWENTY-NINE

The parish priest of Aups, a small village of southern France not far from Carcassonne, looked nervously out of the window of his tiny cottage, and then back at the coarsely-written pamphlet he held in his hand. It was made of paper, but the priest did not know that. It was printed rather than written, but the priest did not know that either. The priest only owned one book, and that was his Missal for conducting services. He knew the services by heart in any case. Besides his services, the priest knew the Lord's Prayer, the Apostles' Creed, the Ten Commandments and the Seven Deadly Sins. On these he preached to his parishioners.

And now this had come, brought to him by Gaston, the mule-driver who came and went between Aups and Carcassonne with loads of oil and wine, charcoal and cloth, trinkets and fripperies. Such few things as the village could not produce for itself and had the few coins to buy. He had brought it back and said it had been given to him—given not sold—by a man in the market. Gaston could not read. He had thought the priest might like it.

It was the priest's duty to denounce Gaston—for though he could not read, it was unlikely that he had taken something and not asked what it contained. Then the tormentors of the bishop would come, and torment Gaston, and draw from him the name, or the description, of the man he met in the market. And if that did not satisfy them, of some other man. And if that did not satisfy them—who knew what tale they would put in Gaston's mouth? Maybe that his parish priest had sent him for the book. The heretic book. Merely holding it put the priest in deadly peril.

Do not denounce him, then. Throw it away. The priest hesitated to throw away any piece of writing. They were too scarce, too precious. And besides:

the tale this one told had about it a strange charm, a seduction. Maybe that seduction came from the devil, as the priest was continually telling his parishioners about the wiles of temptation. But then this book said that the devil was actually the one that the Church called God. The Father who had sent His Son to death. What kind of a father was that?

There was another reason the priest did not want to destroy this book. If he had read it correctly—and another strange thing about it was that it was written, if not in his own dialect, in a dialect very similar to his own and very different from the Church-Latin of which the priest had learnt some fragments in his ineffectual schooling years ago—if he had read it correctly, this book said that it was a part of Heaven to live happily on earth, man and woman together. The priest had been in trouble more than once with his bishop and his archdeacon, because of Marie, the housekeeper who lived with him and who consoled his middle age. Priests must be celibate, he had been told again and again. Or they bring bastard children into the world and spend the Church's good on them. But Marie was a widow, and past child-bearing. What harm did it do, what she and he did between them when the nights were cold?

The bishop was wrong, thought the priest with the first flare of independence his life had ever known. He would keep the book. He would read it again. It might be a work of heresy, or so they might say. But it was not the heresy of the heretics beyond the mountains, with their evil denial of the flesh and their insistence that men and women became perfect only by not breeding children. Though this book did say that men and women were not condemned to breed children for ever and ever. That there were ways of taking pleasure in each other, going to the Paradise on earth, as the book called it, without running the risk of childbirth. Guiltily, but determinedly, the priest opened the little eight-page booklet again, started once more to spell his way through the passage which described, in terms as plain as Shef had been able to make them with the assistance of Svandis and Alfled, the technique of the *carezza,* the prolongation of pleasure for woman and for man.

The parish priest of Pontiac, not far away, did his duty and reported both book and the parishioner who had given it to him. Days later, as the bishop's agents attempted once again to force him to admit that he was part of the heretic conspiracy, he made a silent vow never to admit anything again. When he was released, bent and walking like an aged man, to return to his village under the strictest supervision, he said nothing. When his parishioners who had been called to the Emperor's army returned, however, and spread their stories of demons in the sky and the might of the pagan or heretic sorcerers, their priest made no attempt to contradict them.

The bishop of Carcassonne, who had made great efforts to collect all such material entering his diocese and root out all transmitters of it, finally sent all he could find together to his Archbishop in Lyons, and asked for help against the spread of heresy in writing. He was condemned severely for allowing such material to exist. No other bishopric had recorded so much, and most none at all, he was told. His see must be rotten with loss of faith. And if the sheep are poxed and scabby, railed the Archbishop, who shall we blame but their shepherd? Look to Besançon! You will find no heresy there.

The bishop of Besançon, indeed, had obtained not only the Occitan but also the Latin version of the pamphlet, and had read both through with care, several times. The bishop was poor, by now, having had to pay a year's revenues into the Emperor's coffers for the brawl with the baron of Béziers. Besides that, his back still smarted from the days of scourging he had had to endure from a grinning German prior, till the money arrived, money acquired at a ruinous rate of interest to put an end to the scourgings. In any case the bishop had not one widow mistress, but a small stable of young women. Their constant pregnancies were almost a despair to him, so many children to be provided for, left for adoption in the church if the mother would agree, but so often she did not, found in food and clothing while they were young and furnished with dowries or apprentice-payments as they grew up. The thought that pleasure might not lead to children, even with young women, and that young women might be pleasured satisfactorily even by a man past the flush of youth, if that man knew the secrets of the *carezza*—this fascinated the bishop to a degree that no fear of heresy might quash. The fate of his brother of Carcassonne only rubbed the point home.

The truth was that in the whole of the Langue d'Oc, as in their kindred realm of Catalonia beyond the mountains, Christianity had shallow roots. At the first coming of the Faith in Roman times, the Church had taken hold in the towns, where the urban classes followed the fashions of Rome and of the Empire, and where bishops could be appointed from noble families who saw the Church as another way of consolidating power over land, through its written leases, its acceptance of donations which paid no tax to the secular authorities but still might be kept within the family. Outside the towns were the *pagani,* in Latin, those who dwelt on the *pagus,* the land. In Italian the word became *paesano,* in French *paysan*—the peasant, the one who dwelt on the land, the one outside the Church. The three meanings were at bottom the same meaning. The Church meant little to the country-people, except as a force from the towns that from time to time disrupted their lives. In Northern France, in Germany, one might meet the enthusiasm of the convert or the Crusader. In the South, Mary was hard to tell from Minerva of ancient Rome or the three nameless Ladies the Celts had worshiped generations before, before the *pagani* were made to learn their poor and garbled Latin. Nor was the Easter procession easy to tell from the age-old weeping for Adonis, the legionary cult of sacrificing the ram, or lamb, to Mithras. In a land where written books were rare, and what they said was taken literally as gospel, there was little inherited resistance to the seeds that Shef and Solomon and Svandis had sown: but there was fertile soil in abundance.

In Andalusia, a different situation, but no more stable. Islam had not set foot in the Iberian peninsula till the year 711, when the Ummayads landed at Gibraltar, or Jeb el-Tarik in their tongue, burned their boats, and were told by their leader, "The sea is behind you and the unbelievers in front of you. Truly you shall conquer or die!" And conquer they did, overthrowing the short-lived rule of the Germanic Vandals who gave Andalusia its name and taking their place as rulers. Beneath the veneer of Vandal or Arab aristocracy, however, the mass of the Iberian population remained the same. Most of them were converted from the Christianity of the late Roman Empire without great difficulty, attracted by the benign rule of Islam, which remained free of the desperate and deadly theological squabbles of Rome and Byzantium and demanded no more than the *shahada,* the five daily prayers, abstention from wine and from pork.

Yet while there might be little to disagree with or provoke rebellion in the rule of the Caliphs, there was at the same time little charm. Little mystery. Under er-Rahman, less and less inquiry permitted. The surgery of Cordova would have been the wonder of the world if the world had known it, as would the discoveries of bin-Firnas, or the great work of al-Khwarizmi the mathematician, his *Hisab al-Jabr wa'l Mugabala,* or 'Book of the bringing of unknowns to knowns.' But few did know of it, eagerly though its practical aspects might be seized by traders and bankers. The Wisdom House of Baghdad had been closed thirty years before by those who asserted there was no wisdom outside the Koran, and the Koran was to be memorized, not considered. To some, the intellectuals, the ceasing of inquiry was a pain. To others, the unpersecuted but taxed remnant of the Christians, every call from the *muezzin* was an offense. To most, religion mattered little. But if by any chance some restrictions might be eased, decision in the court of the cadis might relax from the strict interpretation of the Koran and of the desert asceticism that had created it—well, let the learned dispute over whether Allah or the Koran were more or equally eternal if they would. Peace, good governance, and a fair distribution of water through the irrigation channels were what they most demanded.

"I do not think Ghaniya will do," said bin-Firnas one day to his cousin bin-Maymun. "He is half a Berber after all."

"I do not think there is a pure-bred child of the Quraysh left to us," replied his cousin.

"My pupil Mu'atiyah might have done," ventured the philosopher. "He was of high birth, and easily guided by me, if by no other."

"Too late," replied the cavalryman. "We of the army of the Caliph-that-was accused him before the Cadi of bearing false witness. The fathers of many of those he sent to the impaling-poles brought their voices to the court. He was fortunate. Because he had been your pupil the Cadi adjudged him only to the leather carpet and the sword, not to the pole or the stoning-ground. He fought with the guards and died raging, without dignity."

Bin-Firnas sighed, less at the young man's death than at the failure of what had been promised. "Who then?" he asked after a decent pause. "We cannot just pick one of the provincial governors, all the others would rebel immediately."

Ishaq, Keeper of the Scrolls, drank from the cool water which was the greatest of refreshments in this, the tail-end of the scorching Spanish summer, and spoke into the thoughtful silence.

"It seems to me that there is no great need for a hasty decision. The Roman Emperor has turned away from our borders, having found his foolish relic of the Nazarenes, or so I hear. We do not need a single ruler. Why do we not send to Baghdad, and ask the descendant of Abdullah to send us a viceroy?"

"It would take forever!" said bin-Maymun. "Forever to send the message and longer for them to come to a decision. Nor would the governors accept whoever the Abbasid Caliph sent to us."

"But during that time provisional arrangements might be put in place," suggested Ishaq. "Rule by a Council. A Council of the Wise. Strictly temporary, of course. Still, during that temporary state institutions could be set up whose value would be so great that no later Caliph could overthrow them. A House of Surgeons. A House of Mathematics."

"A Tower of Astronomers," proposed bin-Firnas, "equipped with far-seers with larger and better lenses for study of the stars.

"A new system of water-works, running down from the mountain springs to the coast," put in bin-Maymun. "The landowners would pay for that—if they were certain that all would pay and all would share."

"A library," said Ishaq. "One which contained the works of the Greeks as well as of the *hadith*. Translated into Arabic for all to read. Or into Latin as well. If any doubted our aim, we could say that we wished to convert the *Rumi* to our faith with sound arguments as well as by the sword. And our cousins the Jews as well."

"I have heard," noted bin-Firnas, "that this business of the relic contains some terrible blow to the Christian faith. There is rumor of it among the traders from the north in the *souk*."

Ishaq shrugged indifferently. "Such a faith hardly needs a blow. But let us agree that our faith shall be confirmed by reason. And that a Council of the Wise may be the way to do it."

"We will speak to our friends in the morning," agreed bin-Maymun.

"Let Ghaniya the Berber follow Mu'atiyah the fool, and the matter can be arranged."

The Way-fleet lay at anchor in the bay of Palma off the island of Mallorca, exactly where the Arab fleet had lain earlier the same year, before the Greek fire came to destroy it. Fishermen had already given a graphic account of what had happened then, and Shef had been concerned enough to order a standing kite to be raised, with Tolman and three or four of the others taking turns to spend an hour in the sky, not flying free—no-one had attempted that since the deaths of Ubba and Helmi—but strung out peacefully on their lines in the moderate breeze.

Shortly after Shef had tried his own flights, the Mediterranean had indeed proved that it could generate a storm, and the back-eddies of it were still with them. It had been a blessing in disguise, however, in that it had covered the approach of the Wayman fleet till they were almost at anchor. The raiding parties swarming eagerly ashore, led by Guthmund and full of experienced pirates, had immediately seized the Christian cathedral and found in it an accumulation of plunder. It had been first stored there by the Christian lords of the island, continued during the brief Islamic conquest, and stepped up to a higher power, it seemed, by the following conquest by the Emperor and his Greek allies, working in tandem. The troops left behind by the Emperor had fled into the interior. The Waymen, operating under strict orders of gentle conduct and supervised closely by their priests, reported that there was little chance of them acquiring allies from the natives, nominally Christian though they were. Solomon reported further that the booklets he carried in Occitan and in Latin were accepted readily, with great curiosity, by the Christian priests: the natives of the island, trapped in their own dialect of Mallorquin, had never seen a book that they could begin to read in their own language before, and the Occitan was close enough for them at least to try to make it out.

Solomon had not remained at hand, though, to watch the trials that Shef was now preparing. Thorvin too, intensely disapproving, had disappeared on his own errands, as had Hund and Hagbarth. For interpreting, Shef was now dependent on Skaldfinn. Farman too, the visionary priest, was prepared to observe.

The Greek fire apparatus had been unshipped bodily from the half-sunk galley, with immense care not to crack or bend any of its pipes, and had been carried carefully stowed in the hold of the *Fafnisbane,* a man watching it on Ordlaf's orders day and night to warn of any leak or scrap of fire. When it came to a trial, though, Ordlaf had mutinied. Shef had in the end taken a small Mallorcan fishing boat, stowed the apparatus in it, and taken it a decent quarter-mile out to sea. For hours he and Steffi had brooded over it, examining every part of it, theorizing about their apparent functions, reminding each other of what they knew for certain. They were now at least of one mind.

The big tank found separate from the rest was a fuel reserve, they agreed. Its connecting hose clearly matched the smaller copper dome: but the only function of that connection was to transfer fuel once the operating tank was emptied. In operation the pipe at the upper end of the dome was connected not to the reserve tank but to the apparatus actually found in place. Careful removal of this had persuaded them that it was a sort of bellows: a piston forced down a cylinder which, however, did nothing but force air into the operating tank. "It seems," muttered Steffi, "that air has weight." Remembering the strength of the wind under his kite, Shef nodded. The thought was ridiculous, for how could anyone weigh air? But the fact that one could not weigh it clearly did not mean that it had no weight—a thought for the future.

Another mystery was the valve attached to a short length of pipe on top of the dome. The pipe was plugged at the end but had an opening cut in one side. It made no sense.

What, then, was the function of the brazier and the conventional bellows below the dome? Obviously, to heat the fuel in the dome to operating temperature. But why? Neither Shef nor Steffi had any word to express the concept 'volatile,' but they had seen water boil, had seen kettles boil dry. Shef, too, remembered the experiments of his former shipmate Udd with distilling a kind of winter ale. "Some things boil with less heat than water," he explained to Steffi. "It may be that this stuff in the tank is one of them. What comes out of the nozzle when you turn the valve, then, is the lighter stuff, like the drink that Udd makes out of the steam from ale."

"Isn't steam just water?" queried Steffi.

"Not if you heat ale or wine," said Shef. "The stronger stuff comes off first, before the water. The opposite of winter wine. Water freezes first in the cold, boils last in the heat." As he said the words he stiffened, the words of Loki coming back to him. What was it he had said, had offered him as a token? "It is best on a winter morning." He did not understand, but it had something to do with this problem. He would remember it. If it worked . . . Then he would owe Loki something. Put into practice the plan he had considered. It would be a fair test, a fair return.

All their actions had been watched with tight-lipped scorn by the Greek *siphonistos* taken from the captured galley.

"We're going to try it," said Shef to Skaldfinn. "All those who aren't necessary had better leave the boat." The Greek turned immediately, reached for the painter of their dinghy.

"He understands our language a bit, then," said Shef. "Ask him why he will not help us."

"He says you are barbarians."

"Tell him barbarians would lash him to the dome so that he would feel the fire first if anything went wrong. But we are not barbarians. He will see. He will stay with us, take the same chances that we do. The rest of you— over the side with you all, and lay off ten strokes. Now—" Shef turned back to Steffi and his three-man gang with a confidence he did not feel. "Light the match! Bellows-man, stand by and start when the flame is alight."

"It's this pump that worries me," muttered Steffi in an undertone. "I can see what it does, but I don't know what it's for."

"Me neither. We still have to try it. Start pumping on the handle."

The Greek edged away, watching the preparations with increasing fear. The very thought of the fire exploding made his bowels cringe within him. He had seen several demonstrations of what happened when an apparatus was overheated. They had turned the safety-valve closed, without realizing what it was for. He knew, if the barbarians did not, that they were not far enough off to be safe.

Competing with the personal fear was fear for his faith and his country. The barbarians seemed strangely sure about what they were doing. They had spent a long time observing, making simple trials, doing very little and nothing roughly—not like the barbarians of his imagination, but like skilled men. Could it be that they would solve the problem? Even if they did, a voice within him reminded him, there was one thing no ingenuity could find: the strange seepages of Tmutorakan far beyond the Black Sea, where the oil welled up out of the ground.

The fire was burning, the pump was operating, the barbarian with the squint sweating as he worked. In his bones the *siphonistos* could feel the pressure increasing, building up. It had to build up, it must not be allowed to grow too great, heat and pressure had to be balanced just so.

Observing carefully out of the corner of his one eye, Shef watched the signs of tension grow in the captive Greek. He feared the fire perhaps more than they did. And he knew, as they did not, when the likely moment of disaster would be. Had he the resolution to face death unmoved? Shef felt sure that he would make some sign of betrayal. If he did, he and Steffi and the others would be over the side and into the water in a moment. But the Greek did not know that.

"Keep pumping," he ordered.

Shef felt the warmth coming now not from the burning match beneath but from the dome itself. As the heat increased the Greek writhed in fear. The barbarians had no fear because they had no understanding! In the end he could not control himself. He seized up a rag, leaped forward and turned the valve on top of the tank. A shrill whistle sounded from the slotted length of pipe.

"The valve! You must open the valve at once!" he called, in suddenly-discovered English, backing the words with a frantic gesture.

Shef shouted "Turn!"

The last of Steffi's three-man gang turned firmly on the valve that led from the bottom of the copper dome—the valve that led to the nozzle. Shef felt an instant wave of something jetting through the brass nozzle in his hand, a reek of something stinging and acrid. He drew the lit slow-match from behind his back and at arm's length held it to the nozzle.

The dragon's breath flared out, belching flame fifty feet out over the sea, landing on it and blazing with clouds of black smoke even on the water itself. For long moments the sea itself seemed to be ablaze, Shef and the valve-hand stepped back, cringing automatically from the fierce heat.

Shef collected himself, shouted "Turn!" once again. The valve closed, the flame stopped. Instantly Steffi ceased to pump, the bellows-man pulled his bellows away, the brazier-hand pulled the charcoal flame away from under the dome. All five men fell back from the dome to the very edge of the ship's tiny deck and stared tensely at it. Had they pumped it too strongly? Would the flame come back from the sea and ignite some stray spill? After a while Shef felt them all releasing their breath together.

"It's a kind of oil," he said.

"Not olive oil," said Steffi. "I've tried lighting that and it doesn't work at all, hardly."

"Might be whale-oil," ventured Shef, remembering the way Queen Ragnhild's fire-arrows had lit up the harvest of the *grind* in far Halogaland.

"Doesn't smell like it," said the valve-hand, once a fisherman in Ordlaf's village of Bridlington.

"I don't know what in Hel it is," said Steffi. "But I bet we can't get no more of it once this is used up. But at least we know now when to open the valve. That whistle on top, it sounds the warning."

"You may know how this work," the Greek shouted angrily, still in the broken English he had till then refused to admit. "But there is one place on earth for *naphtha* and you never find it. Nor I tell you, no matter how you torture me."

Shef looked down at him coldly. "There is no need of torture, and now I have the machine I know where to get the fuel. It is found best on a winter's morning, is that not so?"

The Greek's heart sank within him. They had mastered the *siphon* with ease. Now it seemed they had the oil as well. After all, in the barbarian West, who could say that there was no Tmutorakan, as there was in the barbarian East? And if they had both halves of the secret, how might Byzantium stand? And he could be sure he would find no welcome in Byzantium once it was known the secret was out. Any Greek should know there was a time to change sides, and this was it.

"Listen to me, one-eye," he mumbled, "that for a price I correct your errors."

Shef nodded calmly, as though he had expected this response, and fumbled for a moment in the pocket of his breeches. He had had these things made by a silversmith in Septimania, made secretly and paid for from his own purse.

"Steffi," he said, "I want you and your men here to wear these." He produced the silver pendants from his pocket.

"What, and give up what we got already?" asked Steffi, putting a hand up to the Thor-hammer round his neck.

"Yes. You have Thor, and so does one of your mates, and the other two have a Frey-phallus and a Rig-ladder like me. But they are just the signs that took your fancy, or that you copied from others. I must stay with my own *kraki,* for it is the mark of my father, but you should wear the signs of your trade, now you have a trade. It is a sign of honor too, for your courage."

"What is it?" said the valve-hand, face glowing with pride. He had been a slave most of his life. Now the One King was speaking to him as if he were a great warrior.

"It is a fire-sign, for the men who trade in fire, in flares, in the marks of war."

The men took the pendants in silence, removed their own, put the new ones round their necks.

"What god is the patron of us fire-warriors?" asked the bellows-hand.

"It is Loki the fire-god, once chained, now free."

Skaldfinn, coming back over the side, froze with horror as he heard the words, saw the fire-sign displayed openly for the first time. He looked back at Farman just behind him for support, saw the visionary pause, and then nod slowly in acquiescence. Steffi and his gang, all English and all former Christians with the scantiest knowledge of the holy myths of the Way, heard the name without alarm.

"Loki," Steffi muttered, fixing the name in his mind. "Loki the fire-god. Good to have a god of our own. We will be his faithful servants."

CHAPTER THIRTY

The Emperor gaped at the small book put into his hands. He could read himself, if slowly, but this time he had no need to. The substance of the booklet had already been explained to him in careful detail by his trusty comrade.

"Where in Hell did it come from?" he asked finally. The Emperor never knowingly blasphemed, took the name of the Lord in vain, or used religious words in other than their literal meaning. This time too, Erkenbert realized, he meant that the book in front of him was literally diabolic. That was good. Answering the question was not so good. Erkenbert had realized some time ago that the sniveling heretic who had betrayed the Grail and earned death for it had not told the truth when he said that there were only two copies: he should have kept him alive. No need to confess that mistake now.

"A Brother found it in a priest's house. Oh yes," he held up a warning hand, "the priest has already been dealt with. But I have heard these things are everywhere, produced with diabolic speed. And they are being believed too. Men say that the very *graduale* which you carry with you and proclaim to be the true ladder on which Our Lord was carried to the Sepulchre, they say that its appearance after so many centuries is proof that what these doctrines say are true. The Lance is death, men say, the Grail is life. It proves that Jesus came back to life in reality, never left this world rather than came back to it. So there is no resurrection, no after-life, no succession of Saint Peter, no Church or need for a Church. Some of those who say that are priests themselves."

The Emperor's face was purpling rapidly, but he was no fool. He realized all this was being said to him for a purpose, not merely to enrage him. Or maybe enraging him was the purpose.

"Well," he said with sudden mildness, "we can stop people saying these things out loud, I suppose. But we want to stop them even thinking about them. I am sure you have an idea how that might be done. Let me hear it."

Erkenbert nodded. They were old allies now, working partners. It was still a relief to him to work for a clear-sighted ruler.

"Two ideas," he said. "One is easy. We need a body of reliable men with no duty other than that of seeking out heresy. They will have to be given powers greater than present law allows. Powers of rope and rack, stake and pit. I suggest we call them the *Inquisitio Imperialis,* the Imperial Inquisition."

"Agreed," said Bruno immediately. "What's the hard idea?"

"Do you know when Church and Empire first came together? For the Empire of the Romans was at first a pagan one, you know, which persecuted Christians."

Bruno nodded. He remembered the stories of Saint Paul, and how he went to Rome for trial before an Emperor who must have been hostile. It had not struck him that somewhere down the line the Empire must have changed religions, but now that Erkenbert mentioned it, he saw it must be so.

"The first Christian Emperor, you know, was Constantine, who was proclaimed Emperor in my own city of Eboracum—York, as the vile pagans who hold it now call it."

"A good omen," said Bruno confidently.

"It is to be hoped so. What happened was that he was beset by rebels— like you, Emperor—and in the night before a battle he dreamt a dream. In that dream an angel came to him and showed him the holy sign of the Cross, and told him, *In hoc signo vinces:* 'In this sign thou shalt conquer.' He did not know the meaning of the sign but the next day he ordered his men to put it on their shields, and fought and won the battle. Then, when wise men explained to him the meaning of the sign, he accepted it and the Christian religion, and imposed it on all the Empire. But he did one other thing, Emperor. He made the Donation of Constantine.

"On this document both Church and Empire are built. From it the Church receives authority in this world. From it the Empire receives legitimacy from the world above. That is why Emperors are the Lord's Anointed. And Popes should be the Emperor's creation."

"It sounds a fine thing," said Bruno with a certain scepticism, "but I make Popes without need of a document. And my authority comes from the relics I have recovered—we have recovered. Why do we need this Donation?"

"I think that as well as the Imperial Inquisition we need also a new Donation."

The Emperor's eyebrows rose warningly. He had already seen that this conversation was urging him to put down the troublesome John by force, and lock the College of Cardinals up until they voted in the correct way for his own candidate. Though Erkenbert did not know it—Bruno did not wish the new Pope to have any hand in the disappearance of the old one—he had already sent a strong squadron to deal with Pope John, and firm messages to the wavering Cardinals of Germany that they had better see sense themselves, and bring their Italian colleagues to do the same. But he did not like the idea of donations. The Church was rich enough already.

"It will be a Donation of Church to Empire," said Erkenbert firmly. "Not of Empire to Church. A tenth of the Church's temporal possessions will be handed over, for set purposes. The defeat of the heathen. The stamping out of heresy. War against the followers of the Prophet. War against the schismatics of Byzantium. New warrior-orders to be founded in all the realms of Christendom, not Germany alone. The establishment of the Imperial Inquisition, against rebels and heretics. We will call it the Donation of Simon Peter."

"Simon Peter?" said the Emperor, mind still racing at the implications of what had been said.

"I will take the Papal name of Peter," said Erkenbert firmly. "It has been forbidden to all Popes throughout history since the first. But I will take it not in pride but in humility, as a sign that the Church needs to begin again, cleansed of its weakness and its surfeit. We will find a document in the vaults of the Vatican, in the Catacombs, written by Simon Peter himself and setting out his wish that the Church should be the loyal servant of a Christian Empire."

"Find a document?" repeated Bruno. "But how can we find it if we don't know it's there?"

"I found the Grail, did I not?" said Erkenbert. "You can rely on me to find the Donation of Peter."

He means he's going to fake it, thought Bruno suddenly. That is against every law of God and man. But a tenth of the Church's possessions . . . Fat monks and idle nuns evicted, their lands made over for the support of warriors . . . No more counting the *Ritters* and the *Bruderschaft* in hundreds . . . And surely, a pious end may justify impious means.

It's a fraud and he knows it's a fraud, thought Erkenbert. But he's going to go through with it. What he doesn't know is that the Donation of Constantine is a fraud too, any scholar can see it, the Latin is quite of the wrong period for what is claimed. It was written by a Frank, or I am an Italian. How many more documents, I wonder, are frauds? That is the true danger of things like this: he took the heretic booklet from the Emperor's hands, tore it across and threw it carefully into the glowing brazier. They start people thinking about whether books are true. We must stamp that out.

Few books, and all those holy ones, that must be our goal. Whether they are true or not—that shall be for me to decide.

The plume of smoke leaking lazily into the air off the port bow held Shef's gaze like a fly struggling to escape the spider. The cruise had gone well, extraordinarily well. The islands of the Mediterranean had been much fought over, but did not seem to have been thoroughly plundered for many years. Perhaps the contestants had been eager only to change the religion of the islanders, not to leave with a profit. The ships in the fleet were low in the water now, not only with renewed food and water, but with church plate, brocades and cloth of unknown dyes.

Most important of all was the tribute exacted from Mallorca and Menorca, Ibiza and Formentera, then Corsica and Sardinia, tribute in gold and silver coins of the Arabs, of the Greeks, of the Franks and the Romans and countries of which Shef had never heard and whose script neither Skaldfinn nor Solomon could recognise. Sicily next, lying only a little to the south, below the island of Vulcan with its smoky mountain? A descent on the Italian mainland? Even Guthmund had been heard to talk of quitting while the going was good, and before the equinoctial gales set in on the long passage home.

Meanwhile there was Steffi to satisfy. He had taken his conversion to the fire-pendant and the Loki-god with great conviction. His conversation was now about nothing but fire, and he had grasped a principle that Shef himself had often stated. There was more knowledge in the world than people realized. Steffi had set himself to find out everything that anyone at all knew about fire and about things that burnt, or lit, or even glowed in the dark. Their Greek captive had been a disappointment. He knew his trade, it was true, and he had told them all he knew of the black oilfields beyond the Black Sea, of the process of draining and refining the stuff that oozed to the surface, fluid and light in the cold, sticky and tar-like in the heat. But though he knew how the trade was carried out he had little curiosity about substitutes, alternatives. They had concealed from him the fact that they had no oilfield in the West as the Greeks had in the East, but without such an alternative they had the half-tank of oil they had captured and no more.

Steffi was not discouraged. He talked to the Greek, to Solomon, to Brand, to Shef, to Solomon, to the fishing boat crews they intercepted, interrogated and released, to his own mates. His monologue continued as he stood in the bows watching the smoke like Shef, but watching it like a lover watching his mistress's window.

"Funny, you know," he repeated. "Once I got asking them you'd think half the fleet knew that if you lit a fire on earth that had been cleaned out of a stable or a cave or whatever, then it burned real fierce. So I asked them what else did that, and they come up with all sorts. Solomon says the Arabs have some stuff like what our Greek calls *naphtha,* but the Greek says it's different. Solomon says the Arabs used to make fire-bundles out of their stuff, like our flares, but they used to throw them not launch them from a catapult. I'd like to get some of that *naphtha,* but meanwhile we got fish-oil, we got the saltpeter stuff, we got wax . . .

"And then one of the lads reminded me of what you get on rotten logs, that glows in the dark, though it doesn't burn. Solomon says that's called *phosphor,* and he says if you get the real stuff, it burns so hard water can't put it out, you have to scrape it off the skin. The Greek says he's heard of that and they tried mixing it with the oil they use, but it's not safe, they sometimes mix in a kind of resin."

"They put that in the wine too," put in Shef.

"Only because it's what they caulk the barrels with. But resin burns, and so does amber, one of the boys was telling me."

"We can't afford amber flares," said Shef.

Steffi frowned at the levity. "No. But I had another idea. You know that winter ale and winter wine they make at Stamford, where they steam it off and catch the steam? Well, one of the lads had a bit left and I bought it off him. That burns too, burns pretty well. Solomon came up and told me the Arabs did that too, they call it *al-kuhl.*"

"The Arabs can always do everything, if you hear them talk. Fly, make lenses, invent algorism, make fire devices, *al-kuhl, al-jabr, al-kimiya, al-qili* . . . Thing is, they never seem to do anything with it." Shef too had listened to Solomon and grown rather tired of it.

"Well, I'd like to get all that stuff, whatever it is, the naphtha and the phosphor and the alcool and all, and the saltpeter, and start mixing it. See what happens. And charcoal too, we all use it, why does it burn better than wood? But most of all I want to see what they've got up there. A fire-mountain, they say. Burning rock. And the smell. Everyone says there's a strange smell comes from the mountain. Sulphur, they call it. But you know something, in the Fens where I come from . . ."

"Me too," Shef reminded him.

". . . we got this thing they call the will o' the wisp. Fires that light and lead you into the swamp. Comes from dead bodies, they say. Well, that smells too. I'm sure we got this saltpeter at home, in barns and piggeries and what not. Maybe we got this sulphur too. I want to see it. Start putting them together."

A pillar of fire by night and a cloud of smoke by day. That was what he had been trying to think of. It was something to do with one of Father Andreas's lessons from the Bible. The Children of Israel escaping from bondage? Father Andreas had said it was an image of the Christian soul seeking heaven. Shef did not think the pillar of smoke they were steering for was the Promised Land, somehow. But Steffi did. Maybe Steffi was the one whose opinion would count.

For some time the fleet had been steering for a fishing-boat running easily under its light lateen sail. It had made no attempt to escape them, the word must have got round that the strangers did no harm to the poor, even paid for news. Indeed the boat was heading towards them, had now rounded and lay easily to leeward. Skaldfinn and Solomon were shouting back and forth, calling one of the fishermen on board. Shef waited for a translation to emerge in good time.

It seemed as if he had said something important. Skaldfinn was coming over with a strange expression on his face.

"He says there's a new Pope in Rome, though the old Pope is not dead. More than that: he says the new Pope is a stranger, an alien, a foreigner. He calls him an *Anglus*. That's when he spat on the deck and Ordlaf hit him."

"An English Pope?" The word had been heard and was spreading through the crew, with general laughter and derision.

"A little man, not even a priest. The fisherman says he has proclaimed a state of holy war throughout the Empire against all heathen and heretics and unbelievers. Soon, the fisherman says, the Emperor will come with his fleet of fireships and his army of iron men and destroy all those who do not bend the knee to Saint Peter. Then Rome will rule the world."

Fireships, thought Shef. Maybe they are not so far off after all. Nor is Rome now. He remembered unbidden the map his divine patron had shown him months before: the map that centered on Rome. Rig had told him that at Rome his troubles would cease. He had no wish to go there. Like Guthmund, his thoughts were for home.

"My grandfather Ragnar tried to sack Rome once," said Svandis. "He sacked the wrong city by mistake, but believed it was Rome because the plunder was so great."

"If Erkenbert is at Rome preaching holy war and another Crusade, it can only be against us," said Thorvin slowly. "Better to fight in another man's country than in your own."

We have not quite three thousand men in the fleet, thought Shef, the Emperor will have many more. But mine are all picked men, crossbows and catapults and flares and even the Greek fire. They want me to fight again. But I have made my peace with Loki, or so I thought. I want to avert Ragnarök, not bring it about.

"Let's hear what Brand has to say," said Skaldfinn diplomatically.

"All right," Shef replied. "But keep heading for the fire-mountain, for the Vulcan-isle. We'll anchor off it tonight."

Shef lay that night in his hammock in the gently-heaving cabin of the *Fafnisbane*. He felt as he had felt when the decision was taken to come on this journey to the center of the world, that opinion was against him, was pressing on him. He was being manipulated. They wanted him to find and fight the Emperor. He was not going to do it. He was going to go home, set his land in order, wait for fate and death to come to him in their proper season. Svandis, who lay in a hammock touching his, was pregnant with his child, he felt sure. The glow on her face and in her eyes was not merely that of sun and sea-air, it was the glow of new birth. He had seen it on Godive years before. This time he would see the child born and know it was his.

They would try to persuade him otherwise, he knew. Not just men, but gods. He was braced for the dream that would come, and whether it came from the gods, or his own mind, or from the wolf that grew amid the rye, he did not care. The night was his enemy, and he would face it.

The dream began abruptly, directly. A man hurrying through city streets, in the dark. The man was afraid, bitter afraid, and ashamed at the same time. He was afraid of something he had seen done before. He was ashamed not just because he was afraid, but because he had been afraid before, and given in before, and vowed never to do so again—and yet here he was, scuttling through the streets to get into the open country, to lose himself, to change his name. His name was Peter. Peter who had once been Simon.

As he came to the walls of the city tension increased. There was a gate, and inset in the gate a little door, one that could be slipped open without the ponderous process of lifting the great bars and thrusting back the gates on their rollers. The little door was ajar. But where was the sentry? There. Asleep, head thrown back. His spear, the Roman infantry weapon that Shef had held in his hands as the Holy Lance, was propped between his thighs. No one else around, the guard-hut shut and lightless. Creeping forward like a shadow, Peter who had been Simon and longed to be Simon again set hands on the door, inched it open waiting for the betraying creak. None came. He was through, the walls behind him, life and safety ahead of him. Just like me, thought the Shef-mind.

There was a shape in front of him. He had known there would be. A human shape, but round its head a crown of thorns. It moved forward, shedding a pale corpse-light around it. Its eyes looked down on the cringing disciple. "Petre, quo vadis?" it said. Peter, where are you going?

Tell him, the Shef-mind urged. Tell him you're escaping! Tell him he isn't even dead, the whole thing's a mistake, he's alive and well and living with Mary Magdalene in the mountains! Writing a book!

The Peter-figure had fallen back, was returning to the door, shoulders drooped. Going back to the city, to Rome, to arrest and death and crucifixion. He would ask to be crucified upside-down, Shef recalled, as unworthy of the same death as the Savior he had betrayed. That won't work, Shef thought. You can say quo vadis? to me as long as you like.

Another picture, flicked into shape like a screen being thrust in front of the eyes. Another man set on flight, but asleep this time. In his dream he saw, not the Christ-figure of the previous vision but the Peter-figure. But not shamefaced and drooping this time, rather stern, majestic, a grim look in his eyes. He was shouting, though Shef could not hear what he said. In his hand he held a scourge, the monastic disciplina, *a whip with many cords and knots tied into every one. He stepped forward, knocked the sleeping man's eidolon down with one bony fist, tore his robe from his back, began to strike again and again with the* disciplina, *blood springing out as the man rebuked struggled and cried out.*

The scene vanished and Shef found himself once more looking into the eyes of his patron. Clever, foxy eyes.

"I don't do that kind of thing," *remarked Rig.* "If you want to shirk your duty, go ahead. I will not deceive you into obedience, or beat you into it. I just want you to see what shirking will mean."

"So show me. You're going to anyway."

Shef was braced for immediate horror, but it did not come. He saw his own city, his own foundation of Stamford. There was the Wisdom House, there its accumulation of workshops and forges and storehouses. Bigger than he remembered them, older, lichen encrusted on the gray stones. Silently, without explanation, the Wisdom House sprang apart. A flash, a crack that he knew would have been ear-splitting if there had not been some barrier between him and the substance of the dream, a cloud of smoke rising and in the smoke stones arcing up into the sky.

As they came down Shef saw what was going on in the ruins. Soldiers everywhere, wearing white surcoat and red cross: Crusaders, such as King Charles and Pope Nicholas had once brought against him. But these soldiers were not wearing the heavy mail and horsemen's boots of the Frankish knights, or the Emperor's Lanzenritter. They were lightly dressed, moved quickly, carried only long tubes in their hands.

"Freedom for Loki as well as for Thor," *said Rig.* "Well and good. But whose side will Loki be on? Or stay on? Naphtha and phosphor, sulphur and saltpeter, alcohol and charcoal. Others besides Steffi can put two and two together. Or one and one and one. In the end Church and Empire united will win. Not in your time. But you will live your life knowing it will happen—and that you could have averted it. I will see to that."

Shef lay dumb and defiant. "Let me show you some more," *the clever voice continued.* "Here is the new city."

A marvel slowly opened before Shef's closed eyes. A white city, with shining walls, and in the heart of it a cluster of spires reaching towards heaven. On every spire a banner, on every banner a device of holiness: Crossed Keys, Closed Book, Saint Sebastian and his arrows, Saint Lawrence and his gridiron. Beneath the spires, Shef knew, lay a multitude of men whose duty it was to praise the Lord and study the Bible. It was not his Bible, but the yearning for such a life, of contemplation and study, of peace and tranquility, swept over him like hunger. Tears began to spill from his shut eyelids, at what he did not have.

"Look closer," said the voice.

In the lecture-rooms stood men reading from their books. The students listened. They wrote nothing. Their duty was to remember. As the lectures finished the lecturers went to a central room, handed over their books. They were counted, checked against a list, placed in an iron chest, the key turned. Safely stored, till next time. In the whole city no man owned a book for himself alone. No man wrote a new word, or thought a new thought. The smiths beat out what they were told to, as their ancestors had done before them. The itch Shef so often felt, to hold a hammer, to beat out an answer for a question in his brain: that itch would remain unappeased for ever.

"It is the Skuld-world," said Rig. "Where Loki is freed at last to serve the Church, and then cast into ever stricter bonds, till he too withers away from starvation. And the world remains the same, from one eon to the next. Ever-holy, never-changing. Every book become a Bible. Your monument, your legacy."

"And if I fight?" asked Shef. "Will Loki be with me instead? Will he weep for Balder and release his brother from Hel? What will that look like?"

In an instant the limited sight of a single city faded, expanded to become an image of the Nine Worlds of which Middle-earth is only one. Shef could see the dark-elves below the earth and the light-elves above it, could see Bifrost bridge that leads to Asgarth and the Giallar-bridge that takes the souls down to Hel. All was—not dark, but weathered, stained somehow, as if all seen through a dusty glass. Somewhere deep down Shef could hear a massive creaking, a noise of rusty machinery forced open, forced into life.

It was the Grind opening. The Grind-gate that separates the dead from the living, the metal lattice through which Shef had once seen the shapes of the child and the women whose bane he had been. Through which the slave-woman Edtheow had urged him to go on. The Grind was opening for Balder. And not just Balder. Once it was open, Shef knew, the souls might come back. Be born again in their descendants, live the happy lives that had been robbed from them. The slave-girls he had found in the old king's mound, buried alive with their backs broken. The old woman whose death he had once shared, as she strove above all to die unnoticed. Edtheow who had died in the wolf-waste, and the poor slave dying of cancer in the Norse village far from her home. Cuthred. Karli. The child Harald.

As the gate opened something leaked from it. Not light, not color, but something that seemed to wipe the dust away, to restore to the world the light and the color that it should have had. There was a noise inside, a noise of laughter and a great clear voice calling others to share new life with him. Balder the Beautiful. Coming to make the new world, the new world that should always have been. Shef was aware from the corner of one eye that all the Asgarth gods were *staring at him, Thor with his red beard and fierce face, Othin with the face like a calving glacier. And standing next to Othin, Loki the traitor-god, the exile-god, now standing once again next to his father. Waiting for his brother to be released from Hel. Released by a victory. And by a sacrifice.*

Shef was awake once more and lying in his hammock, tears still wet on his face. He did not come round with the familiar heart-wrenching shock and outcry, rather with one deep indrawn breath. I'll have to do it, he thought. There are too many lives on my soul already. To have them out, to give them another chance.

Not much chance for me, though. Will I be released as well? Or am I the sacrifice for the others? He put a hand out, rested it on Svandis's warm hip. That is what I am giving up. In the dark night he knew with complete certainty that no-one would make the sacrifice for him, remembered with wry fellow-feeling the cry he had once heard from Christ on his cross: *Eloi, eloi, lama sabachthani.*

My god, my god, why hast thou forsaken me?

CHAPTER THIRTY-ONE

Tolman was signaling frantically from the end of his five-hundred-foot line. Closing warily on Ostia, the port of Rome, in double line abreast, the Wayman fleet had developed the habit of keeping a kite always aloft and floating out to leeward. The hundred yards of extra height that Tolman had at the end of his line increased his horizon by miles, gave them needed reassurance. No one had managed however to work out a way by which Tolman could pass on what he saw, other than by waving colored cloth—white for any sail, blue for land, red for danger. Specifically, for the red galleys and the Greek fire. It was red this time.

The winchmen were hauling him in already, with no need for the order. No need to bring him all the way in, he would go aloft again as soon as he had spoken. Barely fifty feet above the *Fafnisbane,* the kiteboy hung in the wind, a stiff one-reef breeze with a hint of oncoming chill about it.

"The galleys!" he shouted.

"Where?"

"In the harbor. In a long line, other side of the right-hand harbor-wall. Moored."

"How many of them?"

"All of them."

Shef waved a hand, the kitemen reeled out, sent Tolman slanting back to his position. Shef looked round, calculated the distance to the wall that marked the entrance to the harbor of Ostia. Two miles, he thought. They were making seven knots by Ordlaf's log-line. Would that give the galleys time to man the oars, light their braziers, steer to meet him? If every man was ready in place already and they had seen him at the same time as

Tolman saw them. He thought not. Shef looked at Hagbarth and Ordlaf waiting for orders in his own ship, looked across at Hardred in the *Wada* leading the parallel column fifty yards to windward, and pointed firmly to the harbor-mouth. The galleys had caught him by surprise once, in the open sea. Now he would reverse the roles.

As they raced in under sail, the ships shook into their attack formation. The mule-carriers in the lead, in a single file as close as seamanship could make it, the longships to the left of the line and to windward. If Shef had misjudged and the enemy met them with streams of fire, then the Vikings at least ought to be able to turn and escape. But the mules should have done the business before that was necessary.

"Wind Tolman in," Shef ordered as the harbor-mouth opened up in front of them. Tolman was still pointing firmly to the right, relieving Shef of the fear of sudden attack from an unexpected quarter. Cwicca in the forward mule-emplacement was behind the sights, training his weapon round with every heave of the bows, keeping it fixed on the very lip of the harbor-wall. What was on the other side? A galley already heading for them? If there were, she would be sunk in moments. Her fire could be launched in less than moments. As the wall came up, close enough now to be reached by a stone-throw, Shef left his place by the steering-oar and walked forward to the mule-platform in the prow. If the fire was there, the king must face it first.

As the *Fafnisbane*'s bow nudged through the fifty-yard gap Shef saw Cwicca drop his hand. The release-man jerked the lanyard, the mule-arm smashed up, as always too fast to see, the sling on its end whirling round like a demented bowler. Shef heard a crash of timber, waited for agonizing moments as the *Fafnisbane* cruised on and brought the inner wall of the harbor into his vision. Then, relief like cold water. The nearest galley was thirty yards away, still moored bow and stern. There were men aboard her, and arrows flicked from her as he watched, zipping into planking, one into a shield hastily thrust in front of him. But no smoke, no roaring of bellows. They had been taken by surprise.

The first galley was already settling by the head, moored as she was, prow and keel broken by the first mule-stone. Shef ran back hastily to the stern platform, pointed out the second ship, ordered Osmod to hold his release till the widening angle gave him a clean shot. As ship after ship of the Wayman fleet poured through the harbor entrance, they swung into a long curving line, headed by *Fafnisbane* and *Wada*, and poured a rain of mule-stones on to the galleys lined up as if for target-practice against the wall, just beyond weak arrow-shot.

Shef let them shoot on and on till his enemies were all but kindling wood, prows and sterns dangling from the mooring ropes but between them more smashed planking, with here and there a glint of copper. There was no resistance from the galleys. Shef saw men running from them—astonishingly few, he judged. Such opposition as there was came from Steffi, who seized his king's arm again and again, begging for the stones to stop, for permission to take a party ashore and seize the siphons and fuel-tanks of the enemy. Shef shook him off absently each time like a heifer shrugging off a horse-fly. It was beginning to look as if the enemy fleet had simply not been manned. But he would take no risks for Steffi's curiosity.

He raised both hands finally in the 'Cease shooting' order, turned to Ordlaf. "We'll moor over there, by the wall, where it's clear. Four ships abreast. Then we can start getting the men and the supplies off. Well, Steffi?"

Steffi's eyes were genuinely full of tears, he was begging now, imploring. "Only twenty men, lord king, twenty men for the time it'll take to moor and unload. That's all I ask. They're sunk now, but there may be something we can salvage, one tank of oil full and not split by those stones, that would do for me."

A memory came back to Shef of himself on the walls of York, begging Brand in similar style for twenty men to retrieve a catapult, to see how it worked. Brand had refused him, ordered him to join in the sack of the city instead. There had been no sack, but now he was the incurious one, fixed on his own purposes.

"Twenty men," he agreed. "But have them ready to march as soon as the others."

Farman was by his side, eyes wide and unblinking as if he saw something far off. "Will you take every man with you?" he asked.

"I will leave a guard on the ships, naturally."

"I will stay with them, then," said the seer. "You have men of war enough."

No time to argue or enquire. Shef nodded agreement, turned his attention to the problem of getting his army ashore and his fleet secured. There seemed to be almost no-one at Ostia, certainly no hint of resistance. The few Greeks that had been with the fleet had fled. Shef removed the gold bracelets from one arm, held them temptingly in his hand, called Cwicca and three crossbows up as bodyguards, and walked towards the nearest huddle of huts by the dockside. Surely greed would bring him news. Not that he needed to know much about his goal. This was Ostia, and fifteen miles off was Rome. Reach it, sack it, kill the English Pope. Even trying to do that would bring down on him the Emperor, and then their long dispute would be settled. The strange thing was that Shef could not bring his imagination to think of the charismatic Bruno losing. Perhaps he was already fey, as the English said, already gripped by the paralysis of approaching death. He walked towards the huts, waving the gold and a plucked-up weed in sign of peace.

The Emperor of the Romans received the news of his ally's fleet's destruction in a Rome bearing the marks of his own heavy hand. Smoke rose in a plume into the sky behind the Capitoline Hill, was blown away on the rising wind. Bodies lay unburied in the streets: the loafers and gutter-rats of Rome had been able to put up little resistance to his heavy-armed troopers. They had their bludgeons and cobblestones and cart-barricades, and they had tried, defending their Pope against an alien interloper, and they had paid the price. Neither the City nor the Church of Rome had gained anything so far from the Emperor of Rome sworn to their protection.

Just for the time being, thought Bruno. "Cheer up, man," he added to the Greek admiral Georgios as he saw the latter's stunned expression. "Time to rebuild your fleet this winter. Your Emperor will not lose by it, you have my word."

Cheer up? thought Georgios. All my galleys sunk in one morning, destroyed like so many Arab fleets. My marines committed to street-fighting against guttersnipes for an alien Emperor. And the secret of the Greek fire — surely that is not lost. Yet it might be. The man is mad.

The best of his advisers looked thoughtful, Bruno realized. For Georgios there might be reason enough. But Agilulf too . . . His spirits rose in perverse opposition to their mood.

"All right," he said. "They caught us unawares down at Ostia. We are still having a little trouble with the city scum. Pope John keeps escaping my hand. Now, listen. *None of that matters.* Does it, Erkenbert, Your Holiness? Remember what Arno the chaplain used to say. You have to find the *Schwerpunkt* in any campaign, the bit that is important. There is only one thing important here, only one thing that has ever been important now that we have the Grail. That is to defeat my enemy the One King once and for all. If we do that, everything becomes easy. The city will be under control in a week. John will be brought in by some traitor. The fleet can be rebuilt. But if we *don't* do it . . ."

"All the others will be on our backs," summed up Agilulf, "and we will fall apart too." He said the last words with a sideways squint at Georgios. Agilulf had not forgotten who had lashed him and his men with fire, nor believed Georgios's explanation of an unfortunate accident.

"But we will do it," said Erkenbert. Pope Peter II, as he now styled himself. He had not yet shed his faded black robe, traded it for Papal robes. The true regalia had not been recovered, nor had his accession to the apostolic throne been anything but a rushed and irregular affair, attended by a bare third of the College of Cardinals. Yet the Emperor was right. The

Cardinals could be convened again, the regalia recovered or remade. Given victory.

"I am ready to put the papacy aside and return to my duties as comrade in the army of the Emperor," Erkenbert went on. "War-wolf's successors are ready. They will take the field as soon as ordered."

"How can we use a siege-train against a marching army?" asked Agilulf.

"Who knows?" replied the Emperor. "We are not facing an ordinary man, never forget that, any of you. He has tricked every enemy he has faced. Tricked me, even. But he did not trick me out of the Grail, in the end. We must be as tricky as he is. Thank you, Your Holiness. If every man in my army had your heart, victory would be assured."

"Victory *is* assured," said Erkenbert. "*In hoc signo vinces,* in this sign you will conquer." Through the broken window of the plundered villa he pointed to the banner with its device of the *graduale* worked on it, planted above the golden reliquary that now housed the Grail itself. Four *Ritters* stood forever around it, fully armed, swords drawn, emblems of the new Church Militant and the Donation of Peter.

That is the enemy's sign too, thought Agilulf. Two sides with the same sign. Two clever leaders. Two, maybe three thousand real men on each side, and God knows how many dross as well on ours. This is a battle it will take very little to decide.

The Wayman army tramped steadily along the great stone road that led from the port to the City of Rome itself, center of the world. The men's cries of mirth and astonishment had died as the march continued, their spirits dashed by the immense size of the stone blocks that lined the road, the stone houses on every hillside, the air that the country wore of great age and strength long gone by. They had seen Stamford, and it was a mere village in comparison. They had seen Cordova too, and it was no village but a metropolis that dwarfed even Rome for numbers and trade and wealth. Cordova, though, had been a village while Rome ruled the world. There was a sense that every spade turned in this land would bring up the dust of greatness.

The men were bunching in their nervousness, Shef thought. He had sent a hundred Vikings forward under Guthmund, always eager to be first to any chance of loot. He had meant them to keep off the road, investigate the side ways for ambush. There were too many hedges, too many walls. In the strong sunlight they had reverted to the middle of the road, were walking along in an armed gaggle a mere hundred yards before the crossbows escorting his catapult-train. When the sun had moved another hand's breadth he would call a rest halt, change the formation.

On the hill to his right, trumpets blew. Others answered from the left. An ambush, on the long winding trail of men and machines? He hoped so. Any ambush from the flanks would have to cross furlongs of rough ground under five hundred ready crossbows.

The light horsemen burst instead from an olive grove a bare fifty yards in front of the Viking advance guard. Shef had barely time to see them, to note the wide-brimmed hats, the long ten-foot goads of the Camargue cowboys, dragged from home by the Emperor's edict, when the goads dropped from the vertical to the charge, and all vanished in an instant pall of dust.

The Vikings were surprised but not dismayed. In instants swords were drawn, axes shifted to the striking hand. Automatically the loose straggle of the march shifted to a narrow front of raised shields and poised javelins. The cowboys made no effort to charge home but swerved and pounded down each flank. From the column of barebacked horses the goads darted, flicking at face or throat. Men screamed, reeled back into their messmates. The two columns of horses swerved round behind the footmen in a bewildering criss-cross, darted back, goads stabbing again at the weak points in the shaken line, at men still facing the wrong way, shaking their weapons and crying their war-cries to defy an enemy to stand foot to foot.

Crossbowmen had cocked their weapons, were running forward to find a place to shoot, running forward further in the hope of getting through the dust. Shef saw one kneel, take careful aim at a horseman curvetting twenty yards in front of him. The horseman slipped from his seat—he had no saddle—hung the other side of his horse by mane and ankle. As the crossbowman shifted aim to bring down horse if not rider, another screaming Centaur burst from the dust, speared him between the shoulders, dipped the goad to clear the point and swept away, clearing a wall like a hunted stag and disappearing among the trees.

The trumpets blared again from either side, and men faced hastily in all directions. Nothing happened. Through the silence Shef could hear the wheezing noise of a man speared through the lungs. The dust settled on bodies lying in the road. Not many, a dozen, and as many more with their mates bending over them assessing the depth of a thrust. No sign of the enemy. Not a man or a horse left behind, and hardly a bolt shot at them or a blow struck. They could do it again any time. Shef began to shout orders to rally and re-organise his formations.

A long, hot delay on the dusty road while the wounded were loaded on to mules or carts, and the column began to move forward again. Shef had thought a little harder about the ambush problem. He had eight hundred crossbows, mixed in with another three hundred English halberdiers as close support, more trusted by the crossbowmen than their Viking allies. There were perhaps a thousand of the Vikings, heavy infantry of the sort that had decided so many battlefields before the coming of the Way to England. All the mules had been left aboard ship, their ton-and-a-quarter weight making Shef reluctant to move them unknown distances. Instead a dozen of the torsion dart-throwers, the weapons the Waymen called twist-shooters, trundled along behind their mule pairs, crews marching alongside. And then there was Steffi's gang. Shef was no longer sure what they had with them, for they seemed to have become more and more secretive with the establishment of their own pendant and trade. They certainly had half a dozen catapults of the old lobbing traction type, knocked down into beams and rope for easy transport. No use on the march, but they had to be protected just the same.

The column moved forward now with a solid body of crossbowmen at the front, interspersed with halberdiers. More crossbows moved to the flanks, causing continual halts as they negotiated the walls of private villas and the gullies that occasionally ran in culverts under the stone road. In the center of the column, marching rather sullenly under the unwonted slur of needing protection, the Viking sword- and axe-men straggled along either side of the mule-train. If the cowboys came again, Shef reckoned, the crossbows would empty a few saddles as they charged and many more as they retreated. The halberds would hold off light horse, at least.

The cowboys did not come again. The column breasted a slight slope, began to move down at a quicker pace: and there, in the middle distance, Shef saw the shining walls of the Eternal City, a cluster of hills seemingly covered with stone buildings, spires and domes catching the sun. As he gaped into the distance, his eye caught the sudden, familiar, rising and falling streak of an onager stone. No time to guess where it was going. Shef threw himself instantly sideways off the road, rolling painfully on stone, straightening up on bleeding knees to see where the stone had gone. A puff of dust still hanging in the air thirty yards ahead of him, stone chips flying where the rock had broken up on the stone surface of the road. But in front of it, a lane beaten through the marching crossbows, five deep, men lying to either side of it, one struggling to look down at a caved-in chest which would kill him in moments. As the survivors stared in shock at the men smashed down, Shef saw another lane open, and another, men going down like stalks before the sickle. And still they were staring around, some of them cocking crossbows uncertainly against an unseen foe. Shef ran towards them, shrieking at them to spread out, move off the road, lie down, get behind walls. As they did so another flying twenty-pound rock shattered the road surface, sending splinters flying. Twenty, thirty men down already and still no-one had seen the enemy. But there they were, Shef could see the battery set up half a mile off on the side of the hill, the men moving unconcernedly round their machines, winding ropes and training round. They would shoot again in a moment. Shef ducked as another boulder hummed by, pitched well up this time. Behind him the mule teams were scattering off the road, Vikings were crouched in undignified positions behind trees and walls.

There they were all right. Shef focused his far-seer, caught a clear image of the men round the machines. He could not see Erkenbert, as he had half-expected. But he must have trained many men by now to take his place. How to get to them? His only weapons with the range to reach them were the twist-shooters. They would do, better against men than against machines. Shef shouted back, saw the catapult-teams unharness the mules, run their weapons, round, start the slow business of winding and aiming. And while they were doing that . . . As stones hummed over his head, the onagers concentrating now on the dart-throwers, Shef ran forward to his shaken crossbows, shouting.

For long moments they would not move, obeying the instinctive fear of missiles flying from a distance. Get down, don't move, crawl away. Shef shouted, kicked a man to his feet, appealed to their honor and their pride. The sight of one man on his feet without being instantly knocked down restored some sense, reminded them of the mules' doubtful accuracy against single person targets. In a shambling run the crossbows began to move forward. Shef shouted at them not to keep running. Run ten steps, twenty, get down while another ran, when he took cover run forward again. Don't run straight. Make it impossible for anyone to take a steady aim.

From the hillside to one side of the onagers, Erkenbert and his Emperor watched the hastily-organized attack. To them it looked as if the slope facing them was covered with swarming ants, no one of them moving steadily onward, but the whole mass continually edging closer. Meanwhile the missiles of the catapults flew backward and forward. One of Erkenbert's crew was hurled backwards, spine shattered by the five-foot flying dart. A twist-thrower, hit square on by a mule-stone, flew to pieces, its overwound ropes lashing at arms and faces.

"I saw him there for a moment or two," commented Bruno. "Pity he didn't stand long enough for your men to get a shot at him. That would settle this immediately."

"As would your death," replied Erkenbert.

"He hasn't even seen me yet."

Crossbow bolts at extreme range were beginning to clatter among the rocks round the onager battery. The winders were flinching, looking behind them. No way to hitch up a ton-weight onager and drive it out of trouble, Shef thought, not in a hurry. If he pressed on he could capture the whole battery, maybe they had not expected instant attack.

Or maybe they had. They had determined everything else about this battle so far. With a fear so deep it was like a spasm in his breast, Shef remembered King Charles the Bald and how he had pressed on and on in an attempt to capture machines temptingly waved in front of him. Now he was doing the same. But it was his enemy, this time, who knew the ground and had a plan, he who was thrusting forward confident in superior weaponry.

"Hold it," he shouted, "steady, close up and shoot. Stop running!" His voice reached only those nearest to him, the rest saw their enemies wavering, rushed on to close with them and take revenge for their fear.

"That'll do," remarked Bruno, and nodded to his trumpeter. Out of the dead ground between crossbows and onagers, from behind olive groves and villa walls, came the heavy horse which were the glory of the Imperial army, mail gleaming, steel hooves striking sparks from the stone, lance-points lowered. Each group drove straight for their enemies, making no attempt to form a concerted line. Their charge came home from no more than fifty yards, five terrified heartbeats to an unarmored man charged by war-stallions.

Shef, a little behind the rashest of the crossbows, saw them stop, hesitate, and then almost to a man turn and run, leaping from side to side on the stony hillside to avoid the lances behind them. One man dropped to one knee, swung up his crossbow. As he pulled trigger a lance struck him, lifted him off the ground, the bolt flying straight up in the sky. The lancers came on with the skill of men in the saddle from childhood, lances driving, then as they broke or remained fixed in sprawling bodies, whirling broadswords from the scabbards on their saddles. Shef realized suddenly that one rider had singled him out as a target. Their eyes met, and then the horse was leaping towards him, foam flecking its muzzle as the rider drove home the long spiked spurs. Shef groped for a crossbow, reached towards his belt, realized that he was once again unarmed except for a belt-knife. Running was a disgrace, he would be hacked down from behind, a laughing-stock to the future. Try to dodge the blow?

An arm thrust him stumbling aside, a broad metal-clad back filled his view. It was Styrr, run gasping up in the heat from the Viking column behind. The Frank—he did not wear the Lance of a *Lanzenritter* on his shield—swerved his charger with knee-pressure alone to pass Styrr on his right, sword high for the downstroke. As he did so Styrr's own right arm swung with terrible force, the axe-blow with all a man's weight concentrated and flung with hatred behind the iron head. Aimed at the horse—not the rider. The chunk of cleaver on butcher's block and the lancer was falling forwards over his horse's head, rolling in a ball and coming up at Shef's very feet. Without thought Shef hit him with clenched fist on the side of the jaw, as the long-dead Karli had shown him in the swamps of the Ditmarsh. As the lancer staggered back Styrr freed a blade, stabbed him in the back of the neck, turned instantly to face any new foe.

The hillside was clear again, horsemen vanished as if they had been sorcerers' illusions. Back into cover. As Shef looked around to see what had happened an onager stone passed his head so close the displaced air snapped his neck back. All too fast, he thought dazedly. Before one thing's settled another's started.

Styrr grunted as he tried to free his axe from where it was buried deep in the war-horse's skull, grunted again, worked a corner free and dragged it loose. He looked at the blade with concern, then grinned.

"Never done that before," he said. "What's next?" The Vikings, Shef remembered, could be beaten but never panicked. He looked round, began once more to call out orders. One thing was clear. He would advance no further into a maze of traps. The question was, could he now disengage?

CHAPTER THIRTY-TWO

T he well is poisoned," said Hund.

Shef stared at him, stared down into the bucket Hund had just examined. Green slime caked the bucket, the water was filthy. That did not matter, he could drink it. He had thought he was about to die of thirst when he reached the village of the heretics, had refused to drink. This was worse. There was no pride involved, it was water, it looked all right . . .

Hund dashed the bucket from his hands, looked at him with bitter enmity. "Poisoned, I said! And if it is bad for you, what about my wounded?"

Shef passed a tongue over dry lips. It was night already. The whole long afternoon and short evening had been a struggle over baking dust and stone, they had rallied round a hilltop villa which must have its own well. As had happened every time that day, the enemy had thought quicker. He did not know if it was a dead man down the well or something more certain, poison berries maybe. He had to take Hund's word. He had to have water. There was a train of wounded lying ominously quiet. Styrr, who had saved his life, was looking at him in silence. Styrr could resist heat and thirst less well than most men. Outside the night was filled with a deafening chorus of crickets from the olive trees: sound enough to cover any ambush. That was what the enemy wanted.

Brand was propelling someone forward, an old man, a graybeard. There was always someone, Shef remembered Brand telling him, who decided to stay put no matter what threat was coming.

"Ask him where the nearest water is," he ordered. "Skaldfinn, translate."

The chatter that followed sounded like Church Latin to Shef. These were, he supposed, the degenerate descendants of the ancient Romans, still speaking their language, but badly, if not as badly as the French.

"He says, in the aqueduct at the bottom of the hill. It comes from Rome, which is fed by its own aqueducts."

"What's an aqueduct?"

"Like a canal, only made of brick or stone."

Did the graybeard stay behind out of folly or weakness, Shef wondered, or was he left to tell me just that? He will lie. I need to know the truth. Ragnar, Ivar's father, Svandis's grandfather, he knew how to deal with people like this, Cuthred once told me. I wonder if I can do it myself?

He stepped over to the old man, jerked him to his knees, shoved a thumb firmly into the corner of one eye. Ragnar used to grow his right thumb-nail long for just this purpose, he remembered dully. Must have made the job easier. He used to gouge one out *before* he asked a question, just to show he meant it. I can't quite do that.

"Tell him I will have his eyes unless he can tell me why I should trust him," he said, voice flat.

"How can he make you believe that?" answered Skaldfinn.

"I don't know. That's for him to work out."

The old man was weeping now, he could feel the tears under his thumb, tightened his grip a fraction to compensate as the gabble went on. Hund was staring at him, face twisted with hatred, hand ready for a grab to save the old man, but unable to do it without risking a slip. Svandis was there too, looking uncertain—she boasted often enough about her grandfather, let her see what it was really like. Brand's eyebrows were raised. Styrr was grinning.

"He says there is no better place, but the Emperor's soldiers will be waiting, he heard them talking, not all are Germans. I think he's telling the truth," Skaldfinn added. "He's not trying to lay a trap. He's telling us the trap's there."

Shef let the old man drop to the floor. Today he had done everything wrong. Time to make up for it.

"We'll get the water," he said. "Find Steffi, and Cwicca, and Osmod."

"Nothing for us Norsemen to do?" asked Styrr huskily.

"Business for Loki," Shef replied.

"What have you got that we can use?" Shef demanded. No-one spoke more words than they had to now. Their throats were too dry.

"Plenty of flares," replied Steffi. "We improved them. The last lot, I had to light them and then hold them, you remember. Now we know that rope soaked in a solution of that saltpeter stuff burns well and doesn't go out in flight."

"What else?"

"I've been trying to make kind of—Greek fire balls, that we can throw, not squirt."

"Do they work?"

"I can't get them to spray out when they land. But they'll set anything on fire, and water doesn't put them out, just spreads the flame. They're made of bark, with sulphur and saltpeter, and soaked in the Greek oil. All sewn into waxed cotton. Fuses to set them off."

"That'll do." Shef coughed again as the dust settled on his throat. Outside the slope leading down to the aqueduct was pitch dark, no moon as yet. Trees and walls and the shacks of the poor gave cover. He had no doubt the enemy were waiting there for their break out. Shef started to husk out his instructions.

As the wounded were assembled, walking or on stretchers, the sentries watching the other sides of the camp called back, Cwicca's catapult teams set to work. No need for silence, but little wish to talk. The twist-shooters were set up in a rough arc facing downslope and angled right, towards the sea. Behind them Steffi had set up his pull-throwers. On the word his men began to lob the prepared fireballs down the hill, down the hill and to the right. On Shef's instructions, only every third missile was a fireball, the other two rocks from the supply train or from the villa's rock garden.

"We won't hit anyone except by accident," Steffi protested.

"They don't know that."

"We'll have none left to throw later."

"We're leaving them behind in any case."

Steffi protested no longer. His teams hurled the stones out into the blackness, to crash and clatter away down the hill. Amongst them the fireballs made no noise, emitting just the faint red streak of the glowing fuse as they flew away. As the barrage continued and nothing happened, no response from the dark, no cries or orders or counter-missiles, the watching crossbowmen began to mutter nervously.

Behind a wall Agilulf listened to the stones whistling down around him. None had so far come within twenty yards of where he stood. He did not understand what was happening. That, he knew now, was the dangerous time. What were those glints of light through the air? Fireflies? He could face steel, but not flame again. The Emperor should have remembered that.

Steffi nudged Shef and indicated a sudden crackle of fire a hundred yards off. The first fuse had reached the fireball-core. In the light of the flames a tree sprang out, looking as if it were leaning over to the blaze. A branch caught, fire beginning to run back from its twigs to the main trunk. There were more sparkles of fire here and there in the dark now, and they were springing up faster than they could be counted. Such wind as there was was blowing up the valley. Anyone between the fire and the Waymen would have to retreat in their direction.

Suddenly a black shape moved, the first time they had seen a sign of life out there. His *Ritter* helmet showed up clearly in silhouette. Then it was gone, and Shef shouted angrily at the twist-shooter teams for missing a target. But just as the flames had appeared out of nothing, so all at once the hillside was beginning to crawl with movement. Men forced out of their ambush places, men trying to duck through the gaps in the fire to reach the other side, even men, Shef saw, stepping forward to try to beat out the blazes before they got established. Beating them and scattering them, not putting them out.

To the crackle of flame and the noise of the crickets were added the sharp snap of crossbow releases, the heavier twang of the torsion dart-throwers shooting off their heavy missiles at what was for them point-blank range. Shef could see men falling now, or writhing, but some trick of the air kept him from hearing any human noise above the increasing roar of flame. The men dying and twisting were like a shadow play on the walls of a hut.

Shef tapped Brand sharply on the shoulder, jerked a thumb. Move now. Brand led his sixty men, two ships' crews, sharply and directly down the hill. A squad of crossbows followed immediately, then another body of Vikings, all the contingents told off to follow in set order. It was tempting to angle left, away from the flames. Shef had ordered them not to do it. Head into the flames as near as you can. The ones who should stop you will have moved and been shot or fled. Get down hill as fast as you can before you too are silhouetted against the fire.

The men were pouring down slope now, even the stretcher bearers moving at a jolting run over the uneven ground. It was the thought of water, Shef realized, more than any new obedience. Steffi's men had shot off their missiles, stood uncertainly by their catapults.

"Take them apart and carry them?" Steffi pleaded. "Just two of them?"

Shef shoved him on his way. "Leave the catapults. Carry your fire-gear if you can. Move."

The twist-shooters were still keeping up good practice, as the flames lit up a wider and wider area. The easy targets had gone, fallen to the crossbows, but there were still men moving. Did they think they were out of range? They were trying to help their own wounded, Shef realized, running to them to drag them out of the path of the spreading fires. Shef stepped to a machine, pointed to a man trying to crawl out of a tangle of scrub already alight. Sure enough, two men ran in to help him, he could see white faces turning towards him. They were not losing many men down there, Shef thought, but they were being hit out of the dark by men they could not see. A slight movement of the trail, another thick twang, one of the rescuers was hurled aside as if by a giant's finger, the other stumbled grotesquely and turned sideways for an instant. The watchers could see the giant dart driven clean through both thighs. The would-be rescuer fell back into the blaze just as it reached the man he had been trying to rescue.

Shef felt a fierce joy. He slapped Cwicca on the back, jerked a thumb to say "Move." No time to harness up the mules, but the wheeled twist-shooters were easier to handle than Steffi's machines. Without orders Cwicca's gangs seized them by the trails, ran them jolting and bouncing down the hill. With them ran the last squad of crossbows and halberdiers assigned as rearguard. All of them running at full pelt down the slope, Shef in their midst, weapons ready for someone to try to spring the ambush. The ambush that had already been sprung.

A clash of blows in the dark as a few *Lanzenbruder* closed with their enemies instead of falling back behind the flame. They were coming out of the light into the dark, never saw the bolts or blades that cut them down. And then there was the aqueduct, a long line of stone four feet high, with behind it the blessed smell of water. Shef's men poured over the wall, their chief among them, and ignored pursuit as they buried their faces in the cold and gently-running stream.

As he pulled his face up at long last, Shef saw Brand looming over him. "Which way?" he said curtly.

Shef looked for the first time at the aqueduct. The stream itself, built to supply the rich merchants' villas along the Ostia road with purer water than the polluted Tiber, was no more than six feet broad, much of it roofed over with slabs of stone to cut evaporation in the heat. Not all of it, though. He could not take the wheeled machines along it. There was a walkway either side, but barely wide enough for two men, no room again for carts or machines. What Shef wanted above all was to get back to his ships, abandon this failed attack.

Something told him that would not work, the same fighting instinct that had made him keep them shooting down wounded men. This fight would be to a finish now. If he fell back they would pursue him and destroy him. One end of the aqueduct led to Rome, about the other he had no idea. The god had told him—what was it? He would find his peace in Rome. Peace in death, maybe. So be it.

"That way," he said, pointing left. "Get them moving fast. Cwicca, ditch those machines."

Cwicca had nursed his machines over a thousand miles of travel. The machines were what had raised him from slavery. He began automatically to argue with his master, as he had done, to the astonishment of King Alfred, so many times before. This time Shef was past the point of tolerance. As the gap-toothed man began to expostulate, Shef, afraid and overstrained, stepped forward and hit him squarely in the mouth.

"Move," he shouted. "Or I'll have you back in a collar like you were before." His old comrade spat blood, pulled loose another tooth, gaped at it incredulously. Turned to obey the order.

"All masters are the same in the end," remarked one of his mates, hacking at the ropes to make the dart-thrower at least temporarily useless. Cwicca did not reply. In the darkness Tolman and the three boys with him hesitated over their bundles of cloth and canes and rope. Light enough for boys to carry, but a burden just the same. Cwicca seized two bundles from them, slung one over each shoulder.

"I'll carry thothe," he said, lisping badly. Tolman eyed the tears rolling down his face, said nothing.

Hours later the weary column struggled up the aqueduct to the walls of the Eternal City itself. They had run through the night like travelers chased by wolves. Their long thin column had been attacked again and again by men coming in from either side, men who had ridden ahead of them and then swerved in to a line which could not be missed. The crossbows had taken heavy toll of the attackers, but several times the column had been cut in two and there had been fierce work with blades in the dark before it could be reunited. Every time men had been left behind, lost or crippled or unconscious. Their comrades threw the dead into the running water, and as time went on threw in those they were not sure of as well. Few of the wounded were being carried now. In the hot night death by drowning seemed a delight to the sweating and exhausted men who were left. Shef was aware several times of Hund raging and struggling in the darkness as his charges were abandoned or given the warrior's death. He had no time or strength to intervene.

The light was beginning to show in the east as Shef led the rearguard up the final gentle slope to the lodgement that the advance guard had made on the walls of Rome itself, on the very slopes of the Aventine Hill. Light, he thought. And shelter. A chance to see what was happening. To seize the initiative, control the battle instead of reacting to it. He yearned for time more than for food or rest or water. He needed it as an outmatched wrestler needs a foothold.

As he reached the wall, saw the remains of his command spread out along the inner, undefended battlements, he turned and looked out, stepped on to the parapet to feel the dawn wind on his sweat-soaked tunic.

Two hundred yards away Erkenbert said with vindictive relish to his catapult captain, "Launch." The short arm dropped, the long arm shot up, the sling dragged along the ground and then whipped round in its vicious swing. Its load shot into the sky, not neatly but in a confusion of twisted limbs.

Shef, on the parapet, saw nothing except a momentary glimpse of movement coming towards him. He threw up an arm, felt a body-shaking thud, found himself sprawled on the ground, a weight on top of him. He tried to thrust it off, found his hands caught in something tough and sticky, clawed at it in desperation. It was off him and men were lifting him to his feet. He realized his hands were caught in human entrails, from a burst-open body at his feet. It was Trimma the crossbowman, his dead face set in a rictus of torment.

"They're shooting our own dead at us," explained Brand. "They must have known where we were headed and brought the big catapults round to meet us. These are men who were killed in the night."

Ahead of us again, thought Shef. Ahead of us again. I do not know what to do next.

"They're all round us," Brand added. "I doubt there's more than half of us left."

"The worship of Loki has brought us little good, then," said Thorvin. His tone was bitter, his white clothing torn and blood-stained. He had fought with his hammer in the night. He had not been able to save Skaldfinn, cut down by the aqueduct. Solomon the Jew had vanished, no-one knew how. Of Shef's immediate council only six remained: he and Thorvin, Brand and Hagbarth. Hund was there, his face cast down. Svandis too. He should have given her a thought at least during the night, Shef reflected, but he had not. The blood of Ragnar could usually look after itself. But she had within her now the blood of himself and of Rig. Why had he not stayed by her? He had had other duties.

And he had them now. Every now and then the battlements beneath them shook as another boulder landed from the counterweight machines Erkenbert was using: he had improved them, Shef had seen through the one remaining unbroken far-seer. He had hardly needed to, for there was nothing to oppose them with. Shef's council appeared sunk in apathy or despair. Even Brand had his heart set, it seemed, on making a noble end, no more.

Wrong, something said inside Shef's heart. They knew what they were suffering. They did not know what the other side was suffering. They must have lost heavily in the night as well, from fire and shot, in the innumerable scrimmages in the dark. It was an axiom that heavy horsemen should not be used at close quarters and at night, where valuable and highly-trained men could be brought down by mere kitchen-boys. Yet that was what the Emperor had been doing. The Wayman army had lost its machines, that was all. It had once known how to fight without them. Nor had they lost everything.

Shef's eye fell on the long bundles someone had stacked against the parapet. He had not known anyone had carried them, would have forbidden it if he had seen them. But now they were here . . . Yes, there was Tolman, lurking in the lee of a buttress, ducking his head incongruously every time the stonework shook to a new blow.

Shef got to his feet, setting his face into a mask of good cheer and encouragement. He walked over towards the frightened boy.

"Fancy a flight?" he remarked. "Safer up there than down here. Get aloft and let's see what the other side is planning. Cwicca! Unpack the gear and assemble a kite. What happened to your tooth, did you bite someone tough?"

The freedmen eyed each other as they began to assemble canes and cloth. Their experience of slavery was longer than their years of freedom, the habits came back to them readily. "He's forgotten he hit you already," muttered one out of the corner of his mouth to Cwicca. "And the bairn's terrified."

"Shut up and fix that line," Cwicca replied. Were all masters the same in the end, he wondered. He looked down at his wing-pendant, now the mark of the flier-caste. Master or no master, he had done things that no other man ever had.

Within minutes Tolman was in his familiar harness, held by six men just inside the wall. The wind was strengthening and they were a good forty feet up on the battered ramparts of Rome. It would take him out over the semi-circle of machines and men hemming them in from the outside, but Shef wanted him to use his eyes on what he could not see, the forces surely gathering for an assault within the walls.

"We'll reel you out quickly, pull you in as soon as you wave," he repeated. "Be as quick as you can."

The scared face nodded, the launchers held him aloft to take the wind, waited an instant, threw him up and out all together. For a moment he seemed to drop, and Shef noted that the wind eddied round the walls. Then he was reeling away backwards, on the stout mooring line and the cluster of thinner control lines—control lines the boy hardly needed now, so expert had he grown at working the vanes. Shef admired his skill as he swept upwards and outwards. His own best flight had lasted bare minutes. One day, when the world was at peace, he would do better.

"They're still up to their tricks," said the Emperor Bruno to his new-appointed Pope, Peter-that-was-once-Erkenbert. The two stood in the cover of a sacristy outside the walls, wrecked years before by the Moors. The Holy Lance was still by Bruno's left hand, in its holder beside the shield-grip. Behind him the four knights of the Grail stood round their relic and its banner. All had been held back from the fighting, not from personal fear but from the Emperor's fear that the precious relics might fall into enemy hands. He could not hold back much longer, the Emperor thought. Rage at the

enemy's defiance was beginning to overcome him. They were defying not
only him but their Savior, His Church and His relics on earth. The heathen
had penetrated to Rome itself, were in catapult distance, almost, of the
Leonine Wall and Saint Peter's Basilica, heart of the Faith. It must be
finished today.

"If they try it again, I will have a trick too," replied Erkenbert. "But they
are reeling him in. Lucky for him."

"What did you see?" asked Shef.

The boy spoke from his harness, not bothering to climb out. "Inside the
walls, there are men on foot, in armor, on that side there," he pointed.
"About two or three hundred. There were none in sight the other way."

No more than that, Shef thought. There will be more out of sight, of
course. But they have lost heavily.

"No horsemen anywhere?"

"No. I saw the Emperor. Behind me, near that ruined building with a bit
of white dome left. I think it was him. There was a man in black standing
next to him, and a banner by his side."

"What emblem was on the banner?"

"It was yours, lord." Tolman jerked his chin at the ladder-pendant
dangling now outside Shef's torn tunic.

If only we could shoot from the skies, Shef told himself. Or rain down fire
from Steffi's mixtures. Then the Emperor would be dead and the war over.
All wars would be over.

The trouble with machine wars, something within him replied, is that
both sides end up with machines. The same machines. That is the true
meaning of the *Song of the Giantesses,* which Farman once sang for me.

"Go up again," he said. "See if there is a door in these walls anywhere
near the Emperor, a door we might reach. We could try a sally out."

The small scared face nodded, the launchers moved back to their places.
Two hundred yards away Erkenbert exclaimed with satisfaction as he saw
the kite appear again on the parapet. From the shade of the ruined sacristy
men came out, hammered a stout five-foot post into the ground, set on it a
device like an upturned iron stirrup, and on that a crossbow. A giant
crossbow, six feet from tip to tip.

"It is yew-wood," said Erkenbert. "Vegetius does not explain the secret
of the steel the heathen make their bows from. But nor does he explain this.
I had it made when we saw the kites fly from the Jewish city. But this shall
be its first trial, in defense of Saint Peter and Saint Peter's city."

Tolman had seen arrows curve up at him before, shot hopefully by the
besiegers of Septimania. He knew that the range of an arrow shot straight up
is far less than one shot along the ground. He had no fear of breast-bows,

even of the heavy crossbow quarrels of his own side. When the first yard-long shaft zipped past his side and tore through a side-vane he did not understand what it was. Then, almost directly underneath him, he saw the bow bent again and his danger with it.

"He's signaling to be hauled in," Shef said, watching through the far-seer. The man at the mooring-line began to haul in, coiling the rope round his elbow for want of the winch.

"Something's wrong." The second arrow had driven through the body of the kite, all the archers could see to aim at. It had caught Tolman through the knee. His first start and twist of agony had almost turned the kite away from the wind. Then he had recovered himself, was trying to spill the wind enough to help the hauler, but keep it under the top of the box-shaped kite to keep him aloft. As they hauled him in, the elevation fell, the range for the heavy yew bow shortened. It was slower to reload than a goat's foot crossbow, as the two men operating it heaved the cord back by main strength and fitted it over the releasing ratchet. They still had time enough for the third shot.

Tolman was barely ten feet from the wall and safety when the men reaching out to seize him heard the whistle of the arrow, saw the small face contort and the small body jerk to the blow. They still could not see what had hit him. As they hauled him over the battlement, hands reached to pull him from his sling. He could not move, seemed wedged. Then Shef, reaching inside to cut the obstruction free, saw the great arrow driven through sling and body and out the other side. With four ripping slashes he cut away the material and the cords, pulled the boy and the harness and the arrow together all free. It was impossible to lay him down, the arrow would have been driven further through. He stood clutching the boy as blood ran down over his tunic.

"Where is Hund?" he called.

The little leech was already there. He took the boy from Shef's arms, laid him down carefully on his side, cut quickly at the sling and the clothes inside.

He sat back on his heels, patted the boy's face reassuringly. Shef had seen him do that before. It was a death sentence.

"No need to talk," he murmured soothingly. But the boy's face showed worry now, more than pain. He was trying to say something, face turned towards Shef. The king bent forward, trying to pick out the dying words. Something to do with the Emperor . . .

"What? What was that?" he said.

The boy's head turned sideways and Hund let it fall, rolling down the eyelids with professional hand. He looked up at his lord and one-time friend with the disgust and hatred that had come upon him again and again on this voyage. Shef paid no attention.

"He saw something. He tried to tell me something. Something vital. Have we another kite? Someone else to go aloft?"

"They dragged your kite along, the big one," said one voice.

"You could look for yourself," said another.

"Unless you want to thend another bairn," said a third. It was Cwicca, still lisping through his broken front teeth. Shef remembered suddenly that he had struck him in the night, threatened to send him back to slavery. But he could not remember why. All the faces turned towards him betrayed anger, even contempt. He had never seen that before, not from his own men, whom he had freed from their masters. No, he had seen such a look once. In the face of Godive. It was what had sent him on this expedition.

"Rig my kite then and put me in it," he said, his voice sounding in his own ears as if it came from far away.

Moments later, it seemed, he was in his harness, held up by a dozen men, lines attached. His face was a bare foot from Cwicca's just below.

"I'm sorry," he said.

They launched him into the rising wind.

As had happened with Tolman, he dropped instantly below the wall. For seconds he could see nothing but the great squared stones flashing past in front of him, while he thought of the man who had jumped from the tower of the Wisdom House, jumped and gone straight down. Then there was the feeling of lift again, and he felt the wind take him. They were reeling him out as fast as they could, he was beginning to climb, already he could see over the wall. He could see Brand shouting and lashing out at the men who had launched him, could see crossbows lining the wall and starting to shoot down, to kill or distract the men who had shot Tolman. Time to look round and see what it was that Tolman had died for. There, yes, the troops of the enemy forming up for the attack. Not where Tolman had said the first time, but massing behind a villa from which two flights of steps led up to the city-wall where his remaining command was strung out. He leant forward as far as he could without tipping the whole flimsy contrivance into a downward swoop, shouted at the top of his voice, far stronger than Tolman's pipe.

"There! There!" He struggled a hand free and pointed. Brand at least had caught his meaning, was off in the right direction. Steffi was on the wall too, doing something with his gear and an armful of earthenware pots.

"Burn the bastards alive," said Steffi gleefully as he poured his deadly mixture into the pots he had taken from the nearest guardhouse kitchen.

"Let 'em get halfway up before you shoot," bellowed Brand, arranging his defenses. "Don't shoot to kill, shoot 'em in the belly. Frightens the rest of 'em."

Hund stood up from his crouch beside the dead boy, thought of his patients lost in the night, thought of the burned and scalded men he had treated all through, thought of the death and chaos and the worship of Loki.

He twitched the heavy sax-knife from Cwicca's belt, stepped over and hacked through the mooring-line. The kite on the end of it jerked, began to rise and drift away. One of the men on the handling-lines tried to jerk it in, over-compensated, instantly let go before he pulled the kite into a dive. Hund slashed out at the other lines, men ducked, tried to avoid him. In moments only one line held, at one corner, it was tugging the kite over with no pressure from other lines to resist it. The man let go.

Trailing rope, the kite stood on its tail, banked clumsily, turned away from them, drifted off across the open country, losing height all the way as its unskilled operator tried to bring it under control.

With a blare of trumpets the Emperor's stormers surged forward towards the stairways, the stairways held now by axe and sword alone.

CHAPTER THIRTY-THREE

As the lines jerked and parted to the struggle below, Shef felt the kite lurch unpredictably this way and that, felt the instinctive bowel-loosening fear of falling, of empty space beneath him. Then the last line went, and the air was under his canvas again, holding him up like the warm sea under a swimmer. At the same time Shef realized that he was being blown backwards and upwards, the walls of Rome receding, already too far for him to see more than white dots of faces following him from the wall.

To fly free, he remembered, you had to turn away from the wind, not into it. Tolman could do it—Tolman had been able to do it. His nerve quailed at the idea of trying it. Better just to sag backwards, let the wind take him, perhaps bring him down far from the war and the everlasting pain.

It wouldn't happen like that. The wind would change, dash him on stone or drop him into some ravine, to die with a broken back of thirst. He had to turn now. Tolman had said it was like a ship turning fast under oars. Raise one side-vane, lower the other, roll your body as the kite rolled and go round in a bank, just far enough to straighten up. Before his fear had a chance to stop him, Shef worked the controls, trying to do both smoothly and at once. The kite rolled immediately, his body automatically trying to tip the other way, to correct the sickening heave. Override it. Do what Tolman said. Shef tried to point with his back and belly-muscles in the way he wanted to go. He was diving now, still tipped over to one side. Correct it, work the side-vanes, swing the tail with his ankles. For a few moments he was swooping down like a hawk over the villa-dotted slope, his shadow running ahead of him away from the city and the rising sun. Flight! He was the flying man, the Völund escaped from his enemies, the smith who hung in the air while those who had tormented him lamented below. In a moment of ecstasy Shef shouted out the lines from the *Völund Lay* that Thorvin had often sung, the despairing lines of the evil king Nithhad unable to reach his crippled but escaping enemy:

"No man knows how   to knock you from your horse,
Nor has wit so sharp   as to shoot you down,
There where you hang   high in the sky,
Sporting like a salmon   in spawning-season."

The ground was coming up fast, much too fast, his dive had given him speed, he knew no way to brake it. Tip the nose of the kite up like a skier in soft snow? He worked both vanes, felt the nose lift, cut off his view of the ground. Was he rising again? Or sliding along in the air, belly exposed to the rocks?

The kite's tail kicked upwards as it hit the ground, Shef saw the rocky wall of a terraced field hurtling towards him, tried to . . .

The crash smashed the breath out of his body, he felt himself sliding over something in a tangle of cloth and broken frames, tried to jerk his hands free to protect his head. Something slammed him in the face. Then all movement stopped.

For several moments he lay perfectly still, not unconscious but dazed. He was down anyway. And alive. How badly hurt was he? Slowly Shef ran a tongue over his mouth, counting his teeth. Got his left hand free to feel if his nose was broken. All well so far. Both hands free now, and he groped for the razor-sharp belt-knife. Cut the cords, cut through the leather harness, at least he knew now which way was up, he was lying on his face behind a wall over which he must have somersaulted. Now try to crawl free.

Shef looked down at his left ankle, knew it was broken. The foot stuck out at an impossible angle. No pain there, no feeling at all, but he knew not to damage it further before the pain-warnings came back. He rolled on to his right side, edged free of the jumble of canvas, careful not to knock the damaged foot on any projection, rolled on to his back.

Now. He had seen Hund do this. Set a bone quickly and firmly before the patient had a chance to scream or set his muscles. It was easier if you did not have to bend forward. Legs straight out in front of him, Shef bent forward, feeling an immediate pain in his ribs that told of further fractures, seized the foot sticking out at right angles to one side, and pulled foot and leg firmly straight.

Still no pain, but he felt a terrible grinding deep inside the joint. If Hund were here he would cut me open, set the bones straight with his fingers, cleanse the wound with Udd's spirit that the Arabs call *al-kuhl.* Maybe I would walk again. Now I have to crawl from this hillside. At least I am alive.

Shef pushed himself up with his arms. He would reach the wall and hobble along beside it till he could tear down a branch from an olive tree. Make a crutch. Try to get back to the road, find a mount or a cart. And head back to the ships in the harbor, where Farman waited with the rearguard. His fight was over.

As Shef got his hands on the wall, faces appeared on the other side of it. Helmets. Mail. Two men vaulted the wall, came in on either side of him, swords drawn. There was no chance of resistance, he could not even let go of the wall to stand unaided. Perhaps they were Italians, friends of the deposed Pope, he could bribe them with his gold armlets . . .

"*Wi habben den Heidenkuning gefangen,*" said one of the men, "*den Einooger.*"

Close enough to Shef's own native English for him to follow. We've caught the heathen king, the one-eye. Low Germans. Lance-brothers.

They would take him to their Emperor.

If their Emperor were still alive. Shef had been right to think that one side's weakness is rarely known to the other side. As the day dawned and the Emperor counted his losses, he had realized that while his enemies were in a position that would soon be untenable, he himself had barely enough force left to make his advantage tell. He had begun the battle with three thousand men as the core of his army. Now he had less than two—not all the result of casualties, but also of secret desertion in the night.

Yet he had been clear enough what to do. While the giant catapults of Erkenbert harassed his foe, he had spread out his lower-grade troops in a rough semi-circle outside the wall, Greek marines and French archers, the cowboys of the Camargue. If the Waymen came out they would be decimated again by ambush and charge in the broken ground.

His high-grade troops he had sent inside the wall. Some to form strong barricaded blocks either side of the enemy, on the high walkways. He did not want them escaping to left or right. The rest massed out of sight and in cover, where there was best opportunity for what he meant to be a final escalade, up the broad steps to where the Wayman remnants clung to their parapets. There to finish them for good, and their apostate king with them. The *Lanzenbrüder* and *Lanzenritter* were all there, except for the small guard set on the Holy Grail and on His Holiness outside the walls. Such of the Frankish knights as were left alive and still prepared to fight grouped behind them. Perhaps six hundred men all told. The last reserve of the army of Christendom, Bruno thought. But he was prepared to use up his last reserve in what would be the last struggle. He walked through the ranks, dressed in his own fighting gear. The Holy Lance was still inside the cover of his shield, strapped next to the central grip. The Lance-brothers and Lance-knights reached out to touch its projecting head as he passed between them, and he granted them the favor smilingly. At the sound of a bell his entire force fell to its knees, each man took into his mouth a piece of grass, or straw, or even dirt, and swallowed it as a last communion before death while the priests pronounced a general absolution of their sins, gave them the penance of fighting bravely, promised the delights of Paradise to those who fell in battle against the heathen.

Then the army rose and split into its two columns, each one to assault a flight of stone steps, eight feet wide, thirty feet high. Bruno's remaining archers formed line and began to shoot up at the walkways with their weak breast-bows. Their duty was only to hinder the crossbowmen, prevent them from shooting down the armored men making the foot-assault. For a few moments arrows and quarrels went to and fro, then the answering shot died down: most of the crossbowmen had used up their missiles in the night, could not fit the enemy's arrows into their specialized weapons. Bruno's trumpets blew for the charge.

He did not take a front-rank place himself, had ordered Agilulf to hang back likewise in the second, parallel column. The charge was spearheaded by the youngest of his *Ritters,* anxious for glory, afire with devotion to Savior and Emperor. As the armored men strode swiftly up the steps, the Viking swordsmen moved to block them, five men against five men on each of the two flights. Guthmund sub-king of the Swedes headed one blunt wedge, Brand's cousin Styrr the other. As the Lance-knights came on, Styrr faced them, ignoring the arrows that skipped on the stones around him, took his axe in two hands by the handle, held it horizontally with his hands shoulder-width apart. He leapt suddenly through the hoop he had made with his knees up to his chin, held the axe behind him and leapt back again. His men laughed and cheered, Styrr threw the axe gleefully high in the air, caught it as it came glinting down.

The leading *Ritter* sprinted the last few steps to try to catch the bearded fool while he was in mid-gambol. His sword licked out in a stab from below, aimed at the thigh. Styrr, two steps above, leapt high into the air again, above the blade, came down on his feet and swung with all his force. The *Ritter* caught it on the shield, as Styrr had known he would, but the axe's upper horn drove through wood and leather and metal and deep into the arm behind. Styrr was ripping back almost before the stroke had landed, too great a follow-through would leave it embedded in a shield. He parried a slash with his axe-handle against the flat of the blade, swung again backhand, saw another gash open up along the young knight's shoulder. A feint, another feint, and the third blow went home between shield and sword, splitting his enemy's breastbone.

Watching critically, Brand nodded in approval. He had spent a long time showing his cousin how to fight with axe against sword, trading the weaker wood handle against the heavier final blow. He had learned well. In a clangor of metal the Vikings heaved forward, pushed their enemies back down the upper steps, fell back again to leave a space between them, encumbered now by the dead and the wounded crawling back to each side.

Bruno looked from one side to the other. Both columns blocked, he saw, and the archers making no impact against armored men well above them. Time to take a hand himself, render his own service to God. He reached across to remove the Holy Lance from its holder, changed his mind and left it where it was. It was God's service he was doing today, perhaps the greatest he had ever done. While the Lance was with him he was invincible. He stepped forward from the massed ranks at the foot of the stair.

Brand recognised him instantly by the breadth of his shoulders, that made his medium height seem squat, ape-like. He felt a shock of cold through his belly, where Ivar's sword had driven through it. Fear, the fear he had not felt in skirmishes against lesser men. But now a real champion had come. Perhaps Styrr was the man to face him. He had the strength of their shared marbendill ancestry, the blood of Barn Troll's-son. He had never felt a serious wound, was young and confident as Brand himself was not.

Bruno went up the stairs like a leopard, taking them two at a time at first, then springing up them, leaping from side to side between the corpses as if he were on flat ground and his armor had no weight. Styrr took two steps down to meet him, his supporters hanging back to let him face the challenge alone. As the Emperor sprang up and up, Styrr whirled his axe and struck for the shield. Too soon, thought Brand, too hurried. He began to force his way through the block of watching Vikings to come to the help of his kinsman.

Bruno took the axe-blow on his shield, but the shield was already slanted, knocking the blow away instead of letting it sink in. Before Styrr could recover Bruno's own stroke was launched, parried with the iron shield-boss, the backhand recover already in motion. For ten heartbeats the axe and sword flashed back and forth, while the shields rang accompaniment. Already Styrr was bleeding from gashes on arm and shin, each time he had beaten the stroke off before it could sever bone, but in moments he would be overpowered. He stepped back to a groan from the Vikings behind him, Brand now almost at their head, the Emperor followed before he could take the breathing-space he needed . . .

Steffi, busy since dawn with his laboriously-hauled fire-gear and the clay pots and tankards he had rifled from the guard house, flung his first fire-ball at the Emperor's head. Without thought the Emperor blocked it with his shield, it bounced off the leather facing, struck a corpse, rolled harmlessly down the stone steps. Steffi gaped disbelievingly. If he had merely dropped it on the ground it would have shattered, the lit fuse would have caught the contents . . . Now, when he needed it to shatter, it behaved as if made of iron.

Styrr threw his round shield in the Emperor's face and followed it with a disemboweling stroke from below. His enemy stepped sideways like a dancer on the narrow stairs, let the axe-blow go wide, stabbed the overbalancing giant neatly in the mouth, through teeth and palate and brain, stepped back to steer the falling body past him down the stair with a twist of the wrist.

A moment's silence while both sides took in what they saw, and then a roar as the Lance-knights came on, jostling each other in their eagerness. Beside himself with rage, Brand thrust his way through and swept up 'Battle-troll' to avenge his kinsman.

Steffi, ignoring the combats and their unwritten laws of honor, tried again. This time he hurled the clay tankard, its top stuffed with cloth, not at the man but at the stone steps in front of him. The clay shattered, the glowing fuse fell into the mixture of sulphur, saltpeter and oil. A flash and a gout of flame beneath the Emperor's feet. He sprang through it, aimed a blow at Brand, took a return stroke. Suddenly fell back, dropping his sword, leapt back again, beating with gauntleted hands at the flame running up his legs. Brand followed, axe raised and thoughts of *drengskapr* cast aside. Another tankard burst, this time at his feet, then another and another as Steffi's gang, delighted with their success, showered down the clay firepots at every strip of stone they could see on both flights.

The Lance-knights had the Emperor among them now, were stifling his burning clothes with gloves and bare hands. On the other stair Agilulf, who had come forward like his Emperor to deal with Guthmund, had frankly turned his back and fled, hurling a dozen men in front of him down the stair, panicked by the flame that had already marked him to his grave. The Vikings surged forward, met the flame underfoot themselves, hesitated.

Both sides continued to draw back, the only sound now the roar of flame on stone, an eerie flame that poured black smoke and seemed to burn on nothing. A crossbowman who had spent the morning straightening and filing a damaged quarrel lifted his weapon and sent its last shot deep through shield and body of one of the *Lanzenbrüder*.

"Put me down," gasped the Emperor to the men who were hustling him out of bowshot, "put me down, throw water on me, we must try again."

"No luck this time, *Kaiser*," said Tasso the Bavarian. "You got the big bastard but they were ready for us. That's enough for now."

There was a man pushing his way through the storming-party. One of the knights left to guard the Grail, he would not have left his post except in dire emergency. But he was smiling.

"Erkenbert, I mean His Holiness, says to come to him at once. He has something you want to see. Or someone."

The numbness in his ankle had gone now, and pain was coming up from it in steady throbs, each beat of his heart seeming to jar the swollen joint. His

bare foot was red and puffed. He had held it off the ground till his leg
muscles were on the point of failing, but the thought of it touching anything
filled him with nausea. He was still trying to stand up and look composed,
as a *drengr* should when facing death, but his body was beginning to tremble
with shock and pain and weariness. They would say it was fear. What was it
Brand said? 'A man should not limp while his legs are the same length.' He
would try not to.

The muttering of the guards ceased, and Shef, left leaning against a wall,
his hands lashed to a bracket above him, tried to straighten up.

Then the Emperor was there in front of him, Erkenbert at his side.

They had not seen each other since the Braethraborg, though each had
thought of the other every intervening day. Now they stared, to check their
memories, to see what time had done.

The Emperor was hurt too, Shef realized, his harsh bleak face twitching
from time to time with an involuntary pulse of pain. He smelled of blood
and of burning, and the grooves in his face were deeper. The Emperor saw a
man not yet thirty, with the white hair over the temples and the care-
lines round the eyes of one twenty years older. Round his missing eyeball the
flesh was shrunken, indrawn. He seemed in the last throes of weariness,
held up only by the rope round his hands. Each man had spared the other's
life, once. Each recognised in the other the marks of decision and
responsibility.

"You are an apostate and a rebel against God," said Bruno.

"Not against God, your God or any other. Only against your Church. No
priest is persecuted in England, no Christian harmed for being Christian."

The Emperor's voice sharpened. "You hid from me the Holy Grail.
Tricked it from under my eyes."

"I found you the Holy Lance. It would never have come to you without
me."

The Emperor seemed unsure what to say. The voice of Erkenbert the
fanatic cut across his uncertainty.

"You have made false books and false gospels and sent them out across
Christendom!"

"How do you know they are false?"

"You see!" said Erkenbert to his Emperor. "You are minded to forgive
him even now, in your kindness. Think of this. Other heretics sin against the
Faith, but this man—if man he is—he casts doubts on all faiths together. If
he had his way all books would become mere words, to be turned this way
and that. Treated like the oaths of a horse-dealer or the promises of a
harlot."

"Books *are* mere words," said Shef faintly, his senses beginning to leave
him. "Only you cannot ask a writer if he is telling the truth. Cannot look
into his eyes."

"He doubts the Word of God," said Bruno firmly. "It is the sin against the Holy Ghost. How shall he die, Your Holiness?"

"This is Rome. Let us do as the Romans did and crucify him."

"Does he deserve Our Savior's death?"

"Saint Peter was crucified upside down, because he was not worthy to imitate his Lord. Nail this one with his hands over his head."

Just don't touch my foot, thought Shef. A futile thought. They would nail that too. He was putting more and more weight on the rope now, less and less on his one good leg. The sooner he fainted the better.

"Shall we do it where his men can see?" asked a voice somewhere off in the blackness that was closing in.

"No. No. Better that there is no story of this, that he should just disappear. Take him into a garden somewhere. Use the Grail-knights to guard him till he is dead."

The rope round his wrists was slashed free, he stumbled, came down on his injured foot, and fell headlong. The Emperor looked after him as the knights dragged him away. "He might have been a great warrior for the Lord," he said.

"Satan was once Lucifer, brightest angel in Heaven," replied Erkenbert.

His hands were stretched out above him, his feet stretched out below. He had not felt the nail driven through both wrists. As soon as the iron point had touched his shattered ankle he had bitten deep into his lip to keep from screaming, but after the first blow he had felt nothing at all. The cunning soldiers had fixed a tiny ledge below his feet, no more than three inches out from the tree-trunk to which he was fastened, and on this he could rest his weight. Much of his weight. When his one foot would support him no more he would sag again from his wrists, feel the stifling pressure on his ribs. When he fainted the weight would fall again on his ankle, the pain stab him awake once more. As the sun rose towards noon, Shef drifted in and out of consciousness.

The gods were looking down at him from Asgarth, without pity or concern, but with interest and calculation. There was his father Rig, fox-face and cunning eyes. Völund, the lame smith whose place Shef had once taken, once a man but taken to Asgarth for his skills. In front of them all, the one-eyed Othin, who had been Shef's enemy and the supporter of his enemies. The one standing next to him: yes, he could tell the marks of pain and poison on his face, but they seemed smoothed out, half-healed. Of all the faces he could see, Loki's was the one least hostile. Least human, too. Not for nothing was he the father, and the mother also, of the monster-brood. Shef had brought monsters into the world as well.

"He hangs as you once did, father," said Loki. "You hung for nine days, to gain wisdom. It is too late for him to gain it."

"He may not gain it," replied Rig. "He has bred it in others."

"As you did when you bred from Edda and Amma and Mothir, mother and grandmother and great-grandmother," said Loki, truthful but sharp-tongued. "You cuckolded their husbands, made a better breed. But this one's seed dies with him. What good is that?"

"Not quite with him, it may be," said Rig.

"In any case," growled Völund the hamstrung, inventor of flight, "his true seed is not of the body, Loki. His sons are the slaves become men. Udd the steelmaster and Ordlaf the seaman. Cwicca the kitemaster, who wears my token now. Steffi with the squint who wears yours. You should thank him, Loki. You are freed and growing strong, and you will grow stronger, but you would still be mad beneath the serpent's fangs if he had not given men a reason to believe in you."

"There will still be no sons of Shef, no Sheafings, as there have been sons of Shield, Shieldings," said Othin.

Rig said nothing, but Heimdall heard his thought, and the dying man heard it too. Your Shieldings failed when Sigurth died, thought Rig. My son has set the world on the Sheafing path. Not of peace alone, nor war alone, but a path where our sons and daughters will be free to make themselves, and make gods in their own likeness. For good or ill, as they choose.

Maybe Völund will keep a place for me in his smithy, thought Shef, ignoring Rig's silent thought. That would be a better place for me than the kennels of Rig my father.

The vision faded, Shef came back to the world of hot sun and pain. The sun was no longer in his eyes, it was over his head, seeming to burn even through his thick whitened hair. Would they give me water? he wondered. The Roman soldiers gave it to Jesus, I saw them do it. What of the White Christ then? I do not believe in him, but he must be my enemy now.

It was his sometime king, King Edmund of East Anglia, who came to him the next time. They had waited for death together one summer's night ten years before. The king had gone before him, died under the knife and chisel of Ivar and his blood-eagle. He had come to Shef as he too lay in pain from his half-blinding, imagining then that he hung from Hlithskjalf with a spike through his eye, as he hung now in reality spiked through wrists and ankles. But where had the king gone? He had fought and died for his Christian faith, refused to abjure it under torture. If the White Christ could save anyone, surely it would have been him?

The king no longer held his backbone in his hand. He seemed to be looking down from far away, far further than Hlithskjalf, where the Asgarth gods watched the affairs of men with keen interest. Edmund King and Martyr had no such interest, no longer. He had gone elsewhere.

"In the beginning was the Word," he said, his voice drifting down like ash-seeds on a breeze. "And the Word was with God." His voice changed. "But the

Word was not God. The Word was made by men. Bible, Testament, Talmud, Torah, hadith, Koran, commentary. They are the works of men. It is men who made the works of men into the words of God."

"*Greater is work than the naked word,*" replied Shef in his mind, quoting the English proverb.

"*That is true. And so you may be forgiven. What you have done may make the words pass away, lose their authority, the authority no-one would grant their authors, mere men as they were. The authority that comes from faith—that may remain. Those who wish to believe in the salvation of the Christians, in the shari'a of Islam, in the Law of the Jews—that is still open to them. But they may not tell people that their words are holy, not to be challenged. Every interpretation may be challenged. You showed your friend Thorvin that. Your friend Svandis showed you that. There is truth in the Word, but not a single truth.*"

"*Can I believe in your word?*" Shef tried to say to the fading figure. "*Is there truth in my visions?*"

"*Ask Farman,*" said the king's voice in a shrill receding pipe. "*Ask Farman.*"

He's by the ships, Shef thought. By the water. Is there any water here? The sun is on the side of my face now. He tried to call to the knights guarding him, for water or for death, but his voice came out only as a rusty croak like a crow's. The knights were talking, they did not hear him.

"If he does not break them this time, they will break him."

"He will break them."

"The Italians are gathering to defend their anti-Pope."

A bark of laughter. "The Italians!"

"They say an Arab fleet has been sighted . . ."

"The Greeks will sink it. Where is your faith?"

A silence. The doubtful voice said, "I wish we could fight with the Emperor."

"We are here to guard the Grail. And this heretic here."

"Who from?" muttered the doubter.

Shef knew he was near death now, and thirst had ceased to bother him. What did he wish? That he could see Godive again? No, she would live and die happily, as far away from him as King Edmund. That he might see the child he and Svandis would have? If the child was born, with such a mother it needed no father to protect it. He wished he had not struck Cwicca. He wished he could see the Wisdom House again, and what Udd had made in another peaceful summer.

He could not see the Wisdom House, but he could see the Head of it, Farman Frey's priest. Strange. He had seen other men he knew before in visions, but only one man had ever seen him, responded to him as if he had been there, and that had been Farman in the smithy of the gods. Now he was there again, talking urgently.

"Where are you?"

"I don't know. In a garden somewhere."

"Rome is to the east of you," said Farman. "The aqueduct is to the south. Look at the shadows."

Shef opened his eye, saw the shadow of the tree he hung on stretching away, quite long now. If he had his beads and wire he could calculate, could calculate . . .

"That will do. That will do."

Shef's foot slipped from the little ledge, provided not in mercy but to prolong the agony of dying. His weight came on his wrists, on his ruined ankle. This time the pain did not wake him but sent him mercifully down below any level of consciousness at all.

CHAPTER THIRTY-FOUR

The Emperor massed his remaining troops beneath the stair from which he had been pulled earlier that day. There was no attempt at concealment or surprise this time. It was like the game the soldiers played. Two men sat each side of a table, gripped hands, and each tried to push the other's arm down. A test of strength, a test, between evenly-matched men, of will. When the soldiers did it and they were drunk enough, they hammered nails up through the table to impale the wrist of the loser. That was a great improver of the will. And that was how things stood now. The whole day had been full of rumors and sudden panics: the Italians had risen, there was an Arab fleet at the coast, the pagan king had escaped with magic wings to bring up a new army. None of that mattered. The pagan king was dead, or soon would be. His army would be destroyed before sundown. After that Bruno was ready to fall back into the hills, retreat all the way to Germany before he gathered strength and returned. But he would leave no unfinished business, no center to grow a legend of victory.

Brand had spent the afternoon polishing his armor and considering his weapons. He was of the same mind as the Emperor. Most of his army, such of it as was left, was reduced to spectator status by wounds or loss of ammunition. Most of the opposing army, he reckoned, was much the same. He had seen the guard-posts outside the wall shrink all day, from desertion, from call-up of the reliable units to face the immediate danger inside the wall. It would turn, now, on a clash of a few men. Maybe, he thought, two men.

The question was, what to fight the bastard with. Brand did not think the

Emperor was as quick as Ivar, or as strong as himself. But he was certainly quicker than Styrr, or Brand, and stronger than Ivar. Brand had decided to abandon his axe 'Battle-troll.' Against a really good swordsman, rather than a fair or moderate one, it was a disadvantage. He had borrowed a sword from Guthmund, flexed it a few times, rejected it. In the end he had decided to rely on main strength, in which he was every man's master. He had taken one of the English pygmies' halberds, sawn off half the shaft, and constructed for himself an axe of massive proportions. No other man could wield something like this one-handed. That would be his advantage. The axe one side, the spike the other, the lance-head on top of the shaft. Three weapons in one, and all of them clumsy. He had abandoned his shield as well, taken instead a dead man's and cut it down to half the diameter, strapped it immovably on his left forearm, leaving his left hand free. Round his waist and over his mail he had strapped another dead man's leather jacket, doubled over on the left side to cover more of the area that a proper shield would have protected.

As the enemy trumpets rang out again, Brand slouched to the head of the stair. He was hot, he was thirsty—they had blocked the aqueduct earlier on. He had ceased to be afraid.

The Emperor was at the head of his usual troop of heavy-armed German foot. Mixed in with them were strange contrivances. "What are they?" he muttered to Steffi, standing by him holding one of his three remaining firepots.

"I can see the hoses," said Steffi. "I think they're for water. Some way of pumping water. To put out fires, maybe." They were indeed the municipal fire-guardians of the city of Rome, dragged from their hiding by Bruno's agents.

"No need for them," called out Brand in Norse. He knew Bruno understood it from his long wanderings in quest of the Holy Lance. He turned Steffi round, shoved him gently away.

"Let me come up and fight, big man," shouted Bruno.

"I'll come down."

"Will your men surrender if I win?"

"If you win, you can ask them. If I win I'll ask yours."

The mailed Germans fell back a little from the foot of the stair as Brand walked down it, to leave a space twenty feet across.

Not all eyes were fixed on the scene. On the parapet, high up, Cwicca and Osmod whispered together.

"What do you reckon happened to the boss?"

"He crashed. They'll have picked him up."

"Dead, do you reckon?"

"Up to us to see," said Cwicca, still lisping through his broken teeth. "Whether it's win or lose down there, I reckon as soon as it starts to get dark we throw the lines over the wall—I've made half a dozen strong ones from the kite stuff—and we all go down it. All us English, anyway. Then we can butht out and look for him."

"They'll cut us to bits on the flat. The crossbows are useless now."

"They're like us, a lot of 'em have had enough. Three hundred of us, whatever it is, with knives and bad tempers—we'll go right through 'em. Head for where those damned machines were, till they gave up, and see who we can catch."

"I heard you," said Svandis, breaking in on the whispers. "I'm coming too."

Behind them there came the sudden clash of metal.

The usual formal swordfight turned on cut and parry, use of sword and shield together, on speed of reaction and strength of wrist. Brand did not mean to fight like that. If he did, he would lose.

The first clash came as the Emperor, without salute or warning, sprang across the space between the duelers and cut low at the unshielded side. Brand met the blow barely in time with the iron head of his halberd, and ducked his head under the instant vicious back-stroke. Then he too was in motion, on his toes, moving round always to the right, away from the Emperor's sword and towards his shield, the Lance-head once more showing above it. After the first blow Brand made no attempt to parry, only to avoid the stroke, keep out of range. Even against the long-armed and ape-shouldered Emperor he had the advantage in reach. He kept back, feinting every few seconds with his ponderous weapon. As the Emperor braced for another forward spring he stepped forward and lashed out. He flicked the twenty-pound iron head with its sharp-filed edge like a boy sweeping a switch at the head of a thistle. The Emperor took it full on his shield, was beaten sideways, stumbled and recovered. He glanced for an instant anxiously at the inside of his shield, where the Holy Lance rested in its holder. Still there, though Bruno's own blood was running down it now from a gashed arm. It ran where his Savior's had eight hundred years before.

"Relics don't help you now," grunted Brand, his breath beginning to come hard. He was still moving lightly, but the spike of the halberd rested now on his right shoulder, ready to strike again.

"Blasphemer!" replied the Emperor, and stabbed low for the groin.

Brand twisted away from the thrust, slashed at the face, was blocked again. But the Emperor's shield had taken two monstrous blows, was cut deep and splintered. Two more and he would be unprotected. Unprotected both by shield and by relic. The Emperor's left hand was free of its shield-grip, groping across to seize the Lance, to hold on to that even if the shield should be cut away. Brand saw his uncertainty, stepped forward swinging forehand and backhand, high and low, the massive steel head singing through the air as he used the full strength in his forearms, thick as a bear's. The Emperor's turn to dodge away, raising his arms high as a cut hissed past his belly. He was back almost among his own supporters now and Brand backed away, taunting him with his retreat, urging him back into the center of the cleared space.

Not all eyes were on the fight. As the short Italian dusk began to fall, Hund had been seeking his opportunity. He too had heard the whispered exchange of Cwicca and Osmod. Stealthily he took one of the lines Cwicca had prepared. Svandis, looking down at the fight from the edge of the crowd of men on the battlements, felt a hand on her shoulder. Hund beckoned to her, and she turned silently away. In the growing twilight the two padded soft-footed away, reached the aqueduct up which they had come the night before. It was unguarded, the watching sentries turned the other way. Hund motioned to Svandis to drop on all fours. At a scuttling run the little man made off down the line of the channel, hidden from view by the four-foot walls. A few yards down she caught up and whispered to him, "There are guards at the other end!"

Hund showed her the line. "We will go over the side before it reaches the ground. In the shadow of a buttress. They may not see us. The Emperor's best men are with him now inside the wall."

The dropping sun was affecting both combatants now, but the Emperor more. Brand had the sun behind him in the west, only just above the city wall. His head and shoulders were in the light, his body already shadowed. He was striking sometimes out of the shadow, sometimes out of the sun, and the Emperor's shield was a fragment, one strap cut through, the Holy Lance itself hanging loose. But Brand was tiring visibly, while the Emperor seemed as quick and deft as ever. The watchers had been silent at first, anxious and unsure on both sides, but now they were beginning to call out in their excitement, in a medley of tongues.

"Use your own shield, Brand!"

"Use the point, *herra!*"

"Keep moving!"

"Stab him with the Lance!"

Erkenbert too thought that the moment of decision had come. In his own mind it was he who had determined the outcome on the day of the destruction of the Kingdom Oak at Uppsala, by his timely attack with the axe. When the time came for his hagiography to be written there must be something to mark his presence on this second day of the heathen's destruction. Seizing the Grail banner from its holder, he stepped a pace forward from the crowd, lifted it high and shouted with all the force of his lungs, *"In hoc signo vinces!"*

Brand saw the Emperor respond to the cry, and for the first time caught his halberd-shaft in two hands. He blocked the blow at his head with a furious upward drive, took two paces forward at his retreating enemy, now backed once more almost to the enclosing ring, and unleashed a full-armed swing backhand at the body. Too high to jump, too low to duck, no room to dodge.

The Emperor stepped inside the blow and swung his razor-edged sword of finest Spanish steel not at the halberd, but at the wrist. For an instant the blow seemed to continue, the halberd-head met the Emperor's shattered shield, knocked it and the Lance with it from his grasp. Then it was spinning on the ground, still clutched in a severed hand. Blood spouted instantly from Brand's wrist, a deep groan rose from his supporters.

The Emperor dropped his sword-point, realized the shield was gone from his grip, turned anxiously to where the Holy Lance lay next to the severed hand. As he did so Brand stepped forward again, right arm trailing help-lessly. On his left he still had the small shield strapped, the shield he had never yet used. Fist clenched, he swept the left arm down in a chopping blow. The thick edge of the shield met the Emperor's neck as he stooped to pick up his talisman. The snap of breaking bone echoed clearly between the walls. Then, in dead silence, the Emperor fell forward on his face, his head at an impossible angle.

Brand stooped instantly, twitched the Holy Lance away from the dead left hand. A dozen *Lanzenritter* moved forward automatically, hands groping for their holy relic. Brand stepped away as his own men crowded forward, turned towards them and with his left hand threw the Lance up and over the wall, the dropping sun catching its gold-inlaid crosses with a last flash of light.

"Your God has failed you!" he shouted as hands gripped his arm, began to twist a cord round the wrist.

Some of the *Ritters* understood the words, some did not. All felt the same superstitious horror. They would not fight now. They needed to understand first. Knights and brothers alike, they fell back into the alleyways up which they had come, meaning only to retrieve their horses and flee the ill-omened city.

Two of them, Tasso the Bavarian and Jopp the Burgundian, delayed long enough to seize their Emperor's body from the ground. Tasso slung it over his shoulder, Jopp drew his sword and backed away as a rearguard against any rush from the enemy. As he backed away he saw the Grail banner still stuck in the ground. Where is the little deacon, the one our master made Pope? he thought in rage and despair. He has deserted him, he and his false sign! He hacked at the banner's shaft, sent it tumbling with the last light to earth.

Shef knew he was dying now, the dark was all around him. He did not know if it was night or his one eye failing him. He could hear still. There was a voice calling out of the darkness, a voice he had heard first many years before, in York, the day of Ragnar's death when his own true life had started. It was Erkenbert's voice, and it was calling out, "The Emperor is dead!" Now how could that have happened?

A confusion of voices below him. His mind was perfectly clear now at the last, and he could understand what they said, but he paid little attention. The Grail-knights were arguing, unable to believe that their holy cause and leader had failed. Then there were accusations of treachery and betrayal, a scuffle over the golden case in which the Grail had been kept, blows struck. He did not know who won.

Some time later he realized that the clearing, now perfectly dark, was empty. His guards had gone. They should have stabbed him before they left, shouldn't they? Not quite empty. He opened his eye, saw a figure standing at the foot of his tree-trunk. Somehow he had got his foot back on the little ledge that had kept him alive so long, he could see and think. It was Erkenbert the deacon, he recognised the tonsure and the black robe. The little man had found a spear from somewhere, was poising it inexpertly, about to stab him under the ribs as the German centurion had done to Christ, long ago in his vision by the Norwegian fjord.

"False prophet!" hissed the voice from below. "False Messiah!"

There were other shapes behind Erkenbert in the gloom. Hund and Svandis, well ahead of the rest of the Waymen now grouping and marching out of the city under Cwicca's urgings to rescue their leader, had heard the commotion round the Grail and crept up through the groves and gardens to see what it was. Hund carried no weapon, Svandis only the long pin that fastened up her hair. It was enough for a descendant of Ragnar and of Ivar. As the sometime-deacon braced for a two-handed thrust, the thin point drove between his vertebrae. He fell forward at the foot of the tree.

"How do we get him down?" asked Hund.

She pointed silently at the old wooden *graduale,* used long before for a similar purpose, now thrown aside as a betrayal by the furious knights who had looted its casings.

Hund propped it against the tree, climbed up, struggled with the long nail through both wrists, well above Shef's head and his own.

"I need tools," he said. "Thorvin will have some."

"I have what you need," said another voice. Svandis sprang round, pin out. Two more figures had drifted out of the gloom. To her surprise she recognised Farman the visionary-priest, whom she had thought still at the ships, and Solomon the Jew, who had vanished in the fighting the previous night.

"I met Solomon on the road," said Farman. "He saw much of what happened today from hiding. But I already knew your man was here, and what they had done to him. Not all vision comes from the mind, Svandis. Here, I have pliers ready."

After a few minutes of grunting struggle Shef was stretched on the ground, Hund listening to his heartbeat, pouring water on to the cracked lips. Sniffing at the blackened wounds in the crushed and swollen feet.

"I will go for Thorvin and the others," said Svandis. "He needs shelter and protection."

Farman blocked her with a raised hand. "He does. But not from Thorvin. Not from the Way. If he were nursed back to power and kingship now, think what they would say. The one-eyed king, crucified outside the city wall, the lame smith, brought back from the dead. They would make him a god.

"No. Let him go into the dark now, and let the world have rest. He has set the world on its new path, and that is enough."

"You mean to leave him to die?"

"Let me have him," said Hund from the ground. "We were friends long ago. He often spoke of having a hut somewhere in the fen, where he could trap eels and grow barley and live in peace. If he lives, I will take him back to the fen. I do not think he will live through what I shall have to do, but he may."

"Norfolk fens are a thousand miles away!" cried Svandis.

"Septimania is not so far," said Solomon. "I can hide him there, for a while. My people have no wish for any more Messiahs to trouble the world."

"The three of you, take him," said Farman. "He has the gold on his arms still, and here is more from the ships." He dropped a bag on the ground. "Hide here till the Emperor's men are all gone, and ours, and the natives of the place return. If he lives, take him home, but do not let him be seen again. The Way needs him no more."

He bent down over the body, pulled the Rig-pendant from round its neck. "I will leave this to be found somewhere. Then men will think he is dead."

"But they won't know," said Svandis.

"So they will tell tales instead. Of how his faithful friends took him away from the battlefield and were never seen again. Went to Asgarth, to Valhalla, to Thruthvangar. Were taken by the gods, for him to be a god. Not a god who became a man, but a man who became a god. That will be a good belief for men to have, in time to come."

Farman turned and faded without more words into the gloom. Not far away shouts could be heard, torches were flaring. The Waymen, with Cwicca and Thorvin at their head, searching for their lost leader.

"We must go," said Solomon.

"How shall we carry him?"

...he *graduale* again. It can perform one last service, and then we will bu... it... ...ight for firewood, before it kills more men."

As the two men strapped the still-unmoving Shef on the old ladder, the body stirred, spoke.

"What did he say?" asked Svandis.

"I couldn't hear," said Solomon.

"I could," said Hund. "His mind is wandering in far places."

"What did he say, then?"

"He said, 'Up the ladder and into the light'. But I do not know from what prison he thinks he is escaping."

The two men and the woman carried their burden away from the searching torches and into the dark.

ENVOI

The slow wheel of the seasons turned. Five winters passed; now hard frost gave way to slow thaw. An early spring. The plowmen were drawing their furrows across the green fields of an English spring: white hawthorn blossom bloomed from every hedge.

The King of the West Saxons, Alfred *esteadig,* walked with his wife in their private garden, their children playing under the eye of nursemaids not far off. "The Embassy today," he said abruptly. "It was from the Pope. Finally."

"The Pope?" said Godive, surprised and a little anxious. "Which one?"

"The real one. John VIII, I think he is. The one they tried to depose in favor of the Englishman. Restored at last, the eternal squabbling of the eternal city finally over, at least for now. The last pretender Pope banned— or murdered. It is hard to tell. The new Pope's first official act was to offer to repeal the interdict England has lain under. To bring us back into community with the Church."

"Will you refuse?"

"I will tell him we will pay no taxes, we will restore no Church property, the Way will still have the right to preach here and make conversions. If after that he chooses to say we are once more in communion, it will make no difference to us. I think it is a good sign. The Church has learnt humility. I think it will learn more yet."

"What do you mean?"

"I think power has shifted for good, now. All the reports for the past years say that there is no Empire left, or even the thought of one. Christendom is breaking up into smaller states, under local rulers. No more threat in the south from the followers of the Prophet. The Greeks are no danger. There is no need for great empires, armies of conquest."

"But our Empire too, such as it was, it is breaking up. Since we lost . . ."

"Since we lost the One King," Alfred agreed. "It is true, the old agreement he and I made, it cannot stand. Guthmund and the others would not submit to me, nor I to them. Yet we have learned to work together these last few years. I think that that will endure. There will be no war, or the Vikings back on our shores again. We know each other's strength too well. Besides, the veterans of the One King's army, they would not fight each other. They speak the same language now, no-one else understands them. They will keep the peace, and make others keep it too. In loyalty to their master."

A long pause, while Godive considered the name they had not spoken. "Do you think he is dead?" she asked. "They never found the body."

"I think so. So many were never found. The kite fell to earth, he was dragged away and killed defenseless, in a field somewhere. They found his pendant, with the chain broken. You have asked these questions far too often," he added gently. "Now let the dead lie in peace."

She did not hear him—or perhaps did not want to hear what he said. She still worried at her memories like a tongue worrying a sore tooth. "Hund never came back either," said Godive. She, more than anyone else, knew the bond between the two men.

"We have talked of this too often before. They say that he fled over the wall, perhaps from remorse. I expect some straggler killed him too. They looked hard for him, you know, Brand and Cwicca and the others, for they felt remorse as well. When Cwicca refused the reeveship I offered him, he said he would never serve another master. He has gone back to his farm, like so many of the others."

"And Brand holds York for you as jarl of Northumbria."

"Better him than the descendant of one of their old kings. It will take a while for the northern parts to accept rule from me. I like this new capital of London. It is nearer the center of England than Winchester was. But Stamford was Shef's city and like Cwicca will take no other king. It will always be the town for the Way. The Way that grows ever stronger. No wonder the Pope feels he needs to make an alliance!"

Godive did not answer. She was thinking of Cwicca, refusing to take another master. An old saying came to her mind, 'First love is last love.' It was true of Cwicca. Would it be true of her?

"I hope he is dead," she said barely audibly. "Not poor and lost, wandering alone somewhere or begging his bread."

Spring. A spring morning far more gentle than the cold bluster of an English one. The night's storm had almost died away, and the storm-raised waves breaking against the cliff below were already losing their strength in this shallow sea. The tall man, wrapped in a cloak against the last warm showers of rain, sat on the base of a broken stone column looking out to sea. His left leg was stretched out before him to ease the pressure of the wooden stake against his flesh; the leg ended just below the knee. The shower died away and sunlight burnt through. An arching rainbow cut across the bay, seemingly ending near the summit of the smoking volcano. The man pulled the sodden hood from his head, pushed back into place the dislodged patch that covered his empty eye socket.

With a warrior's reactions he turned instantly when he heard the snap of a twig behind him. Smiled when he saw the graceful figure coming towards him through the pines.

"The boy is asleep," Svandis said. "If he wakes Hund is there."

"Come, sit beside me," Shef said. "It was a storm like this that brought our little boat here, almost wrecked us on these cliffs."

"Five years past. Don't you . . . think ever of leaving."

"Yes, in the beginning. Now, very rarely."

"Every day when I wake I think of the north. Of the sharp frost and the white snow—"

"Do you want to go back?"

"Sometimes. Then I think about how happy we were that first winter, when we sheltered with Solomon. Happier than we had ever been before, once we knew you could be healed."

"Maybe we should have tried harder to follow Solomon to his homeland."

"Maybe." Svandis hesitated. She had not lost her convictions about the gods. Yet she had begun to believe, too, in luck, in some kind of direction from elsewhere. "But I think it was a fortunate wind that blew us to this isle of goats. The people, the peasants, at times I am so angry at them. But it is warm, the wine is good and—you are happy."

"I think that I am. When I work with my hands again, I know that I would rather be a smith than a king. And if I beat out something else that is strange and new—well, we will find someone else to take the credit. No one asks what happened to Völund after he made his wings and flew. Maybe he got back his swan-maiden wife, his own Svandis, and lived happily in secret."

"If he did that, you know what I think his great pleasure would have been, after all the pain and blood and triumph?"

"His craft?" suggested Shef.

"His children," said Svandis.

"Yes to both. But also think of him watching what others did with his legacy. Watching from the fireside, from the forge or the ingle-corner. I have said it before. Let others deal now with Loki and Othin, with Balder and Christ and Rig."

"But you have had the power and have ruled from the seat of power."

"That is finished—nor do I miss it." He pointed at the stumps of the broken row of columns, the traces of the mosaic floor between them. "Did you know that this was once a palace built by an old Emperor of the Rome-folk? One of twelve he built on this island because he loved it so. That was over eight hundred years ago and the people here still talk about him as though it were yesterday. Hund says his real name was Tiberius, but here they call him Timberio, like a member of their family."

"Is that the way you wish to be remembered?"

"Perhaps. But it doesn't really matter, does it? If the world is set on a better path, as Farman said, a path that leads away from the Skuld-world of the Christians, then I am happy. But most of all—" he patted his rough tunic. "I am happy because I wear no pendant now. No slave-collar, no king's crown, no god's token. And that is enough for me."

"For me as well." She held his arm, leaned closely to him. "Even Hund seems at peace. His reputation as a leech has spread, to Napoli and beyond. They come to see him and seek his cures. He writes everything down now. Says that he is writing a book recording all his knowledge. He wants to see it printed one day."

Shef reached inside his cloak, reminded by the mention of printing, took out a folded paper.

"Hund asks always for news of the world, prefers these printed papers to payment in gold. So far all have been in the Latin dialect that he puzzles over. But now, look at this."

She smiled, touched the quill-pendant of Edda, the great-grandmother, which she still wore. "Old tales are my study. Not news from Rome or rumors from Napoli."

"But this is in English—printed in London. It tells of grave doings, great events . . ."

"Does it speak of war?"

"No. The peace holds."

"Then that is enough to know. And we are at peace here as well. Our son grows straight and strong. Peace now after a lifetime of war. That is enough for me. But is it enough for you?"

Shef did not answer. Perhaps he could not answer. He looked at the trail of smoke from Vesuvio, now flattening and stretching out in the wind. Then nodded his head.

Below them, flying with steady grace above the sea, the first storks from Africa returned to Europe at winter's end.

Stamford
London
Puigpunyent
Septimania
Corsica
Mallorca
Cordova
Sardinia
Jeb el-Tarik